POCKET KII

♣ ♠ ♥ ♦

POCKET KINGS

a novel by

Ted Heller

ALGONQUIN BOOKS OF CHAPEL HILL   2012

Published by
ALGONQUIN BOOKS OF CHAPEL HILL
Post Office Box 2225
Chapel Hill, North Carolina 27515-2225

a division of
Workman Publishing
225 Varick Street
New York, New York 10014

This is a work of fiction. While, as in all fiction, the literary perceptions and insights are based on experience, all names, characters, places, and incidents either are products of the author's imagination or are used fictitiously.

Library of Congress Cataloging-in-Publication Data
Heller, Ted.
Pocket kings : a novel / by Ted Heller. — 1st ed.
    p. cm.
ISBN 978-1-56512-620-6
1. Novelists — Fiction.   2. Writer's block — Fiction.
3. Internet gambling — Fiction.   4. Poker players — Fiction.
5. Cyberspace — Fiction.   6. Satire.   I. Title.
PS3558.E47625P63 2012
813'.54 — dc23   2011038771

10 9 8 7 6 5 4 3 2 1
First Edition

POCKET KINGS

♣ ♠ ♥ ♦

PART I

Hole

(The first fifty-thousand)

I

Welcome to Purgatory

It is a cold and harrowing morning in the life of a man the day he wakes up, looks at himself in the mirror, and finally realizes that he is not, has never been, nor will ever be George Clooney. A magnificent, eternal ideal had been floating out there; it was a paragon of the perfect human being this man had wanted to become. He wanted to look like him, act like him, talk and think like him. He wanted to *be* him and shed the creaky body, cranky soul, and unexciting past of the man he was. And now he realizes: it isn't happening and it's not going to—*Damn it, I am just going to go on being me.*

Perfection will not only forever elude this broken man; it won't even get close enough to tickle his bald spot, pinch his love handles, or tug on his double chin. If he were as much as half-perfect, he wouldn't be here; he wouldn't be looking at his reflection in his smudged bathroom mirror, wishing with all his might that he were someone else. And it's too late: it won't ever happen. He knows it now. Excellence, courage, wit, grace, confidence . . . they've all slipped away. The luminous spirit of the ideal man has fled the scene and isn't coming back. It's all over now, Baby Blue. James Bond is long gone, my friend. You will never play centerfield for the Yankees, you will never be Tiger Woods or Spider-Man, you won't win an Oscar and own a large yacht and sleep with famous women. The closest you'll ever get to being Jimi Hendrix or Eddie Van Halen is playing Guitar Hero. You've always been you and will always be you and now there's nothing left to do but ride Life's Moving Sidewalk Unto Death.

In these harsh terrible seconds, the truth slowly twists into him like a corkscrew, and in the mirror he sees the lights going out, one by one, on his future.

I have been that man, looking into the mirror. I have heard the strains of "Taps" tooting mournfully out of the bathroom faucet. And in short, I was terrified.

The lights were going out and I had to do something—I had to find something, anything, no matter what—to prevent everything from going dark.

Then I found poker, fortune, glory, and for the first time in my life, self-confidence, and suddenly the world was bright again.
Celebrity

♣ ♣ ♣ ♣

I want to go home. Where it's warm and cozy and where I am, I hope, still loved.

But I can't. I'm no longer welcome there even though I, of course, was the one who sprang for the fuzzy welcome mat. (How cruel is that?) So here I am in Purgatory.

It has finally stopped snowing, but it's still freezing out, and if the furniture inside the Purgatory Inn had teeth, they would be chattering. In all my life I've never seen so much snow. White as far as the eye can see. Snow covering hills, trees, roads, fields, and whatever the hell else out there that it's covering. Underneath that rolling furry blanket of white and silver are many more sheets of it.

This motel has ten rooms but right now I'm the only guest, so mine is the only light on. From the dark, empty road outside, my one light might make it look as if something nefarious is going on, but inside there's nothing more sinister than a humming laptop, a moldy carpet, a lot of faded plaid, and sitting on the rickety night table alongside a plastic glass ("Sanitized for Your Protection") of Scotch, two autographed paperback books, both written by Frank W. Dixon.

minute now Wolverine Mommy, my cherished long-friend, will be joining me here. She and I have never met.

Not in the flesh at least. She had no idea I was coming out to her frosty Michigan oblivion, but here I am.

I want to go home. I miss my wife and it's killing me and I want her back. With all my heart and soul I do.

This is what all my newfound self-confidence has wrought?

The motel TV is on and I'm flipping between March Madness and the usual catastrophes on CNN and paying no attention to any of it. In two or three days I am planning to drive back down to the Detroit airport, if my rented Hyundai Cilantro doesn't crumble on me, and return to my normal life, which has shattered into, yes . . . *A Million Little Pieces.* Where I'll go from here, nobody has any idea.

It's past six-thirty. Wolve told me she'd be here at six. Her husband teaches history at the local high school and loves to hunt and hopefully he won't pop in on us with an Elmer Fudd cap and a 12-gauge Winchester over/under. (I assume she hasn't told him I'm here.) She has three young boys and sometimes, when I'm playing poker with her on-line, I swear I can hear them running, yowling and knocking over things in the background.

Hell, Michigan, would have been a better name for this desolate place, but that was already taken. Only a person in transit from one nowhere to another would ever find out that such a town even existed. I had to leave New York quickly, and it is a measure of how far America's 711,653rd most popular novelist has fallen that the Purgatory Inn is the best I can do for refuge. But there wasn't anywhere else to go except to a clinic. And I'm not ready for that.

The problem isn't that I've hit rock bottom. The problem is that I haven't.

A few hours ago I turned on my laptop and played poker for about an hour and a half. Thanks to four miracle 3s, I finished ahead. (It was terrific: a cocky guy named Element Lad thought he had a sure winner with a club flush; while he gloated, I quietly showed him my quad 3s . . . he was crushed.) Then I saw Wolverine Mommy log on and joined her at her table. "Guess where I am?" I

IM'ed her. "Where?" she said. "In Purgatory," I told her, knowing she wouldn't believe me, "just a few miles away at the Purgatory Inn!" She said, "No way . . . you're kidding me," and I said: "Wolve, I swear to God I'm really, really here. Any way you could come over soon?" She won $300 with two Jacks and, after I swore on my parents' graves I was actually here, she told me: "Okay, I think I can be there at 6 but this better not be a prank."

There's a knock on the door now . . . it could either be the good-natured Sikh proprietor, who has suddenly remembered he owns and operates a motel, or Norman Bates. Or it could be . . .

"It's Wolve!" I hear from outside.

I turn off the TV, get up, open the door. I see that she has bright red shoulder-length hair and is wearing a navy goose-down parka and Timberland boots. She's about thirty pounds overweight, and, no, she's not Miss Upper Peninsula but then I'm no Mr. Teaneck, New Jersey, either.

"I can't believe this!" she says, shaking her head of all its disbelief and snow. "You're really you?"

After I assure her that I can't help but be me, I bid her in with a gentlemanly wave of my arm.

She dances a little jig to shake loose the snow from her shoes and pants, and I close the door. Hours and hours online chatting to each other, of winning and losing money to each other, and finally we meet.

"I can't believe this, Chip!"

"Me neither."

After a minute of nice-to-finally-meet you pleasantries she sits on the bed and I ask, "So, did you tell your husband you were visiting me?"

"Uh, *no.* He wouldn't understand."

It isn't hard to see that she also doesn't understand. And I don't know if I do either.

"He doesn't," she says, "get our whole world. He just likes it that I win sometimes."

I tell her that Wifey has thrown me out of the house, although I don't tell her why, and that I had no place to go and so I came here. To no place.

She looks at me and I look away. *What am I doing here*, she's probably thinking. I know for a fact that I didn't come all the way here to be a cad, and I'm pretty sure she hasn't come to the motel tonight to be an adulteress and has come only as a friend. But still, it's awfully cold out there.

The wind wails and the motel's walls and floorboards shudder when I hand her my two novels, *Plague Boy* and *Love: A Horror Story*, neither of which I am able to think about without being overwhelmed with pride, despair, bewilderment, and rage.

She examines the books, reads my brief inscriptions to her, and starts to cry—I've had some negative reactions to my work, but nothing quite like this—then dabs at her eyes with her huge purple faux-shearling mittens.

"I'm really miserable, Chip Zero," she whimpers. "You have no idea."

"But I'm here," I tell her.

She looks up at me . . . her big blue eyes are her best feature, other than her chest. Many times over the course of the last year she's told me how lonely she is, and right now, in the same way that some statues are meant to personify Perfect Beauty, Total Victory, or Absolute Piety, this woman represents Abject Loneliness.

"Are you going to leave soon? Any idea how long you'll stay?"

I tell her I have no return ticket and no plans to either go or stay. "Right now I may be the world's wealthiest homeless person," I say.

I join her on the edge of the bed, which sags, exhales, and nearly gives way when I sit. You'd think that beds in motels and hotels in the American Heartland would better tolerate the heft of large people.

"Please stay for a while, Frank," she says. "It would be nice."

It surprises me for a second, her using my real name. Hardly anyone does anymore.

I lie and say, "I don't want to go," and as soon as I hear myself say it, I realize it might not be a lie at all. *Maybe*, I think, *I'll stay here for a week or two. Or three. It's barren, it's freezing, it's on the outermost edge of nowhere, but it's certainly endurable. And right now in my life, "endurable" doesn't sound so bad.* I also think: *I hope Cynthia doesn't ever find out about this!*

She takes off her mittens — one drops to the dismal mint-colored carpet — and holds out a hand and I take it. I expect it to be ice cold but it's very warm.

I can stay here in this frozen-over, snow-domed limbo and start writing again. Yes, that's what I'll do! I'll write! And maybe, just maybe, my wife will take me back! There's hope!

She squeezes my hand and says, "NH."

"Huh?"

"NH, Chip."

Ah. I get it now. *Nice hand.*

I put my arm around her puffy North Face coat. She rests her head on my shoulder and I see a warped, dark gray reflection of us in the TV screen. What are we doing, I wonder, the four of us?

"You have no idea," she says, "how lonely I am. There's no . . ." She stops to compose her thoughts. "I really love my husband, my kids are the most precious things to me in the world . . . but none of this is any fun."

I squeeze her shoulder tighter and tell her everything will be all right. More than anything I wish I were sitting next to my wife, on my couch, in my apartment.

"Where does your husband think you are now?"

"At the Kohl's."

For a second, before I realize what she means, I imagine Wolverine Mommy warming her hands over a pile of glowing coals in the evening blizzard.

She looks at her watch and says, "I need to be getting back" and then puts her purple mittens back on. They're as big as lion paws.

She really does have a nice face, sort of like Ellen Burstyn in her heyday but with a few extra pounds.

She wraps her goose-down arms around my neck and we hug for a half a minute and when we separate her face is quite flushed. No, it can't go any further than this. A hug or two. A kiss on the cheek. That's it. Anything more would be nuts.

I close the door and hear a car drive off, crunching through the choppy sea of snow.

This trip to Michigan—the plane fare, the car rental, the gas, the motel—is costing me about nine hundred dollars. If I stay here for a week or so, I'll be able to afford it. Easily.

All I have to do is log on and play a few hands. That'll take care of it.

Because, despite all my recent losses, somehow I still have to believe I'm a winner.

2

A Long Out

This journey of starts, stops, victory, loss, and reshuffles began innocently enough last March in Las Vegas at the Luxor hotel. Had I not been exactly where I was when I was, doing exactly what I was doing, perhaps I would not be here in lonely, frigid Purgatory, one year later.

I was with Wifey, our bellies full of mediocre, overpriced Vegas food—cooked by a famed New York chef who wasn't anywhere within two thousand miles of the place—leaning over a ten-buck-minimum craps table. To my left stood Wifey—Second Gunman, my poker buddy, was the first to call Cynthia that—ever so slightly spilling out of a tight red silk cheongsam. The dress, bought only hours before on a whim, featured a long trickle of gold dahlias falling gracefully down the right side.

The stranger immediately to my right, a male about thirty years old, said, "Hey, you know who you look a lot like?"

Is there a chance, I wondered for an instant, *that this guy actually recognizes me from the black and white portrait on the backs of my two novels?* That would be impossible for three reasons: hardly anyone remembers author photos, hardly anyone bought my two novels, and there were no author photos to begin with.

"I have no idea," I answered. "Who?"

But he was talking to Cynthia, not me. He elbowed his buddy, who stood on his right, and said, "Richie, who's she look like to you?"

Richie examined, unlecherously, Wifey's long, wavy black hair, tight Asian garment, and hint of sun-bronzed cleavage and said, "No idea. Who?"

"The Dragon Lady on the Poker Galaxy site!"

"You're right," Richie told him.

Cynthia and I looked at each other and shrugged. I had no idea what they were talking about.

"Who?" I asked as the dice came up a 7. "What Dragon Lady?"

There was a collective groan, chips were gathered, the dice changed hands, and I plunked a few red chips from my stack onto the pass line. I was still up over $300.

The two men—salesmen of some sort, most likely—told me there was a site called Pokergalaxy.com (aka the Galaxy) and on this site there were "characters" (or avatars): you logged on, went to a poker table, and became a character for the duration of the game, until you left or changed avatars. One of the characters, Richie said, was a foxy Asian woman in a red silk dress.

"People play for real money on this site?" I asked them. So innocent.

"Oh, it's real all right," the one to my right said. "Believe me, it's real."

"You can check it out," Wifey chimed in to me, "back in the hotel room."

That would be easy to do. I'd brought a laptop to write a book on, I'd brought a pad and pens and index cards to make notes for this book. I'd brought everything but a successful career, any trace of a readership, an idea for another book, or the will to ever write another one. (One thing gamblers, writers, aging athletes, and repeat victims of adultery must be able to admit to themselves: *I know when I'm licked.*) So for the last few days, while Wifey was working at the Convention Center at the Venetian (she's head of ad sales at *Soles*, a footwear trade publication), I'd been relaxing by one of the Bellagio pools, drinking Coronas, eating lousy hot dogs, watching women jiggle in swimsuits, and cursing: cursing my (possibly former) agent Clint Reno; cursing my (definitely) former publisher; cursing the *Times* and *Time* magazine and *The Boston Globe* and readers the world over, except for England, where I am, for some reason, understood and appreciated. (Yeah, I know: so are Benny Hill, Robbie Williams, and cricket.) It was an unusually torrid March, even for the Nevada desert, and, after three Coronas and gazing at women in bikinis rubbing SPF 2 all over themselves, it begged the question: Is global warming really so bad? Every day I'd log on to my e-mail, hoping there would be a message from the Reno Brothers Literary Agency—I hadn't heard a peep out of Clint for three months—telling me he'd sold *Dead on Arrival,* the book I'd turned over to him the previous December, to a publisher.

There was no such e-mail.

When Cynthia and I returned to our hotel room from the Luxor, I immediately went to Pokergalaxy.com. Having never been there before, it took a few minutes to navigate the site. I had to register and do this and that and, in a way, it was like becoming a citizen of a new country. But finally I made it to a poker table and saw . . .

"This must be her," I said to Wifey. "Take a look."

I was sitting on the corner of the bed and she peered over my shoulder, her long earring tickling the hair on the back of my neck.

"I guess," Cynthia said, "you could say she looks like me."

Sure enough, a sultry Asian woman in a tight red cheongsam was sitting at a table and playing cards. Although my wife is not remotely Asian, there was a resemblance. But my gaze drifted to the player sitting next to her: a portly dude in a bright yellow Hawaiian shirt with a peroxide-blond Caesar haircut and a pair of round sunglasses tinted a very hip rose pink. I watched this character, the Big Man, as he confidently made his moves, his actions controlled by some stranger in Dubai or Dublin or Durbin or Des Moines. It was No-Limit Texas Hold'em and the Big Man just sat there coolly. . . . There was no movement other than crude jump cuts and no sound other than the clacking of chips and the crisp snap of playing cards.

He won seven hundred dollars with two 2s. Real money.

From out of my mouth there slipped an elongated curious *Hmmm . . .*

♠ ♣ ♠ ♣

The day after Wifey and I got back to New York from Las Vegas, I went into my study and logged on to the Poker Galaxy again and nosed my way around cautiously. There were dozens of places on the site to go to and, I saw, 30,000 other people were logged on at the same time I was. Alongside their handles or nicks (their online nicknames) you could see where they were calling in from: Sydney, Singapore, Cairo, Paris, Kiev, Baghdad, Seattle, Quito. Time zones didn't matter here. It was midnight in Manhattan but some burly yobbo waking up late in Perth and chugging a Fosters for breakfast could get a few hands in against a tea-sipping spinster in Surrey who was just trying to win a few quid before hitting the hay.

In Vegas I had created my nick: Chip Zero. It was the first thing that came to me.

Now I went to a play-money table. Although there were no instructions on how to raise, check, fold, etc., it was easier than putting a round peg in a round hole. You simply had to move the cursor to the correct box and click—a four-year-old could have figured it out. The dollar amount rose when you clicked RAISE, your avatar (I chose the Big Man) folded when you clicked FOLD. It was easy, all too easy.

The game was Pot Limit Hold'em and I watched from the sideline, not taking part. After a while I clicked PLAY and there I was, wired in to all corners of the gambling globe.

The low blind, I got a 6 and a King for my pocket cards. Not good, not terrible. There were three others at the table, and the flop came up 10, Jack, Queen. The betting began and, even though it wasn't real money, my hands quickly got clammy. After a raise and a few calls, the pot rose. I stayed in with nothing but a possible straight. The turn came up another 6, giving me a weak pair. Everyone was passing—they didn't have much either, it was easy to surmise. Or they might be bluffing; someone might have the straight or two or three Jacks or Queens and be slow-playing me, sucking me in. But what did I care?: It was play-dough, not even as tangible as Monopoly money.

The river card was a 6. I had 6-6-6.

I raised. One person folded, the other called. One of them reraised and I saw it. The thought that there were two pocket Queens lying in wait for me flashed across my mind and my hands got colder, clammier. Then it was time to show the cards.

I won. Some man (I assume it was a man . . . online, you can never really tell anything) from Topeka named Topeka Tim had two Queens. But my devilish trips had bettered him.

I won over seven hundred bucks in that first hand.

The money was fake, but the pride, shock and 5,000-volt thrill were not.

"That was just too damn easy," I said to Wifey sometime later that day.

♥ ♥ ♥ ♥

Other than poker, I've never excelled at anything. And it's not for lack of trying.

I wanted to be professional athlete. That was Plan A. If that didn't work, then I would, I thought, become a great artist. That was Plan B.

But I was never good at sports. To observe me playing basketball is to watch a great unforgivable insult to the game itself, and generations of Naismiths have spun in their graves whenever I lofted up an air ball from three feet, dribbled the ball off a shin (my own or an opponent's), or jammed an elbow into the temple of the man I was putatively guarding. I am still a Teaneck playground legend of sorts for not being good at it but for never giving up. Five on five games, three on three, one on one—I played them all, and I've shot hoops by myself a thousand times. I tried so hard but never got good, and it became as common a sight in the neighborhood as the Mr. Softee truck rolling down the street in summer, me slumping my way home from basketball courts and playgrounds, baffled, sweaty, and thoroughly distraught.

was a third-string wide receiver on my high school football

team but never got into a game and quit the team in my senior year to dedicate myself to smoking pot and chasing stoner skirt. In my twenties I played on a Garment Center softball team and once hit a ball high over the left field fence . . . but I stood at home plate too long admiring my majestic wallop and was called out at second base. It ended up just being a long out. At summer camp I was on the B team in soccer and swimming. I was lousy at golf, tennis, and ice-skating and have never won one single game of chess. I was like a clumsy third baseman who lets the ball go between his legs every time it's hit to him, in that I never picked up the signals that the Gods of Success were sending me: some people, no matter how hard they want something and no matter how much they work at it, will forever be relegated to life's B team. Where we belong.

A perennial mediocre student, as early as my teens I found myself staring at the ceiling and wondering: *Is it really asking so much to be good at something? At anything?*

When I finally came to accept that I wasn't ever going to be a professional athlete I switched over to Plan B. My major in college had been Art History. The tests were easy, most of the students in the classes were girls, and I loved what I was studying.

So two years after graduating I flew to Paris with all my savings and found a run-down apartment in a seedy section of town and moved in. Never having studied drawing or painting, I was going to teach myself from the ground up. I would be a *naïf*. If I led a miserably Spartan life, which I did, I had enough money to live there for a year. There'd be no numbered ducks at Tour Argent for me, nor any Le Big Macs; my lone extravagance would be the *International Herald Tribune* every day and a whore on Rue St. Denis once every two months.

I needed to go to a place where I knew no one, had not one distraction, could barely get by with the language. The starving Artist-in-Paris fantasy may seem hackneyed, but perhaps there is something to that fantasy after all, which is how it became so hackneyed. To make matters even more stereotypical, I was fleeing

a scarring breakup with Diane, my college girlfriend, whom I'd
caught in bed one day snatching away my little brother's virginity.
I had to go someplace far away and immerse myself in something
so I'd stop thinking about her.

Once there, I created a serviceable atelier out of my living room
and soon the living room ceased to exist as such: it was a windowed
box containing rolls of canvas, an easel, tubes of paint everywhere,
brushes and pastels on the floor, and me. There was no phone, TV,
or radio. Once a month I made the long walk over to the American
Express on Rue Scribe to get mail.

Weeks passed without my saying a word to anyone, other than
"Un vin blanche, s'il vous plaît" to a bartender. The prostitutes on
St. Denis cost $40 a throw then, and I painted a nude of one of
them, a bulky, crossed-eyed blonde. (I was classy enough to uncross
them in the picture.) I'd begin drawing and painting at eight in the
morning and some nights I'd paint until 3 a.m. Once I got going,
I couldn't stop. Even when I wanted to, I couldn't. Looking back,
this must have been my first battle with addiction and it was one I
didn't want to lose.

As I worked and struggled, I dreamt ahead several decades.
My paintings would hang in museums all over the world and in
the homes of the stinking rich, those despised clients of mine who
saw my work as investments and not as unique works of unparal-
leled beauty. I had a house in Maine, a loft in SoHo. In books and
monographs, black-and-white photographs of the much-younger
me in Paris ran alongside the paintings I was executing at the time.
In these photos my paintings can be seen hanging on the dimly lit
wall and propped up on the floor behind me. My sad, lonely eyes
stare out and I am haggard and hungry, my jeans and sweatshirt
are splattered with paint, and a cigarette dangles from my hand . . .
even though I've never smoked.

Needless to say, no such picture was ever taken.

e time flew by and I wanted to slow it down just so I could
more. I would sit down at my easel and focus in on the work

at hand, focusing as I'd never focused on anything in the past, and before I knew it, ten hours had elapsed. If anyone had been there to ask me how much time had gone by, I probably would have said ten minutes.

It may have been the greatest time of my entire life.

But it was time that went right down the drain. It became Zero Time, a year of my life that just did not happen. Because I wasn't any good. I made no progress at all and was just as bad on Day 350 as I was on Day 1. I denied my lack of ability every day and every minute, I denied it even as my arm, wrist, and back ached from painting twelve hours straight. I denied it when I hung my completed canvases on the walls of my Parisian apartment and stood back to take them in. I denied it as I sketched at two in the morning, did watercolors at noon, and gouache and Conté crayon at nine at night. I denied it right up to the moment when I had only enough money left to make it to the airport and for my plane ticket home.

There was no Plan C, which is how I wound up becoming me.

◆ ◆ ◆ ◆

Taking into consideration the myriad items on List A, which contains those things I'm not good at (sports, painting, carpentry, anything musical, cooking, being charming at parties, anything of a financial nature, crosswords, computer know-how, conversing about indie films and alt rock bands), and the items on List B, which contains those things I *am* good at (writing novels that don't sell and screenplays that never get filmed and plays that never get produced, playing poker, not doing volunteer work), you would think that List A would feel sorry for List B and perhaps send a couple of things over just to boost morale. Sort of like a talent mercy fuck. But List A is merciless, takes no prisoners, brooks no quarter, and the end result is I might very well be a no-talent bum of the first order.

So that was my life the day I won that first hand of fake money: I had two books under my belt, and while they had not sold well, one (*Plague Boy*) had been optioned by Hollywood (the red-hot director Pacer Burton was slated to direct). I'd written a third novel but its fate was unknown and possibly extremely dire. On the plus side, I had a great job. My wife and I had enjoyed seven truly wonderful years of a yin-yang marriage. However, we had been married for ten, and lately (ever since my books began withering on bookstore shelves), my irritable and shabby New Jersey yin had been clashing with her carefree and classy Park Avenue yang. Because I could no longer bring myself to start another book and because I had so much free time on my hands, the stage was set for me to become a semiprofessional poker player.

At least I was doing something I was good at.

I refused to let all the lights go out.

♣ ♣ ♣ ♣

A week or so after I got back from Vegas, I opened up, with Wifey's approval, a separate account at my bank and put a thousand dollars in it. When I got home from work one day I went into the Galaxy and set the whole thing up, linking the new account to the site. In the eyes of over 50,000 winners and losers around the world, I was now Chip Zero, Man of a Thousand Dollars. I would either grow my stake into two or three thousand or fritter it away in a week. If it turned out to be the latter, then so be it. I'd have learned my lesson.

Things would be different now: I wasn't gambling with play money. Play money was Whiffleball; this was hardball. Of course, I didn't have to play for real money—I could shuttle between the play tables and the real ones, hone my skills in the former to unleash them in the latter.

Cynthia hadn't come home yet, and after ten hands with the fake stuff, I made the move into Real Money World. I went to a table in "Low" with five- and ten-dollar blinds; my hands were ice-cold and my armpits were like sponges. As is possible on the site, before I took my "seat," I observed the game and the players for a while. It was not surprising that play here moved slower, that the players deliberated longer: money really does change everything. This was like going from playing checkers with a ten-year-old to playing chess against Big Blue.

I had also noticed—the site informs you—each player's winnings (or stacks); that is, how much money players brought to the table. For example, Foldin' Caulfield (an orthopedist from, ironically, Council Bluffs who either plays poker between surgeries to relax, or performs surgery between poker games to relax) might have a stack of $150,000, while Halitosis Sue's stack was a modest $450. For this, my first game, I chose a table where people didn't have that much, took my seat and played as the Big Man again. I don't know why, but I was drawn to that avatar. (If Wifey resembles, as she thinks she does, Ava Gardner a year past her prime, I resembled Gérard Depardieu then, circa the 1980s, albeit with moppier, grayer hair and not as big a galoot. I was ten pounds overweight but, in my defense, it had been the same ten pounds for twenty years.)

Chip Zero was now in the house.

I dumped five bucks the first hand, folding two fours. The winning hand was three Jacks. *Okay,* I thought, *so now I'm down to $995.*

I dumped twenty the next hand, hoping that my nines and eights would prevail. But three nines kicked me right in the teeth and I let out a groan that sounded like a Bassett hound being neutered by a failing veterinary student.

Well, this isn't that much fun.

But I had nothing else to do. There were no books to write. If I wrote them, there was nobody to publish them. If I wrote them and somebody published them, there were no readers to read them.

In the third hand, not only did I win all the money back with a full house, Kings full of tens, but suddenly I was ahead a hundred dollars.

I vowed then that, as God is my witness, I would never be behind again.

When Wifey came home she put a pot of water on the stove to make pasta for dinner, but simmering with glee I ran over, turned the burner off, dumped the water into the sink, and whisked her out for dinner. In the restaurant I said to her, "I think I may finally have found something I'm good at" and told her it was poker. She wasn't as happy for me as I would have liked, but when I told her how much I'd won and how easily I'd won it, well, I think she came around. I didn't pay for dinner that night and neither did she—a few faceless poker players whom I'd never met wound up paying for it. We downed an eighty-dollar bottle of wine and when we returned home I was still so excited I couldn't sleep. So at about three in the morning I went into my little study, flicked on a small light, and made a list of the things I could do to resurrect my literary career.

Go to book parties and sucker-punch the likes of Jonathan Franzen, Jonathan Safran Foer, Jonathan Lethem, Michael Chabon, David Eggers, David Mitchell.

But this might be a problem as there is no chance at this point I'd ever get invited to such a book party.

In lieu of the aforementioned Jonathans and Davids, I could punch out an old coot like Phillip Roth or Joyce Carol Oates and hopefully not kill them. Or I could take on a career-dead writer like Marty Amis or Sal Rushdie, both of whom could use the publicity, too.

But Joyce Carol Oates once wrote a book about boxing and could possibly beat me up.

In a profanity-laced article in *The Atlantic* or *The New York Review of Books*, I could drill the above Jonathans and Davids new assholes. Why, it would be the literary *scandale* of the decade! I'll write unending comma- and semi-colon-filled sentences about their books and their abundant lack of talent. Pick one single ungainly sentence of theirs—just like the real critics do!—and use it to skewer their entire oeuvre. Use words like "pullulation," or short fancy-ass words like "fictive" so that people take me seriously. It would make *Mailer v. Vidal* and *Hellmann v. McCarthy* look like the undercard of a Golden Gloves featherweight bout! One of the offended geniuses would go on Charlie Rose and, after belittling my inconsequential output and poor sales, dare me to a boxing match (or, if it's Marty Amis or Sal Rushdie, a tennis or cricket match), and I would go on *Charlie Rose* and come up with a lame excuse why I couldn't go through with it ("Charlie, I'm not going to dignify that juvenile challenge with a comment.").

But in order for me to pull this off I'd have to read their books . . . and I didn't want to.

I could burst into the Reno Brothers Literary Agency and pummel the hell out of Clint Reno, my agent (if he still is my agent). In this wacky world, not only would that get *Dead on Arrival* published, it would also land me a reality TV show on Bravo.

Start a blog. Tweet. The final desperate cries for help of wretched losers everywhere.

Write a *new* new novel, get it published; the novel gets good reviews in the *Times*, I go on *Oprah* and *Charlie Rose*. But who am I kidding? The *Times* hates me so much that they Photoshopped me right out of my wedding announcement picture, turning me into the conspicuous gray blotch hovering over my blushing bride's shoulders.

Write a book about my dog. My lovable dog Max, Molly, Spanky, or Duffy. He or she could be a gorgeous purebred or a big ol' scruffy mutt who followed me home one day. The dog keeps my marriage intact and happy, and saves my troubled daughter from drowning one day. Because of the dog, my severely autistic son sinks twenty shots in a row in a high school basketball game, and the dog sees my wife through menopause and a cancer scare. Spanky gets old and blind and dies in my arms. For the first time in my adult life, I—ever the cold-blooded stoic—cry. Ultimately not only has the dog taught me the true meaning of Love, it has rescued my literary career.

Pen a poorly written trilogy of mysteries set in Stockholm and then die of a heart attack.

I could get a job in advertising, then get fired. Then get a job at Starbucks. Write about the whole wonderful, fulfilling experience, and quit the job when the book gets sold to the movies.

Confess in one memoir that I was once a young, homeless, drug-addicted but still ravishingly beautiful transvestite prostitute who serviced truck drivers and the squealing livestock they transported. In the next memoir confess that I wasn't, that I was really my sister, a tough white kid who hung around with murderous but tender-hearted black L.A. gangbangers and who had once escaped the Holocaust, after meeting my wife in a concentration camp, and been raised by wolves in the Brussels woods.

I could write an *A Million Little Pieces*–like memoir, all of it pullulating with exaggeration and falsehood. Concoct my very own crack whore, whose shattered life I later save. I'll pass myself off to the literary world as a tough guy, a bad boy, a ticking time bomb, the kind of brooding, barbwire-skinned punk who calls a bartender "barkeep" and befriends mafiosi and boxers and corrupt clarinet-playing Negro judges.

Or I could write a real memoir, about losing out as a novelist, discovering poker and winning tons of money and adulation but losing everything.

But with so many phony memoirs getting published these days, it has become almost impossible to publish a real one anymore. The world prefers the fake stuff.

I printed out my list, looked at it, tore it up, and threw the pieces out. Then I logged on to the Galaxy and played a few hands. I crept back into bed with my wife, who was curled up and sound asleep and had no idea that her husband was now five hundred dollars richer.

3
Big Slick

<hr>

Where else but on the Galaxy could I find camaraderie at any hour of the day or night? Where else could I find a place where failure was not only expected, but was *hoped* for? For when you're sitting around an online poker table, you're joined by at least one other and possibly nine other likeminded souls and, though they are out to take your money, you are, for a short time, willfully and inextricably bound to them. If you stick around long enough, you will witness them fail miserably and they will be courteous enough to return the favor.

The first friend I made online turned out to be my best: Second Gunman, a hotel receptionist in Blackpool, England. For the first few days I played, I was so nervous that I refrained from any on-line chatting. I'd noticed the chat going on (there's a small oval box where players talk to one another) but I wanted to concentrate on the cards and make sure I made the right moves: it was one thing to channel Doyle Brunson, another to channel me, but I wasn't ready to do both at the same time. It wasn't until my sixth day playing that I noticed I was often playing with the same people.

"Chip," Second Gunman said to me one day, "how are ya?"

I panicked but only mildly. I had been playing in the shadows, an unseen puppeteer pulling the strings of my poker-playing bull-dog. When I'd win hands, players would say "NH" (nice hand) or "VNH" (very nice hand); I should have sent them a "TY" (thank you) but was too locked into the game to do that.

I IM'ed back, "Hi, Second Gunman," and he quickly responded:

"Talking today, I see. The other day the cat had your tongue." I wrote back: "Well, the cat coughed it back up."

This conversation took place while the cards were shuffled and dealt, while we players examined our pocket cards (I had two 4s, usually the start of a go-nowhere hand) and while the flop was revealed. I had to mentally toggle between checking, raising, and possibly folding, and typing the next sentence and reading his words to me.

"I had a feckin cat once," he said. He raised five dollars and I called.

"I don't really like cats," I told him. "More of a dog man really."

"I LOVE cats!" someone at the table, appropriately named Feline Lucky 2Nite, said.

"Well, neither do I, Chip," Second said to me, "but I also don't like mice and that's why I had a cat once. That cat took care of the mice asap."

The turn card was a 3 and everybody passed. There was only the river card left.

"So the cat killed the mice," I said, "but then you're stuck with the cat."

The river card came up a 4. I now had three of them and won sixty bucks. Not bad for four minutes' work. There was a break in the action while the program shuffled the cards, the blinds were automatically paid, and the next hole cards were dealt.

"I made fluffy slippers out of it," Second told me. "Dyed 'em pink. Very comfy."

I had an Ace and a King, unsuited. Big Slick, they call it, probably because it promises more than it delivers and more often than not you end up slipping and sliding.

"That cat was either," I replied, "very big or you have awfully small feet, Second."

The flop came up Ace-King-2, giving me a strong two pair. Money was bet and the pot went over $100 after the flop.

"So what cards do you have, Chip?" Second Gunman asked me . . . as if I would tell him!

"I've got Big Slick," I told him.

The turn card was a 5. No help to me. But what if someone had pocket 5s? My Aces and Kings would go down, like Brazil losing to Lichtenstein in soccer. But I had to stick with them and I kept checking. Gradually, day by day and hand by hand, I was developing a system.

"Big Slick?" Second Gunman said. "Don't get it."

A player named Gloomy Gus 17 dropped out . . . maybe he knew what Big Slick meant.

The river card came up a Jack. Second Gunman passed, I raised, and Feline Lucky folded. It was just me and Second now. He saw the raise.

It was time to show the cards. I had the Aces and the Kings . . . but Second had pocket Jacks: the river Jack had given him three of a kind. He won . . . and Big Slick, that arrogant, strutting cock of the walk, had fallen on his face once again.

"NH," I grunted to my new Anglo-Irish friend.

"Uh oh," he said. "Arsehole hotel manager coming. Gotta go!"

By the end of the first seven days—I took Sundays off—not only had I made over $1,000 but also a new friend who worked at the Four Swans, "the second best hotel in Blackpool, England." ("You ever need a place to stay in B-pool, just tell me," he said. "Wow! I could stay at the hotel for free?!" I asked him. "No," he answered, "but I know a nice alleyway nearby.")

I was still working then and was only playing a few hours a day. And not writing a word.

♠ ♠ ♠ ♠

If I was going to play poker for real money, then I had to concentrate, get totally locked in, locked in to *the Zone*. I had to be like a batter at the plate tuning out all the crowd noise, empty seats,

John 3:16 signs, and the white sky or silver dome above and beyond the pitcher. If Kim Kardashian were descending naked by parachute onto my face, I had to ignore her: There was only the ball. I had to tune out the world and weigh my own hand against what others *might* have and pay attention to their wagering and decide how to act.

When I told Wifey/Cynthia, at the end of the first week, how much money I'd won, she didn't believe me. I logged on to the site and showed her I wasn't pulling her leg.

"So does this mean," she asked me, "that I won't owe you my half of the rent this month?"

I thought about it. The $1,000 seed money had been my stake; it had been my idea to play for real dough, it was my poker skills and luck that had reaped this largesse. She had no more to do with it than I had to do with her earning her weekly nut from her footwear trade mag. *This was all my doing!* (Did Mrs. Isaac Newton ever once ask for a share of her hubby's gravity proceeds?)

"Okay," I told her. "I'll pay it all this month."

At first I reserved my poker playing for between eight and eleven p.m., which is when I used to write. By playing at the same time each day, I discovered, I would see the same players.

One day, in the second week of this new avocation, I was at a table with three other people. My hands still got cold, my pulse still quickened. Second Gunman was present but wasn't saying much. I was having a run of tremendous luck when a Texan named Amarillo Slim-Fast said to me: "Hey, Chip, what's the deal? Stop winning!"

There was a 4, 6 and 8 on the table. I had a 5 and a 10.

The turn card was a 7. I had an 8-high straight now. So, too, might anyone else.

"Slim?" I said, as I raised, "I have an 8-high straight. So if you wanna bail, bail now."

Slim-Fast checked. Neither he nor anyone else believed me. This ultimately became one of my trademark moves: bluff by telling the truth. It may seem cruel but in that crush-or-be-crushed world, it's what I had to do, although it still brings me pangs of guilt to think about it.

"Hey, I got a straight too," announced a player named Toll House Cookie, making the first appearance of what would be many in my life.

Miraculously the river card was a 9 and now I had a 10-high straight. I told everyone present, "Hey! Correction! Full disclosure! I now have a 10-high straight!" I raised again.

Again, nobody believed me. All the others, including the slightly gullible Cookie, called. I took the pot (which by then was over 400 bucks) and left everybody chomping on their fingertips.

"Dang," said Amarillo Slim-Fast. "You was tellin' the truth."

I won six of the next eight hands. Over 1,200 bucks in thirty minutes.

I knew to quit while I was ahead. So much of this was luck: I'd been playing as the Hawaiian-shirted, champagne-blond-haired Big Man; it was his seat and body that I'd chosen to occupy. Had I chosen any other seat at the table, I would not have gotten the same cards. Cartoon character was destiny.

"Last hand, guys," I told everyone. "And then you can all start winning again."

"We appreciate that," Cookie said.

I drew pocket Kings and there was another King on the flop. Pure magic.

Slim-Fast asked me, "Whattaya got?" and I told him, "This one I'll keep to myself 'cause if you knew I had 3 Ks, you'd fold, right?"

Someone new, whom I'd barely noticed, a player named Artsy Painter Gal spoke up. "Sharing is caring, Chip. Do tell. I insist."

The turn card was a 2. With the 2 on the flop and this one, I now had a full house. Fortunately, nobody at the pixilated poker table could hear me chortling at my desk like a madman.

"Artsy, let's just say I have this hand all sewn up," I said.

Artsy Painter Gal's avatar was the cool, curvy blonde with the

Godiva-length hair falling all the way to the floor. That was not all that was plunging: her tight gold-lamé dress barely contained an enormous bosom. The dress was the one Marilyn Monroe wore when she sang "Happy birthday, Mr. President," but the explosive rack belonged to Jayne Mansfield.

"Oh," she said, "you like sewing, do you, Big Blond Boy?"

The river card was a meaningless 5. I'd been slow-playing this last hand; that is, I'd been letting others do the raising, letting them think they had me. And when they did raise, I'd wait a few seconds before I called, making them think I was mulling over the decision to stay in or not.

"No," I confessed, "I can barely thread a needle."

"Too bad," she said, "'cause there's a rip in this gown. And I'm sitting on it."

The pot was now over six hundred. A third of my rent, or my cable bill for four months, or one-half of a large HDTV, or round-trip airfare to somewhere possibly very pleasant. When my full boat was revealed, I was met with a chorus of *grrrrs* and "VNH"s, another "dang" from Amarillo Slim-Fast, and a "Do you have any idea how much I loathe you at this very moment?!" from the fetching Artsy Painter Gal.

I clicked the SIT OUT box, which meant I was still at the table but couldn't play. Artsy Painter Gal, having dropped $200 in one hand, was gone with the wind and her chair was empty, leaving neither a dimple in the cushion nor a stray long blonde hair to be seen.

"I think she liked you, Chip," Second Gunman said. "She had spunk," Cookie said. To which I replied: "I hate spunk."

When Wifey came home that night she could tell right away that something marvelous had happened. Though our marriage was now fairly routine, we still could pick up each other's signals, no matter how faint, and still loved each other very much.

Limpid green eyes glimmering, she asked me, "Did they renew the rights to the movie?"

She meant the rights to *Plague Boy*. Every few months a check

would come for me from an outfit in California called Egregious
Motion Pictures. That was always a sweet windfall, but if the movie
ever got made life would have been a lot sweeter and windier. (But
forget about the money. My hope, my prayer, my pipedream, was
that the movie would start a Frank W. Dixon Revival. Magazines
and newspapers would write articles about my books, which would
be reissued with new, lustrous, star-studded covers. And, yes, there
was the money too.)

"No . . . I won some more money."

She waited a long second before smiling.

I wound up paying for all the electricity, phone, and cable bills
that month, too.

❤ ❤ ❤ ❤

A month into my Galaxy citizenship, I found myself one evening
at a table with someone from Illinois called Grouchy Old Man. It
was just the two of us. I'd played with this *altacocker* once or twice
before but didn't know much about him. I was in my small study
and the lights were out.

"This crazy thing happened to me a few days ago," he said to me
during a game. I looked at the grimy buildings across the street and
asked him: "Here? Or in the real world?"

"The real world," he said. "Out there."

I clicked the SIT OUT button so he could talk, and he sat out, too.
We were two people only halfway there. In the ether of the ether,
twice removed from all things earthbound.

"My wife, she's got Alzheimer's disease," he said. "Had it for
years now. She's in a nursing home a few miles away."

I told him I was sorry and looked more closely at the avatar he'd
assumed. It was an old man in a tattered argyle cardigan with thick
glasses and a furrowed brow. Gramps.

"I visit her a few times a week . . . sometimes she recognizes me,
sometimes I can't tell."

The site sounded a bell: we had to play a game or else click out and then click back in. Both of us clicked back in, cards were dealt and he continued. "So I'm there yesterday and she's in the lounge sitting on a couch and I'm sitting next to her. She says to me, 'Remember the time we went to Lake Michigan? The motel?'"

I had pocket Jacks and bet and Grouchy saw it.

"I say to her," he said, "'The one in New Buffalo? That wasn't a motel, that was a hotel.' She says, 'No, George, the motel! In Saugatuck!'"

The flop was a 3, a 7, another 3. Confident with my two Jacks, I bet again and he called.

"She's calling me George, see?" Grouchy Old Man said.

"Yeah? So?"

"My name is Len!"

The turn card was another 7, giving me Jacks and 7s.

"She says to me," he went on, "'The week that Len was away, George, in New York at the stationery convention and you stayed.' Then I realized, Chip, she was talking about George, who was my business partner. For thirty years. We sold stationery in the Chicago area."

The river card was an uneventful 5. I bet, he called.

"I says to her, 'Yes, honey! I remember now! The motel in Saugatuck, right on the lake. For a week. I remember.' See, Chip, now I'm pretending to be George, who's dead fifteen years, that bastard. Pardon my French."

We showed our cards and the program's mute ever-present "narrator" informed us:

Chip Zero shows two Jacks and two 7s and wins $300.

We clicked out. Back into the ether. He continued:

"The upshot was, Lynn had been having an affair with George for thirty years. I had no idea. They did it in my bed, they did it in my living room, they did it in his bed, they did it on the desk in my office. For thirty years this went on. I had no goddam idea."

I waited a bit. I didn't know what to say. Finally, I asked: "What about George's wife?"

"He never married," Grouch told me. "A real Lothario type guy. And guess what? Everyone at the company knew it but me. I found this out. Everyone. They all kept the secret, those momsers."

We clicked back in and didn't say a word to each other than "NH" and "TY" and "VNH."

We were soon joined by Irma La Deuce in Hartford and Cali Wondergal in Yorba Linda and someone named Bjorn 2 Win from Gothenburg, Sweden. Then two more people came in. Then another three. Grouch kept playing, winning, losing, folding, and hanging in there, and I, sitting alone in my hushed, dark den, realized that all these people at this table, on this site, in this world . . . *are real.*

◆ ◆ ◆ ◆

One Monday morning it was a slow day at work. The previous Saturday I'd spent about six hours online playing poker, winning, then losing. I was still on the plus side but had taken a serious bath. I'd begun the day five thousand dollars in the black but by evening I'd sunk. It's amazing to me how you can do everything right, make every play by the book, and still lose. Al Gore must know the feeling.

It was early and nobody was around. I wanted to see just how much money I'd made in three weeks and I logged on. It was the first time I'd ever visited the site at work. Near the words CHIP ZERO, it said: $5,421. That was a nice bundle, sure, just for deciding when to hold 'em and when to fold 'em, but the $7,476 I'd had two days before was a hell of a lot nicer.

I went to my office door, looked down the hallway in both directions. Nobody.

I sat back down and within a few seconds I was at a table. There were four other players there, including Wolverine Mommy, whom I'd only recently met.

"Hey Chip!" she greeted me.

(In the Galaxy, people are sometimes deliriously happy to see you. "Hey, you!" they'll say. Or: "Hi! How are ya, buddy?!" It's flattering, reassuring, and a bit exhilarating.)

I told Wolve I was at work and couldn't stay too long and that my stack had shriveled badly. She told me she couldn't stay on long either: "Baby very colicky today."

After folding three hands I was met with my new nemesis: pocket Aces. (They just never seem to prevail.) The Kiss of Death. Right away I assumed I was in trouble and I groaned aloud.

After the first round of betting the pot was up over two hundred bucks.

The flop showed two 4s and another Ace. I had a full boat. There was no way anyone was going to beat me. Money in the bank.

The betting resumed and someone—Bjorn 2 Win again—raised. I called, did not raise.

The turn card was a 3. Someone checked, then Wolverine Mommy checked, then it was my turn: I raised. A few people called and Wolverine Mommy folded.

"So where is the baby right now, Wolve?" I asked.

"Bouncing on my lap," she said. "Crying his little lungs out."

She was in Michigan playing poker and her baby was on her lap, probably looking at the screen, at the chips and baize and the Big Man, whose body and loud yellow Hawaiian shirt I was occupying. I wondered how much worse playing poker with a kid on your lap was than smoking cigarettes with kids in the house. But I didn't wonder too long. Besides, the kid had to learn some time, right?

The river card was a 9. The betting began again and I raised and everyone called. A player from Utrecht called Hands Brinker raised again. Which gave me the chance to re-raise.

My full boat won, and I took the next hand with a pair of lousy 4s.

I made, on the average, about $250 a day at that job. But in less than ten minutes I'd won over $1,600. I played for another ten minutes and not only did I make up for most of Saturday's losses, but I easily tripled what I usually earned in one week at work.

I liked my job. It was enjoyable, satisfying, and lucrative enough, and I treasured the company of my coworkers. It was a dream job and I was lucky to have it.

But that morning I wondered aloud: *What the hell am I still doing here?*

4
Start Your Engine

I t took me two years to write *Plague Boy* but not for one second did I ever think it would get published.[1] This was because by then I'd already written about twenty plays, thirty screenplays, hundreds of atrocious poems, and five other novels, and nothing had happened to them. Failure was my Siamese twin, a writhing, unctuous viper joined to my hip who plotted against me in my sleep on those rare nights he was kind enough to let me sleep.

My scheme—in terms of audacity and cunning, the plan was positively von Schlieffenish—was to publish three minor novels, then publish my *American Nightmare Trilogy*, which I felt would be my one true bright, shining masterpiece.

Plague Boy had gotten, with the exception of *The New York Times* and *Time* and *The Boston Globe*, mostly favorable reviews. (According to the U.K.'s *Observer*, the book was "coruscating and blistering . . . masterfully ugly and unsettling . . . almost brilliantly upsetting.") Cynthia lovingly scrapbooked the good reviews but she

---

1. "Are you really going to use your own name?" Cynthia asked me when the book was, to my astonishment, bought by the publisher. "Maybe you should come up with a penname?" My given name is Franklin W. Dixon and, yes, that is the name of the man (it was really a committee of men) who wrote the Hardy Boys detective novels back in the twenties and thirties. Either my parents had no idea about this (this is what they told me when, at eight, I discovered the Hardy Boys) or they had a sadistic sense of humor. The way I saw it, being named Frank W. Dixon might help me get started as a writer and I wouldn't be the first to cash in on a famous name (look at Leicester Hemingway, Joanna Trollope, Auberon Waugh, Martin Amis, Zoë Heller, Kate Chopin, and way too many others), so I told Cynthia: "Yeah, let's go with it."

needn't have: I admit that I've memorized them all and can rattle them off whenever anyone asks. (Nobody ever does.)

And then, after *Love: A Horror Story*, my second book, died its quick and quiet death, along came the idea for *Dead on Arrival*, an idea so obvious that I was afraid to write the book just in case it had already been written. The story: suburban married man bored to numbness, into fantasy football; moribund relationship with wife; one day the wife purposely drives her car, with both kids in the back, off a cliff. Hilarity and high jinks ensue. The man gets a plump check from the insurance company, goes on a senseless, euphoric spree of debauchery (sex—including sleeping with his dead wife's sister—booze, drugs, gambling, the works), then the sad truth of the matter finally settles in. Slow fade to black.

("This sure is some grim and gloomy stuff," my buddy Lonnie Beale said to me after he read the first twenty pages.)

How Nick Hornby hadn't already written a book like *DOA* was beyond me. It seemed like the sort of thing he would do. For all I know, he still might.

Well, this was finally going to be it for me. I was already a forgotten author, but when I typed the final period of *Dead on Arrival*, my career would be reborn. In my beleaguered soul, it was Monday morning in America! The *Times* would *have* to review *DOA*. . . . They might love it or hate it (probably hate it, as the book doesn't begin with a sentence like "In the small village in which my grandmother was born, the giant men flew down from the violet mountain mists after every monsoon season to take our women away."), but they'd have to give it notice. Perhaps I'd even be invited back on NPR's *Fresh Air*, as I'd been for *Plague Boy* but wasn't for *Love: A Horror Story*. All the newspapers and magazines that had admired my first two novels would note the "sudden maturity" in my work and—easy marks that they are—have to start taking me seriously.

There would be other rewards.

I'd be invited to join PEN, and I'd attend their gatherings and make statements against harsh totalitarian regimes that didn't really bother me or that I didn't know existed. *The Times Book Review* would offer me money to write reviews and I'd politely refuse. (*They* may think I'm suddenly qualified to review another author's work; me, I know I'm not.) The *New Yorker* would offer me top dollar to write pithy 1,500-word essays about my favorite album for their Music Issue, the best meal I ever had for their Food Issue, and the most mind-blowing socks I ever had for their Style Issue. My Sally Field moment was close at hand: They would like me, they would really, really like me!

And I'd nail the most prized reward of all, something every writer covets more than a big contract, a movie deal, or a gorgeous second wife: *Freedom. This* is why writers write. Freedom from having to work in an office, from being told what to do by people they smugly regard as their intellectual inferiors. Freedom from having to teach creative writing to kids who can barely compose text messages. A has-been writer once told me he was moved to write "by my demons," but Demon Number One for every writer is having a job and having bosses. (Can you possibly imagine Jonathan David Safran Franzlethchabeggars working in an office?) William Carlos Williams may have been blissfully content teaching Jersey Girls how to breastfeed, but the last place any writer wants to be is at a desk taking orders from The Man.

(If anyone doubts the veracity of this assertion, submitted for your approval, the words of Stephen Dedalus in *Ulysses:* "Count me out, he managed to remark, meaning work.")

I handed *DOA* to Clint Reno on a blustery morning two Decembers ago. I was dead certain this was a life-changing moment and that within days Clint would be telling me of publishers on their knees pleading and offering top dollar for my work. For weeks the words "bidding war" floated in front of me like the wobbly lettering on a toy Magic 8 Ball. I'd eat meals with Wifey and see in my asparagus the words "a darkly comic masterpiece . . . the best American novel I have read in quite some time." Every day and night I would write reviews—I'd write new ones, repeat the old ones, tweak them into perfection—as well as my defiant statement refusing the National Book Award. William Faulkner would rise from the grave to hand me the PEN/Faulkner Award, and Richards Price and Ford and Don DeLillo would number me in their illustrious company (writers who don't write great books but who are treated and paid as though they do).

I have not heard a word over the phone from Clint Reno since then.

♣ ♣ ♣ ♣

By the end of April, after one month playing poker online, I was up $15,000.

One warm evening in my study I logged on to the Galaxy and sat down, for the first time, at a High table. Here the blinds were $500 and $1,000. This was not quite the Upper Stratosphere—there were Ultra-High tables beyond that—but it was close. At this point I was up nine grand and, as far as I was concerned, every penny over my original one thousand dollar stake was the house's money. There, sitting alone at a table, was Bjorn 2 Win. It was 6 p.m. on a Saturday in New York; it must have been midnight in Gothenburg, his hometown. I told myself, *Okay, I'll play* one *hand at these high stakes, see what happens, then get out.*

Bjorn, whom I knew from his terse profile page was a horse butcher, was playing as the old man with the wrinkled brow, and I played as the Big Man, who had become my regular go-to avatar. Bjorn, I was soon to find out, is one of the most obnoxious fuckers ever to stare at a poker hand, online or off. He constantly criticizes other players' playing styles even as he dumps hundreds of dollars to them, and if he is aware a player has a personal tic or physical defect, if he knows something about their past, he won't stop harping on it. Sometimes when he shows up at a table, players say, "Oh no" or "Ugh" or "I can't stand this guy" and leave immediately. In the Galaxy there are no insta-plebescites to eject rude players, the chairs are not ejector seats, and thus you are stuck with these scolds, scourges, and irritants.

I was dealt a King and a 3 of hearts. There was no pre-flop raise, which, at these prices, I dreaded. The Butcher of the Baltic kept mum. The flop showed two more hearts, a 5 and a 2. And a King of clubs. So I now was four cards into a flush and, failing that, I had two Kings. I just needed a heart on the turn or the river to ice it. I raised, he called. My hands got so clammy that it took a while before the cursor budged.

The turn card was another King. Now I had three of them and I raised and Bjorn called. The pot was over two grand now; this was the most I'd ever played for in one hand with only one other person. I was squirming in my swivel chair. The river card came up a 3 of clubs. I had no King-high flush but still, I had the three sovereigns, the hand they call the George Clooney (*Three Kings*). The pot rose and rose. Even though it was the house's money, it now dawned upon me: Wait . . . I *am* the house! I didn't want to lose one cent of it.

I didn't. He never folded. I won $2,300 in about one minute and forty seconds.

I clicked out but Bjorn stayed on. ("That Swedish bloke," Second Gunman had told me, "may be detestable but he is dead money. Whenever you need a few quid, play him.") Understandably, he wanted another shot at me. . . . I could almost see him salivating.

"You're leaving?" he asked me. I felt a chilly gust of Scandinavian incredulity sweep over me. (Was he at work, I wondered, surrounded by hundreds of reeking horse carcasses?)

"Gotta go, Swede." I did have to go: Cynthia and I were going out for dinner.

"That's not right. You cannot just go."

I said, "Watch me, Sven," clicked on the word LEAVE and was gone.

Sometimes I did feel bad for the people I beat (but not the

Swede). They all seemed like nice people. But I'd finally found something I was good at and this was the way it had to be.

♠ ♠ ♠ ♠

After giving Clint Reno my manuscript, the weeks turned colder and the days shorter. A massive cold front from the North moved in on my life. *Why begin a new book,* I reasoned, *I might as well give myself a little time off.* Three books in seven years . . . I deserved a break.

In the middle of January, I sent an e-mail to Clint:

> I know it's been only a month and that no work gets done in publishing in December but I was wondering if you've heard anything re *Dead on Arrival*?

(And what type of business is publishing, that no work gets done in December? In every other job I've heard of, save baseball and lifeguarding, work gets done in December. Do they all go to St. Bart's together to shred manuscripts, toss up the confetti, and pretend it's snow?!)

A day went by without an answer, then another day, then a few more. I checked my e-mail the way I used to check the Amazon rankings of my first two books: every few minutes. At times, every few seconds. After two weeks of silence, I sent Clint another e-mail:

> I wrote you a few weeks ago re *DOA*. Can you tell me who you sent it to? And if you've heard anything? Thnx.

I wasn't worrying yet. Somewhere in the Hamptons, I assumed, a man in dungarees was painting my name onto a mailbox. The book was what a gambler would call a gimme or a lock. Even though my best friend and former cowriter Harry Carver (he gave up writing and is now a real estate lawyer in Beverly Hills) had read half of it and told me it was so dark that he could barely make the letters out against the paper ("What font is this in?" he asked. "Death, 5-point?"), I was certain this baby was going to get published. The typical male reader, publishers would assume, would love the book and laugh along with it because it would remind him of how truly contemptible he was, and the average woman, publishers would assume, would lap it up because she only suspects how truly contemptible the average man is; this novel would confirm it. *DOA* was as blatant a chick-pleaser as were the words LOSE 40 POUNDS IN 10 DAYS on a magazine cover.

When Clint still didn't reply, I began to fret for his health or for the fate of the tiny literary agency he ran with his identical twin, Vance. They didn't handle any of the Big Boys (the Jonathans, Davids, Richards or Shteyngarts); they only handled struggling mediocrities-with-mostly-good-reviews-but-poor-sales such as myself. (I often thought that when the Reno Bros. took on *Plague Boy* they presumed they were getting the next David Sedaris and didn't realize that not only could I not stand David Sedaris, I wanted nothing to do with people who could.) I Googled "Clint Reno" and "Vance Reno" and "Reno Brothers Literary Agency" to see if the three of them were still alive. Perhaps a chopper carrying their entire staff to an off-site retreat had gone down a few weeks ago. Perhaps they'd been purchased wholesale by a large Shanghai conglomerate interested in cornering the market of middling American literature, or maybe it had dawned upon them that in ten years all novels will be written in 3D text-message form. There was no news of the sort. It seemed Clint was still alive and kicking and so was Vance (he works in L.A. and handles the movie and TV end) and that the Little Agency that Could (but wouldn't) was still around.

The eight-cylinder engine of my Joseph K. nightmare was only getting warmed up.

Lacking the onions to call—and also thinking that being Mr. Nice Novelist and not bothering my agent would somehow be to my benefit—I sent another e-mail.

Hey, is everything okay? Hope it is. Did you get my last couple of e-mails? Any news on *DOA*?

There *had* to be news, for when I was writing *DOA* I didn't feel like I was a novelist or an "artist" so much as a cat burglar sneaking into the jewelry box of a much better novelist and pocketing a priceless gem. I hadn't ever done anything to deserve such a good idea.

Clint didn't answer my e-mail. There was no news, and when you're trying to make something of yourself, no news is never good news and is a lot worse than even bad news.

♥ ♥ ♥ ♥

After winning the first fifteen grand, I didn't get so nervous playing anymore. I usually played for about ten minutes for fake money before moving into the real-money rooms, where I'd work my way up the tables, going from Low to Medium to High. I was Spider-Man crawling up a building, moving from the cheaper lower floors to the posh penthouse apartments.

Slowly, I began making friends in the Galaxy.

This was at a table one Wednesday night: I saw that Bjorn 2 Win, Wolverine Mommy, Y. A. Spittle, History Babe (who was new to me), and a few others were present, so I joined in, this time playing as the suave James Bond character, a tuxedoed Clive Owen look-alike with a sleek gold cigarette case frozen for all cartoon eternity in his hand. I folded crap the first two hands but won $900 the next one with only a pair of 6s.

Bjorn 2 Win: Can I get my money back, Chip?

Chip Zero: Huh? From just now? I won that fair and square, Swede.

Wolverine Mommy: So History, what do you do for a living?

Bjorn 2 Win: No, from the other day. You think you're a good poker player, you're not.

History Babe: I just got a certificate for teaching but haven't found a job yet.

I had a 4 and 5 of clubs and the flop showed two more clubs, a 7 and a Jack. Of all the dilemmas in Hold'em, for me the biggest is getting two pocket cards of the same suit. I always stay in and have probably lost more than I've won vying for the flush. (Which would prove what I've always suspected: hope and enthusiasm usually get you in trouble.) And sometimes, of course, even when you get the flush, you can still lose to a higher flush or a full house. If you've ever lost a with a King-high flush to an Ace-high flush, you know the feeling of there being no justice in this world.

Wolverine Mommy: My husband teaches history!

Chip Zero: [trying to avoid Bjorn] Oh yeah, Wolve? Then when was the Battle of Hastings?

Wolverine Mommy: History is the hubby's thing, not mine.

Bjorn 2 Win: You play predictable, Chip. Also, you think you're funny, you're not funny.

History Babe: 1066. Awww, that's an easy one. That's the pi=3.14 of history. Toss me something tougher than that.

Bjorn 2 Win: How many more childs will you have, Wolverine? You should have stopped at 1. I cannot believe your husband even desires to make more childrens with you.

Wolverine Mommy: GFY!

The site informed us:

Dealing the turn card: an Ace of Hearts.

The Ace didn't help my flush at all but I still had four clubs. As soon as he saw the Ace, Bjorn 2 Win raised two hundred bucks, and a few others folded.

History Babe: When was the Diet of Worms, Chip?

Chip Zero: Diet of Worms? No thanks, I'll stick to Weight Watchers or Jenny Craig.

Dealing the river card: an Ace of Clubs.

I had my flush. There were three clubs in the community (the five cards on the table) so it was possible that someone else would have a flush. But there were two Aces and Bjorn leapt in again, raising two hundred. I figured he had three Aces, but kept in mind his best-case scenario and my worst: he might have a full house, Aces full of something. But I had an Ace-high flush and would be a moron to surrender it.

> **History Babe:** C'mon, Chip, take a guess. If you're wrong I won't spank you.
> **Chip Zero:** This had something to do with Martin Luther right? Or was it Lex Luthor?
> **Fifth Beetle:** History, I think he might want you to spank him.
> **Chip Zero:** Well, I wouldn't turn it down, no.
> **Bjorn 2 Win:** It's just not right to leave so quickly after winning, Chip.

I raised. Fifth Beetle (he's an entomologist) folded, so it was just me and the Horse Slaughterer of the North. The pot was approaching two grand.

> **History Babe:** Martin Luther, yes. I don't think Lex was involved.
> **Y.A. Spittle:** Was this before or after he nailed his forty feces to the door?
> **Wolverine Mommy:** He so did not do that!
> **Chip Zero:** Yes, Lex Luthor did that. He was mad at Superman for making him bald so he nailed his feces to the little door on the Fortress of Solitude.

Grouchy Old Man is waiting to enter the game.

Bjorn reraised. Maybe he did have a full boat. It would be me being force-fed my just deserts if he did. But I called.

Chip Zero wins $2,600 with an Ace-high club flush.

Wolverine Mommy: NH!

Fifth Beetle: VNH, Chip.

Chip Zero: Thnx. No props from you, Bjorn? Where's my dap at, Ingemar?

Bjorn 2 Win has left the table.

(I pictured him taking a cleaver and cutting off the scrotum of a dead horse and then hurling each grapefruit-sized nut as far as he could into the Scandinavian snow.)

I stayed at that table for an hour and added a cool six grand to my stack. Players came and went, but the history chatter did not.

History Babe: So Chip, who's your favorite character from history?

Fifth Beetle: Always liked Julius Caesar. I was born on March 15, the day he was killed.

Chip Zero: Wow, you must be over 2000 years old! You seem awfully spry for a man your age.

Grouchy Old Man: You know, just for the Caesar salad alone, you gotta hand it to Julius.

Chip Zero: The hell with the Caesar salad. I mean, what about the Orange Julius? And if you're going to go by history and foodstuffs, what about the Napoleon?

Grouchy Old Man: I guess if you're a conqueror or something to that effect, you get a food named after you, huh?

Chip Zero: It's a good thing the Nazis lost or otherwise we'd be having little pastries called adolphs or himmlers or something.

Meanwhile another hand was underway. I had two twos, usually a loser hand. But—and I had noticed this a few times by now—the other players were now more involved in our conversation than with their hands or with the money at stake. I kept up the inane chatter.

Chip Zero: All right, History: Desert island? Ethelred the Unready or William Pitt the Elder?

History Babe: Hmm. Can't I just have Brad Pitt? I wouldn't be
Unready for him.

Chip Zero: Grouchy, Betsy Ross or Marie Antoinette? Desert island?

Grouchy Old Man: That's a tough one.

Chip Zero: Betsy could probably sew you a loincloth out of coconut
hairs but Marie would probably give you much better head.

I raised, they folded, and I won with only a pair of 2s. When all
was said and done, I would've gotten beaten by Grouchy Old Man,
who revealed he had two 9s, and by Wolverine Mommy, who was
so busy LOLing that she hadn't noticed she had 9s and 2s.

I had developed an M.O.: keep 'em talking, keep 'em laughing,
win their money.

I was playing too much, I knew. But because I was winning, it
wasn't easy to stop.

◆ ◆ ◆ ◆

Plague got negative press before it was even finished. An article
had run in *Publishers Weekly* about the purchase of the book; this
was immediately pounced upon by a weasely media pundit (one of
those parasites who spends all day writing about people who spend
all day writing about people who spend all day writing about . . .),
who, on a seldom-read and no longer extant website, called my
novel "the lowest form of trash, the rankest kind of rubbish, the
grossest sort of detritus, and worthless mind-polluting slag at its
absolute worst." Now, at this point, the book hadn't even been set
in type and I hadn't yet earned a dime out of it. *And already the
reviews were negative?* Two hundred years ago this would have been
enough to challenge someone to a duel; those days are gone but
nowadays, in place of pistols at forty feet, there is e-mail at fifty
words a minute. I fired off a quick one and it was curtly responded
to by the weasel. In the response he had the temerity to call me
thin-skinned! The following day I found out where the Web site
offices were (only five blocks away, as it happened) and stormed

past a receptionist and confronted him in his office. I figured he'd be a 110-pound Ivy League twerp, and that the years of pent-up fury I had over him—plus my menacing Gérard Depardieu scowl—would be enough to make him piss his Old Navy chinos. He turned out to be tall, muscular, and well-dressed and could have knocked me out easily, but it didn't matter. "You call me thin-skinned?!" I yelled at him. "How dare you?" His stunned coworkers rushed to his cubicle as I continued. "YOU DARE CALL ME THIN-SKINNED, YOU SNARKY GODDAM CHATTERING CLASS FUCK?! WHO THE HELL DO YOU THINK YOU FUCKIN' ARE?!" Eventually my inner Teaneck, New Jersey, and I were asked to leave by the petite office manager, who said, just as the elevator doors opened for me, "You know, Mr. Dixon, you do sound a tad thin-skinned."

I had little knowledge of the book business before I was published, and now I have a lot less. Everybody seems so scared to do the wrong thing that they wind up doing nothing. I worked in the clothing business once, and in those days the Mafia was all over the place—they were at the airport clearing the goods through customs, in the trucks delivering the cartons from the airport to the warehouse, and delivering the goods to the stores. It was dirty and people were frightened, but at least you knew the rules. In publishing, everyone is governed by a sort of invisible, elastic British constitution that has never been written: nobody knows whether there *are* any rules but everyone pretends there are and that they know them.

It is impossible for me to read "great" books anymore without seeing the ink of an editor's blue pen throughout. When I pick up something like the nap-inducing *The Ambassadors* by Henry James, I see blue lines slashing through whole sentences and large blue Xs on paragraph after paragraph, page after page. The whale sections of *Moby Dick* are covered by huge blue Xs (today some astute publisher would just publish the whale parts and the book

would wind up on the "Who Knew?" table in Barnes & Noble).
I see written in the corner of the page in blue: "For God's sake,
GET ON WITH THE DAMNED STORY!" Honestly, would
any cost-conscious editor today permit this extravagant waste of
paper from *Ulysses:*

"Sinbad the Sailor and Tinbad the Tailor and Jinbad the Jailer
and Whinbad the . . ." and on and on until finally: "Linbad the
Yailer and Xinbad the Phthailer."

And yet . . . and yet . . . there are hideously pretentious and shock-
ingly juvenile portions of Jonathan David Foster Safroenzthem's
Everything Motherless is Infinitely Heartbreaking and Corrected
(which I have not read and which I will never read, but I have seen
the reviews) that somehow made it into print, that some editor—
thanks to a three-martini lunch?—okayed.

(On the other hand, can you imagine the parts of these books
that were left out?)

One day, a few weeks before *Plague Boy* hit the stores, I got a
phone call from Abigail Prentice, the chief publicist at my publishing house. "Frank," she said as though she was telling me I'd just
given birth to twin messiahs, "you just got a grrrrreat Kirkus!"

I had no idea what the hell a Kirkus was and my first reaction
was that it sounded like a kind of mole; yes, it sounded as though I
were being told my kirkus mole was benign!

In a few minutes the brief review, about as long as a *Times* death
notice, from *Kirkus Reviews*, the Bible of Pre-Publishing, was being
faxed to me. I don't know which was the more glowing of the two
of us, the review as it regurgitated out of the machine or me when
I read it.

Favorable reviews kept coming in. Looking back, I should have
been unnerved by this, I should have seen the thunderclouds behind the silver lining. But I didn't, and this must have been how
Ted Williams felt, swatting hit after hit; surely, before he ever
made it to the Major Leagues, Teddy Ballgame imagined himself at

the plate spraying balls all around the park. And now he was doing it. This must be what it's like to actually be with the young Sophia Loren for the first time (even though that first time would most likely last only three seconds). That is how I felt. After decades of failure and futility, dreams finally were coming true, and I had to pinch myself to make sure I was still alive.

Hey, Mister, maybe I can really do this here novel-writing thing!

I had developed the first man-crush of my life that wasn't on an athlete. It was on me.

❖ ❖ ❖ ❖

February, last year. T plus two months since I'd nudged *DOA* over to Clint Reno during that fateful breakfast. (He had pancakes, I had French toast. I paid for the meal, an ominous sign that I failed to note at the time.) I have not yet begun playing poker. . . . I'm about four weeks away from discovering it exists online. I have sent five e-mails to Clint asking about *Dead on Arrival*. Finally, a week ago, I call. I get his answering machine and ask, voice cracking like a sixteen-year-old boy soliciting a prostitute, "Clint, it's me, Frank. . . . I'm wondering if there's been any response yet to the book? Let me know?" Groveling on my knees, throwing my pride into a toilet bowl and flushing it three times just to make sure every last morsel of it goes down.

A few days later came the following e-mail (I'll only leave in the interesting bits):

> FD
>
> So far the news isn't good. I got this from Glenn Tyler of Lakeland & Barker:
>
> "Frank Dixon is a master of the suburban mimetic. . . . I ended up hating his characters as much as any fictional characters I've encountered in a long time. . . . The truth is that these creeps are out there, and a perhaps even more dismaying truth is that any married man with a shred of honesty will acknowledge his secret

sharer status on at least some levels. . . . I'm going to pass on
DEAD ON ARRIVAL. . . . Frank Dixon is terrifically skilled. . . . but his
characters gave me a kind of spiritual rash."

   Sorry, Frank.

   CR

There were three encouraging things about that rejection: (1)
Everything that Glenn Tyler had despised about the book was
what I'd loved about it. *A "kind of spiritual rash" was just what I'd
been aiming for!* I thought that was what art was supposed to do; (2)
the words "master," "truth," "honesty," and "terrifically skilled" had
all appeared; (3) I now had something ("secret sharer") in common
with Joseph Conrad.

But . . . the "Suburban Mimetic"?

What does that mean?

I was a master of the Suburban Mimetic. Was that a good thing
or a bad thing? Was this like being Dr. J. Robert Oppenheimer, the
Father of the Atomic Bomb? Sure, he engendered the eventual end
of humanity and of the planet . . . but at least he was the Father of
something.

Suburban Mimetic. A crash test dummy in a Chevy SUV?

I looked up mimetic in the dictionary but that didn't help any.

Suburban Mimetic Suburban Mimetic Suburban Mimetic
Suburban Mimetic.

For a week I kept repeating those two words over and over again,
and when I was alone I said them aloud, over and over again. Suburban Mimetic. Suburban Mimetic. It was like an infectious pop
song *(I'm ever-eee woman!)* I didn't like but couldn't shake, playing
incessantly between my ears. I repeated them until they became
utterly empty meaningless noises . . . but then again, that's what
they'd been in the first place. One night, Wifey even heard me
mumbling *suburban mimetic* in my sleep and had to wake me up.

In the old days I used to frequent illegal after-hours clubs in
the far East Village with my pals Harry Carver and Lonnie Beale:

seedy, sweaty punk rock clubs that violated every liquor, fire, and
decency law known to man. Bands played until seven in the morning . . . bands with names like Agnostic Front, the Benzene Ring,
Major Dump & the Roaring Ones, the Suited Connectors, the
Del-Normals, Pierre & the Ambiguities, and often you couldn't
tell when one song ended and the next one began. Many times you
wound up only inches away from the drummer or the guitarist;
there were no stages, no curtains, no fancy lighting, just sticky
floors, leather pants, leopard-skin tank tops and gobs of pomade,
sweat, and barf. These places didn't even open their doors until
2 a.m. and I remember Lonnie once curled up and fell asleep on an
amplifier. I am fairly certain that one night, high and drunk and
barely able to stand, I'd once held my hands over my ears and tried
to drown out the shredding guitars, pounding drums, and piercing
indecipherable rage of a band called the Suburban Mimetic.

5
Lovebirds

It was inconvenient for me, in a hi-tech twenty-first-century way, to have to simultaneously check for e-mails from my agent, check my dwindling Amazon rankings, look for anything new about me on Nexis, and also play poker, so in March, three months plus after I'd turned over *DOA* to Clint, I paid an IT guy from work to come over and rig up a system on both my computers. This system would automatically bring my e-mail to the front of my screen every five minutes, then return it to the background; it would then automatically scan Amazon and Nexis. The IT guy charged me $500 for setting this up.

After he left I went to a table with 100- and 200-dollar blinds and where there were strangers to play with, none of the usual friends. "My Poker Buddies" was what I now called them to Cynthia, just as I now called Cynthia "Wifey" to my Poker Buddies (they also called her "Mrs. Chip Zero" or just "Mrs. Zero."). Like the U.S. being broken down into red and blue states, my world was dividing into two camps: the real and unreal.

I folded the first two hands, then won $400 the next hand. The next hand the other players folded and I stole their blinds. Then I lost $200 with three Queens. Very dispiriting. But the next hand I won with trip 9s and was up over $800 since I'd logged on. The fee for the new program was now more than paid for, and suddenly my screen displayed my e-mail. Nothing from Clint Reno concerning *DOA*. Then, without having to press a button, the Amazon rankings for *Plague* filled my screen. Four out of five stars. Twenty-seven customer reviews, ten of them written by me. Sales rank: 547,901.

The screen then switched to Amazon's *Love* page. Two stars. Sales rank: 621,881. (Is there a point when you don't have a ranking anymore, when your book just sails out to the horizon and finally falls off the face of the Earth?)

The new system worked like a charm.

There was no news.

But I kept winning.

♠ ♠ ♠ ♠

Toward the end of March I decided to work only half-days at my job. I didn't tell Diane Warren, my boss, that it was because I was making more money at poker than I was working for her; instead I told her (and it killed me to hear myself say it), "I need to devote more time to my craft." *My craft.* Yes, it sounded like I wanted to fix my motorboat, but I told her I was writing a book, that I had an actual deal for said book, and that I needed to spend more time on it. Diane asked what the novel was about and, since I wasn't writing one, I told her it was Book I of my *American Nightmare Trilogy*. (In truth, Books I, II and III had been written over a decade before and were turning yellow in a tiny dusty closet in a Chelsea storage facility. More truth: I had no idea where on Earth the key for that closet was.)

After much deliberation I opted to not tell Wifey about this half-day move of mine.

Returning home from work one day—I'd usually grab a cheeseburger, fries, and chocolate shake from a coffee shop across the street—at 12:30, I logged on to the Galaxy, played for an hour or two or three and, in the midst of an up-and-down streak (you can play ten hours straight and still wind up with the same amount of money you started with, to the penny), I saw that I had received an e-mail from Toby Kwimper, my editor at my former publisher.

FD:

I have some bad news. I was just laid off.

I just want you to know that it was a pleasure working with

you. *Plague* and *Love* were two of the better books I worked on here.

I'll give you my new e-mail address when I get a new job. *If* I get a new job. In the meantime I intend to do nothing but golf golf golf golf!

Toby

I felt terrible for Toby. Even upon my worst enemies I wouldn't wish unemployment. As anyone who has ever been axed knows, it's a devastating event, like falling into a bottomless pit a second after a ten-ton weight has landed on you.

I sent this to Toby.

Toby:

I just hope it wasn't my two books that got you laid off! Sorry to hear about this.

Good luck wherever you do wind up.

FD

Now, I was only kidding with that first line. Neither book had sold well, but surely Toby wasn't getting laid off because of *me*.

Two minutes later I received:

Frank, I don't know a nice way of saying this but, yes, *Plague* and *Love* didn't help me here. As you know, the books did not perform. Someone has to take the fall.

That was tough to read. I had gotten a man I liked and had genuinely enjoyed working with fired from a job he loved . . . and all I had done was write two books. The most positive thing that I'd ever been a part of had undone the man who had assisted me with it.

(A third of the way through the editing process, Toby fobbed *Love: A Horror Story* off onto another editor, Jerome Selby, who'd been working there forty-plus years. A week later the venerable Jerome Selby blew his brains out . . . and the book reverted back to Toby to finish. While I did not believe that my book was

directly responsible for the legendary editor offing himself, Mrs.
Jerome Selby cast such a brutal glare my way at the funeral—it
was how Mary Todd Lincoln would have looked at John Wilkes
Booth—that I'm no longer so sure.)

I turned off my computer and stared out the window until everything blurred.

After a half-hour of feeling so bad for Toby I could smell my inner organs decaying, I crawled back into the Galaxy. Some college
kid from Columbus named Buckeyes Rule XXX nailed me right
away with two Queens ("Ha ha! Take THAT, Chip Zero!") but it
took me only three hands to erase the scarlet-and-gray-clad frosh's
winnings from that and then some.

❤ ❤ ❤ ❤

One weekday afternoon I promised myself, *Okay, I'm not going to
play poker. . . . I'm going to begin a new book.* Or maybe it was: *I'll
only play a few games today and tomorrow . . . and when I hit the
$50,000 mark I'm going to find the key to the storage closet and I'll go
back to the* American Nightmare Trilogy *and I'll cut it, sharpen it,
make it something I can show a publisher.* After twenty minutes of
staring at my computer screen and doing nothing, I logged back
onto the Galaxy, won three thousand dollars in forty minutes,
logged off, and took a walk.

I know only a few novelists but I ran into one of them that
day: Beverly Martin. Two reasons I know so few writers spring
to mind: (1) I'm not successful and therefore am not invited to any
book events; (2) I'm jealous of every single other writer and it kills
me just to be in their distinguished, superior presence. It's simply
better for my digestive and circulatory systems to not know them.
Had I lived in his time and been introduced to Leo Tolstoy, I believe I really might have asked him: "Hey, could you please tell me
where you plan on being buried so that way I know where to go to
pee on your grave?"

Yes, it's that bad.

(I'm not only jealous of other writers, I'll have you know. I'm jealous of anyone successful in any field. I also resent Caravaggio, Mariah Carey, Warren Buffett, LeBron James, Niels Bohr, Charlie Parker, Lionel Messi, Julia Child, Thomas Edison, and Erwin Rommel.)

Beverly has had two novels published: the first got good reviews and was on the *Times* best-seller list for four weeks, which is exactly four weeks more than either of my books was on it; the second, to my delight, got very bad reviews. ("Loved it!" was what I e-mailed Beverly about the first book. "Couldn't put it down!" was what I e-mailed her about the second. The truth was, I'd never even opened either one.) Her first novel was about the struggles of a wealthy Boston family dealing with false rumors of child abuse, the second was about the struggles of a writer dealing with her family after she'd written a book about a family dealing with false rumors of child abuse. The same old story: hardly any imagination in the first book, a lot less in the next.

Had Bev's second book done well, I suspect she would have stopped acknowledging me completely. But as of now she can't: she's just one more failed novel away from being me.

I walked past a Starbucks and saw her inside, firing away at a laptop. She tapped on the window, beckoned for me to come in. She can spend all day writing and reading now: her first book was just then being made into a movie, so she has the money and the time. No more office jobs for her. She kissed me on the cheek (she's my height and thin and has a nose too aquiline for an eagle) and asked me to sit down, which I didn't. There's something a little insane about her eyes, and she takes books and writing much too seriously, more seriously than terminally ill patients take their own diseases. More than once I've had to say to her: "Bev, calm down . . . *they're just books for Christ sake!*"

"So? Writing anything?" she asked me after being gracious enough to not mention my newly minted double chin. (I had put on about five pounds since discovering online poker.)

Has someone told her, I wondered, *that I'm not writing anything and she just wants to hear me say it aloud?* Conversations between two writers are like two dogs casually sniffing each other's rear ends and then, ten seconds later, gouging out each other's throats.

"No," I said to her, "I think I'm through."

"But your first book was so great!"

Did you catch that? Did you hear what she just said? My *first* book was so great. Implicit in this is: the second one sucked. I could have said the exact same thing to her, but she was the one holding the hot coffee.

Obviously she, like billions of others in this world, never read the second book. She probably never even read the first.

"Hey," she said, "this is so weird seeing you. A friend of mine..."

A friend of hers, she went on, named Jill Conway had a first novel coming out soon; the galleys had just been printed and Jill needed it blurbed. Quickly. Beverly had read it and it was "very promising and funnyish and quite brilliant" and "sure to make a huge splash." This Jill Conway, who's only twenty-seven, "absolutely adored" *Plague Boy* and "practically has whole chapters of it memorized." Knowing that Bev knew me, Jill had asked her to ask me to read it and give it a nice line or two. "I was just about to call you, Frank," she said to me. She reached into her handbag and pulled out the galleys to Joltin' Jill's novel.

The name of the book, I saw, was *Saucier: A Bitch in the Kitchen.* Jill, Bev told me, was a graduate of the Cornell College of Wine and Cheese and Reduction Sauces, or whatever it's called, and this was a roman à chef about toiling in upscale New York restaurants, the kind of places where they spend weeks training svelte, vapid girls how to not answer the phone. The book, Beverly said, "is going to do to restaurants what *Plague Boy* did to fatal epidemics."

"Is it pronounced 'saucier,'" I said to Bev, rhyming the word with *mossier,* "or 'saucier'?" rhyming it with *flossy hay.*

"That's the thing!" she said, dark eyes twinkling neurotically. "You pronounce it the way you want to!"

Uh-huh.

The book, coming in at a slim 198 pages, was placed in my hands, and the smell of a book in galleys quickly vanquished the aroma of lattes, macchiatos, frappuccinos, and the nearby bathroom's suspect plumbing. It's a truly terrific smell, but only when it's your own book. If it's someone else's, it's like changing the diapers of somebody else's baby.

I promised Beverly, who's never done one single thing wrong to me other than have the gall to be more successful, that I would take a look at it. I've got, I said, nothing else to do.

"You're really not working on anything?"

"Well, I have a book out there now. You know, making the rounds."

I told her that Glenn Tyler at Lakeland & Barker had turned it down but called me a Master of the Suburban Mimetic and compared it to Joseph Conrad's *The Secret Sharer,* and she was pretty impressed. (I left out that my book had given him a kind of spiritual rash.) I said I'd e-mail her a copy.

"You know," she said, "Deke Rivers is a friend of mine. He runs Last Resort Press . . . they're the most prominent self-publishing house in New York. You could—"

"Nope. Let's drop that idea right away please."

After being paid money for my first book, after being paid a lot less for my second, paying someone to print my third was doing a face plant on rock bottom and was out of the question. I once worked at a Friendly's and would prefer going back to wearing a hairnet and making Fribbles.

I knew she was just trying to be helpful and I thanked her.

"And the *Plague Boy* movie?" she asked.

"Nothing new on that. The script's been written. Pacer Burton is still going to direct."

"So what do you do with your time then?"

Do I dare fess up? Should I keep this to myself? Ah, why not . . .

"Well, Bev, I play poker online, to tell you the truth."

"You're kidding me, right?"

My lack of words, expression, and movement indicated to her that, no, I wasn't kidding.

"So, uh, do you win at least?" she asked.

"I've won over twenty thousand dollars. I won three grand just before I ran into you. In about twenty minutes as a matter of fact." Shaving off twenty minutes just to make her ill.

I watched her calculate: *Hmm, it takes me two months to write a short story. . . . if the short story gets published I maybe get two thousand dollars for it. . . . this untalented lug who takes his next lunch more seriously than literature wins more than that in less than an hour???*

Fifteen minutes later I was home playing poker. On the wall over my desk hung a post-Impressionist self-portrait of a young, hopeful, homesick man in Paris suffering a headache; on the wall behind me was a smaller fauvist still-life of a pear in a bowl. (These two paintings were mysteries to all who looked at them.) I sat out of a hand (Foldin' Caulfield had just thrashed my two Jacks with his three Jacks, which he slow-played to perfection) and opened up *Saucier*.

This is how it begins:

> An hour late to work I'm riding the D train in a short tight black BCBG skirt and not only do I feel Seth the Sommelier dribbling down my right thigh but I also see some of Antonio the Busboy sticking to my left calf.

Okay, this might be just my kind of book. Food, sex, New York City, food, depravity, and more food. *Maybe I'll actually read it. Maybe I'll even like it.* I hadn't read a book since I'd handed my new one to Clint Reno and have, in fact, had tremendous difficulties buying any other authors' books since the *Times*, *Time* and *The Boston Globe* demolished *Plague Boy*. No, I couldn't even pick up another person's book—sudoku included—until my own was sold.

I gave *Saucier* a shot though. I read fifteen pages of it, about the same length as a *New Yorker* article about the history of the

Ipswich clam or an Adam Gopnik essay about how well-read Adam Gopnik is. By page fifteen Janie Carter—Jill Conway's Ivy League–educated, sauce-stirrin', scallop-peelin', busboy-bangin' protagonist—had already had sex with four men, two of them in a restaurant kitchen and one near the day-boat scallops section of the Hunts Point Fish Market, and had purposely placed a booger, a heaping teaspoon of her own saliva, and a pubic hair in a Béarnaise sauce, an order of cassoulet, and a side of sautéed squid, respectively. Ten more pages of this and I'd never eat anything but a homecooked meal again.

Three days later I e-mailed Beverly:

> Read the book. Loved it! Couldn't put it down! Here's the blurb:
> "Pungent, rich, and delicious, Jill Conway's exquisitely prepared *Saucier* lingers on the palate like a well-remembered ten-course tasting meal. It is the most mouth-watering first novel I've read in quite some time and will leave the reader ravenous for more."
> Hope she likes it.

In the tit-for-tat world of Big Time Literature, I tried to think of some sautéed squid quo pro I could possibly extract from Bev for this. After all, what if the book wound up stinking and sinking, like the aftermath of a well-remembered ten-course tasting meal? If so, I had quite possibly endangered my own good (but rapidly plummeting) name by associating it with this novel. What back-scratching could I get from Bev for the risk I was taking?

A week later—a nice week in which I called in sick two days and won three-thousand dollars online—your bootlicking memoirist e-mailed Beverly:

> Darling Bev . . . need a favor and it's a small one. Can you e-mail Clint Reno and pls tell him you adored "Dead on Arrival"? Pretty please? It might light a fire under his butt. I haven't heard from him for a while. Thanks. He's at: creno@renobroslitagency.com.
> Oh yes, attached is the book itself! Hope you do like it!

And that was the tit that I'd get for the tat. Five days later (it had taken me three days to read *Saucier* and get back to Bev—even though I'd never really read it—but it took her *five* days to read my e-mail?!), she wrote me back, telling me she'd e-mail Clint first thing and that she couldn't wait to read *DOA*. "Soooo excited," she said, "to see the Master of the Suburban Mimetic in action! And don't forget, if all else fails, there's Deke Rivers at Last Resort Press."

Grrrrrr.

◆ ◆ ◆ ◆

There is rarely a time of day when Cali Wondergal and Wolverine Mommy aren't logged on to the Galaxy. They've become best friends and know everything about each other. Whether I log on at 8 a.m. or 3 p.m. or 3 a.m. (a cyberstalker's dream, the site tells you which of your buddies are on and then helps you locate them), they are usually online. They may not always be playing or chatting, but they're on. Even when Cali, her husband, and kids went to Paris for a week, she was still playing poker. While her family was out taking in the town, she was in her hotel room with her laptop, trying to take away people's money and talking to Wolve.

People became friends and sometimes more than just friends.

Another person who seemed to always be on the site was a terminally effervescent player named Bubbly Brit Bird, aka Bubb, Bubbly, or just BBB. She lived in some windy, wet town in Cornwall, was in her early forties, had never married. She was chatty and loved to laugh and was logged on to the Galaxy at times when it was impossible for her to be playing: 10 p.m. my time, which was 3 a.m. time her time. But there she was. Playing. It seemed she never slept. Often she'd be at a table with a player called Pest Control. Bubbly's usual avatar is the Blowsy Housewife, a once milfy but now gone-to-seed woman in her forties, and Pest usually played as the leathery-skinned, flinty-eyed, ten-gallon-hatted Cowboy character. Whenever I'd scroll down the screen of tables to see who was playing where and with whom, BBB was with Pest, who had made a ton of money in the extermination business in Edmonton before retiring at fifty-five. Pest was married and a father of three.

It's a common practice for players to create private tables (or "PTs") in the Galaxy; all it takes is a few clicks. These tables can be for two or for ten; the main thing is that the person who "built" the table decides who to let in and who to keep out. A virtual velvet rope of one's own.

Private tables are the No-Tell Motels of the Galaxy although the walls, ceilings, and bed sheets are all transparent.

Bubbly's round-the-clock perkiness was alarming. Not only was she always awake, not only was she always logged on, but she was always in a great mood; she loved everyone and effused joy the way that George W. Bush did befuddlement. Other than a few flirty remarks, Bubbly and Pest just seemed to be friends, friends who'd never met or spoken to each other.

I was playing for — and losing — real money in Medium one afternoon when Second Gunman appeared. He didn't fully click in to play; he just sat at the table (and watched me quickly dump another five hundred).

"At the hotel now," he told me. "YLO."

(He was informing me his Yellow Light was On; he could talk now but at any moment his boss might show up. GLO meant the coast was clear and he could chat; RLO meant he couldn't.)

The river card was dealt and I lost $300 to two sixes.

"Chip, you have to come to a FMT in L straight away!" Second said. (A Fake Money Table in Low — Low being the very cheapest tables.)

"Why? I'd much rather lose real money here," I said. And I wasn't kidding. Somehow, losing a load of real money is a more fulfilling experience than winning a little bit of fake money.

"It's Bubbly and Pest! They've got a PT. It's just them! You gotta suss this out ASAP!"

Second Gunman vanished and, after losing $200 with another hand of pure squadoosh, I vanished, too.

It only took a few clicks to find Bubbly Brit Bird's PT. She was playing as the sultry Dragon Lady in the red cheongsam, and Pest was the Cowboy, aka Tex, Hoss, or Clint. They had no idea I was watching. Or that Second Gunman was watching. Or that perhaps 25,000 other people around the world may also have been spying on them.

> **Bubbly Brit Bird:** positively sopping wet right now 4u.
> **Pest Control:** you're wearing blk?
> **Bubbly Brit Bird:** blk bra, baby, and blk knickers. nothing else, phil.

Bubb's real name was Georgette. Pest's was Phil.

> **Pest Control:** georgy my georgy. my sweet georgy. r u touching it?
> **Bubbly Brit Bird:** y. but w/what? guess.
> **Pest Control:** your fingers? pocket rocket, lover?
> **Bubbly Brit Bird:** n. a /toothbrush. the bristly end. where the paste goes. ☺

Bubbly Brit Bird wins $80 with two 7s and two 2s.

Something suddenly popped up . . . it was a dialogue box on the lower right of my screen. Second Gunman was IM'ing me beyond the earshot of Bubbly and Pest.

> **Second Gunman:** Can you feckin believe this, Chip?
> **Chip Zero:** This is amazing! I didn't know Pest had it in him. I really didn't.
> **Bubbly Brit Bird:** what would u do 2 me if u wuz here w/me, baby?
> **Pest Control:** i'd turn you over and start massaging your neck. slowly. v slowly.
> **Bubbly Brit Bird:** oooh. can feel your strong hands all over my back. mmmm.
> **Pest Control:** now I'm going lower with my hands. lower, lower, lower.
> **Second Gunman:** Any lower, Chip, and he'll be in bloody France!

They continued playing cards and playing with each other. She unbuckled his trousers and he massaged her. While he kissed her and she moaned, she won the hand with a heart flush. After dropping $300, Pest turned her over and showed her how aroused he was, which in turn aroused her further. He was sexually multitasking all over her body, massaging her back while playing with her nipples and fingering her. Unless he was an octopus, it was physically impossible but they were enjoying it . . . and so were Second Gunman and I.

> **Chip Zero:** Second, I don't claim to be any kinda of expert at these sort of things but I daresay I think these two are going to shag!

The following then popped up on my screen for five seconds:

Plague Boy by Frank W. Dixon
Amazon.com Sales Rank: #590,949 in Books
Yesterday: #584,253 in Books

And then:

Love: A Horror Story by Frank W. Dixon
Amazon.com Sales Rank: #680,158 in Books
Yesterday: #672,273 in Books
Customers Who Bought This Item Also Bought:
The Missing Chums   The Hidden Harbor Mystery   Freedom

Bubbly cut the foreplay short; while he was busy telling her how he was licking her ears, she informed him that he was already inside her. As soon as he said that, all the massaging and licking stopped, though they did continue to play poker.

> **Bubbly British Bird:** still rubbing self w/bristles. getting close, baby. u feel so good 2 me. go slow, go slow. want 2 feel u deep inside me. mmmmmm. o yeah. o yeah.
> **Second Gunman:** This is getting too hot, Chipper. I may sneak off for a wank in one of the hotel's linen closets. GLO btw.

Bubbly British Bird wins the hand with three 3s.

Bubbly British Bird: ohhh baby i'm so close now. so close. o yeah o
   yeah o yeah. yes. yes. your [sic] getting close. cum w/me, lover.
   cum w/me!

Hoss and the Dragon Lady stayed still. They didn't bet, fold, or
say anything. Other than some loud panting I stayed silent. The
silence lasted a minute. It was like a scene out of Ovid: almighty
Zeus and some supple demigoddess were going at it deep in the
woods of Arcadia, and all the mortals and fauns in the world had
stopped what they were doing to peep in on it from behind the
bushes.

*Pest Control, you must act or you will be disconnected. Either call,
raise or fold. You have 30 seconds!*

Pest Control: oh god. i just came. whew. jesus. wow.
Bubbly British Bird: me 2, lover. ☺ w/my toothbrush. LOL.
Pest Control: really? you really did? promise?
Bubbly British Bird: yes, phil. promise.

Pest Control/Phil hadn't really had sex with Bubbly Brit Bird/
Georgette, yet he was worrying if she was faking her orgasm or not.
Perhaps he sensed that a fake orgasm for fake sexual intercourse
while playing for fake money was a fitting climax.

Second Gunman: I just noticed something. She won about three
   hands in a row while she and Tex were doing it. Pest couldn't
   concentrate. You know what I should do? I should get a female
   nick and start playing for RM [real money]. Talk dirty to the
   men players and steal all their quid while they choke their
   chickens.

That struck me as a cunning, strange, and possibly extremely
sick idea . . . but also as a pretty good one.
The lovers' pixilated afterglow was now interrupted.

Pest Control: wife just got home, bubb! c u later?

Of course he would. There never was a second when she wasn't logged on.

Bubbly British Bird: yes. hope so. luv u! ☺ bye!

Like an actual man getting actual action from an actual mistress, Pest had had his fun and now it was time for a swift exit. Who knew if his wife really just did come home? But who knew if he—or Bubbly British Bird—had really been toying with their own body parts? Maybe in reality not only was Bubbly not holding her toothbrush, maybe she didn't even have a toothbrush because she had no teeth or arms at all.

Eavesdropping on private conversations became a regular part of my life. It was just as sneaky, forbidden, and reprehensible as an extramarital affair and probably just as much fun. I would do it for about an hour a day, fifteen minutes here, ten minutes there, sometimes only a minute at a time. I still played poker the same amount of time, though. So the eavesdropping time ate up more time when I could have been writing.

But there was nothing to write and nobody to write for.

♣ ♣ ♣ ♣

When *Plague Boy* came out, in February of 2000, I was booked to do a reading at the Barnes & Noble on Union Square. I couldn't wait. By the time of the reading, *Plague* had only officially been out a week, and so far, everything was going well. The reviews were good, and though the sales were modest, with a few more good reviews, they might pick up. The rotating fan that was my literary career had yet to be hit.

In about half of the reviews, however, I had been referred to as "reclusive." One or two reviewers made comments such as, "Dixon, who guards his privacy jealously . . ." and "The publicity-shy novelist . . ."

There was only one reason for this: There was no photo of me on the book jacket. Because of that and that alone, it was construed that I probably was either a shotgun-toting long-bearded maniac who wrote his little books on an old typewriter deep beneath the ground in a Wyoming bunker, or that I was a vampire whose face did not show up in mirrors and photographs. The simple but embarrassing truth was that ever since *The New York Times* Style editors airbrushed me out of my wedding announcement picture, I have been pathologically camera shy. No photograph, to my knowledge, has been taken of me ever since.

Abigail Prentice,[2] the chief publicist at my publisher, and Toby Kwimper kept insisting that a photo of me appear on the dust jacket, and Abigail told me their art department would hire a sympathetic photographer who would make it easier for me. Toby advised me, "It'll look really weird without a picture. I promise you." He asked me to think about it—and I did—but the more I thought about it the more I resolved not to go through with it. They were getting close to shipping the art to the printer and I still hadn't made a decision. "Well?" Toby asked me, the deadline only hours away. "Well," I said to him, "I . . . I just don't know." The deadline passed and there was no picture and that is how I became, for a few weeks, "the reclusive author."

My reading at Barnes & Noble, I felt, and all future readings would put an end to such talk. I didn't live in a bunker, I used a computer and not a typewriter, and I owned no shotguns and didn't suck blood out of peoples' necks.

---

2. Abigail begged me to not publish under my real name. Can you call yourself Fred W. Dixon, Dix Franklin, or Frank Dix, she pleaded. I wouldn't comply. Then it occurred to her that extra sales might result due to readers thinking the "real" Franklin W. Dixon had written a new book. She was right: 2,000 copies of *Plague Boy* were bought and returned two days later. How many readers bought my book thinking it was going to be a Hardy Boys book but who didn't return it will forever remain a mystery worthy of the two detective lads themselves, but, given the poor sales, it couldn't have been too many.

The *Plague* reading was scheduled for a Monday evening at eight o'clock. I asked Abigail how many people might attend, and Abigail, whose job as publicist, after all, was to always spread the good word (in other words, to tell bald-faced lies about everything to everyone), told me that the room would be filled and that the joint would be quaking with laughter and applause. It would be, she said, a smashing success.

"You do this," she threw in, "and in two weeks I'll get you on *Charlie Rose*. Who knows, if the book gets a great review in the *Times*, which I have no doubt it will, maybe we can even get you on *Oprah*."

"*Charlie Rose?*" I gulped. "*Oprah?*"

Oh lord. Was I also television-camera-shy? I had no idea. It had never occurred to me I'd ever wind up on television and thus had no phobia prepared for it. It was as if someone was telling me I was going to be transported to another galaxy or appointed attorney-general of Burkina Faso. It just wasn't something I had ever thought about.

I picked the ten fastest and funniest pages of *Plague* and, for two weeks, rehearsed aloud for the reading. I imagined hot writer groupies melting the steel of their folding chairs as I slew them into submission. After I was finished, I merely had to point at one of them—or at two of them—and some Barnes & Noble lackey would usher the limp, damp, besotted writer-worshipper over to me.

It was six at night, two hours before the Big Event, and I was shaving. Cynthia had picked out a suit, shirt, and tie combination for me and laid it out neatly on our bed. All I had to do was shave and shower. She would tie my tie and dimple it perfectly, as she always did.

I rubbed hot water on my face, applied a thin layer of gel, put my razor under scalding hot water so that the blade was steaming. The radio, tuned to NPR, was on in the next room and I wasn't really listening to it, but then I heard these words: "... *Plague Boy* is perhaps one of the worst and most depressing American novels to be written in decades. Not one word rings true. How this unfunny, boring, lame novel ever got published is . . ."

At that very second the razor was making its second downward pass over facial terrain I'd already shaved and I cut myself so savagely that to this very day there is faint skin discoloration on that cheek in some spots. The reviewer continued and I continued shaving. He kept ripping my book and I kept ripping my skin. He even, maliciously, gave away the book's surprise ending; up to that moment I'd thought doing that was a criminal act. (I didn't yet know it actually was a tactic.)

Blood was all over the sink. There was blood on the floor, on my chest, over the tiles on the wall. There was blood on all the toothbrushes, and soon, as I began wiping it up while still trying to listen to the radio, there was blood on about four bathroom towels. I staggered into the bedroom and blood dripped onto the suit, shirt, and tie on the bed. Cynthia brought in a roll of paper towels and we used that and then had to use another one. "He gave away the ending!" I hissed as we soaked up the blood. I had not only torn off two and a half square inches of my cheek, I had nicked my earlobe—it required ten stitches later that night— and lips and cut a trail about six inches long into one side of my visage. The bleeding didn't stop. One side of my face was fine, the other looked like chunks of seared salmon.

Cynthia lovingly smeared about a pound of Neosporin on me as, still aghast, I again said, "He gave away the ending!" and then, while she mopped up the remains, I went off—my face now the color of crushed raspberries—to Barnes & Noble to read from my first novel.

"You can't get up there and do it," the store manager said to me. "Not in this condition."

Abigail was there and couldn't look at it, "it" being my throbbing, lacerated face.

"I can do it," I mumbled. But it hurt me just to move my lips up and down.

Two dozen people were already seated . . . they were looking at me and praying I wasn't going to be the author who'd be facing them from only ten yards away.

"Yo, Frankie!" I turned around and saw Lonnie Beale, my good friend, who had come to see me read. "Holy shit!" he said. "Did you walk into a lawn mower?"

I told him that, yes, I sort of had and then I said, "Lonnie, can you do me a solid?"

It didn't take any nudging at all to convince him to do the reading for me. I tried to find Abigail to tell her I'd be employing a body double but, revolted by the sight of my twitching cheeks, chin and neck, all of which now resembled a melted candle, she had already fled.

Lonnie did a great job, I was told. (I rushed off to a hospital emergency room and couldn't stay for it.) Since there was no photo of me on the book, only a few friends of mine present knew what was up.

More than my face was killing me, though. It turned out the man tearing apart my book on the radio, a weakly-voiced, effete short-story writer named Cody Marshall, was the man who'd be reviewing *Plague Boy* for the *Times Book Review* the following Sunday. He gave away the surprise ending there, too. My ship had just struck its first iceberg and, after the review ran, Barnes & Noble never asked me to read again. Nor did any other bookstore.

"Charlie Rose," Abigail told me, "isn't returning my calls. Sorry."

She probably wasn't even calling him.

♠ ♠ ♠ ♠

I was so eager to play poker and chat with my Poker Buddies when I got off work that I'd call up the coffee shop across the street before leaving my office so that the cheeseburger, fries, and chocolate shake would be waiting for me fifteen minutes later when I got off the subway. And when I did get off the subway I trotted as fast as I could go. I'd pick up the food from the counterman, have the exact amount of money ($9.75) ready, then huff and puff back to my building, where hopefully the elevator was on the first floor waiting for me. I always made sure to leave my desktop computer on when I left the house in the morning so that I didn't have to wait the two minutes and twenty seconds it took to turn the unit on, access the Internet, get to Pokergalaxy.com, and log in.

I stopped going to the gym. Those six hours a week were now allotted to cards. Time was money, and running home with my fattening lunch was all the exercise I was getting.

Now I could walk through the front door and be playing poker (and jamming fries down my maw) within ten seconds.

The words *addiction, gambling problem, obsessed, denial,* and *help* hadn't yet occurred to me.

The company that I was (barely) working for had no idea I was winning more money on their dime than they were paying me. It was as if they were paying me to use their office space as my own office space. I felt guilty cashing their checks but still forced myself to do so.

Bubbly Brit Bird and Pest Control kept up their affair, playing and joking around with others but heating it up at private tables. There were dozens of other trysts and flirtations going on (in some ways being on the site is like walking down a high school corridor between classes) and you could witness every sexual activity, from adult toys to group sex to armpits and toe-sucking, known to man. If an anti-American terrorist organization could read some of the sex chat on the site, they wouldn't deem this country worth destroying.

One time I stumbled upon Cali Wonder Gal entertaining a Seattle furniture salesman.

> **Cali Wonder Gal:** So how big, Eduardo?
> **Fast Eddie G:** How's 11 1/2 inches sound to you, baby? Rock hard.
> **Cali Wonder Gal:** No way.
> **Fast Eddie G:** I no lie to you, sugar pie.

Cali Wonder Gal: Oh yes you do.

Fast Eddie G: Just sent you a foto.

Cali clicked out while she downloaded Fast's photo, and I didn't believe Fast any more than she did. (Only a week before I'd over-heard a player named 23rd Century Foxx telling a guy named Buff Stuff Bobby that she was hot. "How hot," Buff had asked her. "Soooooo hot," 23rd told him. "I'm a hi class escort, $3K an hour." Whereupon two minutes later Buff was not only losing $500 to her three 9s but was ejaculating all over her 36D breasts. "I just jizzed," he confessed to her, "all over your gorgeus [sic] boobs, baby." But I clicked on 23rd Century Fox's profile page [where players can, if they so choose, display personal information and a picture] and the truth in all its gory detail was revealed: The woman may indeed have had a 36D chest but the rest of her looked like a cross between Yoda and Teddy Kennedy.)

Cali clicked back in.

Cali Wonder Gal: Holy smokes, Fast, you no lie to me!

Fast Eddie G: Did I not tell you, baby?

Cali Wonder Gal: I'm surprised you could even take a picture of the whole thing!

Fast Eddie G: Can you handle all that?

Cali Wonder Gal: Honey, I can. But I just don't know if you can handle me. I'm very hot.

I happen to know that Cali Wonder Gal is not very hot. But this is one of the crucial things about this site: all the women are Angelina Jolie, Halle Berry, Megan Fox, and Salma Hayek, and all the men are Brad Pitt, George Clooney, Robert Pattinson, and Johnny Depp. A pair of breasts smaller than a C cup doesn't exist, nor does a female waistline larger than a size six or a men's larger than a thirty-two. Hair is silky and wavy, legs are long, smooth, and slender. Baldness is eliminated, as are eyeglasses, limps, birth-marks, lisps, freckles, acne, and cellulite. All the guys are hung like giraffes and have butts that turn women's heads. In this online utopia, Lane Bryant, Rochester Big & Tall, Rogaine, Pfizer, and plastic surgeons the world over would have gone out of business in a day.

You cannot eavesdrop for two hours without seeing an exchange like this:

> **Nash Gambler:** So who do you look like?
> **Dallas Alice:** What do you mean?
> **Nash Gambler:** Like what celebrity?
> **Dallas Alice:** Well, my friends tell me I look like Giselle Bundchen.

One of the saddest sights is to witness a player all alone waiting for his or her date. Their forsaken animated avatars cannot even tap their fingers against the felt or order a drink from an off-screen bartender. They just have to sit and wait, sometimes for hours. It's sad enough to see a person getting stood up outside a theater, at a bar, or in a restaurant in real life, but to see it happen to a person's cartoon alter ego on a computer screen is even more heartbreaking.

Friendships are forged too: it isn't only about Ace-high flushes, bodily fluids, appendages, and *mmmmm*'s and *ooooooh*'s. Second Gunman and I, as the weeks and months progressed, spent hours griping to each other about our lives during and between games. Toll House Cookie, who'd confessed to me he stole money at his job (he works in a New Jersey tollbooth near the Lincoln Tunnel), sent me pictures of his twin daughters when they were born.

I never asked Second his real name but he told me it was Johnny. For weeks I wouldn't tell him *my* real name. "Just tell me your name for chrissake," he'd plead. "My real name is Johnny Tyronne and I was born in Dublin but my family moved to England when I was four and I live in Blackpool and I work at the Four Swans Hotel and . . ." What I truly feared was my fellow card players finding out my Amazon rankings, for isn't that the *true* measure of a man? I also feared them saying, once they knew I was (once) a writer: *Hey, I'm writing a book!* or *I've thought about writing a book* or, the absolute worst, *I could write a book about my life/my family/ this place.*

Second Gunman/Johnny (it must have been four a.m., his time) was telling me one night about his girlfriend woes and we must have IMed for two hours straight, occasionally playing a hand. Then he asked me my real name, for about the hundredth time. Finally I caved and told him. He told me to hold on. I held. "You still there?" he asked me a minute later. I told him I was. There was no reply. A minute later I asked him, "Are you still there?" No reply. He came back a minute after that and said: "331,871 on Amazon UK. Not too good, mate."

❤ ❤ ❤ ❤

A lot of players have prearranged trysting times. For example, Kiss My Ace, a rugged contractor from Cleveland, would meet with Boca Barbie from one to two in the afternoon every weekday. Sometimes they'd allow others in, sometimes not.

> **Kiss My Ace:** You got my poem?
> **Boca Barbie:** Yes! It was so great. I read it over & over again.
> **Kiss My Ace:** ☺
> **Boca Barbie:** I'll send you back one when I get the chance, Tim. Xoxoxo.

Boca Barbie was a nurse and worked long shifts at a large assisted-"living" facility in Florida. Old men and women died on her regularly, and new ones would quickly fill their places, only to perish a few weeks or months later. A never-ending supply of the dying. Kiss was married, his oldest son suffered from severe autism, and his wife was on Zoloft; the Zoloft wasn't working although it didn't bother him that it killed any last trace of a sex drive she may still have had. Kiss My Ace/Tim and Boca Barbie/ Barbara sent hundreds of love poems to each other, some cutesy and corny, others serious, lovely, and meaningful. "Do you know," I once asked Kiss, "what Boca looks like?" The image of the 36D

Yoda/Teddy Kennedy hi class escort was still fresh in my memory. "Honestly, Chip," he said, "I don't care what she looks like."

Boca mailed care packages to a Mailboxes Etc. account that Kiss had set up, though Mrs. Kiss My Ace sounded so zonked out on her meds that it wouldn't have troubled her one bit had she ever opened a package containing Boca Barbie's stained chartreuse panties. Boca would also send Kiss homemade brownies, stockings she'd worn, sexy underwear she wanted him to wear, her home-made macaroni and cheese (his favorite dish), and souvenirs from Disney World for his kids. He sent her cranberry scones, flowers, books, sexy underwear he wanted her to wear. It was intoxicatingly pleasant to be around them and be in love vicariously (a bit like when dieters force-feed their friends doughnuts, chocolate, and pizza while they watch). Even though, of course, I wasn't really around them and they weren't really around each other.

> **Toll House Cookie:** So are you two ever going to meet?
>
> **Boca Barbie:** Maybe some day. You never know.
>
> **Chip Zero:** Tell ya what. How about everyone at this table chips in from their winnings and we donate some $$ for Boca's flight to Cleveland?
>
> **Cali Wondergal:** Put me down for $50 right now.
>
> **Kiss My Ace:** We'll need to put Barb up at a hotel too, you know.
>
> **Chip Zero:** Cali, you've won 400 goddam k. All you're putting in is $50? Have you no heart? Are you all dollars and sense? Have your winnings poisoned your soul?
>
> **Boca Barbie:** Yeah, Cali . . . I wanna stay at some swank 4-star hotel in Cleveland.
>
> **Chip Zero:** Have you no sense of decency, Cali, at long last? Have you left no sense of decency?
>
> **Toll House Cookie:** I don't think there are any swank hotels in Cleveland.
>
> **History Babe:** Ha, Chip! That was from the McCarthy hearings. You can't fool me.

Boca Barbie: I can't wait to melt in your strong loving arms, my
dear.

Kiss My Ace: I have to make sure I don't break you. . . . I want to
hug you so much. All I want to do is hold you in my arms and
kiss every pore from your forehead to your toes.

Boca Barbie: You can start with the toes, darling.

Chip Zero: I hope she wears Odor Eaters.

Artsy Painter Gal: This is getting a bit too gooey for me!!!

Chip Zero wins $800 with two 9s and two 3s.

I could pass hours in the presence of the two lovebirds, who
probably weren't the only Paolos and Francescas hooking up in
this poker inferno. Yes, it was sweet; yes, it was sickeningly gooey,
but even those of us born without hearts need to wade in a tide of
treacle every now and then, just to remind ourselves of how truly
cold and pitiless we are.

There was no doubt that Kiss and Boca loved each other. The
fact that they hadn't met and didn't care what the other looked like
only, in my eyes, meant that they genuinely, honestly, deeply loved
each other. They must have because even as they were exchanging
x's and oooh's they were also winning and losing money to each
other regularly.

Kiss My Ace raises $200.
Boca Barbie calls and raises $200.
Chip Zero folds
Strained Quads folds.
Kiss My Ace shows a Jack-high straight. Boca Barbie shows a club
flush. Boca Barbie wins $1,200 with a club flush.

Having a straight and losing to a flush is a wretched experience,
like biting into what you think is a porterhouse steak and it turning out to be Spam. Ninety-nine percent of the time, you're going
to win with a straight. Were I a multi-millionaire I would keep
a 38-ounce baseball bat nearby at all times while playing poker,

just to smash my computer to bits when a straight of mine lost to somebody else's flush or when a flush lost to somebody else's full house. Then I'd calmly hook up the next computer and start playing again.

But the two lovebirds were so deeply in love that money and pride didn't matter to them.

> **Kiss My Ace:** OMG, did you just beat me?
> **Boca Barbie:** I think I did, Tim.
> **Kiss My Ace:** I had a straight.
> **Boca Barbie:** Yes, I know. I had a flush. Clubs.
> **Kiss My Ace:** It's okay, darling. Still love you, you know that.

Losing $1,200 in one hand with a straight to someone's flush and then just forgetting about it . . . I don't know if I could ever love anyone that much.

◆ ◆ ◆ ◆

By the end of April I had won over $25,000. In two months I had netted about half of my Real Life salary.

I wasn't writing at all. I was playing.

Every morning I resolved to call Clint Reno and demand to know what was going on with my book. *It's my book*, I would thunder (he'd have to hold the phone a yard away from his ear). *It took me three years to write and I DEMAND to know what's going on!* But by the day's end, I'd forgotten all about that and was usually a few hundred or thousand dollars richer from playing cards. And I'd gotten lost in the maelstrom of puerile chat. It was saltwater taffy for my soul. Book? What book?

I checked and checked for any news about the *Plague Boy* movie.

I'm not really sure what Development Hell is, but that's where *Plague: The Movie* seemed to be languishing. Was a film my only hope? The movie gets made, *Plague Boy* gets reissued with a new cover (NOW A MAJOR MOTION PICTURE STARRING TOM . . .) and *Love: A Horror Story* gets reissued (WRITTEN BY THE AUTHOR OF PLAGUE

BOY, NOW A MAJOR MOTION PICTURE STARRING SCARLETT . . .) people start buying the books, publishers are interested in me again, offers pour in . . .?

There was never any news.

Once a week I e-mailed Clint. Groveling like a hungry dog. No reply came.

One warm April afternoon at about 3:30 I was exactly halfway between the kitchen and the couch, heading for the latter, when the front door opened. It was, I saw, Cynthia. Near the couch was a coffee table with frosted green glass, and on the frosted green glass was my laptop, and on the laptop was poker. Millions of colors and seventeen inches of poker. For two hours I'd been enduring, with groans the neighbors may have heard, a terrible losing streak. Cynthia had no idea that I would be home and in the blink of an eye I had to decide whether to dash to the couch to close the laptop or to skip to the door and tell her either that I was only working half days now or that I loved her. Or both. But the blink passed, so did a few others, and instead I stood frozen in the living room, a cold can of Coke in my hand.

She was equally frozen in the doorway, bewildered by my presence.

"What are you doing home?" I asked.

"There wasn't much to do and I decided to come—what are *you* doing home?"

My laptop let out a soft but suspicious *brrrnnng.* I was wanted at a table.

"So you're only working a half-day today?" I asked, almost sounding accusatory.

"Yes. There wasn't any—"

"Well, me too. I'm only working a half a day. Today. And tomorrow. And last week."

I told her more of the truth (and the can of Coke was no longer so cold): I'd affected this historic life-change of mine about three weeks before. I now only worked from nine to 12:30. She asked me why I hadn't told her this and I said, "I've been meaning to but I kept forgetting. Sorry." She moved into our tiny foyer and asked me how I was spending my free afternoons at home, and I told her, "They're not free. I'm writing a book. It's not like I'm not doing anything." She walked farther into the apartment and was straddling the foyer/living room borderline; she asked me what I was writing and I told her that it was Book II of a trilogy. As I'd completed the *American Nightmare* Troika years before Wifey had entered my life, she wasn't aware of its existence. (She hasn't read any of my unpublished books and could barely make it through the first chapter of *Dead on Arrival* because, in her words, "It's just so depressing.") So now, according to my boss Diane, I was writing Book I of the *Trilogy*, but according to Cynthia, I was writing Book II. (It was a good thing they weren't friends.)

"You could have told me this," she said. She looked past me and saw the coffee table.

"I know. I could have."

"You *should* have."

"Well, I just did."

The laptop emitted another *brrrnnng*. There would be no third: Either I resumed playing within thirty seconds or I would be kicked off that table.

"I have to get back!" I said to Wifey. "Things are coming to me a mile a minute and I can't afford to lose them."

"Things?" she asked. "What things?"

Book II. The *Trilogy*! My life's masterpiece! The things were the words, images, dialogue, descriptions, and plot twists of the project that would make me a literary immortal! What I was put on this Earth to do!

"You have to start telling me more, Frank," she said. "This really isn't good."

Frank? *Who?*

It took me a second to realize who Frank was. For the last two hours I'd been Chip Zero.

She sat down on the couch, kicked off her shoes and sighed, and I apologized and told her that from now on I would tell her everything.

I slammed the top of my laptop shut before she could see what was really going on.

6

It's Not My Party

I have so far in these pages kept Artsy Painter Gal's appearances to a minimum. That may be because in the very beginning, she didn't play an important role. The real reason, most likely, is that whether it's in books, movies, or music, love stories bore me.

Artsy Painter Gal lives in Los Angeles. She is a few years younger than I am, is married and has two daughters. Her husband is a successful investment banker (what else?). As a young painter — single, living in West Hollywood with six other bohos — she showed plenty of promise, was mentioned in several magazines; her artwork was displayed in several shows in galleries and small museums.

And then, suddenly, she stopped.

(Sound familiar?)

After our first encounter, I was smitten. Two days after that I found her at a table; she was playing as the Dragon Lady. The Big Man was taken, so I played as the Dapper Bond Guy.

It was a $50-$100 blind table; her stack showed that she had amassed $11,000, which was impressive since she hadn't been playing very long. It was 6 p.m. New York time.

I stayed silent for a few hands — money, luck, and good cards were going back and forth, which is the usual seesaw flow — then she won $1,200 with trip 10s.

Chip Zero: NH, Dragon Lady.
Artsy Painter Gal: TY, James.

She won the next hand with two eights.

Chip Zero: Hey, you called me Big Blond Boy the other day. I haven't forgotten that.

Artsy Painter Gal: Of course you haven't.

Artsy Painter Gal wins $400 with three 5s.

Chip Zero: You're on fire today, Artsy.

Artsy Painter Gal: I'm always on fire when a dashing guy in a rented tux sits next to me.

Chip Zero: I'm sure there's a fire extinguisher in this joint somewhere.

Artsy Painter Gal: Well, while you're spraying, you might want to get your underarms too.

I found her again the next day. There are four female avatars a player can play as: the busty longhaired Jayne Mansfield/Lady Godiva Blonde, the exotic Dragon Lady, the Blowsy Housewife, and the Wrinkly Bag Lady (aka Granny). The table was full when I found APG and I had to do something I disliked: play as a woman. So I sat in as the Blonde, the only available seat.

Artsy Painter Gal: Wow, look at you! Love the dress. Dior? Chanel?

Chip Zero: What? This old thing? I only put it on when I don't care how I look.

Artsy Painter Gal: You'll never be able to sneak an *It's a Wonderful Life* reference past me, baby.

I won $1,500 (the more players at a table, the more you win) with two Aces.

Artsy Painter Gal: Very nice pair, Blondie.

Chip Zero: Thanks. I knew I had that hand won.

Artsy Painter Gal: Oh, I wasn't talking about your cards. I meant your chest.

In Hold Blood: Ugh. You 2 need to get a room.

Chip Zero: I thought you liked them. You haven't stop staring at them since I sat down.

At first it was impossible for me to flirt guiltlessly. I loved Cynthia and she loved me. We were destined for each other and knew it the second we met. "You should have proposed to me the day we met," she often told me. "I would have said yes." It was either an act of divine intervention that she and I found each other or the greatest stroke of luck in my entire life.

With her I may not have been much, but without her, I know now, I am nothing.

♣ ♣ ♣ ♣

One of the reasons I had retained the services of the Reno Brothers Literary Agency for *Plague Boy* was their accessibility. There were no associates or receptionists to intercept the calls. They only put their voicemail on when the office was closed, and it wasn't even voicemail: it was just an old-fashioned answering machine. If I called Clint either he or one of his partners would pick up the call, or the phone would ring and ring and you knew nobody would pick up the call. From what I've heard, other agencies are different. Not only is it common for an agent not to return your call, but it is expected. It is expected that if a secretary or associate intercepts the call that he or she will not relay the message to the agent. With *Plague* and *Love*, when I called the Reno Brothers, Clint picked up. If I left a message on their answering machine at night, Clint would call me first thing the next day. I was hot then. A comer. The next David Sedaris.

(Agents are very weird people. Not as weird as the writers they pimp, but close.)

In May, five-plus months since I'd finished *DOA*, I came down with pneumonia. I'd never had it before: it just came and attacked me with a vengeance. It lasted about two weeks, and I spent two nights in a hospital. My fever went up to 103, I coughed and hacked through the night, I sweated and stank and shivered. The only relief was the two bottles of cherry-flavored codeine my doctor prescribed and the barrage of sincere get-well wishes from my Poker

Buddies. "Hope you feel better," Wolve e-mailed. "Thinking of you, honey," Cali Wondergal wrote. "Any better today? Hope so, kid," Grouchy Old Man said, sounding way too much in real life like James Frey's imaginary wiseguy friend Leonard does in fiction.

Was there a way I could make this malady work for me?

> CR:
>
> Haven't heard from you in a while and I hope you are well. I'm not. I've been deathly ill of late. Very bad. Spent 4 nights in the hospital last week. Fever of 105.5.
>
> With that in mind, can you inform me as to the fate of *DOA*? Anything new on it at all? Bad news, good news? Anything? It really, really would help me to know right now. I'm in a bad way.
>
> Thank you so much.
>
> FD

Clint never responded to that e-mail.

But toward the end of my sickness I got an e-mail from Beverly Martin, who was now done with her third novel.

> hey you!
>
> jill conway really loved your blurb and it's going on the book jacket. you should get an invite any day now to her book party, which is at florian, june 1, 8 p.m. your old editor toby kwimper should be there! can't wait to see you. xoxo.
>
> bev

Not a word from Bev on *DOA*, which she'd been soooo excited to read. But at least she hadn't called me the Master of the Suburban Mimetic.

Am I going to have to take my book to Deke Rivers at Last Resort, I wondered with a few residual coughs. That was miles beneath my writer's dignity . . . but my dignity was sinking lower and lower every day, and it was no longer so easy to compare what was beneath what.

Three more swigs of codeine and soon I didn't care about

anything. (To me the words "as needed" in a prescription translate to "all the time.")

The next day my temperature was normal. The invitation to the book party arrived and I RSVPed. Until this paragraph I have avoided mentioning that the publisher of *Saucier: A Bitch in the Kitchen* was my own former publisher. I had been dumped, cast aside, forgotten about, for books like this, for pink-covered, luxury-brand-name-filled, brainless chick lit. That's not writing, that's cupcake baking! Why couldn't someone be publishing *Dead on Arrival*, the book that was going to resurrect my career and make the Lit World take me seriously, instead of this I'll-blow-you-while-I'm-preparing-a-raspberry-coulis drivel?! It was a gross injustice. . . . This was my personal Sacco & Vanzetti, my Scottsboro Boys and Leo Frank all rolled into one! I had quit writing plays and movies because actors were all vain nincompoops and because I thought that in publishing, things were different. Publishers and agents were supposed to stick with writers through the mean and lean years. They were supposed to be courteous, courageous, loyal, generous, and determined. Was it possible they were just as unmannerly, cowardly, treacherous, venal, and irresolute as I was?

But at least now I had a book party to go to. And a plan. In attendance would be editors, assistant editors, publishers, writers. Wall-to-wall literariness. *I could network there!*

♠ ♠ ♠ ♠

Like me, Artsy Painter Gal didn't have a profile up on the Galaxy. To our fellow players, we were mysteries. People could click on our names, go to our profiles, but learn next to nothing. When I first got a glimpse of her moniker I thought that she might be a house painter.

It had occurred to me that I might be stalking her. Five times, in the beginning of our relationship, I had sought her out and then—poof! just like Barbara Eden's genie popping into a living room—shown up at her table. But this fear was put to rest one day when I was playing at a table and *she* appeared. APG had been seeking me out . . . and when I realized the crush was mutual, for a few minutes I was fifteen years old all over again.

That day I was riding one of those amazing streaks that serious gamblers go to churches to pray for. I remember staying in with one hand when I knew I should have folded. But I'd won so much by then that I figured: *Why the hell not? . . . I'll stay in.* I needed a 7 on the river to make a 9-high straight and sure enough, a 7 I got. As the Big Man in his yellow Don Ho shirt reached over to collect the $900, Artsy, in the guise of the Sexy Blonde, appeared.

We commenced the snappy repartee that would eventually become our daily conversation. It was something out of a Howard Hawks movie, had Hawks been born forty years later with a much filthier mind. Nobody could follow us, nobody could really join in, and, after ten minutes of the banter, nobody wanted to: the four other players left and it was just APG and Chip Zero.

After about ten minutes of absolute nonsense, all of it flirty and fun, she changed the tone.

> **Artsy Painter Gal:** So, uh, am I allowed one serious off-topic question?
> **Chip Zero:** One and only one. So make it count, baby. And I wasn't aware there was a topic.
> **Artsy Painter Gal:** Love it when you call me baby, baby. Okay . . . what's your real name and what do you really do?

If I told her that I had two unsuccessful books under my belt she'd know that I was a novelist, which might impress her unless, of course, she'd already met a few novelists in her life and knew better. (And I still dreaded the possible "Oh, I could write a book about my life . . . !" My answer to that is always: "No. You really shouldn't.") I decided to . . .

> **Chip Zero:** Okay, I'll tell you. I've written 2 books. There!
> **Artsy Painter Gal:** Uh-huh. Everybody's written two books. Were they published?

Chip Zero: Yeah. But nothing for a while.

Artsy Painter Gal: Can I get a title or do I have to torture you by wrapping my incredibly long, thin, recently waxed legs around your neck and tightening them?

I waited a few seconds and thought it over.

Chip Zero: The first book was about a man unwittingly carrying the plague and accidentally wiping out millions. But in the end it turns out he didn't really. He was just the dream of a dead person in Hell. It was sort of a comedy.

Artsy Painter Gal: Was it called *Plague Boy*?

My heart skipped a few beats and I think I even saw my rotund platinum-blond cartoon avatar perspire behind his round, rose pink shades. (Only on one occasion have I ever seen anyone reading a novel of mine in public: *Plague* had just come out and there was a pretty girl on a subway, smiling and turning the pages greedily; when I approached her and told her I had written the book she was reading, she looked for the author photo and, finding none, assumed I was a lunatic trying to pick her up. I quickly shuffled to the next car, then got off the subway at the next station, five stops prematurely.) A writer who's written a book that hasn't sold, when told by someone that they've read the book, will often joke, "Oh! So *you're* the one!" A defense mechanism, a way of grinning through the anguish. But APG had read the book.

Chip Zero: You actually have heard of the book?

Artsy Painter Gal: Oh yeah. Read it and enjoyed it.

Chip Zero: Are you telling me that you really bought this book and you really read it?!

Artsy Painter Gal: Swear to God I did, Frank.

I couldn't resist.

Chip Zero: So you're the one!

Artsy Painter Gal: You really wrote that? And there was another book? A second?

Chip Zero: Yeah. It didn't go anywhere. And neither have I, other
than to this table.

We clicked back in and played a few hands. I won $300, then lost
it. No other players were joining us: could they sense how much we
wanted to be alone, could they sense how dreamlike was the trance
we'd lulled ourselves into?

Chip Zero: So what gives with the nick? Artsy? Painter? Gal?
Artsy Painter Gal: Well, I am all woman, I assure you.

She told me that she no longer painted, did not even keep any canvas, paints, or brushes in the house. "Once in a while," she confessed,
"I find myself doodling but when I realize I'm doing it, I stop." I
asked why she'd stopped painting and she told me, "I was good but I
just wasn't 'something' enough," and that buyers, critics, and galleries
didn't care for the kind of paintings she executed. She couldn't sell,
galleries lost interest, she was ignored, and then forgotten.

Artsy Painter Gal: I really liked painting but I also like my dignity
too. So I stopped. There was no point. It was becoming torture
to do the thing I loved most. And speaking of torture, are you
enjoying my legs around your neck?

We spent the next two hours chatting and playing. It was wonderful, as much fun as I'd had in years, and was an entirely different thrill than winning huge pots from anonymous unseen human
beings. I told APG a little about my miserable time as a down-and-
out no-talent *naïf* in Paris and she appreciated it and we LOLed
and LMAOed. At one point she said to me: "I could talk to you
and play with you like this all day long, it's so fun."

I felt the same way and told her that.

I didn't tell her I was married. And she didn't tell me she was
either.

♥ ♥ ♥ ♥

When the pneumonia was gone and the codeine was alm
knew what I had to do.

I had to wrest the book from the grip of the Reno Brothers and get it to another agent. An agent who would seriously shop it around, who appreciated and understood my work, who would respond to me. Who would care. It wasn't about money and fame. I really did want to—and still do—entertain and transport people, to make them laugh, cry, think, to disturb and delight them. There is nothing quite like it.

Several weeks before Jill Conway's book party at Florian, I e-mailed Beverly Martin and told her of my dilemma. She told me she felt my pain . . . which I didn't believe for one second: a writer whose first book is being filmed feels no pain whatsoever. Crucify them upside down and slowly stick acid-tipped spears into their hides, they won't even ask for so much as one aspirin. During this exchange she told me, "i can't finish your new book, it's so good," which is, I suppose, the literary equivalent of a woman telling a man she doesn't want to sleep with him because she likes him too much. I asked Beverly who her agent was and she told me, but then said she didn't think the book was a right fit for him. She told me she would come up with a name for me right away and when she didn't I e-mailed her and reminded her. Her reply was simple: "ross f. carpenter @ the carpenter group. see you at the party. xoxo. bev."

I Googled this Ross F. Carpenter and saw he was highly esteemed in the Lit World. He had left a larger, more prestigious agency five years before and struck out on his own and was doing well. Since I no longer read books, I hadn't read any of his writers' work but I did remember the reviews; they were yawn-inspiring, sensitive, self-aware novels that I wouldn't like but that the *Times* did. Long sentences with tons of commas and million-dollar, fresh-out-of-the-thesaurus words, or short sentences with very few adjectives to indicate severe emotional detachment. They were all poignant, lyrical, elegiac, melodious, ruminative, self-conscious, cloyingly politically correct, full of pith and vinegar.

At work one morning I faxed an obsequious, fawning, undignified query letter to Ross Carpenter. It was as if I was swallowing the paper, feeding it straight down my own throat, and chasing it with a fistful of pride. I also faxed the good reviews for *Plague Boy* and *Love: A Horror Story* and, though I'd suffered mightily with the letter, seeing those reviews pass slowly before me was as invigorating as a cold shower. I saw the words: "coruscating and blistering . . . masterfully ugly and unsettling . . . almost brilliantly upsetting . . ." Maybe I *did* have talent! Maybe I could write after all! I mean . . . *they loved me in the U.K.!* But when I got back to my desk it occurred to me: *If I'm so coruscating, unsettling, and upsetting, then why the hell am I on my knees begging to whoever the hell Ross Fucking Carpenter is?!*

In my nauseating query I had ever-so-politely asked Ross if maybe there was any chance in the world that he had the time to perhaps take a look at my work so that he could maybe possibly represent me. I told him I knew he was very busy and very successful and very magnificent but that I was seeking new representation and maybe just maybe he would stoop to maybe condescend to perhaps deign to look at my new book for but one second, if he would be so kind, so merciful, so giving. Could he? Would he? Pretty please?

He e-mailed me.

Frank:
  Really loved Plague Boys. Didn't read A Love Story: Horror. Would love to take a look at you're [sic] new book. E-mail it. A few questions. Is Clint Reno still you're [sic] agent? Whose [sic] seen the book so far? I need to know that.
  Ross

I was able to stomach him screwing up the titles of both my books, but I don't know what disturbed me more: that if Ross wanted to shop *DOA* around, I'd still have to deal with the Reno Brothers Literary Agency to find out who they'd shown it to, or that he was no better with spelling than were half the people on Pokergalaxy.com.

I e-mailed him *Dead on Arrival*, all 750 double-spaced pages. I told him that I *thought* Clint was still my agent but wasn't sure. I told him:

> As far as I know, only Glenn Tyler of Lakeland & Barker has seen it. He called me a Master of the Suburban Mimetic and said it reminded him of Conrad's *Secret Sharer.*

Ross wrote back a few minutes later:

> Master of the Suburban Mimetic? Conrad? Sounds great! I look forward to the read. In the meantime, try to find out from Clint whose [sic] seen it, who hasn't.

Damn. Your toadying memoirist knew that Ross F. wouldn't risk sending the book to people who already had read it. If I couldn't get a list of names, I was officially screwed. But there was no way I was going to be able to get that info from Clint via e-mail. He hadn't even responded when I was coughing, shivering, and strung out on cherry-flavored opiates at Death's Door. No, I knew what I had to do. I had to talk to the man. Face to face. On the phone.

I rehearsed what I'd say to Clint Reno, I went over every likely detour the conversation might take and prepared myself. It was like planning for a journey and studying the map not only for the correct, best way to get there but all the wrong ways, too, the hundred possible wrong roads and wrong turns. I would be polite but stern, gentle but unyielding. It was my book, I'd let him know, it had taken me three years to write it and I certainly had a right to know its fate.

I finally called at 7:45 p.m. on a rainy Friday night, a time I knew the Reno Brothers office would be completely empty, cleaning lady included. It was still the same cackly old answering machine, the same old greeting and beep. I left a message for Clint and rattled it off perfectly, which was easy since I'd prepared myself for leaving a message too. "Clint," I urged, "I know you're very busy but please call me back or e-mail me and let me know who has seen the manuscript. Just let me know. That's all I ask. Please? Hope you're doing well."

Leaving that message had taken all my might and when I hung up I had to cling to the night table so I wouldn't collapse.

Clint did not return the call or send an e-mail.

I was officially screwed.

✦ ✦ ✦ ✦

By the night of the *Saucier* book party, I was $34,000 ahead. The weekend before, though, had been a disaster. (Yes, I was now playing on Sundays.) I'd lost five grand on a Saturday, then another five grand on Sunday. The culprit was overconfidence, straying from my Chip Zero Super System. And I did it knowing I was doing it and all the while cursing aloud. "I'm an idiot," I said, raising with nothing. "Why did I do that?" I yelled, calling when I had very little and *knew* the raiser had three 10s. One of my rules is to never stay too long at tables where there are PFRs (pre-flop raises). But I was breaking that rule. Another rule: don't stay in with a lousy pocket pair, hoping that a third 2 comes up on the turn or a third 4 comes up on the river. I was breaking that rule, too. And it broke me.

Chip Zero: Why did I just do that? I'm playing like an idiot today!
Bjorn 2 Win: Yes, you are. Perhaps you are not really so clever like you think.

Bjorn 2 Win wins $900 with two 9s.

But I was sustained by the attentions of—and by my attentions for—Artsy Painter Gal.

Money was no longer the main point of playing, nor was releasing torrents of aggression by pummeling other players. (And make no mistake about it, that's half the joy of poker: unleashing the fury, thrashing opponents, shaming them.) Nor was avoiding writing a new book.

When I got off work now and ran to the coffee shop to pick up my lunch, I was running because the sooner I got home, the sooner I could play with my new e-mistress.

Every day there was either a party with her and my Poker Crew or an intimate session at a PT with only Artsy. Sometimes there was both. I told her about playing poker and not writing, about the downward arc of my literary career. She told more of her past as a failed artist. We talked about parents, siblings, boyfriends, and girlfriends. Everything but wives, husbands, kids. We hadn't reached the dirty-talk stage yet and didn't want to. We were dating, in a way, but not quite at the heavy petting phase yet. We were just holding hands.

History Babe: So I met this totally hot guy last night in 5 card draw.

Mrs. Foldin' Caulfield: And?

Wolverine Mommy: Isn't this the 5th totally hot guy you've met in the last 3 days?

History Babe: This one's different. First of all, guess what?! He teaches history at Yale!

Second Gunman folds. Chip Zero folds. Mrs. Foldin' Caulfield wins $600 with two Aces and two 3s.

Wolverine Mommy: Sounds right up your alley.

Toll House Cookie: I'm sure that's right where she wants him too.

History Babe: He specializes in ancient Rome and Greece.

Artsy Painter Gal: Uh oh. Maybe he likes boys? You know those ancient Romans and Greeks.

Chip Zero: Ah, so *that's* how Plato kept getting all those A-plusses.

History Babe: Oh, he likes girls, believe me. We had a very long steamy session. 3 hours. And let's just say Caesar crossed my Rubicon 2 x last night.

Artsy Painter Gal: 3 hours, Chip. How come we never do that?

Chip Zero wins $600 with two Jacks.

Artsy Painter Gal: Oooooh, your stack just got a lot bigger, baby.

Wolverine Mommy: You know, APG, I did see Chip first.

Artsy Painter Gal: But, Wolve, we've never really seen him.

Which was a good thing. I didn't know what APG looked like and she had no idea what I looked like. She had only recently told me her real name: Victoria.

History Babe: So this prof knew all about the Peloponnesian War and Herodotus and Charlemagne. We have a date skedded for 10 tonight too.

I made a mental note that at ten that night I would seek out History and her new guy, wherever they were, to eavesdrop. A solid poker player, History Babe was by far the best dirty talker on the site. Nobody else came close (or as often). She had coaxed men into sending cell phone-made videos to her of themselves whacking off. A few of the videos, she told me, had sound: you could hear the guys crying out, while they climaxed, "Oooooh, History Babe, the Edict of Nantes!" or "Oooooh Hist, The Second Punic War! Oooooh!"

Mrs. Foldin' Caulfield: Send me a transcript tomorrow? It's all I have to look forward to.

Bubbly Brit Bird: Awwww, poor MFC. Not getting any at home?

Toll House Cookie: And she's married to a bone doctor too!

An hour later APG and I were at a private table. If anyone was eavesdropping on us and counting on exxxtreme nastiness, they were sorely disappointed. She told me about her high school days as the tall skinny Artsy Alterna-Dork, the outsider, growing up in a Detroit suburb. She didn't fit into any clique, she had few friends and hated the jocks and the popular girls. She had a boyfriend when she was a senior—he was six years older and was a designer at General Motors—but he ditched her. No letter, no phone call, nothing.

"I was heartbroken," she told me. "I still think about it."

"But I'm here for you, APG."

"Yes. I know. And I'm glad. You make my day, baby."

Somebody liked me again and the feeling was thrilling.

It was like a book of mine getting a very good review. Well, not quite . . . but close.

♣ ♣ ♣ ♣

On the day of the *Saucier* party I called Clint again, this time during office hours. That cowardly evening call to his office had energized me, made my onions a bit bigger. I still was planning to keep my cool, to do a little groveling. I just had to get that list. Also spurring me on was the possibility that Clint might surprise me with: "Frank, I've got great news for you. Jerry Bathgate at Something or Other Books loves the novel. I think we've got a deal!"

Crouched over in my study with the lights off—had you seen me you would've thought I was suffering from severe intestinal cramping—I made the call, bracing myself for the good or the bad. What I was not prepared for was . . .

A young female voice answering the phone: "Reno Brothers Literary Agency, this is Courtney, may I help you?"

Huh? Wha—? Or as some poker players say when they don't have a clue as to what's going on: *WTF?*

Clint and the other agents . . . *had hired a receptionist!*

"Huh?" I said to young Courtney, possibly a college intern working for school credit.

"This is the Reno Brothers Literary Agency . . . how may I direct your call?"

"They hired a receptionist?"

"Yes, I've been working here for three weeks. Whom do you wish to speak to?"

She sounded like a grad student who loved the Jonathans and the Davids and books like *Infinite Lovely Fortress of Illuminated Bones Corrections* and *Super-sad True Absurd Heartbreaking*

Debutante Clay and was planning to write a serious novel. She'd write it, it wouldn't get published, she'd marry a stockbroker and move to Greenwich.

"Three weeks did you say?"

"Yes. Who's calling and how may I direct your call?"

I thought about it. . . . It had been four weeks since I'd called and left the message on the Reno Bros. answering machine. . . . Clint must have heard that, made a few calls, then hired a receptionist . . . *just to intercept my phone calls!*

I could hang up and she wouldn't know it was me. But I had to show my cojones. I've bluffed and won hundreds of dollars with nothing but a 9 of clubs. This wasn't that different.

"This is Frank Dixon calling. . . . Can I please speak to Clint?"

She didn't say anything for a while. Had Clint instructed her: *If someone named Frank Dixon calls, tell him things are crazed around here and I'm incredibly busy right now but I'll call him back first thing when I'm free even though I won't.*

"I'll put you through," she said.

The Coruscatin' Kid was still hunched over in the dark. Maybe the news would be good. Kip Nowhere at Nada, Stugatz & Squadoosh loves the book. Bob Somebody at Nobody Books loves the book. Annie Nothing at Kiss My Ass Press loves the book. Bidding war, bidding war, bidding war. Or if the news was bad, maybe Clint would give me the list I needed, and my book and I could move on.

Courtney came back twenty seconds later and said: "Things are crazed around here and Clint is incredibly busy right now. He says he'll call you first thing when he's free."

"Okay," I said. "Please have him do that. Tell him I said hi. Thanks. Bye."

The *Saucier* party was in four hours. I went online and quickly dumped $2,500, then passed a delightful hour with Artsy. Second and Toll House Cookie joined us. It was fun but my mind was only half there, the other half was still stewing over how I'd been thwarted by Courtney and Clint. (I just naturally assumed he was boning her.) But it wasn't only that. While I was going to a book party for a novel that wasn't mine, my own book was festering in a swampy limbo that I couldn't even pluck it out of, and my career was somewhere deeper, darker and more impenetrable.

♠ ♠ ♠ ♠

I walked into Florian in the only sport jacket I had that still fit me, and it didn't even fit me that well. I'd gotten a slightly shorter haircut for the occasion: mostly gone now were the Depardieu *Return of Martin Guerre*, Late Middle Ages bangs I'd been sporting since childhood. I arrived five minutes late but saw instantly that I was one of only five people there, not including the wait staff. I didn't recognize the other four invitees—they looked like tourists fresh off a train—who were huddled and giggling together at a banquette.

There were about thirty tables; each table had three stacks of *Saucier: A Bitch in the Kitchen* on it. There were also gimmick recipe cards, deftly designed and index-card-sized, near the books, each one bearing a small portrait of Jill Conway. The recipes appeared at first glance to be legitimate but ultimately were not: a recipe for braised short ribs, for example, was the real thing but the last ingredient was: "Add two teaspoons of venom." For bouillabaisse, the final instructions were: "Stir in 2 ounces nitric acid. Stir and serve hot." And so on.

I ordered a glass of white wine and hung out alone at the bar, waiting for other people to appear. Most likely, I wouldn't know them, but at least I could hide better among them and not look so pathetically alone. I thought about leaving but couldn't: I had to be here and had to schmooze and network.

I drank my first glass of wine slowly and after twenty minutes got another one. Only three more people showed up. I made a call on my cell phone to Wifey, told her that this party was miserable and that I had nobody to talk to. I waited another fifteen minutes, only five more people showed up, I called Harry Carver in L.A. but he didn't have time to talk to me.

I sat down at a banquette by myself and looked at a copy of *Saucier*. I recalled, with a giggle, how when I was invited onto the NPR show *Fresh Air* to talk about *Plague* I'd sent Lonnie Beale rather than go on myself since he had done such a great job filling in for me at my one bookstore reading. Lonnie must have been terrific again because my Amazon ranking soared to an all-time high of 357 after the show aired. Perhaps the NPR staff had found me out and that's why I wasn't invited back for *Love: A Horror Story*.

(Maybe Lonnie should just start writing my books for me, too.)

I was on my third glass of wine and there was no relief in sight. Where was Beverly Martin? Where were the publishing types? Where was Jill Conway so she could thank me for my blurb and tell me as she was shook my hand, "Oh my God . . . I loved *Plague Boy* soooo much!" Whether said sincerely or not, that's what I needed to hear.

By the time I finished the fourth glass, there were about thirty-five people inside the place. I went to the bar, ordered a fifth and saw, near where the bar met the kitchen, a computer. The idea struck me: maybe I could get a few hands in, maybe I could vanish temporarily from the dismal world. I could find Artsy, Second, Cookie, or History Babe and joke the time away.

I drank the fifth glass in less than thirty seconds. *Un vin blanche, si'l vous plait.* No wonder the bartenders in Paris looked at me like I was a jerk.

"Nobody's using that computer now?" I asked one of the bartenders.

He said no and I got a sixth *vin blanche*.

I swung around and saw Bev Martin enter . . . she was holding the hand of a frizzy-haired guy with glasses so chic, so architectonic, and so magenta that they only barely registered in my consciousness. He was the latest entry in the Boyfriend of the Month Club . . . but any man with post-futuristic eyewear like that required a lot of attention, and she simply liked discussions about Magic Realism too much for that (the names Borges, Barth, Barthes, and Barthelme would no doubt be shrieked in their ear-splitting breakup fight). I gave them two more weeks as a couple. A few others entered. Most of them were in publishing, you could tell just by looking at them. Every profession has its own uniform with its own nuances. Real estate people (the leather coats with the belts), lawyers (the vests, the bulky briefcases), editors (gray cloth-ing, the nerdy glasses). Why not just tattoo your forehead: *I am a lawyer and thrive on the misfortunes of others. I sell real estate and am an inveterate snake. I edit books but people don't read anymore, they watch dumb-ass reality TV on their cellphones.*

I walked up to Bev and she introduced me to Kurt, her boy-friend, an editor at a lit Web site that I told him I visited religiously but had never heard of.

"So when is Jill getting here?" I asked Bev.

"Any minute it should be, I'd say."

She asked me if I'd contacted Ross F. Carpenter and I said I had but that there were complications. She didn't mention *Dead on Arrival* itself, which I imagined she'd already dragged to the trash on her computer. Kurt, who was a good three inches shorter than Bev, told me, "I haven't read your book but I'm meaning to." I reminded him that I'd in fact written *two* books, and that was it, he was through with me. I could see myself transforming from a human being to a dog turd in his eyes.

Beverly and Kurt drifted away and waiters in black floated by with trays of finger food and I asked them to come to me first and then gobbled up half the tray. I got another glass of wine, downed it with one gulp. After the *Times* and *Time* and the *Globe* boiled me alive (and all of them gave away my surprise ending!), nobody wanted to talk to me. A leper I was. A financially bankrupt blind leper with SARS and Bird Flu and Tourette's Syndrome and ooz-ing sores and sporting a glass eye and a prosthetic limb with mon-goloid triplet kids . . . cursed with all these afflictions I had become the sort of human being who sweet, compassionate people in polite society go miles out of their way to avoid. At work people didn't talk to me. Lonnie and Harry Carver didn't return my calls and Toby Kwimper sent me an e-mail that said: "Frank, I'm so sorry." It was all over and everybody knew it but me. The ship, Micheal Ray Richardson once said of the Knicks, be sinkin'. Mine had sunk, too . . . everybody had leapt off but I was the last moron standing on the deck, hoping it would float again.

"Hey, I need to use the computer for a minute," I said to the bartender. "It's urgent."

None of my buddies were online but I played three hands, playing as the leathery-skinned Cowboy: I lost $300 the first hand, folded the second, won $600 the next hand with two 9s and two 5s. Up $300 in four minutes. Then Artsy Painter Gal showed up, told me how nice I looked in chaps and snakeskin boots. I told her I was at a book party and couldn't stay. I played two more hands. I felt a pat on my back and turned around and saw it was Toby Kwimper.

"Frank!" he said, surprised to see me. He may have seen the screen.

"I'll be right with you," I said.

I told APG I had to go and would see her soon. "Sure, Tex," she said.

I spent ten minutes with Toby and he told me about how much he was enjoying golfing every day and not working in publishing anymore. His wife was a pediatrician and they'd be okay. "I'll figure something out," he told me. I was happy for him but it was sad to see what had happened and devastating to know that it was me who'd wrought it. (I felt so guilty and sad for him that I had trouble looking him in the eye.) Toby asked if I knew Jill Conway and I told him I hadn't met her but that I'd blurbed the book and that's why I was here.

"You blurbed the book?" he asked me.

"Yeah," I told him. "I attempted to come up with something reasonably clever."

We spoke for another two minutes, then separated, but not before he introduced me to his successor, Scott Heyward, who shook my hand limply, wiped my sweat off on his pants, and walked away. I knew exactly what Scott was thinking: *So this is Frank Dixon, the guy who drove our legendary editor Jerome Selby to blow his brains out. I'm getting far away from him.*

I went back to the computer and played two more hands. Artsy was gone.

When I turned around I saw Toby picking up a copy of *Saucier* and looking at the jacket.

I noticed a few people from my old publishing house, including the Publisher himself: he saw me and smiled like he had a mouthful of razor blades. (Or maybe he didn't recognize me with my new shorter haircut and new ten pounds.) None of them wanted to talk to me. . . . I was a dark cave they didn't want to walk into, a narrow ledge they didn't want to stand on. I understood.

I wasn't going to network with any editors or publishers here. It wouldn't work. I was damaged goods.

I pretended to make another cell phone call, just so I wouldn't look like such a loser. Toward that same end, I sent myself a gibberish-laden text message, then read it, and responded in kind a minute later. Then while I was calling Wifey I overheard a conversation between four people sitting at a nearby banquette. They were the first people at the party, the tourists who'd made it there before I did. They were Jill Conway's cousins, it turned out, up from Baltimore for the week of the party.

"You're Jill's cousins?" I said, slurring my words just a bit.

"Yes, we all are," said Cousin Lena. They were all in their thirties and very friendly.

"I'm Frank Dixon," I told them.

"Okay," Cousin Nick said. He was the tallest of them and the only male.

"I blurbed her book," I explained.

"Oh!!!!" they all said in unison.

"So you're a writer too?" Cousin Nick said.

I admitted I was.

"And what have you written?" Cousin Tina asked me.

I told them I'd written *Plague Boy* and *Love: A Horror Story* and they'd never heard of either book. I was used to that and no longer did it elicit a wince.

Cousin Nick picked up a copy of *Saucier* and began examining it.

"Jill is a big fan of my first book," I told the Cousins sheepishly.

"Are you sure you blrrbrbrbrbrbrbrbrbrbkbkb?" I heard Cousin Nick say. He was drowned out by music suddenly coming on and by the din of the crowd, which was now up to a very loud hundred or so people.

"Huh?" I asked him. I turned to Cousin Lena and said: "Hey, when Jill shows up, tell her I said hello. I'm gonna leave now. Will you tell her that Frank Dixon said hello."

"Are you sure you blurbed the book?" Cousin Nick asked me. He had the book open on his lap.

They began talking among themselves, about what they were going to do tomorrow in New York. *Take in a museum. See Central Park. Don't wanna get mugged though. Hee-hee.*

I picked up a copy of *Saucier*. I flipped it over, looked at the back of the jacket.

There was a brief two-paragraph description of the book, then three blurbs, including one from Beverly Martin: "Not only the sharpest and funniest book written by a woman about working and food that I've read in years, but the funniest book written by anyone about anything." Mario Batali had even weighed in: "I'd never hire Jill Conway to work for me, but I would read any book she ever wrote. *Saucier* is hysterical, sharp and very tart."

I was nowhere to be found.

We could go down to Ground Zero. But that's depressing, I don't want to see that. How about going on the Circle Line? I'd like to go to Saks. Is there anything in Brooklyn?

My blurb hadn't been used. It wasn't there.

Because I didn't count. Nobody had any idea of who I was, so why bother using it?

I walked away to a corner and drank another glass of wine and nearly wept in the dark.

Jill Conway finally showed up, all in slimming black, got applauded, made the rounds. Her face glowed, her eyes sparkled, her smile lit up the room. It was her night. I overheard people wondering who would play who in the movie version.

Anne Hathaway would just be so perfect. . . . No, it simply has to be Reese! . . . No! Scarlett!

Toby Kwimper introduced Jill to me and her face remained expressionless when she heard my name. I said, "I'm Frank Dixon!" but maybe she hadn't heard it above the music and the clamor of the hundred sets of wind-up chattering teeth and her own ego bubbling over.

"I wrote *Plague Boy!*" I reminded Jill, having to yell right into her ear. "Beverly Martin told me it's one of your favorite books? That you have whole chapters memorized?"

She shrugged, leaned in and yelled back: "Huh? *Vague Toy???*" She shrugged again and shook her head, dumbstruck. She was still crinkling her nose when she was whisked away by Abigail Prentice, whose job it had once been to remove me from such awkward situations.

She had no idea who I was. My books meant nothing to her.

Crossing the street two minutes later, a meat truck almost ran me over but swerved at the last instant. "You fuckin' idiot!" the driver yelled at me. Just as I was about to yell back and deny it, I realized he was right.

When I got home, Cynthia was asleep and I went online right away.

I went to the small $5-$10 blind rooms, where people came to the tables with only $300 or so. These were the little guys, the ants, the nervous newbies who were just feeling their way around playing for real dough. I wiped a few of them out and apologized for it, then moved up to a table in Medium and played one-on-one with a stranger, a German guy named Hamburg Deluxe. He'd come to the table with $3,000 and ten minutes later he had not one pfucking pfennig. I played at a small table for twenty minutes in High and thrashed the three other players so badly they all quit at once. I went to another table and wiped everyone out. . . . They were just giving me their money and it didn't even seem like they were really trying. For the first time ever I went to the Ultra-High No-Limit tables, where all the players have cantaloupes for balls. A player named SaniFlush, who many on the site called the Master of Disaster and who was arguably the most feared and talented player on the site—his stack was over $900K at the time—was there. I played one hand with him, won $6,000 with only two 8s and left. I went to a 5 Card Draw table and crushed the five people in there. A guy said to me, "Hey, you're too good," and I told him, "Yeah, I sure am." I played Omaha—I barely knew the rules—and won some more. I won and won and won and it felt terrific. I was stomping over everything and everyone, crushing and destroying and mowing down all that I saw. So this, I marveled, is how postal workers feel when they return with a machine gun to the scene of their disgruntlement and spray everybody to shreds.

By the time I logged off, at 3 a.m., my stack was up to $50,000.

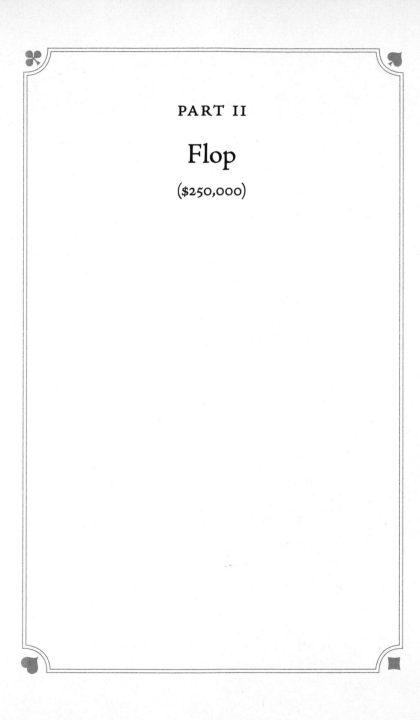

PART II

Flop

($250,000)

7
Chills

I had made $50,000 at online poker in less than six months. It was more than I'd gotten for *Love: A Horror Story*, which took two grueling years to write. And playing poker wasn't work, not even close. It was a game! I remember a ludicrous statement by the much-beloved and vastly overrated sports writer Red Smith about how writing a column was like "sitting down at a typewriter and opening a vein." And how many writers, when they're not griping about their legions of demons, have described a blank page as terrifying? You'll never once hear a housepainter describe an unpainted wall as terrifying. If a blank page is terrifying, then what is it like when someone puts a gun to your head and cocks the trigger or the bank is foreclosing or the doctor tells you your brain tumor is the size of a Titleist golf ball? If rattling off a column about the Dodgers defeating the Giants 5–2 was really like opening a vein, then perhaps Mr. Smith should have sought a different, less terrifying line of work and preferably not at the Red Cross.

In June I quit my job completely. There was no point in even working half-days.

"Are you sure you want to do this?" Diane Warren, my boss, asked me in her office.

"Yes," I said. "Completely sure."

"And how is the book coming?"

She meant the *Trilogy*, of course . . . but I forgot which part of the Triad I'd once told her I was writing: did Diane think I was writing Book I and Wifey think I was writing Book II? Or did

Diane think I was writing Book II and Wifey think I was writing Book I?

The truth was, of course, the whole trilogy was already written. Long ago.

"It's coming along."

She swiveled back to face her computer, but I wasn't through. A working stiff doesn't get a chance to do this that often in his life so I wanted to milk it for all it was worth.

"And then there's the movie, of course . . ."

"Oh yes," she asked, turning back to me. "How's that coming?"

I told Diane what I understood to be the truth: Pacer Burton was going to direct *Plague: The Movie*; the script had been written and was making the rounds with actors' agents. I sprinkled in a dash of untruth: the budget was $150 million, stars were foaming at the mouth to be a part of it. Tom Cruise, Leonardo DiCaprio, Cate Blanchett, Cameron Diaz, and Judi Dench would drop whatever they were doing if the project got the green light.

She turned to her computer again, where an Excel spreadsheet awaited her perusal.

Diane was a little too unruffled to see me go, and it bothered me. But she had no idea (until she reads this) that I was playing poker on company time.

(And now the truth can be told: the Diane who was my boss and the Diane I once caught in flagrante delicto with my little brother are one and the same. At the end of my job interview, years before, she shook my hand and said: "You know, I've never quite forgiven you for walking in on me and your brother that time." *WTF*?)

I had now escaped the clutches of Writer Diablo Numero Uno. I was free! Free as a bird, like the Jonathans and Davids and Chabons and Shteyngarts and Jay Easton McEllisses. No more real work, no more offices, no more bosses. Free at last!

But it was poker, not literature, that had unchained me. That wasn't the plan.

The week I quit I vowed to myself: *Now that I'm free, I'll start writing again. Sure, I'll sneak in a hand of Texas Hold'em every now and then, maybe win a few thousand here and there, but I'll write a book. I lied to my boss and my wife about writing one, so that will compel me to actually do it!* I was like a bride-to-be buying a wedding gown three sizes too small, hoping that in two months I'd lose the weight and be able to squeeze into it.

The prospect of buckling down and writing again was bracing and exciting. I couldn't wait to get started.

On my last day there was no going-away party; a manila envelope did not travel desk to desk and no present was bought for me. I had no exit interview with Human Resources and thus could not complain about the thousand imagined injustices inflicted upon me by all my coworkers. I simply tossed my company key-card into the trash and left.

After much deliberation—okay, not that much deliberation—I decided to wait before telling Wifey about this gigantic move of mine. I would simply lay low.

❤ ❤ ❤ ❤

The day after the *Saucier* party, I sent an e-mail to Clint Reno. It was one thing for him to ignore me, but what he was doing was systematically nullifying my existence.

CR:

Last night I was struck by a Drakes Cake truck.

I suffered a broken tibia, a bruised vistula, a fractured fibula, a partially separated tiber, two broken metatarsals, several 2nd degree lacerations on the skull, 3rd degree abrasions on both knees. I've lost 2 important teeth. My right tympanic membrane is just about shot and it's going to be a while before I hear anything out of that ear again. I have a temporary patch over one eye now and my leg is in a cast.

I'm e-mailing from the hospital now. But I'll be okay. As for the man in the next bed, he wasn't so lucky. Last night he suffered his

third aneurism in as many days, reeled over to my bed and died
on top of me, not before soiling most of my blanket. It took
7 hours before a nurse showed up to remove the deceased and his
excrement from my person.

Clint, have you heard anything from anybody about *Dead on
Arrival*? Could you please tell me who's read it?

You know, I ran into Bev Martin at a book party and all she did
was rave about how "fantastic and coruscating" *DOA* is. "It's really
your masterpiece, Frank," she said, "your chef d'oeuvre." And Jill
Conway, whose novel (ironically about chefs and hors d'oeuvres!)
was being feted, told me she was and I quote, "slobbering in
anticipation of reading it." *Plague Boy* is her favorite book of all
time, did you know that, Clint?

So please let me know what's up.

FD

Surely even Hardhearted Callous Clint would reply to that!
He didn't.

I had weekdays completely free now, so one Monday morning I
went to the corner of Spring and Lafayette Streets, where the Reno
Brothers Literary Agency is located. There was a Dunkin' Donuts
across the street and I sat on a stool near the window. It was 8 a.m.
I waited from 8 to 10 o'clock, drank four coffees and ate a box of
Munchkins, and stared out, keeping my gaze fixed on the building
entrance and looking for any sign of my agent. He'd be hard to
miss: six foot four and slender, a full mane of carrot-colored hair
always kept in a ponytail, clad always in unwrinkled bespoke Savile
Row suits. I saw his three partners go in, at 8:43, 9:18, and 9:48. But
there was no sign of Clint Reno.

Am I really stalking someone? I asked myself. *Yes, you are*, I
answered.

I waited another hour, drank more coffee, ate another box of
Munchkins. Nothing.

After returning home, playing some poker and eavesdropping

on an unbearably torrid session between History Babe and some seventeen-year-old named Royal Flash 89 ("I'm licking your warm cum off my hard nipples," she purred), I e-mailed my would-be agent Ross F. Carpenter:

> Hey, Ross. Just wondering if you've gotten a chance to read *Dead on Arrival*. If so, hope you like it. Pls let me know if you can.

Ross wrote me back within ten minutes:

> Not yet, Frank. Did you get that list from the Reno Bros. yet?
>   Was at the *Saucier* party last night. (Jill is one of my authors.) As I understand it, so were you. Too bad hour [sic] paths didn't cross.

The e-mail blurred to a steamy highway mirage, then came back to me.

At least Ross, unlike Clint, had responded to my e-mail. That was a positive sign.

I went back to the Dunkin' Donuts and stalked Clint every morning of the second week of my new full-time freedom. By Friday the women working there knew I wanted a box of Munchkins. . . . I didn't even have to ask for it; they just saw me and started loading them up.

I never saw Clint or his ponytail.

That Friday I called up the Reno Brothers. It was now six-plus months since I'd handed over the *DOA* manuscript. A half a year of waiting and virtual silence.

"Hi, I'd like to speak to Clint please?" I, voice cracking nervously, said to Courtney.

"Clint is in California now," she said. "May I put you through to his voicemail?"

Fifteen boxes of Munchkins, about forty cups of coffee, a few low-fat muffins here and there . . . and Clint had been 3,000 miles away the entire time.

"You . . . you have voicemail now?"

"Is this Frank Dixon?"

"Yes, it's me," I stammered. I was being reduced to jelly by a grad student (probably) who answered phones and filed paperwork and mailed back unsolicited, unread manuscripts and got coffee. The lowest entity on the publishing food chain was causing me to stammer, perspire and tremble.

Make that the *second* lowest entity on the food chain.

"Clint wanted me to relay something to you," she began. "He said that when the movie of your book gets made and if the book was ever reissued . . . ?"

"Yes?"

"He wanted to ask if his name could be removed from the acknowledgments page . . ."

"Okay. Sure. I could do that. Yeah. Definitely."

When we hung up, an alpine fog wafted into the apartment. But the fog swiftly scattered because I realized . . .

She'd said *when* the movie gets made! She hadn't said *if*. She'd said "when." Was that why Clint was in California? His identical twin brother, the ponytail-less Vance Reno, handled the movie end of their business, but since I was Clint's fair-haired boy perhaps Clint had gone out to L.A. to iron things out and finalize everything. The movie gets made, *Plague* gets reissued in paperback with Leo and Brad and Scarlett on the cover and hits the best-seller list; the all-pro shitheel who rejected *DOA* and called me a Master of the Suburban Mimetic calls Clint and begs to publish it. *Please, Clint, please! I'm sorry what I said about the mimetic! Please, Clint! I take it all back! I'm on my knees now, Clint. Tell Frank I'm sorry about the mimetic! Please, Clint, please!*

There was still hope.

❖ ❖ ❖ ❖

I continued to win and continued to not write. But I swore that once my stack hit $100K I would start writing again.

Sure, there were times when the Poker Fates were not smiling at me, when Lady Luck was so furious at me for not believing in her that she kept plunging ice pick after ice pick into my heart, when everything wrong that could happen did happen . . . but those times were few. The biggest loss I incurred was three weeks after I quit working: I'd been on a mini-losing streak and Second Gunman told me that Bjorn 2 Win was sitting alone at a table in High, waiting to drop a ton of cash. I quickly found the Offensive Swede. We folded a few garbage hands but then, with a full house, 3s full of Queens, I kept raising and reraising. But the Butcher of the Baltic had Queens full of 3s. I lost over $4K. If you've ever seen a boxer get punched so many times that he has no idea who he is, where he is, what day it is and that he is even partaking in a boxing match, then you have some idea of how I felt.

Flabbergasted and wounded I sucked it up and said, "NH, Swede."

"You do not even means that. You are too hurt right now. This does gladden me."

He vanished before I had a chance to win it back.

I lost $2,000 more dollars that day in a frantic effort to win the money back. I took a walk—it was June and New York was only just beginning to heat up—and went back upstairs. I was steaming, livid, dazed, and my stomach turned inside out. I wasn't used to losing and didn't like it at all. I had no job and my books had failed. Poker was all I had. If I wasn't any good at this, there was no point in being. I went back online and dumped another grand.

When Cynthia came home I greeted her with the sort of grunt an overweight ruminant might offer up to its cud.

She had no idea I wasn't working. In the mornings we left the house together at 8:45, as we'd been doing for years, and walked to the subway. She'd stand on the platform for the downtown train, I'd stand on the platform for the uptown train. But now if her train came first, I simply left the platform and returned home. If mine came first, I boarded and took it two stops uptown, then walked back home.

The night I lost all that money, I couldn't fall asleep. Not for a second. I *had* to get that money back. I was still way ahead, but it was the thought of losing, of my possible newly emerging uninvincibility, that gnawed at my psyche. And there was this concern: what if that loss was the beginning of a long disastrous schneid? I had now made over sixty grand; maybe it was time to lose it all. When I first met Toll House Cookie, his stack was up over $100,000; lately, it was hovering around a paltry $45K.

I knew I wouldn't be able to sleep unless I got that money back.

I went into my study at about 2 a.m. and turned on the computer. Nothing but tighty-whiteys on, my belly (those hundreds of Munchkins hadn't helped matters any) jiggling in the darkness lit dimly to turquoise by the flickering hues of Pokergalaxy.com. On the wall over the desk was a still-life—after Derain—of a pear in a bowl; on the opposite wall, a portrait—after Cezanne's *Portrait of Uncle Dominique as a Monk*—of a hungry, homesick, and ridiculously optimistic young man suffering a throbbing headache. (These two works, executed in Paris, of course, were the closest I ever came to being any good at painting.) I went to a table with $100-$200 blinds. Lots of Aussies were playing, lots of South Africans, a few people in California and Seattle. I lost a few hundred more. I wasn't going to let this happen . . . *I had to win it back!* Then I won a few hands, moved to a table with bigger blinds. More Aussies, a few Japanese, Indians and Pakistanis. Melbourne Loser. Osaka 2 Me. Never Can Say Mumbai. Was it tomorrow on that side of the world or was it yesterday? In one game I smelled weakness and won $800 with two 4s. The next hand I won a grand with a diamond flush. Chip Zero was on a serious roll; where my brain should have been, a juicy porterhouse was sizzling on a hot grill. The next hand I got dealt pocket Kings. I raised and other players checked or folded . . . but to my right I heard a rustling and saw the silhouette of naked Mrs. Chip Zero coming toward me in the darkness. A Paul Delvaux painting come to life, on Eighth Avenue and Sixteenth Street.

"What are you doing? It's four-thirty, honey."

"Writing my book," I told her. "I couldn't sleep."

I still had those two Kings. I didn't want to lose the hand.

"But it's late."

"Uh-huh. I just got hit by a serious bolt of inspiration. You know . . . the Muses, right?"

"Must they sing so late? Just come to bed . . ."

A woman named Lahore With A Heart of Gold raised and I checked. A nice slow-play could net me a lot of money here. I had to get that money back!

"When they sing," I told Cynthia, "I have to listen." Now in the past, when I *was* a writer, it wasn't unusual for me to pen my novels at ungodly hours . . . but this was odd, especially since she hadn't seen me writing for many months.

The river card was another King. I had three of those magnificent monarchs now, three of them! The doomed Pakistani raised and I re-raised. Then I inadvertently let slip the nickname for a hand of three Kings and said: "George Clooney."

"Huh?" Cynthia asked with a yawn.

"Um . . ." I covered up, "Barbara Bennett e-mailed me from Hollywood tonight." Barbara was with Egregious Motion Pictures in L.A. and was spearheading the *Plague* movie. "George Clooney is interested now. The *Plague* flick."

"And what is it you're writing again now?" Scratching her sleepy head.

Was it Book I or Book II she thought I was writing? At this hour I couldn't remember, and neither would she. So I said, "You know, that trilogy deal." If she ever asked to see it I could just go to the Chelsea storage facility where it was rotting in airless silent oblivion. (If I could remember where the hell the key was.) Though she then might ask why something so piping hot off my printer was so yellow and caked with dust.

Chip Zero wins $4,800 with three Kings.

I let out a maniacal giggle, sounding like a cross between an old dot-matrix printer and David Hedison at the end of *The Fly*.

"You okay?" she asked me.

"Oh, very much so!"

She went back to bed. Five minutes later she was joined by her loving, content, supersnugglicious husband, who slept like a baby, knowing how incredibly lucky he was.

♣ ♣ ♣ ♣

Whenever you hear a man complaining how gullible, guileless, and oblivious his wife is, keep in mind that this man is secretly grateful. My own suspicion-impaired wife believed I was still going to work every day and still receiving a weekly paycheck. Further covering my mendacious ass, I went to Tiffany one day and purchased an Elsa Peretti necklace for her. This bauble wasn't cheap, but I figured I could win the money it cost in an hour of solid play. I was wrong about that: it took me only twenty minutes. I went home, stashed the ice in a sock drawer and logged on. I won $600 with two 6s and two Queens, then moved to a higher table; I turned that $600 into $1,500 with three 10s. I took that $1,500 into Ultra-High where I found Foldin' Caulfield, getting in a few hands right before performing some surgery, playing with two others. I played three hands and not only did I have enough for the necklace but I had the money for matching earrings and the taxies to and from Tiffany as well. (I was glad I wasn't the patient whose shoulder Foldin' was about to dismantle.)

Wifey didn't see the jewelry right away, though; I was saving it for a rainy day.

There was another problem. In the middle of June—by then I was up to eighty grand—the company I'd worked for always began its "summer hours." I had to be at work—or so Cynthia thought—at eight thirty, not nine. But Wifey's hours were the same: she still always left the house at eight forty-five to get to work by nine. I had to maintain the ruse.

For the first few weeks, I left before she did, went down into the
subway, boarded and took it uptown two stops before I got off and
headed back home. But it was hot and humid and there are few
places more unpleasant to be in the summer than on a New York
subway car, especially if you don't really have to be. So I began a
new routine. *The hell with the subway . . . I'll just take the* Times *to
the Starbucks across the street and kill the time till Wifey leaves.*

And that is what I did. Every weekday morning I'd get dressed
for work, head across the street and park myself on a stool, where
I'd nurse an iced latte and attempt the crossword, all the time
keeping one eye on the entrance of my apartment building. Like
clockwork, every day at eight forty-five Cynthia would leave the
building, striding with that long purposeful gait of hers, a Fendi
handbag swinging from her right shoulder. She'd walk two blocks,
make a left turn, head for the subway. By this time I'd given up on
the crossword and switched to reading the daily book review. Every
other sentence I'd glance back up, just to make sure Cynthia wasn't
on her way back, having forgotten her cell or needing to take an
emergency pee. The coast clear, it was back to the book reviews.
By the time the iced latte was finished, the paper was a crumpled,
mottled mess, especially if the book of the day had gotten a thumbs
up. If I saw the words "brilliant," "searing," "hysterical," "amusing,"
or "reasonably compelling," a shot of corrosive coffee-scented stomach acid would surge back up into my gullet.

After that, I'd go back upstairs and start playing again. The
system was safe: she and I only called each other's cell phones and
when we e-mailed we used our Yahoo accounts. For all she knew,
I was on Pluto.

(Our new 60-inch plasma TV, a brand new laptop, the new coffee table, her iPad, and our pride and joy, the $1,000 Sleep Num-
ber Mattress—we'd even shopped for these items together, but
never once did she ask me, "So where's the money coming from
for all this?" Had she done so, I would've responded, "Poker." After all, poker had gotten her her magnificent new chinchilla coat,

presently being boarded for the summer at a fur kennel. She knew poker was a source of income; she just had no idea it was my only source.)

One day toward the end of June, Wifey woke up with a fever and a sore throat.

"I'm going to have to take a sick day," she told me.

I'd been dreading the possibility of such an event and denying it so much that I'd never fully developed a contingency plan. I kindly offered to take the day off to stay home and take care of her, but she said no, it wasn't necessary, that I should just go to work.

One of these days, I thought, *I'm going to find that key and get the* Trilogy *in case she asks to see if it really exists.*

"I'd really, really like to stay though. You don't look well."

Fifteen thousand poker players were waiting for me to play with them; Artsy Painter Gal was waiting for me in Los Angeles; all my Poker Buddies were waiting.

"No, really. I'll be okay."

I kissed her forehead good-bye and headed out.

After fueling up on an iced latte I walked around. It was already 90 degrees out and by the time I got to the Barnes and Noble on Union Square I was gasping for breath. I had little interest in literature anymore but usually stopped in once a month there to check up on *Plague* and *Love*. *Plague* was often on the ground floor, in a stack of ten or so, on the Urban Fiction table; *Love* usually was wasting away upstairs in the fiction section. My usual routine was to sign the books, then have someone there slap a SIGNED BY THE AUTHOR sticker on the cover—anything, anything at all, for a sale.

On this sweltering day I saw that there were no *Plague Boys* on the Urban Fiction table. I headed up on the escalator to the fiction floor and looked down and saw the Paperback Favorites table. *Corrections, Infinite Jest, Absurdistan, Extremely Successful and Incredibly Rich*, the Eggers masterwork . . . they were all there. The enemy redoubt. All the clever, coy, convoluted, self-conscious, postmodern, post-post-ironic books the *Times* finds fit to love, books not about human beings but about their own cleverness. You had to squint through the pyrotechnics just to read the words. The only thing more intolerable than reading books about writers is reading a book about itself. To my right I saw beneath me the New Fiction shelves—never again would my name and words besmirch its particle board—and there it was: *Saucier: A Bitch in the Kitchen.* It had recently gotten a rave review—written by a chef who probably hadn't ever read anything but cook books—in the Sunday *Times.* I also saw the stacks of books on the Have You Read a Memoir Lately? table. The absolute fabulist James Frey, the truth-stretching, untalented Augusten Burroughs, and the archfiend of all archfiends, the King of Plop, the Supreme Czar of Lite FM Smooth Jazz Soft-core Comedy: David Sedaris. There were books by other writers who had screwed up their lives and then decided to unscrew them by writing about it. Whiners, public nuisances, nudges, whores for literary fame. The nerve of these people . . . mining every little scrap of their private lives, no matter how uninteresting, and making it public. (And no one had asked them to!) And if the facts weren't tragic enough, make a few up. Add something, multiply, spice it up, stretch and hang-dry it, lift and separate and toss the works into a blender and puree. *No way I'll ever resort to this*, I promised myself. *If I ever sink that low then please dear God just let me drown in a vat of my own self-pity instead.* I'd rather work at Friendly's again. These books shrunk to postage stamps as I ascended. As long as Frey's book was in print, poor Lilly would forever be sucking off a drug-ravaged scumbag in the rat-infested Crack Dens of Eternity, only to be rescued just before the money shot by our fearless and gallant hero-narrator (who a few years later would need to bring his mommy onto *Larry King* with him.) If Sedaris were to read his grocery lists of the last twenty years at Carnegie Hall, I reflected as the novmoirs and memvels faded from view, not only would every seat in the house be filled but everyone present would be pissing themselves with laughter. Yep, a goddam yukfest. Why? *Because they were David Sedaris's grocery lists! Awww.*

Finally on the paperback fiction floor I headed to the D's. There were no copies of *Love: A Horror Story* there. No *Plagues* either. Not even a telltale tiny vestigial gap between Chitra Banerjee Divakaruni and E. L. Doctorow, where my babies should have been nestling.

I had three more hours to kill. Then I could go home and tell Wifey I'd had a really productive day at work.

I went back down the escalator and all the books got closer and closer. *Truckstop Tranny Crack Whore! Babes in Gangland! My Holocaust Wolf Baby Wife!* Could the other customers in the store see the pints of clammy envy oozing out into the armpits of my shirt?

"Hey, you don't have any more copies of my book," I said to the genial store manager, who looked like any number of *Jeopardy!* contestants.

"And what book is that, sir?" she said.

"*Plague Boy?* Usually you have some there." I pointed to Urban Fiction.

She told me to hold on and started typing on her keyboard. She told me to hold on again and chewed on a pencil as she gazed intently into her screen.

"Well, we could get more of *Love: A Horror Story* in," she told me. "I could do that. And we do have *The Missing Chums* in Young Readers."

"Wrong Frank Dixon."

"Right." After a few seconds she said, "Look at this . . ."

She showed me her screen. It took a few seconds before I knew precisely what to look at and when I did I was struck by such a violent shiver that Barnes & Noble could have shut off their mighty AC system—that chill would have kept the place, all five floors, cold for the next three summers.

"It's out of print," the manager told me.

"Ah. I see."

I was too embarrassed to know whether I should have been embarrassed or not.

"But we'll get more of *Horror Love* in here. I'll order them."

"Okay. Thanks."

Slumping like a hairy figure in an evolution poster, I headed for the exit, went past the table labeled Who The Hell Knew? or Who'da Thunk It? or I Had No Fucking Idea! or whatever. Books on the history of salt, oysters, wind, cork, turmeric, helium, the fork.

I staggered out into the swamp of summer again and was walloped by an oncoming wave of "air." I was gasping now not only from the heat but from the failure of my first book. Failure: my oldest, dearest friend. Even when I succeeded, I failed. I'd gotten a book published, it got mostly positive reviews, I did some press, it didn't sell, it died. It was that simple. The thing was dead.

"I have no fans," Mickey Spillane once said of his loyal readership. "You know what I got? Customers. And customers are your friends."

But I had no books anymore. Thus I had no customers. Thus I had not a friend in the world.

But there was the movie. The movie! Surely Pacer Burton and Hollywood would save me.

I walked around and around, shaking my head all the way. What had I done wrong?

I had come so close to being successful. Although, in truth, not that close.

When your book dies, I now knew, it's not nearly as sad as burying a child—nothing is—but I would put it somewhere between burying a grandparent and burying yourself.

I walked toward the Hudson River, fuming and cursing aloud, and happened upon a small cybercafé in far west Chelsea. For ten dollars an hour I could sit down and access the Internet.

I stayed there for two hours. At noon Artsy/Victoria came on and we chatted for twenty minutes. I told her about *Plague* being out of print and she said she was sorry. "Check your e-mail in three minutes," she said right before she logged off. I went into my Yahoo account and saw that she'd sent me an e-mail with an attachment. Her message said: "This is a nude I painted about 10 years ago. Of me. A detail of a much larger painting." I downloaded it and there on my screen was an extreme close-up of a right breast of peachy pink and a small nipple of cherry red.

I won $800 in those two hours, went to a Gap and bought a few shirts that fit me, and went home. (Either I had passed from Medium to Large or they had drastically reconfigured their whole sizing scheme.)

Wifey was still in bed. She was shaking with the chills and was bundled up under two blankets. There were bottles of ginger ale and Tylenol on her night table. As bad as she looked, I don't know if she looked as bad as I did at the bookstore.

"Hw wz wrk, Frnk?" she asked me, the thermometer in her mouth.

"Productive," I told her.

8
Our Mutual Jigs

Frank:

Hey you! Sorry for not having e-mailed for a while but I have very good news!

I think we can get ——[3] and —— to star in *Plague Boy*. They have the same agent at IGT and the agent read the screenplay and really loved it. —— would be perfect to play Luke. —— is very much in demand right now but the agent says that if —— commits, then —— is in. He's perfect for Benny; it's almost unimaginable anyone else playing him. Pacer Burton wraps *Breakthrough*, his new movie, in about 2 weeks and still wants to make *Plague Boy* next and he and —— have wanted to collaborate for years. So this is fabulous news!

I may be in New York early September. We can do lunch!

Barbara Bennett

Egregious Motion Pictures

Los Angeles, California

♠ ♠ ♠ ♠

Second Gunman: Won 4,000 quid yesterday, lads. Not bad for
2 hours work.

Chip Zero: Where? Ultra-High?

Second Gunman: No. Right here in Blackpool. Just a few streets
away.

---

3. For everyone's sake, especially my own, I'm leaving the names of actors blank.

Chip Zero: Huh? You mean, like, playing with real flesh and blood people in real life? Real people with real lives and real bodies, sitting across a real table with real cards? Talking to each other instead of typing? In real time? Are you telling me you really did this?!

Toll House Cookie: You telling us you've never played real cards?

Second Gunman: There must be hundreds of games going on in NYC this very second.

Toll House Cookie: There are. I know of 2 places in NYC where they have games going 24/7, no shit. I saw Halle Berry there one night drop 3 large on 1 hand and throw a serious hissy fit.

Second Gunman: Have you not even played Go Fish with a real person, mate?

Chip Zero: I think so. Yeah. Maybe. Long time ago. Summer camp.

Toll House Cookie: Dude, you need to get out more.

Chip Zero: Why?

♥ ♥ ♥ ♥

CR:

Hey, sorry to bother you but both my computers conked out last week. The desktop died of old age, the laptop overheated and caught fire. The fire destroyed a rug passed down to me from a great-uncle who passed away in Auschwitz only hours before it was liberated. Also, it killed our cat. I was here when it happened but my leg is still in a cast from that Drakes Cakes truck thing and I couldn't do anything but smell my hair singe.

Anyway, all the e-mails I may have received the last seven days were lost. So if you responded to my queries, then I didn't get it. Could you please re-send? Thanks, Clint.

FD

To all:

I am out of the office until the first week of August. If you need to contact me, e-mail my assistant Courtney Bellkamp at cjb@renobros.com.

This is an automatic message. Do not reply.

Clint Reno

The Reno Brothers Literary Agency

◆ ◆ ◆ ◆

Boca Barbie: That last poem was so beautiful. It got me through a very tough day.

Kiss My Ace: I don't know what my life would be like if we hadn't met.

Boca Barbie: But Tim. We haven't met.

Kiss My Ace: I know. But we will. I promise you. You've become my best friend.

Boca Barbie: And you're mine. I've never thought about anyone so much ever ever ever in my life. I live for you now. I feel so happy and young and alive. You're everything to me.

♣ ♣ ♣ ♣

Frank:

No, haven't read *Dead on Arrival* yet.

Going to Martha's Vineyard for last 2 weeks of July, 1st week of August. You get me that list from Clint and I'll read it. Can you re-send the ms.? Don't think I have it anymore. What was it about again?

Did you hear the good news? *Saucier* was bought for the movies. Jill Conway will be a millionaire! She's julienned her last potatoe [sic].

Ross

♠ ♠ ♠ ♠

Artsy Painter Gal: So tell me. When you lived in Gay Paree, you bought your paints there or you brought them all with you?

Chip Zero: I brought them, they ran out, I started buying supplies there. Man, one cold night around Christmas I was so hungry I almost bit into a tube of vermillion.

Artsy Painter Gal: I still can't believe you did that. Lived there and starved and painted.

Chip Zero: In retrospect I should've eaten a lot more and not painted at all. Think of all the boeuf bourguignon and pastries I was missing! Speaking of artsy matters, I Googled you this a.m. Forgive the cyber-stalkage but I found an article on you. There were two paintings I could see. One was a sort of Max Beckmanny portrait of a woman.

Artsy Painter Gal: In a white slip drinking coffee staring out a window? That's my sister Daphne. I painted that up in Mendocino.

Chip Zero: The other was a combo still-life and landscape.

Artsy Painter Gal: Apples in a bowl, ocean in background, periwinkle sky at dusk. Painted under the influence of shrooms in Cozumel. Not my best stuff.

Chip Zero: I'd give everything I've got to have your talent.

Artsy Painter Gal: I'd give everything I've got to *not* have it.

Chip Zero: I liked what I saw. I'd even buy it. Is any of your stuff still around somewhere?

Artsy Painter Gal: Can we change the subject please? Just play a few hands with me, baby.

♥ ♥ ♥ ♥

Saucier: A Bitch in the Kitchen (Hardcover)
by Jill Conway
Amazon.com Sales Rank: #17 in Books (See Top Sellers in Books)
Yesterday: #22 in Books

0 of 9 people found the following review helpful:

Hard to Swallow, Inedible, Unsavory, Tasteless, Not Fit for A Starving Dog
Reviewer: The Suburban Mimetic (New York, USA)

Like 5 week-old moldy pork rinds, this book was lukewarm garbage from the first page to the last. Jill Conway HAD to have been a better cook than she is a writer. Her prose is bland, flat, mealy, unfit for human consumption, raw and overcooked. When I finished the book—which I barely did—I felt I had caught e. coli AND botulism AND ptomaine. Let me FURTHER beat the food metaphors into the ground: Had this book been served to me in a restaurant, I would have returned it after the first half-page. So THIS is the swill that readers consume nowadays? These are the kind of books publishers are churning out? Someone call the Health Department and have Jill Conway condemned! I felt as if I ordered chicken and they cooked up the nearest cat and it's 4 days later and I'm still pulling pieces of this book from my teeth.

Was this review helpful to you? Yes No

❖ ❖ ❖ ❖

Frank Dixon:

Sorry, I wasn't able to find the list you need. I don't know if there is such a list. Clint is in the Lake District in England for a month and when he comes back I'll ask him.

By the way, I read *Plague Boy* when it came out. One day I was reading it on the train and this weird guy walked up to me and told me that *he* had written it! I looked for the author photo to verify but there wasn't a photo so I guess he was just some creep.

Oh well. Just thought I'd let you know that. ☺

Courtney Jane Bellkamp

The Reno Brothers Literary Agency

♣ ♣ ♣ ♣

Bubbly Brit Bird: haven't seen you around for a while, luv.
Pest Control: lost the internet here for a while.
Bubbly Brit Bird: for 6 days?

Pest Control: y. for 6 days.

Bubbly Brit Bird: and you're telling me the truth, philly? promise?

Pest Control: i promise, georgy-girl. i missed you.

Bubbly Brit Bird: too bad you couldn't call.

Pest Control: my wife looks at the bills. don't know how i'd explain
a call to england.

Bubbly Brit Bird: i know. but it would be so sweet to hear your
voice, that's all.

Pest Control: if you heard it right now you might not think that.

Bubbly Brit Bird: oh, of course I would!

♠ ♠ ♠ ♠

Frank:

Hey you! Good news/bad news/good news.

The good news is that —— is still in. His agent *really* wants him
to star in *Plague Boy*. The bad news is that even if —— is in, —— is
now 100% definitely out. He just committed to the sequel of his
last picture.

However, there's a chance now that —— might want to costar.
His agent read the script and really loved it. He told me that ——
and —— have tried for years to get together on a project and this
just might be it. Also, Pacer Burton and —— are friends, so that's
good.

I'm in New York Sept. 5–Sept. 9. We'll set something up!

Barbara

♥ ♥ ♥ ♥

Chip Zero: Are you sure you don't want to fold, Swede?

Bjorn 2 Win: Why? Should I?

Chip Zero: Well, let's put it this way. I have 2 Kings and 2 Queens
right now. One of the Kings is a club as is one of the Queens.
I own this hand so much that I'm holding the deed for it right
this very second.

Bjorn 2 Win: I don't believe you would still use the same tired
tactic.

Wolverine Mommy folds. Mrs. Foldin' Caulfield folds. Bjorn 2 Win
raises $100. Chip Zero raises $100. Bjorn 2 Win calls.

Chip Zero: I don't get it. Do you *like* losing money to me?

The turn card is an Ace of Clubs.

Chip Zero: Okay, so now look at what I got. Ace-high club flush.
Why do this to yourself? I know you slaughter horses . . . but
why slaughter your own bank account? Why make luncheon
meat of what little that remains of your self-esteem?
Bjorn 2 Win: Maybe I have a full house, Aces full of Kings.
Chip Zero: Yeah, and maybe I'm Greta effin Garbo.

Bjorn 2 Win raises $200. Chip Zero raises $200. Bjorn 2 Win calls.
The river card is a King of hearts. Bjorn 2 Win raises $200. Chip Zero
raises $400. Bjorn 2 Win calls. Bjorn 2 Win shows 3 Aces. Chip Zero
shows a Full House, Kings full of Queens. Chip Zero wins $2,800.
Bjorn 2 Win has left the table.

◆　◆　◆　◆

yo, frankie!

long time no see. wanna go out and get a few burgers and
beers just like the old days, booooooooy? we could hit a few of our
old stomping grounds if they're still around.

bad news: i'm getting divorced. very sad. vanessa and i tried
but couldn't make it work. i feel terrible for the kids. when we go
out I'll hit you with all the gory details.

lonnie

ps: does harry ever come to nyc? if so, maybe the 3 of us could
get together and relive the glory days that never were. and then,
what larks!

lonnie b.

♣　♣　♣　♣

Frank

Guess what? I found some tony downtown publishing house just gullible enough to hire me. So I'm back in business! I was thisclose to working at the Wok & Roll in the local mall. Sadly, there will be no more daily golf for me. I shall miss it. I was quite hooked!

Hope to hear from you soon.

Toby Kwimper

TriHo Books, Inc.

Toby:

Every time I see the word "tony" I can't help but think of the posh well-to-do golf-playing, tennis-playing swell Tony Newport in *Love: A Horror Story*. How come not 1 single solitary reviewer ever pointed out that clever pun? What, they didn't get it? And how come not 1 single reviewer mentioned that the name of the coffee bar in *Plague Boy* was Max Perkins and that there was once a very famous editor named Max Perkins? And back to *Love* again: Why did not 1 reviewer mention that the names of the two movie body doubles in the book were Bill Wilson and Golyadkin? Were they not familiar with Poe's doppelganger story William Wilson and Dostoyevsky's doppelganger story The Double, whose main character is named Golyadkin?! Nope. See, Toby, if you're a "good" writer, an "important" writer, if you're "postmodern," if you're "self-conscious" and "post-ironic," then critics appreciate your witty wordplay and cutesy literary references; if you're not 1 of the lucky, the blessed, the darlings, the privileged, the cream of the crop, the proud, the few, the chosen, the elite, the anointed, the sanctified, the A-list, then they find them stupid if they find them at all. Critics! 20 years of schoolin' and you're still writing book reports. Fuck 'em. Fuck 'em all and let God sort 'em out is what I say.

Good luck at your new job. Knew you'd land on your feet.

Frank

♠ ♠ ♠ ♠

Plague Boy
by Frank W. Dixon
Amazon.com Sales Rank: #710,949 in Books
Yesterday: #674,283 in Books

14 of 14 people found the following review helpful:

Not a Book 4 Kids!
Reviewer: Justin J. (Waco, Texas, USA)

I can't believe this book! I thought I waz getting a book about
my favarite detectives from Bayport but this was about a man
in New York who spreads dezeases. I finished it but it wasn't
good and there were a lot of dirty parts. Kids shoudn't be
reading this type of stuff!

♥ ♥ ♥ ♥

History Babe: I'm on top of you now, moving up and down on your
enormous shaft.
King of Kings of Hearts: Ohhhhhh you feel so good. So good. Keep
doing it.
History Babe: I bend down to kiss you, put my tongue all the way
down your mouth, you suck on it and suck on it, and I play with
my clit while I slide up and down your cock.
King of Kings of Hearts: Keep doing it, Hist. Ohhhhh yeah.
Mmmmmmm.
History Babe: Then your wife surprises us and comes into the
room and she's so excited by the sight of my tits and your dick
inside me that she takes off her clothes and jumps in.
King of Kings of Hearts: Hey, I dunno about this! Make her leave.
History Babe: She starts licking my nipples while I fuck you. She's
on fire. You're looking at your wife licking my tits and you get
harder.
King of Kings of Hearts: I don't know. I'm having second thoughts
about this.

History Babe: C'mon, King. Stop thinking and keep fucking me!

King of Kings of Hearts: Oh, all right. I'm fucking you.

King of Kings of Hearts calls. History Babe shows two Jacks. King of Kings of Hearts shows two 4s. History Babe wins $1,200.

❖ ❖ ❖ ❖

frankie-boy

    maybe you're away for the summer? why you no answer my e-mails? let's go out. i need to talk.

    lonnie

Artsy Painter Gal: Do you think we'll ever meet?

Chip Zero: I hope so. I think about it often but maybe it's best we not meet. I'm no Clooney, either George *or* Rosemary.

Artsy Painter Gal: Just tell me: what's your best physical feature?

Chip Zero: Hmm. That would be the void I leave behind me when I leave a room.

Artsy Painter Gal: Zzzzzz. Listen . . . I'm going to be in the Bahamas over Labor Day weekend. Empyrean Island at the Nirvana Resort & Casino. Maybe you could just happen to be there too?

Chip Zero: Yeah. A chance. But Victoria, my dear? I've Googled you. So I know. That you're married. And you have two kids. Sarah and Emily.

Artsy Painter Gal: And I Googled you too, Sherlock Holmes, and found out you're married too. Cynthia. Works at an arch-support tri-quarterly or something. So there!

Chip Zero: And your husband Aaron is a graduate of Yale, where he played lacrosse. He's a hot-shit investment banker. So I guess our mutual jigs are up, eh?

Artsy Painter Gal: Just think about this Empyrean Island thing. I'll be there with Mr. Artsy Painter Gal and both Artsy Painter Gal Juniors. Now, even if it's only for a second at a poolside bar, blackjack table, a limbo contest or it's me "accidentally" knocking a banana daiquiri all over your skimpy Speedo, I'd like to meet you. Think about it? Okay?

Chip Zero: I'll probably think of nothing else.

♠ ♠ ♠ ♠

Frank Dixon

Hi, I'm glad we finally "met."

Barbara Bennett is gonna be in NYC in early Sept and as it happens so am I.

I didn't read your book I'll admit it but Mickey Alba's Plague Boys screenplay is totally off the hook as I'm sure you know. —— would fucking kill to be in the movie and I'd fucking kill to have him do it. I'm having lunch with —— tomorrow. He hasn't read the script but his agent has. I'm going to hand the script to him and he'll read it. Is he perfect to play Benny or what?

I'm also thinking of —— for Benny in case that falls through. He's very C List right now, I know, but he'd be excellent.

Let's have lunch you me and Barbara.

I just wrapped Breakthrough but after all the post-production shit I'm going to do everything I can to bring Plague Boys to the screen. It's gonna happen Frank.

Pacer

Pacer:
Sounds good.
FD

♥ ♥ ♥ ♥

Frank:
The latest . . .
—— is now officially out. He just signed to do two movies and one of them begins filming in three weeks. To be honest, his agent found *Plague Boy* way too dark. —— himself never read

the script. With the way his career is going, he needs to do more cheery romantic comedy Hugh Grant fluff. With him out that means we've also lost —— too. So we're back to square one. Right now the script is with ——'s agents right now. I think they'll like it. They also rep —— and the two of them would be fantastic although clearly not our first choices.

Pacer e-mailed me yesterday and can't make it to New York in September.

Barbara

◆ ◆ ◆ ◆

Frank:

Please don't take this the WRONG way. You know I LOVE you very much. I found out recently that The Plague Boy is OUT OF PRINT now. Your second book DIDN'T DO TOO WELL either. I adored both books. Especially the 1st one. When both books came out I was so HAPPY that you remembered your Aunt Elaine and mentioned me in the acknowledgements. But even though I'm very OLD and SICK now I am wishing that if it's possible YOU COULD TAKE MY NAMES OUT OF BOTH BOOKS in future editions IF THERE ARE ANY. Thank you and much LOVE as always.

E.

♣ ♣ ♣ ♣

Congratulations, Chip Zero, you have now won $100,000 on Poker Galaxy and are officially an ELITE PLAYER. Keep playing and good luck!

9
Fun in the Sun

I have a great idea for a screenplay!" Harry Carver, calling from Los Angeles, yelled to me over the phone one day in late July. "And I need your help with it, Frankie."

"Okay . . . uh . . . okay . . ." I said, with all the enthusiasm of someone offered top dollar to test out anthrax vaccines for a start-up pharmaceutical company. "Tell me more."

Harry, I assumed right away, wanted me—the professional "writer"—to write it. It had been a long time since my former co-writer had put pen to paper other than to work on real estate contracts or property liens, and he dwelled so many income brackets above mine that by all rights we should have required interpreters simply to speak to each other. Harry and I wrote one-act plays, five-act plays, decologies of plays ("The 3rd Street and Avenue D Cycle"), movie and TV scripts, everything. Sadly, nothing that Harry and I had ever worked on together proved successful. As a matter of fact it was only after he moved as far away from me as possible, while still staying in the contiguous forty-eight states, that he succeeded in life. And, sort of, vice-versa.

I played poker on my laptop while Harry related to me his brainstorm. He had me hooked with the first sentence; by the second sentence I was ready to buy the latest version of Final Draft. It was a brilliant idea, the kind of thing that we, years before, could have knocked off in four weeks. He and I used to write at work, then write at his place or mine and in East Village bars and cafes, often spurred on by caffeine, Jack Daniel's, weed, coke. It was the Pre-Laptop Era, and we wrote on legal pads, index cards, the backs of our rent bills, and bar napkins. (One night Harry picked up a pink-mohawked punk-rocker chick at the Mudd Club, got an idea while performing cunnilingus on her kitchen counter on Ludlow Street, and wrote the idea down on her buttocks.) We were proud of the final product and we got depressed when it went nowhere. The only thing that could cheer us back up was getting started on our next foredoomed project.

After I told him his idea was great and after he told me he knew it was, I said: "You're offering this to me to write, but when I finish it, what would I do—"

"No, I'm not offering it. I want to write it *with* you, you ignorant bastard you. I'll come to New York. Or you could fly out here. Take a week or two off from work." He had no idea that I *had* no work anymore. "You could kick it West Coast Style."

I was at a table with Capt. Rehab and World's Slowest Human. The latter was living up to the moniker: every decision took a minute and I suspected he was consulting a fifteen-inch-thick poker manual between moves. I had pocket Jacks; the flop was a 3, a 5, and a 7, and he kept raising and I kept checking. Capt. Rehab folded. The thought of writing again with Harry was very tempting. Writing alone was my favorite thing to do in the world and was like meditation, but writing with another person was more fun. Jamming and psychotherapy all at once.

"Look," Harry said, "I ran the idea by a Hollywood high mucky-muck last week—a very serious pooh-bah—and she got sopping wet just hearing it."

"What are you doing talking to Hollywood mucky-mucks and pooh-bahs?"

The turn card came up a Jack. Now I had three.

"A minor real estate matter. Okay, maybe not that minor. Hey! You know who it was?"

He told me who it was and, though the name meant nothing to me, I could tell by the way he said it that it should have. I acted, though, as if I'd been suitably impressed.

The river card was a 10.

Harry said we could meet in Vegas and stay at the Bellagio or Mandalay Bay and write around the pool all day long and in our rooms at night. He'd pay, he said, for the hotel rooms. (He didn't know it but with just my winnings from the day before I could spring for us both.)

"Remember writing in Yankee Stadium?" I asked. "I completely missed that Mattingly grand slam 'cause I was so busy writing stuff down."

There was about three grand in the pot now. I had three Jacks and raised and World's Slowest eventually reraised. Capt. Rehab said to World's Slowest: "Hurry the bleep up!"

Harry's movie idea was so great that I wished I'd come up with it. "It's *Metropolis* meets *Wedding Crashers* meets the lighter, funnier parts of *Shoah*," he said, "and you and only you can help me write it." He paused and asked me what I was presently working on.

"It's kind of a trilogy-type thing. It's about America during a totalitarian—"

"Wait. You began that fifteen years ago, didn't you? And didn't you finish it?"

"I'm, uh . . . I'm sorta like revisiting it, you know? It could be groundbreaking stuff."

"You said that fifteen years ago too."

I vowed that instant that when I hit the $150,000 mark on the Galaxy I'd forget about poker completely and devote myself to the *Trilogy*. That amount would sustain me for the three years I needed to sharpen and polish my masterpiece. Ross F. Carpenter might not like *Dead on Arrival*—if he ever read it—but this, he and the public would flip for. When the *Trilogy* got published, it in itself would justify why there had been such a long gap since *Love*: because it had taken so long to write each complicated book of the Triad. Only a privileged few insiders would know there was another failed book in between. And they'd shut up about it.

And once the *American Nightmare Trilogy* started winning

prizes and was in its fifth printing, publishers would come begging for all my unpublished work, which I had a ton of.

The Complete Short Stories of . . . The First Five Plays . . . Early Poems.

"You need a break," Harry said, interrupting my reverie. "Think about it. We'll thaw out a bottle of the old creative juices and get them flowing again. It'll be a blast."

Convinced of victory, I showed my three Jacks. World's Slowest had a pocket 4 and 6, giving him a 7-high straight and wiping me out. His manual had worked.

"Well . . .?" Harry asked.

Disgusted, stunned, I told him I'd think about his offer and would get back to him.

♠ ♠ ♠ ♠

After Harry moved to L.A. to become a lawyer, I had decided that writing for the screen and for the theater was just not for me. I didn't even like movies and I pretty much loathed the theater and all the people involved with it, even though I'd barely met any of them. And television was just plain stupid. The fruit of ten years of futility now sits rotting in a bunch of cardboard boxes, along with some oils, pastels, and gouaches, in a dusty storage closet overlooking the Hudson River. That was it for me. Good-bye to all that.

With no idea for a novel in mind I merely took whatever was near the top of my stack of failed screenplays and began a novelization of it.

It took only a few days of lonely 6–8 a.m. and 8 p.m.–1 a.m. writing for me to realize that no simple six hundred-page double-spaced novel could contain this crazy behemoth. No, it had to be either a 2,100-page novel or . . . or *written in three parts!* Now, unless you're Tolstoy or Stephen King you're not going to get a 2,100-page novel published. Even I, ignorant then as I still am to the ways of publishing, knew that. So I would divvy it up into three smaller books.

The ironic thing was that once all three novels were written and had hit the best-seller lists and won prizes and I was dividing my time between the Hamptons and London, some fat movie bigwig would want to turn the whole thing, *which originally had been a screenplay*, into a movie. I'd meet this imaginary sweaty producer at the Four Seasons in New York, he'd ply me with Chablis and Beluga, and during dessert he would say, "Frankie, I absolutely adore your trilogies. All three of 'em. Let's turn 'em into a movie!" And while I was swallowing the last glob of molten valhrona I'd whip out the screenplay I'd written before one single word of the books had ever been penned. "I've already got the script right here, Harvey-babe," I'd say.

Freezing one fleeting moment of a life for all eternity, memory is the Natural History Museum of the soul. Eons and eons ago, some idiot Neanderthal with a long pointed stick protected his family from a bear just outside his cave; little did he know that ten millions years hence generations of school kids would gaze with mouths agape at this eyeblink of his life in a museum window diorama. Such a moment it was when I handed my screenplay over to Harvey. Picture the diorama yourself: my hand is out, my expression is confident, Harvey's tie is undone, three beads of sweat from his jowls hang over his crème brûlée, suspended in midair for all eternity; his gecko eyes pop out, his pockmarked jaw drops with astonishment. Frozen for posterity.

Priceless.

Except it never happened.

For seven years I devoted myself to the *Trilogy*. I wanted it to be good; I wanted to be good at something, for my own sanity. It was all I thought about from the second I woke up to the second I fell asleep, and my magnificent obsession even cost me a girlfriend. The diminutive Hethuh (Bay Ridge-born and bred, Heather could not pronounce her own name too well) and I went our separate ways because I wasn't paying, she claimed, enough attention to her needs. She was right. My life now was all about the project—that was what I lived for, it was what I was created to do. The history of baseball is unimaginable without Babe Ruth having played it, haystacks were only put in that field to be painted by Monet, four strangers *had* to meet and become the Beatles, and as surely as the New World waited for centuries to be conquered by Europeans, someone had to write the *Trilogy* and I just happened to be the one chosen to do it.

Twice a year I took unpaid two-week leaves of absence from work and went to London, settled into a seedy Paddington bed and breakfast and walled myself in from the outside world. I couldn't wait to take my seat and take out my pens and that day's legal pad at the library in Kensington where I wrote. And once I did so, it was as if I wasn't the writer at all but was merely the medium between some mystical force and the words I was penning onto yellow paper. The Muses needed a body, a scribe, some poor patsy with a Bic to bring the words down from the clouds onto Earth . . . *and they'd chosen me!*

At the end of the first two weeks I had well over three hundred pages written. Half of Book I, the first wheel of the mighty Troika.

When I returned to New York I entered what I'd written into my brand-new Commodore Amiga. I printed it out, pored over it again and again, made changes, some small, some vast. After months of tending to Book I, it was time to return to London and finish the first draft.

After the second sabbatical, the rough draft of Book I was just about done. Literary immortality had reached my doormat and was just about to ring my bell.

"So what do you think?" I asked petite Hethuh. She worked in a health food shop in the basement of a midtown skyscraper and made what were then called "health shakes" for business execs and their assistants, who were always too brusque or in too much of a hurry to thank her. She was four foot eleven, and it was this genetic slight that defined her existence and weighed down upon her taut 95-pound frame every second of her life.

"It's really, really good. This *has* to get published. Oh, by the way, my folks are coming into town next week, including my much taller younger sister. You're going to have to spend a lot of time with them. Also, I'm going to need you to . . ."

Her needs again. She had, I think, twice as many needs as I had pages.

Book I was done. Two more to go.

Never off my mind was: *Okay, so how do I get this monster published?*

❤ ❤ ❤ ❤

Keeping up the ruse that I still had a real job and a real place to go to every day, I kept going to Starbucks in the morning, where I would wait for Cynthia to leave our building. (If this seems sad, then keep in mind: this Starbucks is now closed and everyone who worked there was laid off.) Every morning I told myself that later that night I would tell her the truth. And one day, toward the end of July, I did tell her the truth but it certainly wasn't on my terms.

It was 9 a.m. and she'd been gone for fifteen minutes. I was so absorbed with an absurdly positive book review that day that I couldn't concentrate on anything. I read the review over and over again. Everything that they loved about the book—a slow-moving, elegant, and empty novel about post-9/11 New York—was everything that I would hate about it, if I ever read it, which someone would have to pay me good money to do. The book would do well, I knew, and so would the author's next book and the ten after that; it didn't even matter if they were any good (and they wouldn't be). The author was set for life and he had Osama Bin Laden to thank for it. After the fifth reading, the review faded to a rectangular blotch and then suddenly from nowhere, and from everywhere, I heard a voice asking me what I was doing there.

It was Cynthia. Right in front of me. A foot away. Looking at me, at the book review, at the poker on my laptop. She'd had to go back home, she eventually told me, to take a quick pee and, her bladder now emptied, she thought she'd get some coffee for the road.

A hundred lies, fifty of which were fairly plausible (and of those fifty lies, thirty of which she would have believed), occurred to me all at once and as I was weighing them out I heard my voice say: "I don't work anymore. I quit. A while ago. Sorry."

Telling the truth, I thought, was an even more brilliant strategy than telling any of the lies I'd so swiftly concocted.

She snatched the newspaper out of my hand and slammed shut my computer. I thought of Gloria Graham throwing boiling coffee into Lee Marvin's face in *The Big Heat* but realized that Cynthia was drinking an iced latte; if she decided to go all Fritz Lang on my ass, it wouldn't have been so bad.

"We'll talk about this later," she hissed.

I told her that I looked forward to the discussion and that it would be like being rid of a tremendous burden, her knowing the truth I'd been hiding from her all these months.

As she headed for the door, I reminded her that I was writing, not just playing.

She believed me but didn't seem to care.

❖ ❖ ❖ ❖

But at least I wasn't cheating on her.

Although I was. Sort of.

Artsy Painter Gal and I would e-mail soft-core fantasies to each other—always worded in the present tense ("I'm slowly pulling off my panties while you . . .")—and, in hers, she carefully avoided the elephant in the room: what I looked like.

Courtesy of Google Images I was able to find two pictures of Victoria Landreth, her real name. APG had told me that she once looked like a young Joan Collins and I could see it: she had the same cheeks and black hair, the same lustrous eyes and lips. I don't look like that anymore, she informed me. (But who among us didn't look better fifteen years ago unless we've had plastic surgery since?) Every time she told me she didn't care at all what I looked like, I told her that if she knew what I looked like she might start caring. I informed her I had gained some weight since discovering online poker, though I kept the numbers vague. "Don't you think," I asked her, "that if I looked like George Clooney my wife would be keeping a much shorter rein on me?" She said, "If you looked like George Clooney, you wouldn't have gotten married!"

"True, very true."

"Labor Day weekend. The Nirvana on Empyrean Island. We'll be in Tower 1, the hubby, the kids, and me. Why don't you take a few days off and we'll meet. You'll have fun. Maybe you'll get a nice suntan or even—dare I say—start writing again?"

"I'll start doing that when you start painting, okay?"

"Sorry. You're right. But I'd love to meet you."

After that conversation I had trouble concentrating on the tasks at hand: winning money, obliterating the competition, being King of Hold'em Hill. Gambling was now my full-time profession. It was what I did for a living. I was a pokerizer.

But that afternoon, a week after our Starbucks encounter, as I pondered telling Cynthia I was thinking of taking a few days off to go to the Caribbean, I dropped around $18K. It was an ugly onslaught of lousy cards and dumbass moves. Or maybe I wasn't concentrating because I was daydreaming about a lazy river pool and ice-cold Coronas and finally meeting my e-mistress, or I was thinking about heading out to Vegas to work with Harry on his script. When Second Gunman saw my diminished stack the next day he said, "Bloody hell! What happened to you?!" While I was recounting with blow-by-blow detail my run of bad hands, I lost an additional $1,800 to him.

Did I want to meet Artsy? Yes, desperately. Did I want to get out of New York City for a spell? Certainly. Did I want Artsy to see my new wider, plumper self? Hell no. (*Maybe*, it occurred to me, *I could send Lonnie Beale down there to fill in for me!*) Did I want to see Artsy's husband? Nope. He was the robust, outdoorsy L.L. Bean type and not only was he capable of doing many of the things that I wasn't, but he actually enjoyed doing them: wearing a tool belt, camping out, running marathons, making money. When women in showers all around the country fantasized about anonymous, faceless firemen and handymen and brought themselves to orgasm, it was him they were picturing.

"I'm thinking of taking a few days off," I told Cynthia over pizza in SoHo that night.

"From *what?*"

"From New York . . . I haven't been out of town for a while. Not since . . ."

"Since Las Vegas, right?"

Right. The dice table at the Luxor. I told her that I had the Nirvana Hotel on Empyrean Island in mind. Massages. Tropical drinks. Total relaxation. Chillin' like a villain.

"You know," I reminded her, "I *am* working on a book. And I'm exhausted."

(A year ago I would not have been able to pull this off with such aplomb and without even a telltale swallow or momentary look askance. Before this I had really only mastered the white lie, saying things like, "Okay, pork chops are fine," when I really wanted chicken. How had I become so good at subterfuge, deception, at outright lying? Why was I able to pull it off without any slight twinge in my conscience? The answer is easy: poker. Poker had taught me to bluff guilt-free.)

I told her the *Trilogy* was truly groundbreaking stuff. For the hell of it I pinched some twaddle from Hemingway and told her that what Cezanne had done with painting and landscapes, I was doing with literature. To my tremendous relief and great disappointment, she bought it.

"So," I told her, "I need a break from that. And from the poker. Or I could bring the laptop and just work on the book by the pool."

(We'd had our talk. I nearly cried when I said how sorry I was for not having told her I'd quit my job. I told her I was miserable and that all I wanted to do was write. I'd been living a lie. She was still mad. The next day she wasn't quite as mad. The day after that she was only mildly sore. And now . . .)

"Instead of the laptop," she offered, "you could bring me."

"I was just about to ask if you wanted to go," I lied. "You didn't give me the chance."

As soon as we got home, I booked the trip. I went back online, spent five hours playing and won back four thousand. Shaken by disturbing dreams of Joan Collins and Gerard Depardieu, I woke up at four to take a leak and then played some more. I played until Wifey woke up at the usual time, and by that afternoon not only had I won back all the money I'd lost but also enough for our little end-of-summer fling.

No longer did I have to go through the ruse of pretending to take the subway to work, so that morning I walked Cynthia to the subway station. As she was about to descend I said, "Hey . . . I have these for you."

I told her I was sorry for everything and handed her the Elsa Peretti necklace and earrings. Even though it was ninety degrees out and there wasn't a cloud in the sky, this was that rainy day.

"You don't need to do this," she said.

"I know."

We kissed on the lips, she took the jewelry anyway, and we parted.

(Some shameless, no-longer-relevant author once received a shit-load of money for plugging Bvlgari in a novel. I am getting nothing from Tiffany for mentioning them in this memoir but if they wish to contribute, they know where to find me.)

The jewelry was originally meant to be so glittery that it would blind her to any amount of deception and treachery. But we were past that now. For the most part.

♣ ♣ ♣ ♣

It's one thing to be a pariah in the literary world, where I never belonged, but to be a piranha in my own fish tank—Pokergalaxy.com—would be too much to bear. The Galaxy is not only my refuge, it is the Patusan to my Lord Jim, the streets of Persepolis to my Tamburlaine. There the world is a Sunday best-seller list and every weekend I am Mitch Albom. In August I made it past the $150,000 earnings mark. There was no confetti, no streamers, no dancing girls; CNN, FOX News, and Gawker did not report it. Were I the blogging or tweeting kind, I would have given it nary a mention. But the amount was, in six months of work, more than what my first two books had brought me. The problem now, though, was that as I went to this table or that table to play, some players, when they saw the intimidating size of my stack, would leave right away.

I've heard that there are some porno actors who are so freakishly endowed that a few actresses refuse to work with them. This was as close to that as I'd ever get.

I understood what was going on and a few times purposely lost the first hand or folded the first couple of hands. That way the other players present would think I was on a bad schneid and would stick around to move in for the kill. Once in a while I'd declare falsely that I'd already dumped $15,000 that day and was showing no signs of turning it around. When I did that, it was unbelievable how popular I quickly became. All the world, it seems, loves a loser.

The more I won, the more I had to wager and the more confident I felt, and it was difficult to believe that only a few months ago my hands were clammy when I bet $10 of play money. Now I mostly shuttled back and forth between the High and Ultra-High tables. If I was on a real losing skid, I rode it out, gnashed my teeth and shook my legs so much that the floorboards began to splinter. When my luck changed, when I was winning again and all the gears were meshing, I felt confident and moved back up to the Big Boys.

There were people on the site who had won a lot more money

than I did, such as the incredible, inscrutable SaniFlush. Usually lurking silently in Ultra-High tables or at the No-Limit tables (where I rarely tread), by August he had won over a million bucks. I have played against him a few times but prefer not to. Watching him operate is like watching Rembrandt paint although probably a lot more exciting. His avatar is always the Psycho Killer with the Aviator Frames and the Hooded Sweatshirt, and he plays among the super-elite on the site; SaniFlush is frighteningly unpredictable, is a rampant pre-flop raiser and a maniacal bluffer (he may have been born with an extra testicle or two) and those are three things I avoid. He rarely says a word, and Second Gunman calls him the Prince of Poker Darkness. One time I saw SaniFlush foolishly draw to an inside straight and win $15,000. Even though they were disconsolate and must have hated his guts that second, Babe Ruthless and The Great Chatsby, his opponents that game, tossed him a NH and a VNH. SaniFlush didn't even say TY. For all I know he's a real poker superstar such as Jesus Ferguson, Daniel Negreanu, or Phil Ivey and he's just sneaking in a few online games to warm up for in-the-flesh games with real people and real cards.

As I won more money and wagered more money, I often found myself conversing and joking around less. I was spending less and less time with my usual crew.

Because it wasn't just a game anymore. Now it was business.

Grouchy Old Man: We don't see you that much anymore, Chip.

Chip Zero: Hey, I'm here now, aren't I?

History Babe: Yeah, but we know you're just slumming with us small potatoes. So tell me, what's it like up there, Mr. Zero, huh? Is it true that they serve caviar and Cristal and that when a player wins a hand he gets a bj underneath the table from a stripper?

Amarillio Slim-Fast: Just go, Chip. Quit your slumming. Our feelings won't be hurt. You don't wanna be down here with the poor folk.

One time I won $7,500 in one hand—it was quad 7s beating a full house, Queens full of 7s—and I didn't get one NH for it. I was flabbergasted and I missed my old buddies who, every time I took their hard-earned money, always had the good manners to compliment me.

The weird thing was that for me to lose fifteen grand in one day with a stack of $150K was dreadful and would torment me until I won it back, but it felt not one iota worse than when I used to lose $15 when my stack was $1,500. It meant the same amount, to the second, of teeth-grinding; it meant the same amount, to the decibel, of cursing aloud ("DAMN it! God DAMN it!"); the empty soda can I hurled against the wall traveled to the wall at the same velocity; it meant the same amount of lost sleep. It might take ten or one hundred hands or four or forty hours of up and down play for me to win that $15K back, but it also might take one off-the-wall lucky hand . . . and the same was true with the fifteen dollars.

The thrill of victory was no different either. I can only pump my fist so hard so many times or jump up so high off the floor and I can only yell, "YEAH BABY! YEAH BABY!" so loud. If there were such an instrument as a Pleasureometer, I believe it would record that the amount of joy a kid feels when winning the Little League World Series is exactly the same as he feels when, twenty years later, he wins his first World Series.

I was now playing twelve hours a day on the average.

My dream states were crazed by poker, by cards, by players, by chips, all through the night. In the fuzzy half-life just before sleep, when people kick their myoclonic jerks (there is, I swear, a player named Myoclonic Jerk), there glimmered hardworking, soot-faced 3s of Clubs, overly optimistic 9s of Hearts, radioactive Pocket Rockets and the snooty, powdered faces of insolent Queens and Kings. As soon as I closed my eyes, this electric cardshow began. The shuffling of cards and the clattering of chips became the soundtrack of my dream life. Flops, turn, and river cards were being dealt from midnight until dawn. Even though I still had real dreams while asleep, ever distractingly present were cards, cards, chips, cards, players, cards, cards.

Another strange aspect of my new profession: when I looked at possessions I not only saw the things themselves but also saw the hands that made them possible. And not just the hands, but the people I was playing against and the pots I'd won. Every Sunday night Cynthia and I made the bed; it was impossible for me to look at that new $3,000 made-in-Italy bedframe and not think: three Jacks, The Scarlet Bettor, Pearl S. Luck, $3,000. Instead of seeing our brand-new sixty-inch plasma TV and whatever show I was watching, I saw: King-high straight, Folda Meir, Ante Maim, Willie McTells, $3,500. When Wifey got dressed to go to work, if I wasn't already in my study playing, I would look at the shoes she was putting on and think not of Jimmy Choo but of a Jack-high club flush, Derek Cheater, Ministry of Foam, Flush Gordon, $500. Not only did I see the hands, I saw them as they developed, card by card, raise by raise.

I used to imagine playing golf to induce sleep. It was a trick my mind played on my body, and if you're ever having a rough night, try picturing yourself as Phil Mickelson pitching out of the rough at Torrey Pines: you'll be fast asleep in two minutes. But that no longer worked, for as I lay curled up on my Sleep Number mattress (three 3s, Foldilocks, Pest Control, Lindsay NoHand, $1,000) and as I saw myself driving the ball off the tee, the sky hanging over Pebble Beach transformed into a fluttery mobile of playing cards and the fairway before me became the baize and the sand traps were full of millions of infinitesimal chips, not sand.

My dreams were no longer peopled by friends, family, and acquaintances, but by Poker Buddies and their cartoon avatars. In these dreams I was usually the Big Man with the round, rose pink sunglasses. I no longer dreamt on film or on tape. I had gone digital.

There were days when, all told, I played poker for seventeen hours.

Why was this happening to me? Why? Except for my alcoholic

Uncle Ray, there is no history of addiction in my family, and never before in my life had I ever evinced any symptoms of addiction or even the slightest hint of a propensity for any kind of addiction whatsoever—other than for alcohol, sex, and drugs.

So why then? Why had playing cards taken over my life? I didn't even watch poker tournaments on TV—Orange County housewives, Alaskan crab fishermen, and Shark Week were more captivating to me.

When you wake up each morning, you are pretty sure how the day will go. If your life is managed right, there are few surprises in it . . . which is precisely the problem. When you see a movie you usually know within the first half-hour how it's going to end, and usually you don't even have to read the final twenty pages of a novel. But the course and outcome of a hand of poker is *always* a mystery, and even with only a dollar on the line, the suspense always kills me.

The Chip Zero Super System involves folding a lot of hands, which makes for a lot of boredom. Sometimes I'll wind up folding six hands in a row and when this happens there's nothing to do but either watch the other players play and make note of their tactics and tendencies, or daydream. (Some days this new job of mine was just as boring as anyone else's.) During one such lull I sent an e-mail to Toby Kwimper, asking my dear old editor if he was interested in *Dead on Arrival*. I thought that Toby would like the book, I *knew* he would like it; after all, he had liked my first two books and both he and I were still the same people. It would be great, wouldn't it, if he wanted to publish it . . . then I would call Ross F. Carpenter and he'd arrange the deal with Toby's new house, TriHo Books. The key thing was to screw Clint Reno over and make him regret treating me so shabbily. As I folded bad hands I repeatedly imagined Clint picking a copy of *Publishers Weekly* and reading:

> Frank W. Dixon has sold his third novel, *Dead on Arrival*, for an undisclosed sum to TriHo Books. Toby Kwimper, who edited Dixon's *Plague Boy* and *Love: A Horror Story*, will edit.

Reportedly the deal is in the high six figures, although neither Mr. Dixon nor anyone at TriHo would confirm. Calls to
Ross F. Carpenter, Mr. Dixon's new agent, were not returned.
Mr. Kwimper described *Dead on Arrival* as "a coruscating,
blistering, brilliant and disturbingly revelatory journey into
the dark, twisted, wounded, damaged psyche of the Modern
American Male." Several movie companies have approached
Mr. Carpenter for rights and a seven-figure deal is said to be
imminent.

I lived for such a moment. No, not the book finally getting published—and at this point, the undisclosed sum could be a dime—
but for the moment when Clint hanged himself in his office by
either his Hermès tie or his own ponytail, the copy of *Publishers Weekly* still rolled up in his hands. He had let me dangle for
months . . . now it was time for him to do some dangling.

One day an archaeologist will stumble upon some scrawls in
an Eritrean cave or some cuneiform script on thirty-sixth-century
B.C. tablets and publish a scholarly paper that proves what I've long
suspected: writing was invented not as a way to communicate, record history, or effect commerce, but as a way to settle scores with
enemies. A club to the head is great but it only kills once—you
embarrass someone in print, it lasts forever. Hemingway humiliated the writer Harold Loeb in print while Loeb was alive, transforming him into the ex-pat Jewish shitheel Robert Cohn in *The
Sun Also Rises*. It was a devastating drubbing, although Hemingway made one minor miscalculation: had he not used Loeb as the
basis for an unforgettable fictional character, not one single person today, including me, would remember who the hell Harold
Loeb was. James Joyce exacted revenge on his old roomie Oliver
St. John Gogarty by turning him into Buck Mulligan—once again
keeping a mediocrity alive for eternity—and centuries ago, some
Roman guy stole Ovid's girlfriend (or his boyfriend) and so what
does Ovid do? He grabs a pen and some papyrus and turns the
guy into a hyacinth.

I don't have that kind of courage, imagination, or talent. Disgracing a living person in print is like blowing a man's brains out face to face and keeping both your eyes open. But getting back at Clint Reno in the above fashion was as tidy a thing as pressing SEND on my cell phone and blowing him up from a hundred miles away.

So it was too bad that Toby never responded to my e-mail.

It was during another stretch of folding and daydreaming when Harry sent me an e-mail, asking if I wanted to cowrite the script. He had two weeks free around Labor Day, he told me. I e-mailed him back and told him I loved his idea but had plans to go with Cynthia to Empyrean Island then. I'll think about it, though, I wrote. And I did.

He e-mailed me back the next day and attached a file containing a vague scene-by-scene breakdown for the screenplay. "I NEED YOUR HELP WITH THIS!" he added.

I read the scenario and saw what was good and what wasn't and what might be done with it. I opened a page in Word and gazed for a minute into the terrifyingly empty blankness of it. It really did make me shudder from head to toe. I cut and pasted Harry's scenario in. It was now mine to tinker with . . . all I had to was add or subtract a few words, jumble things around, throw in some ideas. I stared at the screen, then played a hand of poker. I went back to the scenario, read it two times and even giggled when I thought of some dialogue and plot twists I'd throw in. Maybe, just maybe, this time something that Harry and I wrote would work! We were a lot older, a lot wiser, a lot less stoned, and now he knew Hollywood pooh-bahs. I played two more hands of poker, did some chatting, then went back. I read it again and thought of which actors would be great for which roles and envisioned them saying the lines that I would write. Leonardo DiCaprio, Scarlett Johansson, Paul Giamatti, Keira Knightly, Jake and Brad and Cate . . . the usual gang. *Hey maybe, if Harry and I cranked this out quickly, I could get it to Pacer Burton and he could make* Plague *and then do this! What a one-two punch that would be!* I played five more hands of poker,

then another five. Then I closed the file without saving it and
e-mailed Harry and told him that I'd look at the scenario and get
back to him.

"Let me know soon," he wrote me only seconds later, "okay?"

I promised him I would.

♠ ♠ ♠ ♠

The words on the Nirvana Resort & Casino Web site describe the
place better than I can: azure, snorkeling, turquoise, white sand,
tropical breezes, couples, spa, lazy river pool, casino, relax, sun,
frozen drinks, time stands still. Empyrean Island is a forty-minute
ferry ride from Nassau; the ferry docks inside the hotel lobby. The
Nirvana *is* the island, from what I could tell: the property occupies
90 percent of the land. You can walk around the island, on the
beach, in two hours and never be out of the shadow of the hotel itself. The Nirvana's three immense towers are connected by bridges,
and each bridge—for the benefit of the incredibly lazy—contains
a moving sidewalk (the tread is made of clear fiberglass, and right
beneath your feet swim hundreds of dazzling tropical fish). The
theme seems to be Indian and Zen (there was a delicatessen in
Tower 3 called Koan's Delhi) with some West Indian thrown in.
The hotel staff, man and woman alike, wear russet brown silk shirts
with Nehru collars but also Bermuda shorts, and the music playing
throughout is a jingly mix of sitar and ska. The logo, an Eastern-
looking cursive *N* escaping from a circle, is everywhere—on the
floors, the linens, the china, the staff uniforms, the casino chips.

(The last time I'd been in the Caribbean was when I had to join
fifty of my coworkers at an off-site retreat five years before. We
were led in trust exercises, which included rock climbing (I passed
on that) and cliff diving (no way). During one drill I was supposed
to catch a coworker named Mimi, an assistant V.P. in her twenties,
in my arms as she fell backward. Our cheery Facilitator counted to
three and Mimi fell. I instantly stepped back and let her fall to the
ground. "Why did you do that?!" the astounded Facilitator asked

me as Mimi dusted the sand off her red polka-dot bikini. "Because to be honest," I told him, "I just don't trust her.")

Cynthia and I arrived at the Nirvana a day before the Artsy Painter Clan was to arrive, but I was already nervous. Cynthia noticed it, while she and I relaxed by one of the hotel's three enormous pools (she relaxed, I didn't), while we ate an enormous and only so-so seafood dinner, while we sat and played blackjack together in the evening and shot craps after that.

"So what's wrong?" she asked.

We were walking along the white sand beach. The moon was enormous, the sky was swimming with stars, the sea was silent. It was summer and midnight and 99 degrees.

"Nothing. Why?"

"Because something's wrong. I can tell."

Ten years of marriage, three years of dating before that. She knew me well.

"I don't know . . . I just don't feel right."

"It's that *Trilogy*," she said, "isn't it?"

Okay, so maybe she didn't know me that well.

We went back to our room, which looked onto two of the Nirvana's pools and the Caribbean beyond. I'd lost $250 at blackjack and won it back at craps. It took three hours. A hell of a lot of work for not that much profit or loss.

So back in the room when Cynthia went to bed I turned on my laptop and logged on.

I played three hands in High and, after folding the first two, won two grand with the last.

Then I opened up an e-mail from Artsy Painter Gal.

"Hope to see you tomorrow," it said. "I'm kissing you long and deep in the pool now under a cool waterfall pouring all over us. We're making the water steam."

"What are you doing?" Wifey asked me groggily.

"You think the Muses," I said, "stop singing to me just because we're on an island? They have found, can find, and will find me anywhere."

When I woke up the next morning I was so panic-stricken that I went to the bathroom, got on my knees and dry-heaved violently. In her Nirvana terry cloth robe and fluffy Nirvana slippers, Cynthia put a cold wet towel on my forehead. I clutched my belly and gagged up nothing but wave after wave of balmy air.

"It must have been that seafood," Cynthia said. "I thought the tuna tasted gamy."

APG and family wouldn't be arriving until seven that night, but throughout the day I kept looking at my watch every five minutes, which Cynthia noticed.

"Do you have to be somewhere?" she asked poolside.

"Oh, it's just a habit," I said.

"A *habit?* You don't ever have to be anywhere anymore!"

I tried everything I could to ease my nerves: swimming in the pool, wading in the sea, walking on the beach, almost dying on one of the hotel fitness center's Stairmasters, drinking four margaritas. I went to the barber shop and got another short haircut (the *Martin Guerre* bangs were now officially all gone) . . . it seemed like I was in the chair three hours. In this glitzy tropical paradise, time, as the hotel's Web site guaranteed, did not stand still—it moved backward. When at one point Cynthia suggested, "Maybe you should go upstairs and write," I couldn't even eke out a grunt.

"Let's try the water slide?" she suggested. "That might be fun."

Wifey and I arose from our poolside chairs, now drenched with a tangy blend of sweat, suntan lotion, and tequila, and walked to the top of the slide, where we deftly cut in front of a few kids. Cynthia went first, then it was my turn. I slithered down and made a large loud splash when I hit the water. It was fun and for ten seconds I forgot that in a few hours my online poker-playin' mistress would be somewhere on the premises, then suddenly I was confronted by one of the hotel's lifeguards, a dark Adonis in a yellow bathing suit not much larger than a Band-aid, who told me, "Sir, I don't think you should be using the water slide." My impact had created too large a splash.

We ate dinner at six o'clock at one of the Nirvana's fifteen restaurants. The menu informed us the beef was Black Angus and was aged for so many days, that the lobsters were flown in live from Maine, and that all the produce was local. (Unless they were growing lettuce on the roofs of the hotel, that didn't seem possible.) Cynthia had salad and prime rib, a baked potato and string beans, I didn't touch whatever it was I ordered.

I was too scared to go into the casino that night. APG might be there. I was scared to leave the room, but when Wifey suggested another walk on the beach I went. The water was warm but my bare feet stayed cold. Walking back to the hotel—all 5,800 rooms—I saw room lights twinkling in Tower 1 and wondered if one them was APG's.

When we got back into the hotel complex—the lobby alone is three acres—Wifey asked if I wanted to go to the casino and I said no. There was a good chance, I knew, that Artsy might be there. "We'll spot each other," she had written me, "at one of the pools or in the casino."

So I didn't see APG that night.

But we did have contact. She had brought her laptop, too. At 1 a.m., while Wifey slept and hugged a Nirvana pillow (it was the size of Santa's toy sack for a family of five), I logged on to the Galaxy. There she was, in a room at a table by herself. Her avatar presently was the Jayne Mansfield/Lady Godiva blonde; I occupied the body of the suave James Bond dude.

Artsy Painter Gal: I have attained Nirvana. You're here too, right?
Chip Zero: I'm here.
Artsy Painter Gal: Tower 1?
Chip Zero: Tower 1.
Artsy Painter Gal: Room #? You must tell me or die, Mr. Bond!!
Chip Zero: 1022. You?
Artsy Painter Gal: OMG.

There was a thud right over my head.

Artsy Painter Gal: That was my suitcase! We're in 1122! I'm on top
    of you, baby. Hope it feels good. So tomorrow, okay?
Chip Zero: Okay (gulp).

Again we kept it vague: one of the pools, the casino, a bar, a
restaurant. She tried to pin me down to an exact place at an exact
time but I refused to commit.

The next day I was even more of a wreck. Every time a new person arrived at the pool my stomach went sour. Half of the people
at the pool were women, two thirds of those were with men, a third
of those were with kids. APG had salt-and-pepper hair, she'd told
me—"a lot more pepper than salt"—and these days no more resembled a young Joan Collins than I did. "But I'm still in pretty
decent shape for my age," she added. She had told me she'd wear a
shiny red maillot on the first day at the pool. Thinking it would be
suspicious to ask Wife out of the blue, "Hey, what's a maillot look
like?" I found a few examples online. On APG's first full day, there
were eight women in red maillots at the pool, four with what could
be construed as salt and pepper hair . . . but none that could be said
to be in "pretty decent shape" for their ages.

I couldn't eat yet couldn't keep anything down. This time my
heaving wasn't dry.

Maybe I was throwing up Cynthia's prime ribs and string beans
vicariously.

"Should we go back home?" Wifey offered. We could end the
trip and catch an earlier flight, she suggested. I shook my head and
told her I'd gut it out.

In the late afternoon, while Wifey was at the spa getting an
oatmeal and aloe-vera enema and having her eyebrows reorga-
nized, I logged on to the Galaxy. APG wasn't on but I saw a new
player named Hibernian Hottie sitting by herself and playing as
the slinky Dragon Lady. I played a hand and she began talking to
me. I lost, on purpose, then won the next. Hibernian told me, "I'm
so hot that if you saw me your screen would melt." I won, she won,

we folded a few hands, I won, she told me she was playing with her enormous tits. I said, "Oh, okay," then she said: "You turd! It's me! Second Gunman! I've been playing as a woman for 3 days and I've been cleaning up too!" I told him, "I'm gonna kill you, you transvestite arsehole!" and he said, "Well, you're gonna get the chance to cuz I'm coming to New York in a few weeks."

"You are?"

"Yeah."

"Oh."

I didn't know how I felt about that. These fake people whose real money I was taking and was spending all my time with were actually real people, but maybe it was better if they weren't.

After dinner that night—I forced myself to eat a quarter of a hamburger—and after chasing a Xanax with a double-shot of Pepto-Bismol, I went down to the casino. "I'll be wearing," APG had e-mailed me, "a tight black dress and red do-me pumps."

I played blackjack—sitting down concealed my burgeoning paunch better than standing at a dice table—and after two hours broke even. How, I don't know . . . I wasn't paying attention. There were too many women in black dresses and red pumps to count, but I did tally ten women with salt-and-pepper hair in black dresses and red pumps that could be construed as "do-me." Of those ten, a mere three could be said to be in decent shape for their ages. Two of them were no taller than five foot three—"I'm five-eight," APG had told me—and the other one's hair was straight and almost fell to her waist. "My hair is shoulder-length and wavy," APG had said.

I gave up at ten that night and went back to the room and suffered the worst stomach cramps and case of nerves I've ever experienced. Trembling hands, sweat all over, cotton mouth, throbbing temples, the whole bit. If a panic attack means breathing rapidly and going in and out of consciousness, then I was having one . . . on the bathroom floor.

"I'm sure," Wifey said, "the hotel has a doctor."

She looked at me with such genuine concern that I wanted to

never meet Artsy or talk to her again. Nobody ever liked me this much. What was I doing?

"I couldn't make it to the casino tonight, damn it," APG IM'ed me that night.

(Had my e-mistress and I, I briefly suspected, come all this way just to narrowly avoid meeting me each other?)

"No problem," I IM'ed back. "RLO. Wifey here. Gotta go!"

Knowing the coast was momentarily clear I took an elevator downstairs, ran to the steakhouse and wolfed down two New York strip steaks, an order of fries, a baked potato, and two pieces of cheesecake in fifteen minutes, and made it back upstairs and quickly fell asleep.

On the third day I was so self-conscious that I wore a shirt by the pool. At some point I *had* to make contact with Artsy and time was running out.

"Why are you wearing that thing?" Cynthia asked me by the pool.

"I don't want to burn," I told her.

"But long sleeves?"

I stayed at the pool from ten until five. I also kept a robe over the chaise longue, for added protection from APG's disillusionment. My shirt still on, I peed in the pool three times.

I didn't go to the casino that evening. On the thirtieth floor of Tower 2, the hotel has a spa, unforgivably named Nirvanspa—there are hospitals in medium-sized towns that aren't as large—and it's open twenty-four hours a day. Manmade waterfalls and hissing pools and the bubbly drone of New Age Music, everything saffron yellow, terra cotta, brilliant turquoise. That night, I got a Shiatsu massage at seven, a Swedish massage at nine, a hot-lava-stone and aroma-therapy combo at eleven. It didn't help me relax.

An hour after I returned to my room, so dehydrated and man-handled that I looked like a peach pit, Artsy Painter Gal told me, live on the Galaxy, that she had spent the day with her daughters on the beach and shopping at the hotel's complex of 150 shops.

Meanwhile Mr. APG, the Rugged Beachy Type, had hang-glided, jet-skied, and parasailed . . . but that goes without saying. (Had a great white shark attacked a young girl, he no doubt would have swam out and killed the evil beast with his bare hands.) Artsy had also visited the casino and gone on an extended futile Chip Zero hunt and won $250 at roulette.

"I'm going to be at one of the pools all day tomorrow," she said. "I may be alone. FIND ME OR ELSE, Big Blond Boy!" She would be back in the shiny red maillot, she told me.

Tomorrow was my last day. I had to find her.

Okay, let us act as if this hard-hitting, pull-no-punches, take-no-prisoners memoir is a movie on DVD. I'm going to press the PAUSE button here for you.

If anyone were to play Cynthia/Wifey in the movie version of this Caribbean getaway, it would not be, despite what she would tell you, Ava Gardner in her delicious prime — for Cynthia just isn't nearly that beautiful (oh, *your* wife is?) — but Ava Gardner's body double's body double. Wavy black hair, dark olive skin, bright green eyes. As Gérard Depardieu's French accent is too thick for him to pass for a native Jersey Boy, James Gandolfini, circa Season One of *The Sopranos*, gets the role of me without an audition (he would need to don a rug, however). Although the Joan Collins of *Land of the Pharaohs* and *Can Hieronymus Merkin Ever Forget Mercy Humppe and Find True Happiness?* might play the younger Artsy Painter Gal/Victoria Landreth in some sexy flashbacks, the adult role would have to go to Liz Taylor right when she was on the wane, post–*The Sandpiper*, in her *Boom* and *The Only Game in Town* days. The part of Mr. Artsy Painter Gal goes to one person and one person only or this movie doesn't get made: George Clooney.

I'll press the PLAY button now and the action resumes.

It is the next day, my final full day at the Nirvana. I wake up, after three hours of card-haunted sleep, knowing that today Artsy and I will meet, *must* meet. Cynthia hasn't slept that much either: my ragged nerves seem to be contagious and she is on edge and the

bags under my eyes are also under hers. Even during our breakfast
(Jacks and 2s, Bet Midler, Stuey Hunger, $50) on the patio, which
I charge to the room, she's biting her nails and shaking her legs as
she sips her Bloody Mary. I'm looking around for APG and family,
but they don't seem to be there.

"I must look like hell," Wifey says, unable to eat another bite of
mango pancake. (It's a line I can hear Ava Gardner saying.) Her pea-
green shades, however, mask most of her hell. The morning sun is
relentless . . . this is a place to come to in January, not the summer.

"You don't," I tell her.

An hour later we're at the pool, sunning and sweating gallons,
and replenishing with ice water, Coronas, and margaritas.

"How close are we to the equator?" she asks me several naps and
dips later.

"Close. I just felt it move under my back. They change it every
day about this time."

After a few drinks Wifey asks me, "You're really writing a book,
right? You don't just sit around and play poker all day long?"

"I only wish," I say, "life were that easy."

I signal for my next Corona.

Wifey falls asleep just before noon and the sun beats right down
upon her pricey Rosa Cha bathing suit (three 7s, Raise The Lawd,
Bumbershoot Bob, $300) and amethyst necklace (two 9s, Gentile
Ben, Playing Mantis, and Chips Ahoy, $450).

I walk around our pool, reeling slightly. The sweating bodies,
some sunning and reading, some sleeping, are stacked in rows of
beach chairs five deep. The air smells of chlorine, rum, cologne, and
coconut. Female buttcheeks dapple the mise en scène, round ones,
pale ones, tan ones, dark ones, buttcheeks of all variety sheathed in
swimsuits of every color. There are all sorts of breasts, too, plump
ones, flat ones, pointy ones, freckled ones, and too-good-to-be-true
fake ones.

No woman fitting APG's description is around the pool.

I walk past some palm trees, tall potted plants, and long,

scuttling chartreuse and lime green lizards to the next pool over. The sweat on my neck is trickling down my back, down my shirt, which is underneath my silk robe. The next pool is the largest: there are children, some with water wings, at the near end, and at the deep end a few adults swim unremarkable laps. There is a pool-side bar and also a few stools in the pool where some bathers sit and drink or nod off under the blazing sun. I walk around the pool three times looking for my secret iLove. There are many women in red bathing suits and maybe one of them is her . . . I just cannot tell. When I abandon this pool and make for the next one—walking around a large Jacuzzi filled with giggling adults holding glasses and bottles—I feel a combination of relief and frustration.

The third pool is the smallest and the most kidney-shaped. Walking only a few inches from the edge of the pool I begin my circumnavigation; I'm so close to the chaise longues I pass that I scrape my calf four times against their metal ends. As it is now after one p.m., some people are eating lunch or at the bar or are back in their rooms recovering from the flesh-loathing summer sun. Only half the chairs are filled.

I walk . . . I pass a flabby man on his stomach and hear him snore, I see two empty chairs, I pass a woman in a red bikini reading an Eckhart Tolle book and improving her life, I see a guy in the next chair slurping a frozen drink, I pass two empty chairs, I pass a muscular stud with a *Wall St. Journal* lighting up a cigar, I see a woman in the next chair in a black bikini spray her shoulders with oil, I pass a chair empty but for a Stieg Larsson paperback, I see an attractive Hispanic couple fiddling with their cell phones, I pass a woman with black hair reading the book *Love: A Horror Story* in paperback, I see an empty . . .

I sit down in the empty chair.

"Excuse me," I say.

Artsy Painter Gal puts the book on her negligible midriff bulge. Not only had my novel been providing a quick fun summer read but also excellent protection against the midday sun.

"Yes?"

"That book you're reading?"

"Yes?"

"I happen to have written it."

"No way!"

"Swear to God."

She takes off her sunglasses, revealing a pair of hazel eyes so intelligent that I feel my SAT scores diminishing retroactively, turns the book over and looks for the author photo.

"How do I know you're telling me the truth? There's no picture."

"I'm not bluffing, I promise."

"This is good," she says, smiling. "But *The Missing Chums* was better."

I notice that my robe is starting to separate around my chest and I pull it closer together even though my shirt is on underneath.

"A robe?" she says. "In *this* heat?"

"I'm . . . I'm a bit . . ."

I cannot find *le mot juste* to tell her what I am.

Suddenly she puts her sunglasses back on and whispers, "Hub coming! Play blackjack with me tonight. Ten-thirty. The five-dollar tables. *Be there, Chip!*"

A shadow comes over me, then two smaller ones, then the shadows join to engulf me.

You have to imagine the improbably cast movie scene: George Clooney, his rugged tan body in a black bulging banana hammock, and his two daughters (Abigail Breslin in a dual role) stand over James Gandolfini, who slouches forward in his sweat-drenched silk robe and talks to Elizabeth Taylor circa *Boom* and *The Only Game in Town* while, two pools away, Ava Gardner's Body Double's Body Double, circa *The Night of the Iguana*, bakes flat on her stomach atop a chaise longue—under which the ice of Margarita Number 3 melts and a pair of Christian Louboutin sandals (9-high heart flush, Bjorn 2 Win, Minnesota Phat, Steve McQueens, $500) seek shelter from the sun.

"Aaron," Artsy/Victoria/Liz says, "you're not going to believe this . . . the book I'm reading? This man says he wrote it!"

"You did?" Mr. Artsy/Aaron/George says, insultingly void of any suspicion.

"Yeah, I guess I did," I say, standing up quickly. Too quickly. The sun's blurry yellow, the pool's shimmering blue, the sky's paler blue, the terra cotta and saffron yellow of the hotel's tripartite façade, the many Coronas and all those encircled Nirvana N's hit me at once and I fall back down to the chaise longue . . .

Five or ten or fifteen minutes later Chip Zero/I/James Gandolfini comes to, courtesy of some smelling salts and a few shoves, in the same spot. I hear splashing, I hear swimming, I hear a smattering of applause (for me being recalled to life). People I've never seen before are standing right over me. Artsy and her family are gone but Wifey/Cynthia/Ava Gardner's Body Double's Body Double is right there with her loving, caring smile and Thierry Lasry shades (two Aces, Trey Scalini, Raisin' Bran, $350), asking me: "Are you all right? Can you get up?"

"Yeah," I mumble as I shield my eyes from the light. "I think so."

"What happened?"

"I was walking and . . . I saw someone reading my book. I saw that and I guess I fainted out of shock."

Wifey and I head back to our room (three 10s, Bjorn 2 Win, Unlucky Lindy, Tally Ho, $2,800) to recover.

I ate a few grains of rice for dinner, then threw up into the toilet and showered. "It must be the water here," Wifey said. "Although I drank it too and nothing's happened to me."

I played poker in the room until ten, got an e-mail from Barbara Bennett in Hollywood telling me she wouldn't be able to make it to New York in September, then went into the bathroom and sat in the empty bathtub for ten minutes.

I told Cynthia I was going down to the casino, she told me she didn't want to go; she wanted to pack for tomorrow morning, watch TV, and read. She kissed me and wished me luck.

Downstairs, Artsy was sitting by herself at a fifty-dollar

minimum table. She had a rich husband and had won over $75K online by then—these stakes were nothing for her.

"I thought you said the five-dollar tables," I said as I took a seat next to her.

"I did. But when I got here I realized how truly short life is."

"Where's Mr. Artsy?" I asked.

"Upstairs with the kids," she said. The dealer busted and she won. I pictured her husband putting the kids to bed, doing three hundred push-ups, gargling with Drano, and calling it a night.

On my first hand I got a nine and a two and doubled down. Then I pulled a nine and APG said, "Nice, baby."

She told me she couldn't stay long.

"So I fainted, huh?" I said.

"I must look pretty terrific in a red maillot!"

"Well, you do."

Her thighs were a little chubby, there were two tablespoons of flab under each arm, but that's nitpicking. She was a fine-looking woman for her age. Nice sturdy rack, piercing eyes, her butt hadn't yet fully collapsed. Here's a coarser way of putting it: if there's such a Web site as losangelesmilfs.com, she'd most likely make the top thousand.

On the next hand we both hit blackjack.

"Sweet," she said, tossing the dealer a five-dollar chip.

She told me she had to get going and we gathered our chips and stood up.

"Well, Chip . . ." she began as we started walking. The place wasn't that crowded. The holiday weekend was over, people had gone home.

"Yes?" I was ready for her to tell me that it was fun being with me but that she saw no reason for us to ever meet again. In a way, that's what I wanted to hear.

"I'd like to see you again some time," she said. "This isn't going to be enough."

"Sure . . . okay."

We walked to the cashier and got our money.

"How are things with Mrs. Zero?" she asked me as we walked toward the casino entrance, the warble of slot machines almost drowning out her words.

I sighed and told her that it was so complicated that it defied explanation, and we walked out.

There were a few people in the lobby, there were a few at the lobby bar. Her floor was in a different elevator bank than mine and we had to separate.

"We'll say good-bye here," APG said.

I stuck out my hand but she put her arms around my neck and kissed me, slipped me the tongue . . . there were about ten people out there who might have seen it but she didn't care.

I couldn't remember the last time I had a tongue in my mouth other than my wife's or my own.

Alone in the elevator, as the in-flight flat-panel TV touted the hotel's restaurants, sun, sea, and spa and plasmically flashed the time and temperature and Dow Jones, I wondered if all the people I'd been spending so much time with lately online were sad, unfulfilled, lonely, and more than just a bit strange and if it was this and not cards, good luck, bad luck, and winning and losing that bound us so closely together. Were we all in it for the collective insanity and not the money? In my dark hotel room, hushed and chilled with air conditioning, Cynthia was curled up and asleep . . . she looked so untroubled and angelic in the deep blue darkness. She was—and is—all I ever wanted. It took a while but after playing three holes of golf at Pebble Beach, each green ringed with an undulant halo of hearts, diamonds, Aces and 8s, I joined her in the spectral, stately clubhouse in Dreamland.

♥ ♥ ♥ ♥

Back in New York a few days later I e-mailed Harry and told him that I just wasn't the man to work with him on the screenplay. I was way too busy, I told him, with my own writing.

But I wished him luck with it.

10
Dónde Está Big Lou?

One day, two weeks after I returned from the Caribbean, I rode a winning streak so absurdly lucky that I was sure something calamitous was going to happen just to atone for it: I'd be walking to get my lunch and a Great Dane would rear up and rip my throat out, or a leather sectional would fall out a window and crush me, or a manhole cover would electrocute me. On Monday I had won $3,500; the next day I won twice that. Wednesday morning I didn't even start off at the low tables—I went straight to the top. The pixelated menace SaniFlush was there, so was Bjorn 2 Win, a few other high rollers. I took my seat and watched the cards as they were dealt to me. A King of spades, a Queen of spades. SaniFlush raised, Bjorn called, I called, two others stayed in. The flop was a Jack, 10 and 9, all of spades. Insane luck. I knew this pot was mine. When I showed my hand I won an amount so high that I am embarrassed to tell you, but I will say it was by far the easiest $7,500 I've ever earned. I could almost see SaniFlush flinching behind his mirrored Psycho Killer aviators.

It was September and the air had cooled and that night I took a subway up to a Barnes & Noble on the Upper East Side. I had seen in the paper that a writer named Cody Marshall would be reading from his first collection of short stories, recently published to much acclaim (to much acclaim in newspapers and magazines for which Cody Marshall had reviewed other writers' first collections of short stories). The name Cody Marshall didn't just ring a bell—it banged a deafening gong right near my ear, for it was this same Cody Marshall who'd shoved *Plague* through a high-speed

shredder in the Sunday *Times* when it came out; it was his voice
that had made me shave half the skin off my face.

I simply had to see this guy in action.

Besides, he owed me a pint of blood.

The reading began at seven. There were metal folding chairs,
posters with Cody Marshall's book and his portrait on them, a
small makeshift dais with a microphone and pitcher of water. Cody
was of average height and wore thick glasses and had dainty, well-
crafted hair. There were about fifteen book lovers present, not including me as I no longer was such a thing.

When he began to read I asked myself: *Do you really have the
courage to embarrass this person and destroy one night of his life since
he destroyed countless nights of yours?*

He read two stories (each time he ended, he had to tell the crowd
that the story was in fact over) to a minor spasm of applause, and
immediately hands shot up, people began asking questions, and
my hand rose as though yanked by someone on the next floor up.

"Yes?" the author said after fielding a few softball queries, looking at me and swigging some water.

"How could you have done that to me?" I heard my voice say.

"What did I do?" Cody said.

"I think you know."

"I'm afraid I don't."

Of course he didn't. He had no idea. People all over the country
didn't buy my book because of his review, but once he had written
it, he was through with me. He didn't even have to wash his hands
of the matter: it had happened so quickly, no blood could collect.

"You even gave away the surprise ending," I said, sitting back
down miserably.

That was not to be my comeuppance for winning so much
money so easily earlier in the day. My great Dane, leather sectional,
and electrified manhole cover were still out there. But it would
come soon enough.

When I got home Wifey was very excited and told me that someone had called and left a message. It was, she told me, a publisher. "I think it's good news," she said.

Good news? Had Clint Reno come through for me? Finally? After nine months of silence? I imagined the message: "Frank, it's So-and-So from Such-and-Such Books. We want to publish your novel."

Dead on Arrival was going to be published! I would get tens of thousands of dollars that I didn't need, but my reputation would soar. I could write more books, which is all I wanted to do. One book every three years for the rest of my life. Books that mattered to people. I would *be* somebody and finally would be satisfied, perhaps even happy, with my life.

"Frank, Deke Rivers at Last Resort Press," the message went. "I had lunch with a friend of yours yesterday—Beverly Martin. I'm a huge fan of your first book, by the way. Huge fan. Anyway Bev told me you had something that might interest me and gave me your number. I'd love to take a gander at it, I really would. My number is . . ."

I deleted the message before it finished.

"So what was it?" Cynthia, still tan but peeling now, asked.

"It was just some guy. Deke Rivers. A publisher."

"But that's good news, right?"

No, it wasn't. I wasn't going to pay someone to publish me. There was putrid, uncooked animal-waste matter I'd rather swallow whole than do that. For a second I was furious at Bev, then I was mad at Deke Rivers, then furious at Cynthia (for being the nearest available human being), but I finally settled on me. The proper target.

"Which book was he talking about?" Cynthia asked me.

"The last one."

"The one I couldn't finish?"

"Yeah. That one."

◆ ◆ ◆ ◆

When I began writing the *Trilogy* I felt invulnerable. There was
a force field around my body: a Cloak of Invincibility had been
draped over me, the Muses would protect me. I'm certain that
when Joyce was writing *Ulysses* he felt the same way. The book,
he knew, had to come into the world, so what terrible fate could
possibly befall its author? *There's no way,* Michelangelo thought
while painting the Sistine Chapel, *that this scaffolding is going to
collapse and I'll fall to my death and not finish this thing. No way.*
He probably hopped up and down on the platform, maybe even
sawed a few pieces off, or dangled off it from a pinkie nail. And I
bet Marcel Proust felt the same way when he went looking for lost
time, although I believe he never once left his bedroom for fourteen
years to seek it out, so maybe he didn't.

   Because of this newfound invulnerability I began doing incredibly stupid things. I was brazen, I was brash, I was a bit of a jerk.
I regularly got into minor bar skirmishes in the East Village; I attempted to pick up women while they held their husbands' hands
at parties; I once stormed into a kitchen at a restaurant and confronted three knife-wielding cooks because Flatbush Hethuh's
cheeseburger had been done medium well and not medium rare. I
did eighty-five in a fifty-five-mph zone, I drank red wine with fish
and ate oysters in months without R's and went swimming within
an hour of eating. Why did I do this? Because I could. The Muses
had my back! One night I tackled a pickpocket on Third Street and
Avenue B and knew he wouldn't stab me because Erato would lop
his hand off in mid-plunge; I bought hard drugs from guys named
Julio and Omar and knew they wouldn't shoot me because Terpsi-
chore wouldn't allow a bullet to penetrate my skin. One night when
a large, tattooed ex-con and I were about to go at it just outside a
bar, even as he informed me that he had enjoyed carnal knowledge
of my mother for the insultingly low price of $25 and as I, in turn,
imparted to him the pertinent information that I, along with all
of the male residents of the Bronx, had had our way with his sister
in her hindquarters ("I don't *have* a sister, faggot!" he yelled at me),

I was thinking: *He can't hurt me . . . nothing bad can happen to me until I finish the Trilogy.*

And it worked. Despite the myriad stupid, suicidal things I did, not once did I die in all that time.

"Why are you doing stuff like this?" Hethuh, exasperated and worried about her boyfriend, asked me the night I tackled the pickpocket. (He wasn't a pickpocket, it turned out. He was just some dude running.)

"Because," I answered her, jutting out my jaw, "I can."

Was Beethoven going to suffer a fatal heart attack while working on the third movement of his first symphony? When I was only twenty pages away from the last page of Book I, were Julio and Omar really going to slit my throat with a box cutter because I was five dollars short for three dime bags? That would have been like John Lennon and not Stu Sutcliffe dying in 1962. When he was writing Molly Bloom's soliloquy I wouldn't be surprised if Joyce dove in front of trolley cars nightly or chugalugged flaming shots of absinthe. He must have known that he wouldn't suffer even a sprained toe until he got to the final "Yes" of that book, and here is as good a place as any to say that I've always found the "Trieste-Zurich-Paris, 1914–1921" ending of *Ulysses* to be about as annoying a thing in literature as exists, even more than that cutesy little flip book of a man falling up into the World Trade Center that David Safran Wallace Foeranzan included in *Incredibly Unbearable and Unbearably Unincredible*. The final word of the most overrated work in modern literature, then, is not the affirming, inspiring, exultant "Yes," but is the word "1921," the year that brought the world widespread labor unrest, race riots, the spread of Bolshevism, the Communist Party in China, Adolph Hitler as the head of the Nazi Party, and the birth of Prince Phillip, Duke of Edinburgh. Perhaps one day the world will see *Ulysses* for what it is: the First Gimmick Book. A whole day in the life of a man, the man is alienated from his surroundings, he is estranged from everyone he knows, all day long he is betrayed, he tries to reconnect with a child forever lost to him. Face it: *Ulysses* is 24 except not as exciting.

When Book I of the *Trilogy* was finally finished, I bought a copy of *Writer's Market* and sent out dozens and dozens of queries and samples of the book to agents and publishers. While I waited (and waited and waited) for positive responses, for *any* responses, I met someone who knew someone who knew someone whose cousin was a recently hired editor at the prestigious publisher Lakeland & Barker. I asked the first person in that chain to ask the next person and so on to ask if the editor would be interested in reading my book. It had been three months since I'd sent out my original queries and I was getting desperate. It only took a week to find out that Martin Tilford, the editor, would be interested.

I dropped off all seven-hundred-plus pages of Book I at Lakeland & Barker.

Later that night I told Hethuh that I needed some time off from her. She had straight black hair and freckles over her entire body but, as she was so tiny, that really didn't amount to so many freckles. (When I used to drop in on her at work I could barely see her: the blender on the counter where she whirled her health shakes was over her head.) The race was on as to what would happen first: my missing Hethuh and making a desperation booty call, or Martin Tilford getting back to me and telling me he wanted to meet me.

Against all odds, Martin Tilford won.

Could I meet Martin, his assistant wanted to know, at Café Quelquechose near Union Square for lunch on Thursday, November 6th, at 1:30 p.m.? I didn't tell her but I would have met Martin Tilford at Café Rien in the Black Hole of Calcutta for a Ritz cracker with hamster turds on it on Wednesday, March 53rd at 3:30 a.m.

I called Hethuh, not for booty purposes, but to tell her I had a meeting with an important editor. She was happy for me. Two minutes of that and then an hour of her unfulfilled needs and I regretted making the call.

I showed up at Quelquechose ten minutes early and had a club soda at the bar. I didn't yet know what publishing types looked like, but the restaurant was full of them. The gray suits, the battered leather envelopes, the furrowed brows and serious-looking glasses. For every editor sitting at a table, there was a writer with scruffy hair next to him or her, wearing jeans or khaki pants, an oxford shirt and no tie and cheap shoes, and expressing something between a feigned grin and an eternal grimace.

The front door opened, Martin approached and asked me if I was me and when I answered in the affirmative, we took a seat at a table near a window. He had a hint of a British accent; either he was American and had been educated in England or was English and had been living in America too long. (Or he just could have been an asshole.) Sitting down, I recognized a famous overrated novelist—he is no longer famous, overrated, or alive—who seemed to have put away all by himself the bottle of Merlot sitting on his and his stone cold sober editor's table.

"Oh God, how I do so love your book! It's a masterpiece. It is without question the finest American novel I have read in quite some time."

That was what I'd imagined Martin saying to me as soon as we sat down. But instead I got: "Do you know what you want?"

When I told him I hadn't decided, he slid a menu over to me.

"The seared peppercorn tuna here is simply extraordinary," he said.

I asked Martin how the hamburger was and he said that it wasn't as good as the peppercorn tuna.

Our waitress asked if we were ready to order. Martin ordered the peppercorn tuna and I ordered a hamburger and fries. But then Martin summoned her back and said, "He'll have the tuna too." When she left, he winked at me conspiratorially.

I didn't argue. How could I when just then he pulled from his battered leather envelope the manila envelope containing Book I?

"I must ask you . . ." Martin began, "Frank W. Dixon? Any relation?"

"A great uncle or something." Who knew? . . . the famous connection might help me.

"So!" he said. He was about thirty years old, on the deathly pale side, and would be gray before he was forty. His smoke-gray Brooks Brothers suit didn't fit him too well but with just three more years of free lunches it would probably be two sizes too small. "A trilogy, eh?"

"I hope so," I told him. A waiter went by me, holding a plate that held a plump drippy hamburger and fries. It went to the no-longer-living author at the table immediately behind us.

"Have you started the second part of it?" he asked me. "Book Two?" (He made quotation marks with his fingers and toggled his head when he said that.)

"Up here I have," I told him, pointing to my skull. "I'm allowing myself a break."

"Ah! A break. A respite. Time off. Rest for the weary, I suppose, eh?"

He took the seven-hundred-plus pages out of the manila envelope. They were held together by a rubber band. As he undid the rubber band, hamburger molecules began wafting up my nostrils, making my nosehairs swoon.

He asked me how I'd heard about him, and I briefly explained I knew someone who knew someone who . . .

The dead writer behind me bit into his hamburger. I could hear it, I could smell it, but I was also gazing at my title page like a mother watching her daughter in a school play.

"Wait until you have this tuna. It comes with wasabi mashed potatoes and string beans."

"I know. I saw it on the menu."

"Well, let's drink. To seared tuna, mashed potatoes and to trilogies!"

The wine was good . . . it would have gotten along just swell with a hamburger.

"So! A trilogy! That's going to mean a lot of work, Fred. It's going to mean years and years of toil and struggle and dedication. Are you committed?"

"Yeah . . . I think I am. And it's Frank."

"Oh yes. Sorry. So you're ready to hunker down for the long haul? You're in it to win it?"

"I guess so."

"Have you read the Anthonys, Trollope or Powell?" he asked me. "Proust? Durrell?"

"No. Those weren't trilogies, I don't think." Well, I knew they weren't, but I didn't want to come across as a smarty-pants.

"At one time, they must have been though. Right? I mean, just after they'd finished book three and hadn't gotten yet to book four. They were trilogies then, weren't they?"

"I suppose they were at that point, yeah."

I turned my head and saw that the dead author had only one bite left of his hamburger.

"Things were very bad then," Martin said, "but still we carried on."

It was strange to hear someone else saying the very first line of my book. Even though it was only a yard away, it was as if the words were pealing through the sky like thunder.

"That is a classic first line," he said. "Simply classic."

I thanked him.

"Just a great classic American first sentence. A little bit Bellow, a little bit Hemingway. I suppose one could call it Bellingway-esque. Where did that come to you? *How* did that come to you?" I was about to answer when suddenly he said, "Look!" and pointed to a waitress walking by us with two plates. "The tuna!"

I finished my glass of wine and Martin signaled for another glass.

"Things were very bad then," he said again, "but still we carried on. Things were very bad. Things *were* very bad. Things were very *bad*. We carried on. We carried *on*. It really draws you in. It has its own peculiar dynamic to it, its own sort of wondrous journey."

Just as I was about to tell him about Books II and III, the pep-percorn tuna, wasabi mashed potatoes, string beans, and second glass of wine were placed in front of me. Martin looked at it as though it was his birthday cake and there were a hundred candles blazing. Within a few seconds I found out that he was not, like me, one of those gifted repulsive people who are able to eat and engage in conversation at the same time. This was good insofar as I didn't get to see string bean between his teeth, but was bad insofar as we didn't talk about the book—or about anything at all—for fifteen minutes. I was so disinterested in my meal that I ate but three small bites of the tuna; the rest I merely cut into tiny pieces and strategically placed in various far-flung arrondissements around the plate, under and over clumps of mashed potato that I had also similarly apportioned.

A busboy took the plates away. The waitress asked if we wanted coffee and dessert, and Martin looked at his watch and said he didn't have time.

"What was I saying?" Martin asked me.

"You were talking," I reminded him, "about the first sentence?"

He pulled the manuscript closer to him, to where his pepper-corn tuna had been only moments before, and said: "'Things were very bad then but still we carried on.'"

He looked at me and I nodded. My knees were knocking each other, my stomach was growling for a hamburger, my blood was boiling, but outwardly I was smiling ever so sweetly.

"Just a classic American first sentence, Fred. So deceptively complex. It really does jar you at first. It jars you, it unnerves you, with 'very bad,' then releases you with the tender, warmhearted 'we carried on.' This sentence alone is a masterwork of sublime Manichaeism."

He pulled out his corporate credit card and signed for the bill.

"Things were very bad, things were very *bad*. We carried on. *We* carried on."

While I tried not to bite my lip so hard that it bled, he stood

up and carefully—no, not carefully at all—put the title page back
in its place, but when he wrapped the rubber band around the
manuscript it snapped and the title page crumpled. So he left the
title page on the table near the ashtray. Then he shoved the whole
thing, now an unfettered and unprotected lumpy mess, back into
his leather envelope.

I followed him outside where he shook my hand and took off
down the street. He didn't even tell me that I'd hear from him
again—I didn't—and I was too brokenhearted and beaten to go
back inside and order a hamburger.

(Not one single agent asked to read the rest of Book I. An editor
that I'd sent a query letter to wanted to read a ten-page excerpt,
but after I sent it, he vanished into a black hole. This book, I told
myself, must be *too* good.)

♣ ♣ ♣ ♣

I'm human, all too human. I have biases, prejudices. I have preconceived notions. I do not expect a three-year-old to be able to explain
string theory to me. I do not expect a 450-pound woman to be able
to run the hundred meters in less than ten seconds. When I walk
into a sports bar to watch a football game, I expect there to be
more men present than women and I expect these men to behave
stupidly. I have, I confess painfully, a few ethnic biases, too, none
of which I will give examples of. So try me at the World Court and
hang me because I'm a racist, ageist, weightist, sexist Nazi.

As I waited on the visitors' side of the baggage claim area at
Kennedy Airport on a Thursday afternoon for Second Gunman, I
therefore had a preconceived notion of what Johnny Tyronne might
look and act like. He would be big, he would be boisterous, he
would have reddish blond hair and a fiery glint in the eye, he would
fancy his pint, his football, and his birds. He might even have a
large moustache. Perhaps I expected John L. Sullivan to get off
the plane, find me, and give me a Guinness-tinged hug that would
break my backbone in two.

Second was going to stay on my living room couch until Sunday, then go home. Tomorrow Cynthia was going to visit her mother in West Virginia for a week, so we would not be in her way. The truth is, I didn't want Second on my living room couch or anywhere in my living room or elsewhere in my apartment, but it's hard to say no to a foreigner coming to your city, especially one you've beaten, all in all, for about $4,000 at poker.

He had won over $200K in the Galaxy. Couldn't he have stayed at a hotel?

It was now an hour after his flight had landed. Maybe, I figured, he was being detained by Homeland Security after a drunken donnybrook with a few customs officials. So who is this guy, Wifey had asked me that morning, soon to occupy our couch and toilet seat? He's just a friend of mine, I answered. He's the one, I told her, who first started calling you Wifey as a matter of fact. And for this, she said, he gets to stay in our apartment? I reiterated that he was a friend but then confessed I really didn't know the man.

"Chip?" I heard. "Chip feckin' Zero?!"

My senses dulled from watching tourists wait for their luggage, I slowly turned around. I was beginning to feel that I, too, had just arrived from a long flight from overseas.

"Second?"

"That's me."

I looked at him and immediately felt ashamed. Because he did look a little like John L. Sullivan. He was about six foot three, two hundred and ten or so pounds. He had reddish blond hair, broad shoulders. He had a fiery glint and even a moustache. I felt terrible and ashamed because it meant that some of my ethnic-, gender-, and age-based prejudices were sometimes based on facts. I had wanted to be wrong and wasn't.

Second and I shook hands, talked about his flight, took each other in. He didn't have much with him, just a beat-up suede jacket, a blue nylon knapsack, a black laptop bag.

"Chip, it's good to meet ya." (It was a bit disconcerting to be called that in person, but as this was my online tag for about twelve hours a day it wasn't that disconcerting.)

He looked at me strangely, eyed me up and down. I looked like someone else to him, it seemed. But who?

We got a taxi and headed toward Manhattan. It was evening now. The whole way home, I could tell, he was examining me and seeing a cartoon character. I didn't mind because for the last nine months of my life, he'd been a cartoon character to me, too.

♠ ♠ ♠ ♠

Cynthia was asleep on the couch when we walked in. The TV was off, the lights were on.

"Is she okay?" Second whispered. "You didn't kill her, did you?"

I gently nudged her awake and saw, as she came to, what had put her to sleep.

Dead on Arrival was on her lap. (After the phone message from Deke Rivers, Cynthia had asked if she could finish reading it. "I don't remember, though," she admitted, "where I left off." I reminded her it was at the second paragraph on page 48.) As she and Johnny made each other's acquaintance—he called her Wifey to her face, which elicited a smile—I espied that she had made it up to page 61. I wondered what was on page 61 that was so boring that it had knocked her out cold, but then I recalled what Harry Carver had said about *DOA*: "It's a lot like reading a close friend's obituary."

Second and I went out that night for dinner: hamburgers, fries, and beer at the indomitable Corner Bistro. I told him about New York. I explained the layout of the city, how addresses flowed west and east from Fifth Avenue, I told him how to get around, what to see, where to go and not go. We could also go to a museum tomorrow, I told him, go to a great restaurant tomorrow night. If he wanted to see Ground Zero I would suck it up and take him and I'd take him across the river to Newark, where my mother and father grew up, or I'd show him Teaneck and the neighborhood I grew up in. I proudly told him about the history of the city—a city whose mere outline on a map sometimes reduces me to sentimental tears—and about Peter Minuit and the Great Fire of 1835 and George Washington at Fraunces' Tavern and how the construction of the Brooklyn Bridge had engendered the great city as we know it today.

I told him all these things and was so proud to live here that I got all choked up and my voice cracked, and when I was done he asked me, "So how far away is Atlantic City?"

♥ ♥ ♥ ♥

"This is where you steal my money?" Second Gunman said when I showed him my study after dinner.

He sussed out the operation, the computer on the desk, the books on the shelves, the view out the window. When Cynthia came in to say she was going to sleep—her plane to West Virginia left early next morning—Second asked me, "So what's this a picture of?"

"You know," Cynthia said, "I always wanted to know that too."

"It's just a pear in a bowl," I told them. "That's all."

"And that?" he asked. "Who's that?"

"Just some guy. Just some guy in Paris, okay?"

"Is he always so touchy?" my visitor asked my lovely wife.

"I'm going to sleep," she said.

A few seconds after she left, Second asked me how an ugly blumper like me could marry a pretty flinny like that. This wasn't the exact slang he used, but it was something to that effect. I told him that years ago I was thinner and had a lot more promise.

"So these are your books, huh?"

He was looking at the shelf with the foreign editions of my two books.

Second told me he wanted to get a few hands in before sleep, and he got on my computer and logged in under his name. He played five hands and stopped when he was up $200, then I logged

in under my name and played. During the second hand I saw that
Plague had slipped 10,000 places on Amazon. Between the second hand and the third an article on Nexis revealed to me that a
Frank Dixon who worked for Boeing had been promoted to vice-
president. During the third hand Toll House Cookie, playing as
the ten-gallon-hatted Cowboy, came to the table.

Chip Zero: Hey, Hoss!

Toll House Cookie: Yo, Chip.

Chip Zero: You'll never guess who's here.

Toll House Cookie: You, me, two other nobodies. Why?

Chip Zero: No, I mean HERE. In my apartment. In real life.
Second is!

Toll House Cookie: The hell he is.

I explained that Second Gunman was standing only few inches
away, then Second played as me for a few seconds (and won me
$300 with two 7s). It took about four minutes before the occa-
sionally ornery Cookie finally believed I wasn't playing a prank
on him.

Second asked him about going to Atlantic City and while THC
was typing, I told the Blackpooler: "Look, you really don't want to
go there. It's a void . . . it's a first-class shit hole."

Cookie, via IM, agreed.

Toll House Cookie: Nah, don't go there, man. Try Foxwoods or
Mohegan Sun.

I shook my head. I didn't want to go there either. They weren't
voids or first-class shit holes per se but they just weren't for me.

Toll House Cookie: Or just go to Vegas.

I told Johnny that Vegas would have to wait until his next trip,
but even though he seemed like a nice guy, hadn't been untoward,
had indeed been quite civil and hadn't groped my wife, I didn't
want there to be any second trip. Still, I had to be nice.

Toll House Cookie: Why don't you try to get into a few local games in NYC?

Chip Zero: Nah. We're okay.

Second Gunman, standing over my chair, poked my shoulder blade and said, "Yeah, get an address from THC. We'll play. You could break your real-life poker cherry, you gobshite."

I looked up at him, at his mischievous eyes and reddish mustache, and it dawned upon me: these next few days might not be so easy. I disliked having visitors stay over even if they were absolute saints, which this one wasn't.

Cookie IM'ed me the address of a poker joint on the Upper East Side. It was just off Lexington Avenue, in the eighties, not far from the posh apartment building Cynthia grew up in.

Toll House Cookie: It's underneath a bodega. Walk in and go to the cash register and say to the guy, "Dónde está Big Lou?" You got that? "Dónde está Big Lou?" That's the password.

Chip Zero: Dónde está Big Lou. Right. But wait . . . what if there *is* a guy named Big Lou there?

Toll House Cookie: There is, dude! That's why I just told you to ask for him! He's downstairs running the show. Lou's cool. Drives through my toll lane nearly every day. Tell him Cookie sent you.

Chip Zero: Okay, but what if the cops come while we're there?

Toll House Cookie: They'll already be there. They're the security guards.

A minute later I said good-bye and logged off.

"Is this," I asked Second Gunman, "really what you want to do in New York?"

I reminded him of New York City's amazingly diverse culture, about the incredible restaurants, the finest shopping in the world, the subtle tints of pink and violet over the Hudson River at sunset, the hot dogs and iconic roller coaster on Coney Island, the Rembrandts at the Met and Matisses at MOMA.

"Let's go play poker," he said.

"Johnny, when did you think you were going to do this?"

"Wifey's asleep. C'mon, Chip. Why not right now?"

I told him no.

Yes, this is what he really wanted to do in New York.

◆ ◆ ◆ ◆

The next morning Cynthia woke me up before she left. *DOA*, I saw, was in her carry-on Furla bag. As soon as she was out the door, it felt like it always did when I knew we were going to be apart for a while: as though all the warmth, goodness, and comfort had been sucked out of me in a flash and that I was living in a cold and lonely vacuum.

Second had a weird list of things he wanted to see in New York. He didn't want to visit any museums but did want to see the no-longer-extant Belmore Cafeteria, where a scene in *Taxi Driver* was filmed. He didn't want to see the Statue of Liberty but did want to see the Chelsea Hotel, where Sid killed Nancy. No Empire State Building, but the subway station where a scene in *Ghost* was filmed. As I've never seen the movie I wasn't sure where that was, so I just took him to any old station and he fell for it.

At one point in the middle of the afternoon I went to my bank and got out $7,000 in cash. Second Gunman didn't have to; he had brought about $20,000 (stuffed into the ripped lining of his suede jacket) with him to New York. We were going to play.

Walking along Union Square in the early evening to get a taxi to go to Big Lou's bodega casino, I noticed there was a reading at the Barnes & Noble. The book, I saw from the window display, was a memoir called *Lost and Found* by Charlie L. Something. The reading would begin at eight. I looked at my watch and saw that eight was only five minutes away.

"Hey, Second," I said. He was still in his suede jacket, even though it was in the forties out and windy, and was wearing baggy jeans and a blue chamois shirt. "Let's go inside."

"What a weird time to decide you wanna buy a book."

"I don't."

We went inside, wove our way through and around the stacks and tables to where the reading was. Truth be told, Second and I had enjoyed a long lunch together and had drunk a bottle of wine; we'd just had dinner and another two bottles. At the end of both meals I was speaking with an unconvincing Irish brogue and an even less convincing burr. We were primed.

We took seats toward the rear. There were only about fifteen people there but one of them looked familiar, even from the back. It was Beverly Martin, I was pretty sure.

Charlie L. Something adjusted the mike to a smattering of applause and coughing, thanked us for showing up and began to read. He resembled a lesser-known president—Polk, Arthur, or Garfield—but without the wig, muttonchops, or beard. His book was about his privileged childhood and preppy adolescence, his descent into drug abuse (including siphoning off his dying father's morphine drip) and living on the street, and subsequent recovery at the Shining Path Clinic in the Southwest and conversion from Presbyterianism to Episcopalism (which for me was like relocating from Park Avenue to Fifth Avenue). I'd read *Lost and Found*'s reviews and, as usual with books of this type, from St. Augustine to Malcolm X to the present, the early screwed-up nasty parts were way more interesting than the later recovery parts. Presently he was going on about how the refulgent façade of Shining Path glittered in the sun "like some splendid, otherworldly cathedral on some lonely, lofty hill, built all of stained glass and drenched in God's great golden light."

"Zzzzzzzzz," Second whispered.

"Could you say that louder please?" I asked. He didn't get it so I whispered: "Snore louder! So everyone can hear it? Come on. I'm giving you a free place to stay!"

"Bollocks! You don't . . . What's this fribblin' kranswaggle ever done to you?"

"Had a book published within the last two years!"

Charlie L. Something droned on and the only person who

seemed as though she might be paying attention was the woman who might be Bev . . . so now I knew it was her.

"Get on with it!" Second called out to Charlie. "Get on with it, gobshite!"

Charlie stopped reading for a second, then resumed. I slid down in my metal chair.

A few sentences later Second called out: "Is this really the best you can do? This is like takin' foiv Ambien CR's!"

People turned around to look at Johnny, and Beverly Martin was surprised to see me at the reading but even more surprised to see me sitting next to the rambunctious boor who was disrupting it.

Charlie resumed but after a few more sentences Second stood up and yelled: "FREEBIRD!"

A Barnes & Noble employee came over and asked us to please leave. We got up and were making our way out when I heard Bev call my name. We stopped—we were deep in the shadowy thick of the Self-Help section—and she approached us.

"Frank!" she said.

I introduced her to my buddy Johnny Tyronne.

"You were heckling Charles," she said to him. "That wasn't very nice."

"Well, it wasn't very nice of him to be so boring," Second said to her.

"I didn't think he was boring."

Of course she didn't. For her if it was in print it was fascinating and sacred. She probably regarded Chinese take-out menus as classic texts.

"Well, I guess we're just not going to be mates then. Pity, that."

"Deke Rivers called me," I said to her.

"Oh yes . . . I gave him your number. How did that work out?"

I thought she got a kick out of siccing a vanity press editor on me and that she enjoyed the feeling of being a bar bouncer stamping an ultraviolet LOSER on my hand for the night.

"I haven't called him back. I don't think I'm going to."

"I better go back."

She spun around and headed back, nearly knocking over a table of Addiction and Recovery books.

Twenty minutes later we were outside Big Lou's bodega. It looked ordinary, rundown, anonymous. Second went inside and bought two quarts of Bud and then we sat on a stoop across the street and drank and watched the place. Everything seemed normal until a limousine pulled up and three well-dressed people got out, went inside, and didn't come out.

"Do you think we should call Cookie?" my guest asked. "He could meet us here."

"Nah, he's on his tollbooth shift," I said. "Doesn't get off work until like three a.m."

Second nudged me in the shoulder and said, "Well?"

Online, there was no doubt that I was a damned good poker player. I could analyze the situation at hand as well as anyone, and my decisions were swift, smart, and sane. It was the only thing I was good at, but for months now I'd been wondering if I'd be any good in person. I was like a singer who could belt out "The Star Spangled Banner" and raise my own goosebumps in the shower . . . but could I do it before the Super Bowl in front of a billion people?

"Dónde está Big Lou?" I said to the guy behind the counter, eyes darting east and west.

He pointed to a curtain near the Progresso and Goya cans and said, "Abajo."

Second and I walked behind the curtain. The light on the stairway was murky and I had to feel around the walls blindly as we descended. The stairs were narrow; twenty more pounds and I wouldn't have fit. By the time we made it to the landing below there was hardly any light at all. There were no knobs, no sliding window panels—it wasn't like the Speakeasy-Swordfish scene in whichever Marx Brothers movie. "Forget this, Second," I whispered. "Let's go back up."

Suddenly one of the walls slid open onto a small antechamber and the landing was flooded with light and noise. I heard music, I heard voices—a lot of voices—and liquor glasses and chips. Real honest-to-God chips, not a tinny reproduction playing out of my computer speakers.

"Who are you here to see?" an acne-scarred, off-duty cop wearing black pants, black shoes, and a black turtleneck asked me.

"Dónde está Big Lou?" Second and I said nervously at the same time.

He looked us up and down, asked us to turn around and put our hands on the wall of the antechamber. As we were packing only cash and no heat, he allowed us to turn back around and directed us into the large room. (For his troubles, I handed him a twenty.)

The subterranean casino was the size of a small high school gym . . . which at one time it might have been. There were no windows, no clocks, just lots of buzzing fluorescent light, cigarette and cigar smoke, and lots of men. Men at Let It Ride and Pai Gow tables, men at craps and blackjack tables, men walking around, men with women at roulette tables. "Rio" by Duran Duran was playing when we walked in; although the music wasn't throbbing, it was just loud enough to be annoying. There was a fully stocked makeshift bar and two bartenders in dull golden brown tuxes at the far end of the room, and Second and I headed over and surveyed the scene as we walked. Against the wall near the cashier window were rows of slot machines, but only one woman, about thirty, was playing (if you choose to call losing your money in slot machines playing). Second and I quickly downed our drinks—they weren't free—and he said he was itching to play. I could see that. He was scratching the lining on his jacket as though the suede was a bad case of hives.

"You've got all kinds of Hold'em games here?" Second asked one of the bartenders, probably also an off-duty cop. We got another round. I had a very nice buzz on.

"All kinds," the bartender said. I know cops are underpaid, I know most of them have families and lead dangerous, stress-filled lives, but not for any amount of money, I reflected, would I wear a tuxedo the color of Gulden's Mustard.

While they chatted I walked over to one of the two dice tables. This one was a ten-dollar minimum table, the other was fifty. All the casino workers were dressed as though this was a legitimate but low-budget operation: burgundy sharkskin suits with a few stains here and there, loose black bow ties, white shirts with ruffles and imitation pearl buttons. The blackjack dealers were mostly Asian women, and no more than 20 percent of the gamblers were women. I threw in fifty bucks and got some chips—they were real, made of clay and not plastic—and played for ten minutes, all the time keeping an eye on Johnny Tyronne/Second Gunman, who was still conversing with the bartender. After ten minutes I was up sixty bucks and I brought my modest winnings back to the bar.

"Chipper," Second said to me, "I think I loov your coontry."

"Yeah, what with places like this, we're a real light unto the world, Johnny-Boy."

We sidled over to a spot near the cashier's window, and "Heart of Glass" came on.

Second Gunman explained to me the baffling setup of real-life poker at Big Lou's and, as we'd already drunk a lot that day and as we were still drinking that very moment, it wasn't easy to follow. The upshot was there were all varieties of poker games going on, tournaments, freerolls, sit and go's, etc. (I had no idea what he was talking about.) There was No-Limit, there was Pot-limit, there was Omaha, there was a lot I'd never heard of. As he was explaining all of it to me I noticed, to my amazement, Scott Heyward—Toby Kwimper's successor at my former publisher, whom I'd met at the *Saucier* book party—take a seat at a table and reach into his wallet. (That wallet couldn't have been too full since he worked in publishing.) Could I possibly, I wondered, not only win a few grand here but also sell *Dead on Arrival* to Scott? That seemed an impossible stunt to pull off: if I was winning, it would be his money I was pocketing and he might not be so anxious to buy my book in that case. I decided I didn't want to play with Scott Heyward, I didn't want to talk to him, I didn't even want him to see me.

"So you should sit there then . . ." I heard Second say to me.

"Huh? Where?"

He pointed to Scott Heyward's table.

"When?" I asked, feeling all the hundred-dollar bills in my pockets shriveling like a scrotum in cold weather.

"Now! Hurry."

He told me he had to go to another table very quickly to play No-Limit.

At this point, Evening Two with my new mustachioed Black-pudlian buddy begins to get fuzzy and very dark gray. We had been drinking since lunchtime and by no means was it Second Gunman's fault: it really was a folie à deux, sort of like how neither Perry nor Dick acting alone could have murdered the Family Clutter but had to be together on the fateful Kansas night that at once cemented and ended Truman Capote's career. When I sat down at that poker table, drinks kept coming, one after the other, then three after the other. It turned out the drinks *were* free, once you were sitting and playing, and they were brought to you by off-duty cops, who, other than making sure you weren't going to get in any brawls if you lost lots of money, were there to keep you as drunk as possible and make sure you lost lots of money. Another reason for my gray-out was simply this: fear. Fear of playing with real people. Real people were at my table, on both sides of me, across from me; real people were all around. Things got very blurry, voices blended into each other. Cards were shuffled and dealt in slow motion and in fast motion at the same time. I believe that Scott Heyward recognized me . . . or maybe I just thought he did, or he didn't and I foolishly reintroduced myself to him. After that—I'm almost certain of it but not sure—he kept bringing up the subject of Jerome Selby to me. *So you're the one who drove Jerry Selby to commit suicide,* he said. And he kept at it. (I think.) *Forty years Jerome Selby is at the company, there's no sign of trouble, he gets your manuscript and wouldn't you know it, two days later he blows his brains out.* Hand after hand Scott kept this up. I had been used to online tomfoolery but this was something else and it wasn't fun. *Toby Kwimper didn't want to edit your book—what was the name of it:* Love Horror, *was it, or* Plague Love?*—'cause he knew it was a definite go-nowhere career-killer, so what does he do? He gives it to poor Jerry, a legend in the business and a man who never could ever say no to anybody. You happy, Frank? Does this make you proud, you untalented, increasingly pudgy fuck? Your book, which sold—what was it, like fifty copies?—ended Jerome Selby's life. Some book!* Then the other players, strangers to me all, joined in . . . and they were saying things like *Wow, you really did this?* and *You must be a real piece of shit, Frank. This Jerry Selby sounds like decent people, like a regular standup guy, and you just go and make him kill himself* and also *That must have been one lousy book to make a guy commit suicide.* At one point a player to my right told me he could write a book about his life, and at another point the player immediately to my left said to one of the off-duty cops, *Hey, Al, this guy here once killed a guy named Jerry Selby by suicide. Homicide should look into that, doncha think?* Then another player, I'm fairly sure, asked me, *So what the hell was Fenton Hardy really like and did you really have a boat called the* Sleuth? So there was the booze, there was Scott Heyward's cruel bullying, there was the spliff I'd smoked with Second outside on the stoop before we walked in that I only just now told you about, there were the humiliation and guffaws, and, ultimately, there was also the fact that I lost all seven thousand bucks by 2:15 a.m., which made me feel as if every ounce of blood in my body had been replaced by flat club soda.

Reader, my whole life up to that point had been spent not being George Clooney . . . George Clooney, who had been put into this world to be the very exemplar of all the things I should be but never would. (My one saving grace might be: just as George Clooney was created to remind me that I was not successful, perhaps I had been created to remind him that he was.) Even in the dark, ignorant years when I didn't know that there existed in the world such a thing as a George Clooney, I, as mistake-prone as a person can possibly be, still had never come close—not even accidentally—to being anything remotely like him. A man can measure his life in many ways—how much money he makes, how he provides for his family and how his children turn out, how many women he's slept with—but my measuring stick is the Clooneyometer. So on the 100 Top UnClooneyest Moments of My Life Countdown, I would put fainting at the pool at the Nirvana somewhere around 11 or 12 and I'd put the seared peppercorn tuna around 13. If my lousy book reviews are numbers 7 and 8 and walking in on my brother with my girlfriend is number 1, then I put losing $7,000 playing poker that night at number 5.

Second Gunman fared even worse. He'd dumped almost ten grand, he told me, and for a few minutes hated my country about as much as your average Al-Qaeda recruit does. Outside, back on the stoop across the street, I sat on a dirty stone stair, bewildered and angry, and rested my head against the cold black iron banister. *What just happened to me*, I was trying to figure out, *did that really happen?* Second paced in a circle and muttered, using all sorts of slang and curse words. He must have walked the same circle fifty times, punched his palm about twenty times, and employed every possible variety of the F-word at least ten times each.

"Jaysus . . . Jaysus . . . Jaysus feckination Chroist."

"I can't believe it."

"Can you feckin' believe this, Chip?"

"Did I just not indicate to you that I couldn't?"

"Nine-feckin'-thousand eight-feckin-hundred-and seven-feckin'-teen dollars! Gone!"

It was, I confess, enlightening and reassuring to see someone as tormented by losing as I was. So *this* is what I was like to be with, eh? It was a pretty ugly spectacle but I couldn't not look at it.

Second stopped his pacing, put his hand on the iron banister, and asked me, "Well, what the bloody hell are we gonna do then?"

"There's nothing we can do. We can just win it back online."

"Bollocks. Takes too much bloody time, man!"

He was going to start pacing again, but I pulled the collar of his suede jacket to stop him. A few hundreds fell out and he picked them up and shoved them back in.

"So what do you suggest then, mate?" I asked.

"Where's this Mohegan Woods? We could—"

"Forget it. It's, like, literally right in the middle of a forest. It's an unnatural act against Nature to frequent a place like that."

"Run by injuns, right? What kind? What tribe? Mohican? Cherokee?"

"Comanch! I dunno. Some made-up tribe."

"Fuck it." He waited, then said, "What about Atlantic City?"

I thought about it. We could rent a car, we could take a taxi, maybe even get a helicopter. We could afford it. But that car, taxi, or helicopter would wind up pulling up or settling down in Atlantic City, the Land that Steve Wynn Forgot. I didn't want to go.

He was pacing again. Hands in the pocket of his jacket. Muttering. I was muttering, too. Goddam Scott feckin' Heyward, I said. The brogue and burr were back and going in and out.

"What about Las Vegas?" Second said, carving circle number fifty-five into the Upper East Side asphalt.

In the corner of one eye I saw a thousand neon lights flashing, and in the corner of the other a lubed-up, top-heavy stripper, her body dripping liquid gold, flopped around a pole like a dying trout.

"What about it?"

"We go back to your flat right now and we pack our bags and go to the airport and take a plane to Las Vegas. We'll win it all back. Come home and nobody including Wifey is the glimphy wiser. And if we lose more, then *pffft* . . . it wasn't our yoopy ploosh to begin with."

I looked up at him. He wasn't circling anymore. Under the wan moonlight and the flickering streetlight, the fire was back into his cheeks and his mustache sparkled like a lit fuse.

In the insane world I was now a citizen of, it made sense. I wanted to win my money back, too, any way that I could, as long as that way didn't involve Atlantic City. Cynthia was out of town for a week. I had no job to go to. There were no responsibilities, no meetings to keep, no books to write.

We took a taxi back to my apartment, both of us wailing "Free-bird" at the tops of our lungs with the windows open, and got home at approximately 2:30, packed some clothing, packed up our laptops and some toiletries, got some cash and hit the road, still singing.

There was a little problem.

No planes were going to Las Vegas at that ungodly hour.

So we took a taxi.

11

Whales, Blowfish, and Walruses

E ver since reading *On the Road* I've always wanted to take a cross-country road trip.

No, that's not true. Ever since reading *On the Road* I've never wanted to take a cross-country road trip.

When Second and I crawled into the taxi that night I didn't tell the driver our true intended destination, not because I thought he would immediately throw us out but because I wasn't sure I really wanted to go all the way to Nevada. I merely told Abdul Salaam, our driver, to take us to the Holland Tunnel toll plaza. In the back of my mind (there wasn't much going on in the front of it) was the hope that once we found the sensible, sober Toll House Cookie he would talk us out of the preposterous scheme that each minute was picking up more and more steam.

"You are just going to the toll, sir?" Abdul said.

"Yep," I said, knowing it was an odd request. "A buddy works there. And please . . . don't call me sir."

"A buddy," Second said to me in the car. "Have you ever met him? In person?"

"Nope. But a week ago I could've said the same thing about you."

We turned west on Seventeenth Street, then went down Eleventh Avenue.

(Ernest Hemingway got to write sentences like "I walked to Place de la Contrescarpe and then went down to Cafe Select where I picked up Brett and we drank two *fines* and then we held hands and walked to Le Dôme where we found Robert and Frances who were both very tight," and I'm stuck with: "We turned west on Seventeenth Street, then went down Eleventh Avenue.")

"If we go through the toll," Abdul said, "there will be a toll, sir."

I said, "Uh-huh" and caught Abdul checking me—the infidel, the oppressor, the enemy—out in his rearview mirror, which he adjusted for a keener view.

When we emerged on the Jersey side, Second said, "So this is New Jersey? Tony feckin' Soprano, eh, and Brucie Springsteen and Frank Sinatra and—?"

"Yeah. Jersey. The Hawkeye State. The Land of Enchantment. The Land of a Thousand Dances. Right here, Johnny-Boy. Did you know that Jon Bon Jovi is the governor?"

(I confess to a deep nostalgia every time I return to New Jersey, my ancestral homeland. As soon as I set foot in the Garden State, my mind is flooded with memories. Just the sight of Elizabeth or Bergen or the Pulaski Skyway . . . it's like once again breathing in the musty body odor of a girlfriend from twenty years ago.)

There were only a few cars around at this late hour and the tollbooths got closer. The sky was the color of muddled blueberries in an expensive exotic cocktail. I knew that Cookie was African-American but didn't yet know his real name. This might be tough.

Abdul took us into an uncrowded lane and we stopped. I handed him the cash to hand to the toll collector and rolled down my window and said: "Hey, are you Toll House Cookie?"

"What?" the man said, putting his hand to his ear to hear better.

"I'm looking for a guy who works here and plays poker online, named Toll House Cookie!" He shrugged and indicated with a wave of the hand that we better keep driving through.

"I think that was him, you gobshite," Johnny said.

"Will you shut up?" I said. But in a friendly, drunken 3 a.m. way. I said to Abdul, "Let's try it one more time, okay?"

We swung around and went back into Manhattan, turned immediately around and came back through the tunnel, and Johnny was just as disappointed with New Jersey the second time as he had been the first. Abdul pulled the car into a different lane and I asked another African-American toll collector: "Are you a guy named Toll House Cookie who plays poker online?"

He looked at me as though I had offended him terribly. Stitched into his blue Port Authority jacket was his name in yellow script: MARVIS WASHINGTON.

He came out of his booth and waddled over to my window and asked me, "Who wants to know?"

All our windows were open and Second Gunman was rubbing his hands together to keep warm. His jacket, lined with his remaining $10K, wasn't doing it for him, but if our Vegas road trip came to pass we'd soon be in a place where he wouldn't need the jacket, only the lining.

"You can't guess who I am?" I asked.

"Foldin' Caulfield?"

"Do I look like a goddam orthopedic surgeon to you, man? It's me . . . Chip Zero!"

"And I'm Second Gunman!" came the raspy voice behind me.

"Shit," Cookie said. "You two come all the way out here at this time of night to see me?"

"Actually we were planning on kidnapping you . . . Marvis."

"Oh yeah? To where? 'Cause my shift just ended. And don't tell anyone my real name, okay? I don't want anyone stealing my fake identity."

Second said, "We're plannin' on goin' to Las Vegas."

Please talk us of out it, Marvis. Please talk us out of it!

"You mean," THC said, "you're goin' to Newark Airport to go to Las Vegas?"

Second told him that, as insane as it sounded, we were going to ask Abdul to take us all the way to "the LV," that I'd just dumped seven grand and that he'd dumped ten, that we were seriously jonesing to win our money back and that we would never have lost it but that he—Cookie—had told us about Big Lou's underground casino in the first place.

"Hey, man, I got three kids at home," THC said, scratching the back of his neck. "Two of 'em's babies. Otherwise I'd . . ."

Good. Talk us out of it, Cookie! Come on! Do it! The kids! Use the kids! Talk us out of it and I'll get 'em all Christmas presents every Christmas for the rest of their lives, I promise.

"And I got four," Second said, astonishing me. "All boys." Until that second, I had no idea Johnny Tyronne had any kids and a day or two later, just outside Abilene, Kansas, I was to discover that he'd made all of them up on the spot. "So are ya coomin' or not, Cookie?"

"Hold on. My boy Donnie's supposed to give me my ride home. Hold on."

Oh no. Oh God no. Please don't let this happen.

He walked over to another booth and pulled out his cell. Abdul, his beard, eyeglasses, and leather jacket the color of the blackening night around him, sat silently. Across the road was a drab place called the Tunnel Motel. It looked more like a prison than some kind of lodging.

"Have you ever been to Las Vegas?" I asked Abdul.

"No. I have never been more west than Detroit."

He told me that he had lived and driven a taxi in America for seven years and had rarely taken a day off. But as of January this shiny yellow tank was his own baby. I asked him where was the farthest any passenger had ever asked him to go; he told me he'd once driven two businessmen from LaGuardia Airport to Baltimore. But that's where you *did* go, I said. Where was a place that someone had once asked you to go but you wouldn't? He thought about it, then told me that one very intoxicated guy, sir, had once asked to drive him to Aruba. I saw that Cookie, talking on his cell phone, was coming our way and said, "Abdul, *please* do not call me 'sir.'" I asked him where was a faraway place that wasn't across a body of water that someone had asked him to drive to but he'd turned them down, and he told me that a couple got in once and asked to go to Port St. Lucie, Florida, so they could watch the Mets play an exhibition game, but that he'd said no to them only because his wife was pregnant at the time, otherwise he would have done it. Is your wife pregnant now? I asked him. No, she is not, my friend, he said. He added that his wife and two children were presently in Riyadh. After telling him that I much preferred my friend to sir, I said, So you'll be able to drive us to Las Vegas then?

Cookie stuck his head into the cab and said: "Aright, I just squared it with my wife. It wasn't easy 'cause I don't ever lie. I told her that my Cousin Cleon had just died in Atlanta from a stroke and I gotta go down there right away. The way I see it is, since I don't really have a cousin named Cleon, I guess he really is kind of dead and I didn't lie to her. And Donnie's gonna cover for me for a few days here. So if we're goin', let's go."

"You got a cousin who's a Klingon?" Second asked Cookie. The very first jab.

"His name, I just told you, is *Cleon* and no, I don't have a cousin named Cleon."

He got into the car and, much to my regret, we were on our way.

♣ ♣ ♣ ♣

I sat up front alongside Abdul in his Crown Victoria; THC and Second—who had never really hit it off online and weren't going to in person—were in the back.

I looked at the meter. It was already up to fourteen dollars and we hadn't even made it out of Essex County yet. Our original deal, I believe, was that we would either pay Abdul the amount on the meter plus $1,000 so he could go back (plus we'd spring for all the gas and tolls), or else $5,500, whichever was more.

"You could stay a few days, Abdul," I said to him as bits and pieces of mortifying New Jersey streamed by us in the chilly September night. "It's nice and warm out there."

"Perhaps."

Behind me Second and Cookie were embarking on a minor countrywide dispute, about leg room, money, manners, stray elbows, belching.

"Well, the weather will be good. We'll get a place with a nice pool." He had already told me he was a Saudi so I didn't feel I was being impolite when I told him, "It's in the desert, it's sunny, it's very hot and dry there, everybody has a lot of money. You might feel at home."

"I will think about it."

Two thousand five hundred miles—he sure had a long time to think about it.

A few minutes later Cookie leaned his big head forward and whispered to me, "Second says he knows a shortcut to get here. He's been in New York how long?!"

I whispered back: "He barely knows where he is right now. We could take him to Vegas by way of Fairbanks, Alaska, and he wouldn't object."

"But Fairbanks," Cookie informed me perfectly seriously, "is way out of the way."

The liquor and weed were wearing off. It was after 3:30 a.m. and the world inside and outside the taxi was all fuzz and bubbles and my inner GPS was on the fritz. To misquote Paul Gauguin: who were we, where were we, where the hell were we going, and why?

"Las Vegas, Nevada, is west," Abdul said. "I will get us there."

Yes but Tijuana and Minneapolis were west, too, and so was Moose Jaw, Saskatchewan, and Pitcairn Island.

Out of nowhere—well, not really nowhere (my main character in *Dead on Arrival* had driven from Westchester to Las Vegas and I remembered the route)—I said: "Okay, this is how it's done, guys. Hear me out. . . . Take Two-eighty. It will become Interstate Eighty at around . . . at around someplace after Passaic or somewhere. You take I-Eighty through Chicago, all the way to Cedar Rapids, I think."

"And what," Second asked, his eyes sinking into his mustache, "Archduke Franz Ferdinand Gobshite Magellan the Lincoln Navigator, happens in Cedar feckinating Rapids?"

"In Cedar Rapids I guess we stop and get a road motherfeckinition map, lad."

"No," Cookie said. "You're all wrong. We take Seventy. Seventy goes all the way to Utah. We should take Eighty to around Columbus and then get on Seventy there."

"Columbus where?" I said, realizing I was dealing with a Directions Nazi. "Missouri?"

"*Missouri?!* Ohio, man!"

"Yeah . . . okay, that sounds good." I turned to our driver. "You gettin' this?"

[Often, over the course of this journey, if the last person speaking was Second, I sounded Anglo-Irish; if the last person speaking was Toll House Cookie, I sounded African-American.]

"I-Eighty to Columbus," Abdul said with a confidant nod. "Seventy to Utah."

"Right." I turned back to Cookie and said: "You sure about this?"

"I give directions all day long in my booth, Chip. I believe I know my way around."

"Yeah sure . . . but admit that we're a little out of your purview here."

"We're out of my *what?*"

"Your purview. Your range of expertise. We're out of your element. Your bailiwick."

"So we should take your way? You ever drove from New York to Las Vegas before?"

"No. But I know someone who did."

"Who?"

"A guy, okay?"

"What guy?"

"This guy. Like, this character I once created."

He rolled his eyes. As I would have. For not only had this char-

acter never really lived and thus never really driven from New York
to Las Vegas, but the book in which he appeared had not been
published either. A heaping triple shot of nonexistence.

"My *purview*. Eight hours a day for twenty years I tell people
where to go and how to get there and you tellin' me about my
purview."

"Okay. Sorry. We're doin' it your way. You're the pro. You're
Hammond and Rand and McNally and MapQuest all rolled into
one."

"I'm just sayin'."

This was the first of about a thousand I'm-just-sayin's that I was
to hear over the next few days.

The Delaware River soon approached and I began to drift off. I
put my head against the cold window and with one eye made sure
that Abdul was more awake than I was. He was.

♠ ♠ ♠ ♠

When I woke up I thought my bladder was going to explode and
take the rest of my body with it. It was just past ten in the morning and the sun was warming and bright; Cookie and Second, his
mouth wide open and dribbling, were still asleep in the back, and
Abdul was wide awake. We were bypassing Youngstown, Ohio,
and the meter was up to $840.00.

"I need a bathroom," I said, my breath so rancid it almost shattered the windshield.

On one side of us there was a KFC, a Popeyes, a Denny's, a
Pizza Hut, and Taco Bell; on the other side was a Bob Evans, a
Motel 6, a Casual Corner and a Super 8. It was as if our taxi was
plummeting down a gigantic artery clogged with trans fats, onion
rings, chili fries, and melted down Kenny Chesney CDs.

"We will find one soon," Abdul said. "And we need gas."

Second yawned loudly, stretched, and in doing so landed a
glancing blow on Marvis's jaw and woke him up, and looked out
the window.

"Good morning, Johnny-Boy. Welcome to Ohio, the Aloha State."

"Ohio, eh? Not very pretty."

"Yeah and this is the nice part."

"The Magnolia State," I said. "Vacationland, USA. The Birth-place of Jazz."

"What the hell is a Dress B*arrrn?*" Second asked right when we went by a strip mall that was so depressing and run-down I almost began to weep.

"Just a place for women to shop, that's all," I said.

"What a name. Callin' it a barn. Do they have a Cow or an El-ephant Department?"

"Most farms," Cookie said, "don't have elephants on them."

A gas station and its ramshackle, skid-marked restroom was up ahead on the right, and Second looked out the window and asked, "So who the hell is this Bob feckin' Evans?"

♥ ♥ ♥ ♥

We refueled the Crown Vic, took our leaks, and had breakfast at an IHOP, where Johnny/Second easily polished off two Rooty Tooty Fresh 'N Fruitys. Following Toll House Cookie's instruc-tions, we got on I-70 in Columbus. We'd traveled about seven hun-dred miles and the meter was past $1,600 and when I saw the exit sign for Spiceland, Indiana, I noticed that Abdul was playing tricks on himself to keep awake and that these tricks weren't working.

"You didn't think you were gonna drive the whole way, did you?" I asked him.

"It is my car, my friend. I am a driver. I am sure that you would want to do the profession that you do."

I don't have a profession. I don't do anything. I don't work, I play.

"Jaysus Chroist," groused Second from the back. "There's no wifi in here?!"

I turned around. His laptop was on his lap and he was pecking wildly away at the keyboard. THC was looking at him warily out of the corner of his eyes.

"Look," I said to Abdul, "we're all good drivers here. This is a long haul. We'll take turns. And the meter can stay on." (When we'd stopped to pee and to eat, Abdul had generously turned the meter off.)

"Bloody hell. I'm down ten K and I can't even try to win some of it back in here?!"

"I'm not a good driver," Cookie said. "So don't include me in on this. I only drive from my house to the tollbooths and that's it. I don't like to drive."

"And we're following," Second said, "your bloody directions?!"

"You know how many people," THC explained, "pass through my booth in the course of a year and then probably hours or days or weeks later, they're dead? Gotta be hundreds. Everyday I stare into the faces of future dead people. Thousands of 'em. People in their cars. More people die in cars than in bathrooms, did you know that? It's like I work on a draft board and they're all A-One and I'm sending them right to Okinawa or Iwo Jim. So I'm not driving."

"That's ridiculous," I said. "And it's One-A, not A-One, and it's Iwo Jima, not Iwo Jim."

"Is there someplace around here," Second said, still fiddling with his laptop, "where we could maybe stop and go online and play?"

There was nothing around us but trees and the chilly autumn grayness above and between them and a million miles of asphalt monotony, but I pointed to a pine tree and said: "I think that tree over there picks up a signal, Johnny-Boy."

"And I think that you're a board-certified card-carrying, A-One, One-A gobshite."

"Can't believe you lost that all money in one night, man," THC said to Second. "I thought you was supposed to be good. Guess not."

I slid down in my seat. The truth was, if that pine tree did receive a wifi signal, or if the clouds above did, I probably would have stopped there and started playing. I wanted my money back too.

"My friend," Abdul said, "I think perhaps it is time you should be driving now."

His eyelids and head were drooping, and a minute later I was at the wheel.

◆ ◆ ◆ ◆

Lunch at an Arby's in Centralia, Illinois, Second flirting with two teenage Hannah Montana wannabes at the next table; a long four-way bathroom break at a rest stop near High Hill, Missouri, and then dinner at Mighty Mo's Ribs on the outskirts of Kansas City, the meter up to $2,600. "I guesstimate we're almost halfway there," Cookie said while eating a pulled pork sandwich, the exposed ends of which glistened and swayed fetchingly. "America's too bloody big," Second said. "They should split it into twelve different pieces. No coontry should be so wide that you can't drive from the head of it to the arse of it in ten hours, if you ask me." "I didn't ask you," THC said. "Well, I didn't ask you if you asked me," Second shot back.

Abdul, of course, did not eat pork and was contenting himself with sides: rice, beans, corn, coleslaw, biscuits. "Aw, come on, Abdul," Second goaded him, "have a rib." Abdul shook his head politely. "What do you think is gonna happen to ya?" my half-Catholic, half-Anglican visitor asked our Saudi chauffeur. "You think you're gonna go to Muslim hell?" Abdul thanked him for the offer but said that it was against the dietary laws of his faith. Second, twirling one end of his mustache, now soaked with a Day-Glo orange wet rub, asked, "In the Mooslim paradise if you get seventy virgins, once you shag one of 'em, is she replaced by a brand-new virgin or are you stuck with her forever? And what do the female martyrs get? Seventy male virgins?" Again he offered Abdul a rib but Abdul repeated, "It is against the laws of my faith." "Well," Second said, "grufflin' me blipty is against the laws of my faith too but I've been doing it since I was twelve feckin' years old."

"If he doesn't want to eat pork, that's his thing," I said.

"How many times in a man's life you think he whacks himself off?" Second asked, picking up his last baby back. "What's three-hundred and sixty-five days times ten times a day times seventy-five years? That's like an Indian Ocean of spunk right there."

"I never did that," Cookie told us. "Not one time."

"You're lyin', Marrrvis," Second said. (His mouth and chin—and my mouth and chin and THC's—were soaked with sauce and there were specks of hickory-smoked swine and cow between our teeth.) "Not one time? Not one time in your life? That's not humanly possible!"

"I'm tellin' you, I never did it. It's a waste of time and energy. It's just wrong. Every time you do that to yourself, the Lord keeps track of it. See, each single person down here has a book on him up in Heaven. You play with yourself or you lie or curse, the Lord writes it down. And if you get past a certain number, you wind up going to Hell. You can't erase anything in that book. It's etched in stone and once it's done, it's done. But most of all, it's a waste of man-juice. You just can't be pourin' that stuff out all over the place. You got to keep it. Store it up. Save it. Use it when you got to. Wasting it on yourself is just dumb."

I tried to picture God opening a massive leather-bound, gold-embossed tome, and such a book for every single person who'd ever lived. Surely by now the Lord had upgraded to computers.

"If God's keepin' a book on me," Second said to me, "for cursin' and spankin' me monkey and all that shite, then he's fookin' roonin' outta paper up there."

"Anyway," Cookie said, "I don't do it. I never have done it. I never will."

"Yeah, but how can you help it?" Second, incredulous, said. "A man refills himself. If he doesn't do it, the stuff'll start pourin' out his underarms, ears, and nose. It's just not possible!"

"I guess I just got more control than you do."

"That kind of control, I never wanted." Second nibbled and sucked his last rib dry, then asked: "When you were a lad, you didn't look at *Playboy* or a *Leg Show* or *Black Playboy* or whatever it is you blokes got?"

"I looked at all of 'em as often as I could. Man, I used to see Pam Grier naked in movies with her big titties all hangin' down. Looked nice. I saw them in *Foxy Brown* on the VHS and I damn near exploded. But I knew I had to save it all up and not waste it. It's why I don't need to take vitamins . . . I got a backlog of all the stuff. How you think I wound up with twin girls?"

"But if you was really potent wouldn't they have been boys?" Second said. He let out a belch that shook every salt and pepper shaker in the restaurant and then resumed. "So if you stored all of it up, Cookie, then you must have plurped your quiffles in like three seconds when you finally were with a woman."

"I did. I admit it. Three seconds. And I passed out from it too. It was a great big shock to my system. Took me nearly three minutes to unload. It was like I was watering the grass of Yankee Stadium. When I got home and weighed myself I saw I lost three whole pounds."

"So when you bluff at poker," I asked Marvis/Cookie, "you don't consider that a lie?"

"No, Chip," he said. "I consider that a bluff."

"But you curse. I've seen you do it online. And you steal from work too. You've told me that. The pages in that heavenly book of yours can't be all blank."

"No man's is. We're all born with the first page filled in, thanks to Adam and Eve. And it isn't technically stealing until they start payin' me what I know I'm worth. Plus, I have to live day and night with the fear of being replaced by EZ Pass. You don't know what that's like."

I signaled the waiter over and told him to bring me the check . . . after I told him to also bring me a pulled pork sandwich with a side of sweet potato fries, for the road.

♣ ♣ ♣ ♣

Second Gunman took the wheel in Salina, Kansas; the closest I'd ever get to having my very own Neal Cassady, he was a surprisingly cautious driver, never going over 65 miles per hour. The meter hit $3,800 in Burlington, Colorado, just over the Kansas state line, and I took the wheel again. We were all in the same clothes, now grimy and wrinkled, as when we started out; we hadn't showered or brushed our teeth and the bones beneath my ass were hurting me . . . it was like I was sitting on a stove, all four burners going.

"Colorado, eh?" Second said. I was riding shotgun. Abdul was asleep in the back and Cookie, who refused to drive, was gawking out the window. As I was.

"Yep. The Land of Lincoln, Johnny. Live Free or Die. The House that Ruth Built."

"You know who's from Colorado, don't you?"

"Who?"

"History Babe is."

"From Colorado Springs," Cookie said from the back, "to be exact."

"She's gotta be the hottest thing on that site," Second said. "God's filled in a few pages of my sin book up there 'cause of her for sure."

APG at her very filthiest was no match for History Babe, who had probably IM'ed five hundred different men to orgasm, two hundred of them while winning their money.

"Let's call her up," Second said.

I didn't deem this ridiculous caprice worthy of a response, but . . .

"And how do we do that?" THC said.

"We'll get her number is how. And call her. Maybe she'll coom to Vegas with us."

"Anyone know her real name?"

"It's Tracey," I said. "Or Stacey or Lacy."

Nobody knew History Babe's real last name. So the matter was dead. For ten minutes.

"Let's go someplace," Johnny/Second suggested, "where we could go online and if she's playin' poker she'll tell us. Then we call her. And also, I need to buy some new underpants. There's more crust down there right now than on an uneaten blueberry pie."

There wasn't much of anything but clear sky and cold air in this stretch of I-70. My main character in *Dead on Arrival* had taken a different route than this. He was fleeing the shocking loss of his wife and kids . . . I was fleeing the loss of $7,000 and what little was left of my pride. But playing poker with Scott Heyward was disappearing back into the primordial pea soup from which it arose and with every mile we traveled westward, the soupier it became.

We pulled into a Comfort Inn, south of Denver. The sign outside said there were vacancies, HBO, an indoor pool, and wifi, and we got a room. Second took a long shower while THC, with our waist, inseam sizes, and shirt specifications, waddled just across the road to a Big K and got us all new clothing and some toiletries. (I said to him, "No boxers please, Cookie!" and he came back with boxers.) It was cold here and there was a sparkly layer of snow on the ground and we could see snow all over the Rockies from the window. When Second was done showering I took a shower, then it was Abdul's turn. I applied three extra coats of deodorant just to make up for the prior two days. None of the clothing Cookie came back with fit right and none of it looked good or went together. My splashy rayon socks had pictures of BMX bikers on them and it occurred to me that, for whatever reason, Marvis was purposely trying to make us look like idiots . . . but in his new threads he looked like one, too. While Marvis showered, Second logged on to the Galaxy and, sure enough, History Babe was online, trouncing five others at a table with two slow-played Aces. Second gave her my cell phone number and told her to call. It was amazing: logging on, finding her, her calling me—it all took less than three minutes.

History said, sure, she could get away and go to Vegas with us; she just had to make a few calls, go to an ATM, get some cash. We'd drive down to Colorado Springs, I told her, and pick her up. In the background, Second and THC were bickering about the clothing the latter had picked out; Johnny, looking ridiculous in tangerine cargo pants and a mauve polar-fleece hoodie that blared I ♥ MONSTER TRUCKS! across the chest, might have done better for himself shopping in the Elephant Department at a Dress Barn than in trusting Cookie. You sure you want to do this, I asked History. She said she was sure. There're nothing much else going on right now, she told me. Her sister, whom she lived with, was an extreme Evangelical and was currently was on a three-day prayer jag. I need to get out of here really quickly, she said.

We stayed in the hotel room for about an hour and a half. Second didn't log off the Galaxy right away and won almost $2,000 at an Ultra-High table.

"Only eight more bloody K to go," he mumbled, closing his laptop back up.

♠ ♠ ♠ ♠

"Okay, gentlemen, let's roll," I said after a perfunctory quickie flossing. I was in blue jeans that were more a lot more white than blue . . . they came down only to just below my knee and there may have been more pockets on this pair of pants than on all my other pants combined. It was something that one of the Fat Boys should be wearing, not America's 1,457th greatest living novelist.

Abdul was back at the wheel, and an hour later we were at the address that Tracey Winters, History Babe's real name, had given us. It was an eerily quiet middle-class neighborhood and she lived above a hardware store, and as I leaned against the lamppost on the corner I felt like a faceless figure in someone's poor attempt at a Hopper painting. It was snowing lightly and it was only us on the street. While THC stretched his stubby legs in his brand-new wide-wale Barney-purple corduroy pants, for some reason I thought of Cynthia. I missed her and hoped that she was thinking of me, too. Then the front door opened and one of the mousiest-looking women I've ever seen came out, rolling a small green suitcase.

"Are you Second Gunman?" she said to me. Her voice sounded mousy, too. She was five foot four, in her mid-twenties, had thin straight brown hair tied back in a tight ponytail; her complexion was grayish, her eyes were brown, she had tiny ears and no curves at all to her waify body, and her round eyeglasses were for a woman, or an owl, with a much larger head.

"No, I'm Chip Zero," I said.

I looked down at her, she looked up at me. If they knew what she really looked like, I wondered, how many of the five hundred men she'd coaxed into orgasm would love to have those orgasms back?

Cookie introduced himself and gallantly put her suitcase in the trunk and we all got in: Abdul was at the wheel, Second rode shotgun, Cookie was at one window in the back, I was at the other, and History Babe was sandwiched tightly in the middle. The windshield wipers went on and swept aside a furry wreath of snow, and onward we rolled.

"Okay," THC directed Abdul, "now go back up Interstate Twenty-five, then get on Seventy going west again."

"Nope," Hist said. "That's not the best way. Take Fifty west. It hooks up with Seventy in Grand Junction. Then we get on Fifteen. You'll save lots of time. I've done it before."

I looked at THC, who sat stone-faced but for rapid eyeblinking. Finally a *hmmph* emerged from his epiglottis.

We were in the home stretch.   Only eight hundred miles to go, which included a hell of a lot of desert. But beyond the quiet limit of the world wasn't absolute silence; there was neon, gold, platinum, silicone, beer, cashmere, lap dances, and prime rib.

♥ ♥ ♥ ♥

A woman's presence in the Crown Vic changed the group dynamic and not for the worse.

There was a sizable decrease in the amount of tomfoolery and cursing in the car, and on those occasions when Second did curse, he was quickly reprimanded by Toll House Cookie. "Hey," THC would snap, "we got a lady present now!" There was a lot less talking in the car, period, and there was also less farting and belching and the air quality improved significantly.

Cookie paid a lot more attention to the awesome scenery of

the American West and was heard to utter the words "wow," "unbelievable," and "look at that!" as we passed the majestic Rockies and then the desiccated moonscape of the Great Basin Desert. These sentiments were echoed by all others present, including History Babe, who said "awesome" so many times that I requested she please employ another adjective. (She ultimately settled on merely "nice.")

Another change: Abdul Salaam drove considerably faster than he'd been previously driving. Perhaps he was discomfited by the presence of a woman. Conversely, when History Babe took the wheel, in Green River, Utah, our speed got up to 95 mph, the fastest we'd yet traveled. She changed lanes as if she was playing an Activision NASCAR: Suicide video game, and Second dug his fingernails into the flesh on Cookie's wrists for support.

Also, the men had chivalrously decided that we wouldn't inflict our lousy eating habits upon Tracey/History Babe and that our next meal would be a good one, a healthy one, consisting of fresh ingredients and local produce, something that took more than two minutes to prepare. But somewhere along the road History Babe said to us, "We could just go to a Taco Bell . . . I really like their stuff."

But we weren't perfect and I heard History Babe say to Second while we drove through Cisco, Utah: "Can you take your hand off my knee please?"

◆ ◆ ◆ ◆

In Utah, I-70 came to an abrupt end . . . it was like shooting a cannonball into a wall and the ball just sticking there. Seventy connected with I-15 and we took that, Abdul at the helm, down into Nevada. As we passed Cedar City, only an hour and change from the Nevada state line, a critical issue that not one of us had yet publicly discussed was finally brought up. It was something that had crossed my mind many times already but one that I dared not mention, perhaps because by not discussing it aloud I was able to detach myself from the outlandish lark I was presently embarked upon, this being that I had hopped into a taxi at 3 a.m. in New York City with someone I barely knew and that we'd picked up two other people I knew even less and were heading 2,500 miles west to win back money that hadn't really been mine to begin with.

"So where we staying?" THC asked.

"Yes," History said. "Where?"

"I could stay in the car," Second said. "I'll stay anywhere. I don't care."

"It's not our car, Johnny," I reminded him.

History Babe said: "I know some okay places way off the Strip. This time of year they'd be around eighty dollars a night or less. They're kinda boring though."

"We're gonna get one room or four?" Cookie asked.

We looked at each other. Nobody, I surmised, wanted to spend too much time with anyone. Had History been a Babe, that might have greatly changed things—there might have been a scramble to be her roomie. Second and THC were never going to get along; I would have been surprised if they ever played online together again. THC and I had nothing in common, other than he worked within two miles of where I lived, and he wouldn't recognize a witticism if it tied him to a chair and waterboarded him for three hours straight. Also, could I ever really be that close to anyone who'd been fourteen and seen Pam Grier naked and then not rubbed one out? To him I was probably just a rich, spoiled, white-boy loser who'd won a lot of dough but who didn't really need it. To me, Second Gunman was interesting, he was a character, he was an eccentric . . . but he was the kind who could embarrass me and make me cringe at a moment's notice. He had done this several times on the road already in fast food joints and at gas stations. ("Hey," he'd said to the two Hannah Montana wannabes at the Arby's, "this guy"—me—"wrote a best-selling novel . . . he could get you big parts in the movie.") He was getting tired of me, too, I could tell; I had surpassed the world's record of getting called a gobshite the most times within a two-day period. Yes, we all needed a little distance from each other. With our online poker winnings, each of us could afford our own room and spend some time apart.

"Why don't I," Second said, breaking an uneasy minute-long silence, "call one of the hotels on the Strip and try to get a fancy large high-roller suite for all four of us?"

♣ ♣ ♣ ♣

Abdul Salaam had never seen Las Vegas before and he let out a deep and extended gasp when in the distance the mysterious contours of the Luxor, the skyline of New York, New York, and the probing needle of the Stratosphere shimmered into view. He whispered a few words of Arabic to himself—whether they were words of praise or damnation, I shall never know.

He dropped us off on a sidestreet near the Flamingo, in the middle of the Strip. The last three hours of driving were like passing through a diorama of a Cormac McCarthy novel, a merciless barrage of russet endlessness. I had certainly felt such desolation in my soul before but had never gazed upon it, and nobody inside the car said a word.

We got out of the taxi. It was in the seventies but the air there, as usual, was dry, and already I was thirsty. Cookie unsnapped his Port Authority jacket, Hist unbuttoned her coat.

It was time to settle. The meter read $5,423 dollars.

"Okay, how are we doing this again?" I said.

"I forgot our agreement when you got in, my friend," Abdul admitted.

Our driver thought about it while the fading sun beat down on his long, black beard . . . it was late afternoon and the mountains in the west were writhing under the coming sunset.

Everyone agreed that $5,500 would be good enough.

Second reached into his jacket and pulled out some money and I went into my wallet. I'd left my apartment with two thousand dollars, but along the way I'd been stopping at ATMs and withdrawing cash—Cookie had been doing the same thing. We were loaded. History had left her house with three grand, but since she only had been aboard since Colorado, we only hit her up for $400. It took five minutes for us to work everything out, including a nifty four-hundred-dollar tip for the most patient, well-mannered taxi driver in New York City history. Everyone seemed pleased, but then a few seconds later, Abdul said: "There is an additional charge, my friend, because I picked you up after eight o'clock at night. A dollar fifty. Plus sixteen dollars for the two tolls."

Cookie rolled his eyes and handed Abdul a twenty and Abdul got back into the Crown Victoria and began his lonely journey home.

♠ ♠ ♠ ♠

My laptop and knapsack on the ground between my feet, History and Cookie right next to me, and Second off looking for a hotel for us, I gazed into the Fountains of the Bellagio as Celine Dion sang the *Titanic* theme song, and reflected: When Man attempts to emulate Nature, Nature usually finishes a distant second. The skies of Michelangelo and Casper David Friedrich are more spectacular than any real sky I've ever looked up at; a suburban swimming pool contains far fewer sharks, jellyfish, seaweed, and tsunamis than the ocean and is a much better environment for swimming; no gust of wind I've ever felt outdoors is quite as soothing as the effect of an air conditioner cranked up to high cool; and let's face it, Las Vegas's Venice is cleaner, smells better, and has much better food than the original one in Italy. Try synchronizing geysers and springs to Celine Dion and you tell me which is more spellbinding, them or the Fountains of the Bellagio. No, it is not Man that cannot emulate Nature, but Nature that cannot . . .

"Okay, I got us the high-roller suite at Jimmy's Hotel and Casino," Second said, interrupting my contemplation. In his hand were a dozen business cards he'd been handed on the Strip: they were all for leggy, busty girls-for-hire . . . strippers, dancers, whores, whatever.

"Where the hell is that?" I asked him.

The hotel was off the Strip, he told us, and wasn't even a half mile away—by which he meant, I could tell, it was four miles away—but it seemed safe and nice.

"I've never heard of this place," History said. "Jimmy's . . . ?"

"A high-roller suite?" Cookie said. "*Us?*"

Johnny looked at us like we were all hopeless sticks-in-the-mud. Behind me, the Fountains and Celine were reaching their grand climax together, bursting into the air as high as they could, pounding like heavy artillery. Her heart, she knew, would go on.

"Smile!" Second Gunman said. "We're whales now! Smile for Chroist sake!"

Our hotel turned out to be one of those places that you only see when your less-than-honest Las Vegas taxi driver isn't taking you the fastest way from one place to the other. A large blue banner with red lettering draped haphazardly over the hotel's flat façade screamed JIMMY'S HOTEL & CASINO but suggested to all those passing by—there weren't many of them—that the place hadn't always been Jimmy's or a hotel and had once been some other sort of enterprise. It was a cube, an ivory cube with four stories and a hundred rooms. Size-wise, it looked like it would have made a good clinic for alcoholics and drug addicts to dry out in. It also turned out there was no casino. Either the sign maker or Jimmy himself had lied.

Our high-roller suite was on the top floor.

The door opened onto a sunken living room with a Jacuzzi right in the middle of it, three flat-screen televisions, cheesy shag carpeting, all the usual stuff. But our cough-syrup-scented rooms weren't large and this only confirmed my suspicion that at one time this place had been a medical facility and had been gutted and renovated, or a lunatic asylum that had gone out of business because most people in Las Vegas were lunatics and it just wasn't needed.

Two bedrooms adjoined the living room, each one had two double beds. The windows in both rooms looked onto the backside of another unlit concrete cube, most likely a Best Buy or Office Depot that the developers had given up on halfway through.

While I was putting away my few personal effects, Second called the front desk and, as dollar bills spilled out of his suede jacket, began complaining: "The safe doesn't work. . . . *Yes*, I followed the instructions. . . . Yes, I know. . . . I work at a feckin' four-star hotel in England, you think I don't know how to use a hotel safe? I've slept in more hotel safes than you've seen! . . . Well, do it soon. . . . And another thing . . . It says the sheets have a six hundred thread count. . . . Now since I work in a hotel, there's one feckin' thing I know and that's thread counts and these sheets aren't six hundred any more than my feckin' IQ is six hundred. . . . I counted the threads three bloody times and even double-bloody-checked it twice. . . . Okay . . . Okay . . . Cheers."

Within five frenzied minutes we had a new safe and new sheets. Second gave the manager and the maid $40 each and it was then decided via flips of a coin that I would be rooming with Second and that Cookie would be rooming with History Babe, an arrangement, as it happened, that seemed the least offensive to everyone.

"If I don't get me a bit of squaff soon," Second Gunman, shuffling his little deck of naked hottie cards, whispered to me, "I'm gonna die."

❤ ❤ ❤ ❤

We took showers and got ready to go out and play.

"We need to get new gear," Second said to me in the living room. "We'll go shopping on the high street tomorrow." He was watching all three TVs at once, not staying on any channel for more than three seconds. (It was, in its own way, a remarkable display of digital dexterity and mental Attention Deficit Disorder.) "The high *what*?" Cookie said. History came out of her room, her hair still wet and with some makeup on. I could tell that Second was disappointed by her looks—he wanted her to look like Carmen Electra or Pam Anderson or some more current sexbomb. I didn't care what she looked like, but I did hope that Second wouldn't hurt her in any way. She seemed like a good egg.

Cookie asked if we were ready to go out and I said: "Should we have a drink first?" As we were high rollers there was a fully stocked bar, but as we were high rollers at an $89.99-a-night joint far off the Strip, fully stocked meant: a pint of Smirnoff vodka, a pint of Dewar's (half of which was gone), some tonic and seltzer, and a six-pack of Fig Newtons (the wrapping of which may have been bitten through by a mouse). Being a high roller here was like being the United Nations ambassador of a country that only the people of that country had ever heard of.

"Where do we go?" Second said. "Should we start out a strip club and then start playing or do it the other way around?"

Cookie, ever the gentleman, looked at History and said, "I'll skip the strip club . . . I'd rather play. I got me enough naked girls at home."

Second scratched his chin and said: "Yeah, I guess playin's why we're all here."

We left our rooms, our plan of assault being to take a taxi to the southernmost end of the Strip and work our way up.

When the elevator doors opened out came a tall, broadshouldered, silver-haired man in his late sixties dressed all in white, except for a black bolo tie, surrounded, as though they were his bodyguards, by five smiling, tanned beauties all about five foot eight. The women were dressed in flashy minidresses or miniskirts and tight, revealing tops. These chicks were state of the art and were giggling when the elevator doors opened. (A note on the exact nature of the giggling: it sounded more like girly pajama-party laughter than adult cocktail-party laughter.)

"You're in the other suite, I guess," he said with a very white, very expensive smile.

We nodded. The women stopped giggling but were smiling. Their teeth were big and white, too, and I don't think there was anything smaller than a D-cup in sight.

"Rusty Wells," he said, introducing himself and lifting his Stetson. "Houston, Texas."

We all shook his hand but when Tracey held out hers, Rusty kissed it.

He introduced us to his five lovely escorts but was unable to remember who was who. There was a Jasmine among them, as well as a Shiloh and an Aurora. They'd just had dinner and you sensed from their collective burnished sheen that they'd eaten and drunk quite well.

Rusty told us he'd been coming to Vegas since the good ol' days when everything was mobbed up, when the casinos took a skim, and when, if you were caught cheating, they took you out to the desert, tied you to a tree stump and let the sun fry your body and the jackals eat you alive. "Yep, things were better back then," he said while Aurora (or Shiloh) straightened out his bolo tie. His five escorts could have stepped out of the pages of *Harper's Bazaar*, had the pages been dated 1969. They were in their twenties or early thirties but came from the era of vinyl boots, pot parties, Polaroid Swingers, blue Corvairs, and much too much makeup.

When Rusty asked us what we did for a living, I told him I was once a writer.

"What books you write?" he asked. "I read a bit now and then."

"Rusty," I said, knowing he never would have heard of me and wishing to spare him the discomfort, "to be honest, I've forgotten the names of 'em and what they were about."

"Tell them what you do for a living," one of the women—she wore a gold sequin mini-dress and her eyelashes were as a big and fluttery as butterflies—said to Rusty.

Rusty told us that ever since he was knee-high to a grasshopper he liked to tinker. During the Vietnam War he was in the Army Engineer Corps but "they didn't take a shinin' to my ideas and I got drummed out honorably," he said. He eventually landed a job in the oil industry in Houston, received three patents for machines that dredged and drilled, but couldn't stand it. "I didn't fit in with that refined, upper crust, golf-clubs-stuck-up-their-asses country-club set and didn't want to." Five years ago, he was struck with "the most brilliantest, simplest idea that ever struck a man since the light bulb" and now he proudly plucked the issue of this earth-shattering idea out of his jacket pocket. It looked like a cook's thermometer, something you'd use to see if a pot roast was done, but the bottom end was more complicated and the readout was digital.

"It's the Stoolometer," Rusty said, handing it to Second. "You drop a number two into the toilet and you stick it into the water and it weighs your product. It's correct to the quarter ounce or your money back. This here is the simplest one. The Stoolometer-Plus you don't got to insert into the water each time . . . it just fixes right into the bowl just so. We got one version out there now that's even got the Bluetooth, too."

He told us how, even though American retailers wouldn't go near it, millions had been sold here and in South America, Europe, and Asia, and about the tons of money he's made and the new life he's living, and I thought of all the books, short stories, plays, screenplays, and poems I'd slaved over. I had once wasted three months of my life writing a twenty-five-page postmodern epic poem called *Thirteen Ways of First Looking into Keats' "On First Looking into Chapman's Homer."* And for what? Big Tex here had a brand-new life and many millions, and all I had was a fragment of my dignity.

"Well, nice meetin' ya," he said with a sly wink. "Hope to see ya again real soon."

We watched him walk down the hallway with his giggly, sparkly, high-heeled escorts.

◆ ◆ ◆ ◆

We took a taxi to the Luxor—Second wailing and air-strumming Led Zeppelin's "Kashmir" en route—where we hung around a dice table, each of us afraid to take the first plunge, and decided not to play. We walked up to Caesar's Palace and thought of playing blackjack—even concocting a reasonably good card-counting system—but didn't, agreeing that, when you've played as much poker as the four of us (combined, had we played over a million hands?), blackjack just seems too monotonous and luck-based. We crossed over to the Flamingo and hung around the dice tables again. Craps had always seemed the safest and most fun casino game to play, but it no longer would bring me any real satisfaction. The pit crew carefully gathering and doling out chips, marking whose chips are where, making sure loaded dice hadn't been slipped into the game—it took too long between rolls. When I used to go to the track with Harry or with my family, the half-hour between races seemed to last two hours; now the minute or so between dice rolls seemed like half an hour. I missed the rat-a-tat blitz of online poker.

And I wasn't the only one.

"Shit," Cookie whispered to me as we looked on, "this takes forever."

"I know," I said. "It's really slow. And you just cursed."

"Yeah, I know I did, but I'm just sayin'."

We walked up to the Wynn, then took a taxi back to Jimmy's and heard slumber-party laughter coming out of Rusty Wells' suite when we walked by . . . my guess is, they were naked in the hot tub, drinking Cristal, doing lines of coke off each others' titties, that sort of thing. Or maybe they were just cuddling in the dark and watching *Pillow Talk* on DVD.

We had two laptops, mine and Second's. From 1 until almost 3 a.m. we all took turns playing poker. Given the time—even with the time difference between Vegas and New York—I played against people I rarely played against. And I soundly trounced them. I won five grand that night and was now only down $2K from my losses at Big Lou's. Whenever that was: at this point Memory was a many-tangled Slinky wriggling clumsily down the Spiral Staircase of Time. History won $1,800, THC a bit more than that, and Second, playing in Ultra-High, recouped half of his losses. I just won, he said, three thousand from Bjorn 2 Win with two 2s! We were so giddy, so pumped, and so flushed with victory that, well, we simply *had* to go to a ...

... a loud, massive, five-tiered, ear-pounding, $40-cover-charge, NBA-arena-sized strip club, inside of which I fell fast asleep for an hour in sort of a crucifix pose under the swaying penumbra of four reupholstered breasts. It was late—or early—almost six in the morning, and after I woke up in my sticky red banquette and after I made sure I still had my wallet on me, I went outside and called Wifey in West Virginia, where she was just waking up.

Never letting on for a second where I was, I told her the weather the past few days in New York was very typical for that time of year, and she told me that she was making her way, albeit slowly, through *Dead on Arrival.* "So first you kill," she said, "your main character's wife and kids and then he *has* to hook up with the sister-in-law and all her best friends?" "If the wife and kids don't die," I responded, "and he doesn't hook up with the sister, then there's no book. Take away the whale, there's no *Moby Dick.*" "Where I left off last night," she said, "he was trying to convince his friends to go to Vegas with him." "Fancy that," I said.

Just as the sun was peeking up over the mountains in the east, she told me she missed me and that, after she was done with *DOA,* she wanted to take a crack at the *Trilogy,* but when I saw Second and History leaving the strip club and coming my way I said a quick good-bye.

In the taxi back to Jimmy's Hotel, four things crossed my mind: (1) How do I know that Cynthia really is in West Virginia? What if she'd been so upset by my lying and pokerizing that it's get-even time and now she's having an affair? (2) She really does seem to be reading *Dead on Arrival.* Naturally, she's repulsed by it ("This is going to be an impossible sell," Clint Reno had told me the previous December, "for women, who read ninety-seven point five percent of all fiction"), but she's reading it. (3) She wants to read the *Trilogy? What???* Only one human being has ever read all three books: me. (4) She's being so sweet. Will her first words to me, when we see each other again back in New York, be "Darling, I've joined a convent"?

When I got back to the room I turned on my laptop and read this e-mail:

> Where are you? Are you okay? Talk to me please. Are you bored of me? If so please do not just vanish into thin air like this. I miss you so much, Chip, that I feel ill.

Not only had Artsy Painter Gal noticed my absence, but it was making her sick!

♣ ♣ ♣ ♣

The next morning our doorbell rang and woke me up. I slipped back into the accursed multi-pocketed pale blue jeans that THC had gotten me and answered the door. Before me stood a woman so suntanned that for a second I thought I was looking at a copper statue. She had a helmet of shoulder-length dirty blonde hair and was wearing white slacks and a pink satin tank top. She was in her early forties and once I realized that, no, she was not a statue, I saw that she had the most leathery skin I had ever encountered. Too many afternoons lounging by the pools at the MGM Grand. Still, despite the Ultrasuede skin, I don't think there was a pore of skin on her face that hadn't received a jigger of Botox. But it was a sad case of too much too late.

She told me, as I wiped the four hours of sleep from my eyes, that she was Laurel Dodge, our personal host: she was going to make sure we were insanely happy and get us tickets to shows and reservations at restaurants and get us past the velvet ropes of the most exclusive Vegas clubs. "I just want to make sure," she said, "that you come back to Jimmy's."

"Are you interested," she asked as she made her way into the living room, "in seeing Cher or Barry Manilow tonight? Or maybe an Ultimate Fighting match?"

Suddenly she formed her mouth into an O and hers eyes opened wide. Due to all the Botox, however, the muscles in her face couldn't fully register shock, but I could tell something was awry. I turned around and saw Johnny/Second stark naked and scratching his mop of reddish blond hair, eyes mostly closed, Jughead-like. He was enviously well-hung, uncut, and had about fifteen pounds worth of ruddy love handles hanging from his sides. He also had a severe case of backne . . . it looked like he had been whipped on his back and chest years ago and the welts would never heal.

Laurel didn't wince or say anything about the nude Blackpooler presently airing out his morning flatulence; instead our socially skilled, suede-skinned hostess fixed her eyes right on mine and never moved them. If her orbs had been burning a hole through mine, my eye sockets would have been hollow and not one eyelash would have been singed.

"Or," she continued with aplomb, "you just name any Cirque du Soleil show and the chances are good I can get you in."

"I'll keep that in mind," I said, "but I don't think we'll be going to too many shows."

"Just came to play, huh?"

Still no change in her expression. She *was* a statue.

"Yeah, I guess so."

Second grunted, grabbed a kitchen towel and girded his loins with it. He looked ready to appear as an extra in a gladiator movie, had they been filming one in the hallway.

Laurel, whose sapphire ring was as big as a doorknob, rattled off the names of a few restaurants she could get us into and gave us four business cards. I thanked her and saw her to the door.

A few seconds after she left, Second drank some coffee right out of the pot and asked himself aloud, "I wonder if she's got the tickets on her?" Then he ran into the hallway in nothing but his jerrybuilt loincloth.

A minute later he came back in wielding four ducats to see Cher. The seats weren't the best, but I wasn't surprised: the water in the Jacuzzi in the room didn't get that hot and barely bubbled, the flat-screen TVs were flat but weren't that big or that good, the shag carpeting was musty, stained and not that shaggy. We weren't truly whales, not if we were staying here at Jimmy's. The truth was we were just blowfish.

"Gee, Johnny," I said, "I don't see you liking Cher. I had you figured more as a U2 or Arctic Monkeys fan."

"The hell with Sonny and feckwad Cher," he said. "I'm sellin' these tickets on the street."

"You're bloody daft, you are, lad!"

He may have been daft but he did get $500 for them.

♠ ♠ ♠ ♠

The four of us had breakfast together at a Denny's on the Strip and with every foul, mealy forkful I thought of calling Laurel Dodge and asking her to reserve me a table, all by myself if need be, at the most expensive place in town. Second finished half his breakfast—the Lumberjack Special—then complained about the steak being overcooked to the waitress, who apologized and then, five minutes later, brought him the Lumberjack Special v.2. In this way he managed to eat, for the price of one, one and one-half Lumberjack Specials and, as he stuffed steak, sausage, and flapjack into his mouth, he told us his Vegas brainstorm. "I think I'm going to call," he said, "Steve Wynn's secretary and maybe try to get an appointment with him. From what I've seen all his concepts are stale lately. The Wynn and Encore don't even have feckin' concepts for Chroist sake—they're just called Wynn and Encore. There's not even a 'the' in front of 'em. Look, there's New York, New York and there's Paris, Paris and the Venetian, the Venetian. Well, these are my ideas . . . Atlantis. The world's first undersea hotel. Ten thousand rooms, all underwater . . . guests all have oxygen tubes, like Jacques Cousteau. Live dolphins in every room. Walruses in the halls. Or how about this? Hell. Ten thousand rooms. All in Hell. The dealers and maids would be dressed up as devils and you could rig it up so they breathe fire. The water in the swimming pools would be black and boiling, like it was tar. Okay, one more. Instead of New York, New York, you do: The Las Vegas. Ten thousand rooms and it's a mini Las Vegas *within* Las Vegas, a reproduction of the city you're already in. You'd have a fake Eiffel Tower and Empire State Building but they'd be fake fake ones. . . . Okay, it was just an idea."

After breakfast History Babe called her fanatical sister in Colorado Springs. She was still praying. Praying for what, I asked History. Well, she answered, now it's for my wretched soul. Toll House Cookie called his wife in New Jersey. Mrs. Cookie asked how Cousin Cleon's funeral was and Cookie told her, "They ain't had it yet." See, he told us after he got off the phone, I didn't really lie. You know, Marvis, I said to him, the Lord may not be filling in your pages for telling lies but he's probably scribbling tons of notes along the margins.

We walked down the Strip on one side of the street, then came up the other, going as far south as the squalid, doomed Tropicana and then as far north as the equally squalid and doomed Circus Circus. Cookie was too scared to take a gondola ride at the Venetian. He was afraid of cars, he'd admitted to us, but that was nothing compared to his fear of gondolas. It was almost noon and it was in the low eighties and his toll-collector outfit was back on.

But that day, we finally bought new clothes. Second sprang for History Babe's new dresses (Valentino) and skirts (bebe) and they didn't come cheap. I was glad we'd picked her up. Her gentle presence alone, I believe, prevented the three males among us from either separating from each other for good or from slitting each other's throats.

In the casinos sometimes we stayed together, sometimes we drifted apart. I watched craps and blackjack, Second hung around the roulette tables over at the Rio, together all four of us stood on the periphery of a poker tournament at the Bellagio, separately I almost started to play craps at the MGM Grand. The table there was boisterous, people were winning and laughing, but they weren't truly interacting, not like they did online. In that world you see the same people over and over again, every day, but these people gathered around the table, I knew, would never see each other again. It was too transitory and was ultimately meaningless, the difference between an empty one-night stand and an actual relationship, and I didn't want any part of it.

After a late lunch we retired back to our suite at Jimmy's, where Second called the hotel manager and let him have it: "The soaps in the bathroom say they're French-milled on them. . . . It says it on the wrappers. 'French-milled.' I'm lookin' at one now. . . . I know French-milled soap when I see it and this soap isn't French-milled. . . . At best this is Belgian-milled or maybe Luxembourg-milled. . . . So either take money off our bill or get some real French-milled soap up here straight away. . . . Okay, cheers."

I went online and sent an e-mail to Barbara Bennett at Egregious Pictures asking if there was any news about Pacer Burton, whose *Breakthrough* was due to open around Christmas. So much for me depended on the *Plague Boy* movie coming to pass. I sent an e-mail to Courtney Bellkamp at the Reno Brothers asking for the list I needed. I sent an e-mail to Ross Carpenter reminding him I was still alive.

Second and I began playing poker on our laptops. We made sure not to play at the same tables at the same time. I was going up and down but mostly winning, he was doing the same. Then History stood over my shoulder, watched what I was doing, and told me she had played against three of the players at my table. She sat down next to me and helped me out since she knew their style of play. Meanwhile, THC was doing the same with Second. After losing three hands (and $900) in a row I called THC and Second over, so it was all four of us playing as one. It was extraordinary, it was teamwork at its best; we were like Secretariat and were *moving like a tremendous machine*. I won ten of the next thirteen hands. I recouped all my losses at Big Lou's and then won $9,400 more. The

four of us then shifted to Second's laptop and our Thumpin' Think
Tank did the same for him. We all worked together, the gears spun
and meshed beautifully, and we were unbeatable. The Incredible
Four-Headed Doyle Brunson. In an hour Second won $7,000. Yes,
a tremendous machine.

At one point I said to Second, "Hey, I could seek out Bjorn and
we could really win a lot."

But he wouldn't go for it. "It's not a good idea," he said, suddenly
agitated. "We've taken enough from him." He told me he felt sorry
for the Insufferable Swede and I dropped it.

We four blowfish then took a taxi to the Flamingo. Only one
of their pools was open and it wasn't very crowded, this being autumn. (I slipped the towel boy a twenty and he let us through.) We
were in brand-new bathing suits: the thoroughly unreliable Cookie
had bought the guys yellow banana hammocks and History an im-
perceptible Corona Beer yellow bikini. Her skin was pigeon gray
but she had skinny legs and a sexy ankle bracelet I had trouble not
looking at. Cookie, Second, and I each drank three beers and History had a peach margarita and while he held a sun reflector up to
his stubbly chin, Second related to me the brainstorm that had just
struck him: "Your writing career isn't goin' too well. As a matter of
fact, it's not goin' at all. Well, there's got to be a university here, like
a College of Las Vegas University, right? So why don't you become
their writer-in-residence? You could live at the Bellagio, some of
your students would be showgirls who wanted to become writers,
the weather would always be great, and you could gamble between
classes, and you could keep writin' all yer books here that don't ever
get published. . . . Okay, you don't have to give me that look, it was
just a feckin' idea."

After listening to that I went inside the hotel and found a cool
pair of round tinted glasses in a gift shop and bought them. I
wanted a new look and this seemed to be a good start.

Then I decided to take a walk around the pool.

The last time I had done such a thing I collapsed.

It almost happened again. And this one would have been a book-related collapse too.

I saw a woman reading *Saucier: A Bitch in the Kitchen* and let out a quiet groan and kept walking. Then I saw another woman reading it and groaned so loud that the people around me assumed I was in some sort of extreme anguish. (I was.)

I had to do something about this. And I vowed that I would.

♥ ♥ ♥ ♥

Back in our rooms the three of us were gathered around History Babe as she sat and won money on Second's laptop, when Laurel Dodge dropped in on us again, looking as suede as ever. Her upper lip seemed a little puffier than the first time I'd laid eyes on her. Either she'd had some work done that day or had jogged into a mailbox.

Johnny pulled her aside, over to the window, and when their conversation become heated I went over and joined them.

"I can't do this!" Laurel said. "Stop it!"

Second said, "Yes you can!"

"I can't and I won't." She turned to me and said, "Your friend here wants me to arrange hookers for him! And for you and the other guy."

"What," I said to Johnny, "Tracey doesn't get one too?"

"I hadn't gotten around to her yet!" he said. He turned to Laurel and asked: "What about that old Texas geezer in the next room? You didn't arrange his harem for him?!"

"Look," Laurel said, "do you want tickets to a Cirque show tonight or what?"

Second: "Fook the feckin' Cirque du bloody feckin' Soleil!"

After Laurel left, Second said to me: "You would've liked it, I promise."

He told me he was going to get one woman for Cookie, two for me, and three for him. History could join in if she wanted. When I told him that those numbers seemed skewed towards him, he told me he was counting on Cookie not taking part, so I would have gotten his girl and then it would have been even. "See, I've always got your back, Chip," he said, "don't I?"

I took the elevator downstairs, found Laurel about to drive away in her red Jag convertible, made nice with her, and took the Cirque du Soleil tickets. Later THC, Hist, Second, and I went to Burger King for dinner. Second, after complaining to the manager that our meal in no way involved all four flavor profiles, sold the Cirque tickets for $200 to a family from Arkansas in the next booth.

◆ ◆ ◆ ◆

After we got back from dinner and combined our uncannily invincible powers to send Toll House Cookie's winnings over $150,000, Second retired to the loo.

Six minutes later he emerged with a very puzzled look.

"How do we know," he asked, "if the thing is real?"

"What thing?" History said.

"Rusty's shite thermometer! The Dumpostat or whatever the hell it is. How do you know it's really tellin' you what's what? I just took a reading and it said three pound, four ounces. For all I know it just goes to any bloody number. It could be off two ounces, it could be off a whole feckin' pound or two. It's not like when the thermometer says its fifteen feckin' degrees outside and every other thermometer says it's fifteen feckin' degrees outside and then you go outside and it's exactly fifteen feckin' degrees out."

"Do you really care that much?" I asked, seeing that he was all worked up.

"You could weigh yourself first and then afterwards," History recommended.

"Yeah, I could," Johnny said. "Or I could get a very accurate scale and just pinch a loaf onto that."

He rubbed his chin. Presently he was wearing, for no reason at all (we'd just been to a Burger King, after all), a gray three-piece Armani suit and a pair of turquoise $700 rayskin shoes. Very sharp, very striking. But the look was spoiled because he still had on the mauve I ❤ MONSTER TRUCKS! hoodie.

"I think I'll have me a chat with that Texas millionaire gobshite . . ." he said.

That night I took a taxi by myself to the Strip and hit five or six casinos, but as soon as I got out of the cab I regretted leaving the room. My place was in the Poker Galaxy. Everything in Las Vegas was fake—fake New York, fake Paris, fake tits and fake skies and mirth-by-numbers—but in the Galaxy, even though nobody was really there, it was a lot more real.

I needed friendship. I needed true camaraderie.

Looking over the Venetian's indoor, air-conditioned, and odor-free Grand Canal, I called Lonnie Beale in New York. His wife Vanessa answered and soon reminded me that she and Lonnie were separated and would be divorced in a matter of months. I apologized for bothering her and she told me to call his cell phone. Then she—perhaps spitefully—asked me, "So, Frank . . . any new books coming out soon?" and I said good-bye right away.

I wanted to tell Lonnie to take a few days off and hop a plane and join me out here. I'd even pay for it. He'd wanted to raise hell with me a few weeks ago . . . well, now I was up for it.

I called him and left a message on his cell.

I walked into the smoky cardboard box that is Harrah's and took in the sights: an eighty-year-old-man with a USS *Yorktown* cap in a wheelchair glued to a Buffet Mania slot machine. A zonked-out rhino of a woman with canary yellow hair smoking two cigarettes at once and playing roulette. Morose, hunched-over players at blackjack tables, getting their cards and grumbling, then losing to the dealer. More chips, more cards. Another cigarette, another vodka, another losing hand.

Out on the Strip, the sky was blue velvet, the insane neon was flashing, and the mountains in the distance, beyond the spike of the Stratosphere, were as dark and still as spilled syrup.

I called Harry Carver and left him a message: Hop a plane right away or drive from L.A. . . . I have my laptop, I have the time . . . we'll write your screenplay . . . *our* screenplay. We'll stay two weeks here, I said, and we'll get it done. We'll live like kings, man.

I tried to get into three very good restaurants but they were booked, and wound up having a Big Mac and large fries at a McDonald's. My cell phone was out on the table as I ate . . . maybe Lonnie would call and say he was on his way, maybe Harry would call and say he was on his way. Maybe it would wind up being the three of us. *And then, what larks!*

But they didn't call.

I got back to Jimmy's at one that night and the place was empty and dark.

There was a note on my pillow, hastily scribbled down on three pages of a Jimmy's Hotel & Casino notepad.

> I'm getting a taxi and going to the airport and I'm going home. I went [out] for a while[,] when I got back 3 hours later I walk into my room and what do I see [but] 2nd Gunman and Tracey naked on my bed and she was on [top of] him. And they wasn't alone[;] there was 2 other women with them naked too. It looked like fun but I don't want any part of that so I'm leaving now and if you want you could keep the new clothes I bought but I don't think they'll fit you.
>
> If you ever meet my wife Chip you have to get my back ok? We was in Atlanta you & me at my cousin Cleon's funeral in case she ever asks, ok?
>
> Cookie

♣ ♣ ♣ ♣

The final night, I slept alone . . . I had the whole suite to myself. Where Johnny and Tracey were, I wasn't able to find out. I still haven't. History Babe, over the course of the ensuing weeks, has hinted they went to an Off-Strip "couples club." I'm glad they didn't invite me because I would have had to decline. Although it would have been nice if they'd invited me.

In the morning I drank coffee, ate a complimentary doughnut, and watched ESPN *SportsCenter* on all three screens; when the show was done, they played it again. And then again. While cornerbacks cracked other people's spines and broke their own knees, I again vowed that I would make vows. *When I get back to New York I will finally take action!* The reason people were pushing me around . . . was because I was letting them. I would call Clint Reno and confront him, I would confront Ross F. Carpenter. . . . I would get up in the grille of any person who had ever stood in my way. I had to stand up for myself!

I hit the street and found an old barber shop in the middle of the desolate nowheresville the hotel was situated in. There was one barber and two chairs. I wanted to do something radical with my look, something that would give me spirit and fierceness. I had to be fierce! There was going to be a new me and I needed to look the part. I told him to dye my hair "very blond, almost white" and, after making sure I really wanted this and shaking his head, he sluggishly got out a bottle of peroxide. He moved reluctantly, as though I was asking him to give me a vasectomy, but while he worked I looked in the mirror and began thinking things such as *Hey, Scott Heyward . . . it's payback time. This time it's war. You want a piece of me, Clint Reno? Bring it! Not In My House. This time . . . it's for real. You, Beverly Martin . . . are . . . going DOWN. Cody Marshall, I OWN you.* I repeated those phrases to myself and then I realized I was just regurgitating what I'd heard over and over on ESPN for three hours.

When I was done, my hair was platinum blond. He combed the fringe of my front hair forward and layered it into a Caesar cut. With the new do and my new round shades and new thirty pounds, I did look sort of fierce, for a change. And it felt good.

On our last day the weather was grim. I had never seen Vegas this time of year and it didn't seem like the same place. One day they will put the whole city inside a bubble and keep the climate always between 90 and 105 degrees with 0 percent humidity, allowing only the cigarette smoke and the light of the Luxor's mighty beacon to escape.

Second Gunman and History Babe (both of whom told me they liked my new look) and I took one last walk up and down the Strip. I was barely aware of what day of the week it was . . . but I knew that Second's plane home to England was the following day, that History had to teach history tomorrow, and that Cynthia was coming home soon, too. If everything went well, Wifey wouldn't ever know I had skipped town.

Johnny and Tracey hadn't slept at all and he had cut off the long sleeves of the hoodie, which was damp with what I hoped was merely his sweat, and History Babe had dark bags under her eyes. We took a taxi downtown and went into Binion's Horseshoe, which wasn't even Binion's anymore, and the Golden Nugget. We gorged on prime rib, Alaskan King Crab, and brownie sundaes and drank a bottle of Dom Perignon. It was our first meal in God knows how many days that didn't taste like it was cooked under a hairdryer on a conveyor belt.

"Where do you think Abdul Salaam is by now?" Johnny asked me, pulling some crab out of his two front teeth. "I wonder if he made it back to New York in one shot."

"No idea," I said. "He may still be driving."

"He's probably eatin' pork somewhere in Kansas City when no one's lookin'."

Back in the room we packed up. None of us had arrived with much luggage so we didn't know what to do with our purchases. Second stuffed his new Armani, Prada, and D&G wardrobe into a large white plastic garbage bag. I left the maid my white blue jeans, BMX biking socks, and a two-hundred-dollar tip.

Cautiously, Laurel Dodge dropped by, asked us if we'd had a great time. I told her we had and thanked her. I could tell she wanted me to hand her scads of money and I would have given her half that amount had she not been so obvious about it.

"So how was Cirque du Soleil?" she asked.

"Oh, it was just so spectacular!" I told her.

When she left I heard History and Second whispering in her room. She was sniffling. I could guess what had happened: he had plucked her from the wintry ennui of her everyday life, pulled her away from her prayer-addicted sister, shown her a scintillating time, entertained her with the force of his huge personality . . . and she didn't want to let him, or the experience, go.

You'll see me again, Trace, he said, *I promise you you will. Soon.*

♠ ♠ ♠ ♠

I had called and gotten two airline tickets for myself and Second back to New York; History was flying back to Colorado Springs. Her flight left an hour before ours.

As we were closing the door to our high-roller suite for the last time, the door to the other suite flew open, and one of the Go-Go Girl escorts, in shocking pink hot pants and a black fishnet halter top, ran out and headed down the hallway toward the vending machine. There was none of the usual silly giggling from inside the suite. Another of the escorts, possibly Shiloh, stepped out and stood hand on hip . . . she still had on the sequin-spangled mini and was telling the other to "Hurry! . . . hurry!" She looked fed up and tired. The hot-pants escort came jiggling back with a bucket of ice and went into the suite. Shiloh looked at me and said, "This isn't all it's cracked up to be, let me tell you."

I looked in and saw Rusty Wells on the floor, not a stitch on save for his white Stetson, on his hands and knees. Two other woman were standing over him while he retched onto the shag carpeting, and the Jacuzzi in the room was hissing and the steam was rising. The ice-carrying escort handed a few cubes to another one, but nobody knew what to do. Rusty's back and arms were as pink as coral and he was vomiting and laughing and there was a handcuff around one wrist and he said, between heaves: "Awww man, it just don't get any better 'n this!"

Twenty minutes later we were at the airport.

Security there did a double-take: the dull, moppy gray hair on my driver's license photo no longer matched the hot yellow hair on my head. But then they figured it out.

I didn't want to be there when Johnny said good-bye to Tracey, so I went into the small airport bookstore and looked for myself in the fiction section and, of course, didn't find any sign I'd ever written a book or even been born. However, three neat stacks of *Saucier: A Bitch in the Kitchen* books were prominently displayed on their best-selling-fiction table. Each copy, I saw, had an Oprah sticker, and a serrated knife sliced through every organ from my neck to my colon.

(My blurb had *almost* gotten into the book. Was this as close as I'd get to ever being published again?)

There was tap on my shoulder and it was Second.

It was time to board and we got on line. We didn't mention History Babe.

"Hey," Johnny said to me as me moved forward. "Did you win or lose?"

"Where? . . . Here?"

His puffy, bloodshot eyes needed a long rest: the flight to New York and then to England might not be enough.

"Yeah. Did you finish up or down?"

I told him that I hadn't bet the entire time. Not on the terrestrial flesh-and-blood plane, only in cyberspace. Not one hand of poker or blackjack, not one roll of the dice.

"I didn't bet either," he said with a little laugh. Then he said something out of place, for him (or for anyone): "Didn't Albert Einstein say that God doesn't play dice? Well, neither did I." Who knew that the night clerk of the second-best hotel in Blackpool could quote Einstein?

We had traveled over 2,500 miles and driven over lolling, shade-drenched hills and down through emerald and teal sunswept valleys; we'd gone past a thousand Main Streets and around spankin' brand-new exurbs that looked as if they were constructed out of Legos, and past redbrick high schools and A-frame Lutheran churches with purple and cherry-red stained-glass windows; we'd seen spewing smokestacks and abandoned factories and mile-high silos and cricket-infested fields with phantom Christinas dragging themselves along the tall grass; we'd driven past sunlit malls that bustled like ant farms, past moonlit ballfields and lonely eternities of cornfields; we'd gone over mountains and through great charred wastes all the way to the desert; and neither Toll House Cookie nor History Babe nor Second Gunman nor Chip Zero had risked one single red American cent.

But I had won—on the laptop, in the flickering etherworld—more than $29,000 in three days.

12

WWHMD?

Wifey never did find out that I hadn't been in New York pining away for her return from the Appalachians. There was no telltale tan, sunburn, extended hangover, or conglomeration of hickies, and the apartment looked just as bad as if I'd been there the whole time. It was perfect. What wasn't perfect was her first impression of my new platinum-blond hair and tricked-out James Joyce shades. (When she first got a glimpse of it, her response was simply: "Okay . . . so, why?") I kept the look and she said, unconvincingly, she would try to adjust.

One night I went to my desk and pulled out *Dead on Arrival* from a drawer and looked at it with fresh eyes. It had been a while. I read the part where the wife kills herself and her children. Twenty pages later my main character was having sex with his kids' babysitter, fifteen pages after that he was doing his late wife's sister. Nick Hornby, I knew, couldn't write stuff like this if he wanted to. And he wouldn't want to. John Updike, John Cheever, and Richard Yates had never come close to this type of ugliness. This was the churning, toxic cesspool behind Revolutionary Road that everybody preferred to agree wasn't really there.

"So," I asked Cynthia later that night, "did you finish it?"

"Not yet," she answered. "It's so dark."

I looked at her blankly and she said, "I don't know what else you want me to say."

She would, I could tell, never finish it. She and thousands of others would never make it to the last page. It was a crying shame.

I didn't know much about the books Deke Rivers and Last

Resort Press put out, but they had to be worse than *Dead on Arrival*. I wasn't going to shell out one cent to have my breakthrough novel published and it would have been nice to have gotten paid for all my hard work, but by now any publisher in the world could have had it for free. *Didn't they know that?*

(But maybe I didn't want them to know that.)

After I reread the first half of *Dead on Arrival* and reflected on how I'd ascended halfway up Literary Mountain only to plummet all the way back down, after I considered that the path back up was now blocked to me, I would venture to say that of the eleven pints of blood in my body, ten and a half consisted of furiously boiling rage. The other eight ounces were merely anger.

Clint Reno had let me down. I had to let him go. Even though he had let me go first.

I wanted to tear every hair out of his head, especially the slick ones in his perfect ponytail, and then pummel him in front of his coworkers who, in this juvenile homicidal fantasy, would cheer me on and claim to the cops that they'd seen nothing, heard nothing. "Great job, Frank!" one of them would say. "We were hoping someone would do that to him one day."

("You really have to stop carrying around these horrible grudges," Wifey has told me numerous times. "It's unhealthy." "You don't understand," I've explained to her, "I *am* my grudges." And it was true: if I didn't have them, then I didn't have me.)

Clint hadn't e-mailed me when I had pneumonia, he hadn't e-mailed me when I was in a hospital with an eye patch over my eye and another patient's excrement all over my pajamas (yeah, I know: that never really happened, but *he* didn't know that!). I thought of sending him e-mails telling him I had brain cancer . . . I wanted to see at precisely which ailment he would be moved to write me back. A stroke? Pleurisy? Food poisoning? Maybe no disease was drastic enough. Maybe he would only contact me after I was dead.

I decided to stalk his sartorially perfect ass again.

I had just sat down at my usual Dunkin' Donuts stool across

the street from his office and thrown back three Munchkins when I saw him strutting down the street. I hadn't really thought about what I'd do if I saw him (I wasn't armed), but I got up, grabbed the box of doughnuts, and trotted toward him, intending to pretend that this was a casual run-in.

"Hey, Clint!" I called out with a friendly Hey-Look-Who's-Here wave from the other side of the street. It was 9 a.m. and blustery out, but his ponytail didn't whip in the wind. He probably spent an hour shellacking it every morning before he left the house.

"Yes?" he called back with a squint, not really seeing me getting closer.

"Clint . . . it's me . . . Frank Dixon!"

We stood a foot apart. As usual, he was dressed impeccably. His tie not only always matches his shirt but also the affected faint freckles dotting the bridge of his nose.

"Aahhh!" he said. "You must want Clint."

"*You're* Clint," I said. "Right?"

"No . . . I'm Vance." His identical twin brother. His business partner. Who works in L.A. and who seldom comes to New York.

"You are?" I asked.

"Heh. This isn't the first time this has happened to me. Or to Clint."

"You're really Vance Reno?" Now I was the squinter and he was the squintee and I was clutching the Munchkins so tight that the box was starting to crack.

"Clint happens to be in London now on business."

I could have asked Vance what he was doing in New York, I could have asked him why he now wore his hair in a ponytail just as his brother did, I could have asked him, "So since when did you start wearing suits?" since the two times I'd met him he'd worn jeans and a T-shirt, and I could have asked him since when did his tie and shirt match so perfectly, but I opted not to. If it *was* Clint trying to avoid me and pass himself off as his twin, then I couldn't bring myself to humiliate him (Clint) by telling him that I knew he wasn't really him (Vance). If it was Vance, then I didn't want to confront him (Vance) either, since he wasn't really him (Clint).

But I did gather up enough courage to say: "Wow, it's amazing how much you look like him now, Vance," my words not dripping with as much sarcasm as I would have liked.

"Yes," he said, just about to enter the building to escape me, "I'm quite often mistaken for myself."

I politely asked him if he could, once he was upstairs, do some quick digging around and find out to which publishers Clint had sent *Dead on Arrival*. Why do you want that information? he asked. Not letting on about Ross F. Carpenter, I said: "Because I just do."

He told me he'd get right on it and hurried inside.

All the Munchkins were on the ground at my feet. The box had broken.

♥ ♥ ♥ ♥

"How much more of this abject misery can one human being take?" the fed-up *Time* Magazine reviewer had remarked about *Plague Boy*. Life was giving me a brutal pasting and I was just taking it. It felt like all ten billion other people in the world were kicking, punching, and biting me and would rather abuse me, shame me, and cause me tremendous anguish than eat, breathe, drink, and have sex amongst themselves. It was their idea of a good time.

(Once when I was about nine, my Uncle Ray and I boxed in his Elizabeth, New Jersey, living room. He broke my nose with a right jab. The blood poured out and I began to cry at the top of my lungs. "Why didn't you put your guard up?" Uncle Ray asked me. "Why didn't you punch back?" As he plugged both my nostrils with tissue and tried to comfort me, I whimpered, "Because I didn't want to hurt you.")

In Las Vegas I had vowed to do something. It was now time to make more vows.

No longer would I let people kick me around. I had to fight

back. I had to wriggle free from the Whipping Post of the World and whip back.

I logged on to the Galaxy, opened up a page in Word, and started playing poker and making my vows at the same time.

At the top of the page I wrote "What Would Herman Melville Do?"

Herman Melville wrote *Typee* (his *Plague Boy*) and then *Omoo* (his *Love: A Horror Story*). A scrappy sonuvabitch, that New York-born and -bred fighter kept fighting back. *Moby Dick* was his undoing, but still he never gave up. They kept knocking him down but he kept getting back up.

> #1: I will call Clint Reno. I will *demand* the list of names I need. No e-mails. No messages. No snail mail. Voice-to-ear contact. Live, as it happens. He *will* comply.
>
> #2: No, I won't call. I'll push my way into his office. If he gives me a dirty look, if he threatens to call the police, I will yell so loud that I'll see his eardrums turn to powder and sift out of his ears.

I won $850 with three 5s at the Medium tables and it put me above $232,000. The next hand, I won $600 with two 8s.

> #3: I will call Martin Tilford and ask him, "Hey, remember me? The seared peppercorn tuna at Café Quelquechose? So, Martin, I was wondering . . . have you made it to the second sentence of my book yet?"

Two 10s and two 5s at the High tables. $1,450. Two Aces the next hand: $900.

Herman Melville was a steel-tough, sea-tested, iron-nail-chewin' battler but wound up working for U.S. Customs. It wasn't going to go that way for me. Why not? Because I had poker to fall back on. No dumb uniform for me other than pajamas or sweatpants. I had to be resilient. The more they knocked me down, the tougher I'd get, until their own fists were bloodied and broken and they couldn't knock me down anymore. This was war! I would become a raging pest, the Mother of All Nuisances, the Annoying Hyperactive Little Brother to everyone who had ever mistreated me; I'd be the bane of the publishing world's existence and *Publishers Weekly* would put me on their cover, my newly peroxided and bespectacled kisser inside a circle with a red X through it. I would be the Fly in the Lit World's Ointment, and my mug shot would be pinned to the walls in PEN offices around the world (if there are such offices). You rejected me? You snubbed me? Well, guess what. *It's clobberin' time!*

A 10-high straight in High: $1,600. Two Queens, two 9s: $1,300.

#4: I will buy a *Writer's Market* and deluge agents and editors and I *will* be published again! I do have two books under my belt and it's not like I'll be coming at these book peoples from nowhere. Listen, you fuckers, you screwheads . . . here is a man who would not take it anymore. Here is a man who stood up. A man could stand up! I won't be ignored! Attention must be paid. I can coruscate, blister, and unsettle like nobody's business. I can lick any man alive and give him the kind of spiritual rash to end all kinds of spiritual rashes!

Three 10s in Ultra-High. $3,100. What did some ten-year-old bully once say to me while he was beating me up after a basketball game: "You fuck with me, you fuck with the best. You fuck with me, you die like the rest."

Back down to Medium. Two Jacks. $500. Two hands later, a club flush: $700. Van Morrison once sang, "Listen to the lion in your soul." I was listening to mine with the volume cranked, and the lion was roaring so loud the neighbors would soon be banging on the wall.

#5: I will track down this "actress" who had only two speaking lines in a play I once cowrote that was workshopped in

Minneapolis but who went off on her own one day and wrote a five-page monologue for herself. I'll track her down at whatever restaurant she's slinging hash in or office she's temping at and ask her: "So, uh, how's the whole acting thing working out for you?"

Back up to High. Leopold Gloom, Sam Spades, Bjorn 2 Win. Full house, 8s full of 3s. $3,800. In the real world I was a deuce or a lowly 4, but here I was a face card, a puissant, swaggering, omnipotent King barely noticing his subjects as he trampled them. Maybe it really was better to reign in Hell than serve in Heaven, especially since Hell paid so much better.

If you ever cut me down, if you ever ignored me, if you ever disrespected me, then, pal, I am about to become the worst hemorrhoid you will ever have! *You die like the rest.*

I took a breather. For ten seconds. I reread my vows. It was becoming a manifesto!

#6: I will call and e-mail editors in the U.K. and they will publish my book over there and I will win the Man Booker Prize and *then* I will have Deke Rivers publish my book here and will thus be able to keep 90 percent of the profits and share not one cent of it with all the American publishers who rejected me. If they reject me in England, then I will visit upon them something so wicked and so downright irritating, that they'll *wish* it was just the Black Plague coming around again and not me.

Two Queens. $2,400. Back to Medium. Two 9s, two 7s. $450. The world was full of ants and I was a size 18EEE shoe. It was Hiroshima and I was the *Enola Gay*.

#7: When I see writers on the street I won't let them just walk by. Oh no. If some priss like Julian Barnes or the doughy has-been Salman Rushdie should cross my path, I will get right in his face and tell him, "You should have stopped writing twenty years ago. What's it like to do nothing but read and write all day long?" "Hey, you! Joyce Carol Oates! I could take you!" "Hey, Richard Ford! How my ass taste?"

Four 7s in High. I repeat: *four* 7s. $2,250. I was Ralph Kramden and everybody else was Alice and I was going ballistic all over her apron. "Get something in your head, Alice! I'm the king here! Remember that! This house is my castle! I'm the king! Remember that! King, king, king! You are nothing! A peasant! This is my house! My castle! I'm the king!"

My next vow was that when I went over $300,000, I would stop playing poker and work on the *American Nightmare Trilogy.* That amount would certainly be enough to tide me over. If I couldn't stop playing poker, I also vowed, if I found I was hooked, then I would seek treatment. I Googled the words "gambling treatment addiction facility," and among the thirty pages of results, the first and foremost was the Shining Path Clinic. I went to their site, which was sophisticated and well designed, and looked at the photos of their perfectly manicured grounds in the arid Southwest, of patients talking to therapists and to each other and playing Ping-Pong, I looked at the ads for Atavan and Paxil, and then went back to my Declaration of Principles and returned to #7, which was becoming my personal favorite.

If I ever see Calvin Trillin I will say to him to "Do you honestly believe that that novel you wrote about a guy and his New York parking space would *ever* have gotten published if you with your fancy *New Yorker* pedigree hadn't written it?! Joe Blow writes that book, it don't get published. *A guy and his parking space??* Fuck you . . . *Bud!*"

An Ace-high heart flush in High. $1,500. Was this a dream? Was some other poker player dreaming *me?* Now I knew what it was like to be Mike Tyson when Mike Tyson was still Mike Tyson, before he became . . . Mike Tyson.

If I ever see Dan Brown on an airplane I will follow him into the restroom and I'll barge in on him just when he's closing the door and yell, "Do you realize that you're not any good and that you're just lucky?" I will stalk Mitch Albom and lunge at him and when I've got him down on the sidewalk I'll say, "Hey, you know how you always write books about dying or dead people? Well, guess what? Your next book can be *about yourself!* 'Cause as of now you're dead!" I will fear nobody. "Hey, Cody Marshall, you gave away my ending once? Well, it's payback time and now I am ending *you*." I will drop a 90-pound television on Jonathan Franzen's already swelled head from ten flights up and yell down: "Hey, Franzen! Guess you finally got a TV now, huh?"

Ultra-High. A table for three with Ante Maim and SaniFlush, the baddest player on the site. I had squadoosh. The Big Doughnut. But I kept raising and raising. They finally folded. $3,600. Fireworks were going off and "Ode to Joy" was blasting and millions of people were on their feet applauding. To echo Rusty Wells in mid-puke: "It don't get any better 'n this."

I logged off at 4 a.m. and, according to Wifey, I giggled in my sleep all night long.

◆ ◆ ◆ ◆

Two weeks later I logged on, as usual, at eight in the morning and a mostly blank page came on my screen and told me that Poker galaxy.com was closed for repairs but would be back up soon. *Soon?* When is "soon"? Is "soon" five minutes, five hours, or five weeks?

How could they do that to me?

I checked every few minutes to see if it was back. Sometimes I just clicked on the refresh button so I suppose I was, from time to time, checking every few seconds. I went to the kitchen, opened a box of Froot Loops, checked the site, went back and got the milk out, checked the site, went back to the kitchen and poured the milk over the cereal, checked the site, then brought the bowl into my study and kept checking with every spoonful. Two hours later I interrupted a pee halfway through, checked to see if the site was back up, and then went back into the bathroom to finish. It still wasn't up at two, so I brought my laptop to a restaurant near my apartment that I knew got wifi. But it never did come back up that day.

When Cynthia came home from work I was a pale, shaking ruin and I told her I wasn't feeling well, which was not a lie.

The next morning the site was back up.

There were e-mails from my Poker Buddies. They had all, they told me, gone through a similarly rough twenty-four hours. Kiss My Ace told me that his one day without any contact with Boca Barbie was the worst twenty-four hours of his life. "And i once did," he added, "this marine corps training in the desert when we had no food or water and had to eat these scorpion things we hunted down."

> **Artsy Painter Gal:** I don't ever want to go a day without you ever, ever again!
> **Chip Zero:** I thought the site would never come back up, that you were gone from me forever.
> **Arty Painter Gal:** I thought the very same. I was really panicking! I can't bear the thought of losing this! It would kill me.
> **Chip Zero:** Look at us. We're just as sickeningly sweet as Kiss My Ace and Barbie. We must be making people throw up if they're spying on us.
> **Artsy Painter Gal:** OMG, you're right. Look what you've done to me! You've made me GOOEY!

The next day things got even more serious between us.

> **Artsy Painter Gal:** Chip, what I said to you at the Nirvana I meant. I would like to see you again.

Artsy Painter Gal wins $300 with two 9s.

Artsy Painter Gal: I know it's completely insane and we don't even
know each other but I know what I want, ok?

Chip Zero: I don't think we don't know each other. We do this so
often. I tell you everything.

Artsy Painter Gal: Name a time and a place. Where and when?
And make it soon.

Chip Zero: I don't know. I'll give it some thought, I promise you.

Where and when? Those words stayed with me for days, for weeks.
They floated off my computer screen and hung in the air and followed me around. They loomed over me as I sat at readings in
Barnes & Noble and asked writers annoying questions afterwards
("So what made you write this book, how much did you get for
it, and what did you do with all the dough?"). *Where and when?* I
would be eating with Cynthia in a restaurant and the words un-
dulated over my calamari, onion rings, or sushi. In ghostly hues
the letters shimmied and shimmered morning, noon, and night,
like the weird lettering of "Come to the City" in Murnau's *Sun-
rise*. It was the same situation, too: a woman, not my wife, from
a faraway place was using all her wiles to lure me away from my
loving, devoted wife. If anyone said the word "where" in the course
of a sentence, I saw "and when?" appear, wobble, and then slowly
disintegrate.

I was true to my word to Victoria. Not only did I give it some
thought, I saw it and heard it and dreamt about it and couldn't
shake it.

Ever since coming back from Empyrean Island, my sleep had
gotten even stranger. Lately it was a rare event when a real flesh-
and-blood human being even made an appearance. Mostly animated poker-playing figures populated my dreams. I, of course,
was the Big Guy, the big lug in the Hawaiian shirt. Cynthia always showed up as the dark, sultry Dragon Lady in the red silk
dress, and Artsy Painter Gal was the buxom Lady Godiva Blonde.

Sometimes we sat around a poker table, sometimes we stood on the street around a poker table, sometimes we sat up in bed playing cards and dunking poker chips in onion dip. When I dreamt about Harry Carver, he was the Leathery Cowboy; Lonnie was the Black Pimpin' Dude with the monster 'fro, and my mother was always the Blowsy Housewife. And there was little or no talking . . . now it was mostly instant messaging. The nonsense-speak of dreamlife had been replaced by chat and emoticons. Nobody laughed—they LOLed.

Real life was little different. Or was it that my dreamlife and the doings on the Galaxy and in the real world were mixing into one confused *tricolore* pasta? When I handed over money to real people in the real world, I felt like I was the Big Guy losing a hand and shoving over my chips. When I turned over things, such as mail, magazines, or a bill at a restaurant, I felt like I was turning over playing cards, and it was disorienting to see "$90.00" looking back up at me instead of a 9 of spades. When I heard numbers in real life, or on television ("And Bryant hits another three-pointer" or "The S and P rose five points today"), I always associated them with cards (for an instant I envisioned Kobe Bryant hoisting up a 3 of diamonds from twenty feet) and if someone told me that her father had just had heart surgery, I envisioned a team of doctors in an operating room removing from a gaping, blood-soaked chest cavity an 8 of hearts.

No longer could I say that I was haunted by poker. The Galaxy was now the world I lived in.

♠ ♠ ♠ ♠

A week before Thanksgiving my first book was down to 711,762 on Amazon but my second was holding steady around 768,000. Soon the two books would meet up in a place called Nope. I e-mailed Harry and asked what had become of his movie idea; he e-mailed me back a few days later telling me he'd get back to me soon. Ads were now appearing in the papers and on TV for *Breakthrough,* which wasn't just called *Breakthrough* but was "Pacer Burton's *Breakthrough.*" He had gone from being hot to very hot to being hot shit.

I was in the middle of writing a brief e-mail to Barbara Bennett at Egregious Motion Pictures when—*puff!*—I received a brief e-mail from Barbara Bennett at Egregious Motion Pictures.

> I am so sorry to be the one to tell you this but Egregious isn't going to renew the *Plague Boy* option. Pacer Burton was really excited about the project but he's had a ton of other offers and after carefully considering his choices, he decided not to do *Plague Boy*.
>
> I'm very sorry. I know this meant a lot to you. Please don't slay the messenger!
>
> Hey, you can always have Vance and Clint shop *Plague* around again. I'm sure they'd do a great job.

I couldn't wring from my crushed, deflated soul the graciousness to send Barbara a heartfelt thank-you for all the work she'd done for me, which was a considerable amount. I couldn't even muster up enough energy to close the e-mail, so I just sat there staring at it for thirty minutes. I didn't sob, I didn't wail, I didn't whimper . . . because those are all things that dead people cannot do.

Plague Boy: The Movie would never be made, so there would be no reissue of the book with Tom, Leo, Scarlett, Reese on the cover with the words "Now a Major Motion Picture" beneath the title, and there would be no reissue of *Love: A Horror Story* with the words "Written by the author of *Plague Boy,* now a Major Motion Picture" on the cover. It was over for me. The lights were all but out, and the curtains were coming down before Act I was even done.

It couldn't have been easy for Barbara to send me that dreadful bit of news, but she needn't have because the news came to me automatically, via Nexis, a few hours later:

LEXISNEXIS SEARCH RESULT
Copyright Variety Magazine

Pacer Burton, whose *Pacer Burton's Breakthrough* bows the day before Thanksgiving, has signed on to helm *Saucier: A Bitch in the Kitchen*, based on the best-selling memoir by Jill Conway. (*The Plague Boy*, which he had been planning to lens, has been placed on the shelfola "indefinitely.") The book, which follows in gritty but hilarious detail three years in the life of a sexy, sassy New York chef, is an Oprah Book Club pick and has been on the best-sellers list for 15 weeks. Reese Witherspoon and Leonardo DiCaprio have agreed . . .

I didn't tell Wifey the movie was dead in the water. There was no reason for her to know. If she asked about it in a few months, I figured, I'd just tell her that they were still working out the details and that the movie would get made. The wheels were still in motion . . . it just took time. She would believe it. Because for a long time I had believed it too.

The day before Thanksgiving I went over $250,000.

I had finally found something I could excel at, something I was better at than 99 percent of the rest of the population. I couldn't paint or play basketball. Hedge funds, stocks and bonds and their ilk, were beyond my limited scope. I couldn't write or create iPad apps or be a short-order cook. But I could win an awful lot of money from a lot of people I never saw.

I would have thrown every cent of my stack into the garbage just to get published again.

I had Thanksgiving dinner with Cynthia; her father, who had recently been named by *New York* magazine as one of the city's top fifty divorce lawyers; and his surgically reupholstered second wife on the Upper East Side. I left before dessert, claiming I wasn't feeling too well due to overeating (I swiped some pecan pie on the way out and scarfed it down in the elevator). I just wanted to go home, log on, and play. It was almost seven at night when I left and the weather was windy and drizzly and hardly anyone was on the street. New York City usually seems bleak and empty on Thanksgiving night and that evening it was no different.

PBS once ran an excellent documentary series about Jesus Christ and the early days of Christianity. It follows the path of what we know and believe of the Historical Jesus and His journey in becoming the Savior, the Son of God. One episode ends with the portentous words: "Jesus of Nazareth had become . . . Jesus Christ."

As I walked down Lexington Avenue that night, my hands in my coat pockets, I paid attention to little around me. At a street corner I heard someone say something, call something out. It was a word, one crisp syllable, and there was something familiar and friendly about it. But I didn't pay it any mind and kept walking, stooping over to brace myself from the rain and wind. A half a block later I heard it again but still it didn't fully register.

Five minutes later it was raining harder and windier and it dawned upon me that someone—whoever it was—had been saying my name. They'd called out, "Frank!"

But that wasn't me anymore. Just as Muhammad Ali regarded Cassius Clay as his slave name, "Frank W. Dixon" was now a thing of the past. That person was a relic, an MIA, a cipher. A thing from three thousand years ago who never mattered. Imagine a butterfly sprouting from a chrysalis and then kicking it out of sight. That was me. It was a skin I'd been shedding for almost a year, a tattered and soiled parachute I had buried two miles deep in the ground after falling to Earth. It was my slave name and I didn't want to answer to it anymore. I wanted to change my name on all my billing addresses, on my apartment lease, and on my books, my bank and credit card accounts.

That other person didn't exist anymore. He was gone.

I stopped on the empty street and looked into the window of

a closed shop. I had put on about forty pounds; I had on round, rose-pink-tinted glasses, and my hair was short, champagne blond, and deadly.

I was the Big Man.

I had become Chip Zero.

PART III

Busted

13
Holy War

I t's not in *Poor Richard's Almanack* but it's a fact of life: the longer you live, the more people you meet, and the more people you meet, the more people you'll know who will die. Perhaps Marcel Proust, holed up in his cork-lined bedroom and never seeing the light of day on Boulevard Malesherbes, knew what he was doing.

One winter morning I logged on to the Galaxy and went to a table in Medium. I played three hands there, then Wolverine Mommy joined me. She didn't say hello, she just said: "Did you hear? OMG! It's terrible. Chip, Grouchy Old Man died!"

Since I sometimes had trouble believing that these people really lived, it was inconceivable to me that they could also really die. (Imagine reading Homer Simpson's obituary in the *Times*.) There was a man who was born, who lived, who got married and had kids and called himself Grouchy Old Man; I saw him online at this or that table, he won money, he lost money. And he had, Wolverine Mommy told me, just died of a stroke.

He actually had died the week before, but it had taken a few days for the news to filter through to the tens of thousands of souls inhabiting the Galaxy. Grouch and Cali Wondergal had become friends and occasionally spoke to each other on the phone; when Cali hadn't heard from him for a few days, she made a few calls, did some snooping around, and found out that he had dropped dead on a line at a deli. His addled, Alzheimer's-suffering wife would never realize that she had outlived the man she'd betrayed many times on his desk at work and in his own bed.

Had Cali not poked around and found out the news, would I ever have realized what had happened? Perhaps after a week of not seeing Grouch, I would have thought he'd gone away for a week. Two weeks more, I would've thought he was on a senior-citizen cruise, playing shuffleboard and comparing meds with the other *altacockers*. But after three or more weeks I probably would have assumed he'd had his fill of poker and found something more constructive to do—such as taking up watercolors, knitting, or tap-dancing—with the waning years of his life.

♥ ♥ ♥ ♥

Sucking up my pride, I bought a *Writer's Market* one afternoon and commenced my jihad.

I combed through the Bible of Failed Writers Everywhere and got the names, addresses, and e-mail addresses of every editor I thought might be mildly receptive to *Dead on Arrival*. Some publishers, the book informed me, wouldn't respond to e-mail or faxes—you had to send snail mail and then assume a waiting posture. Some wanted a ten-page excerpt, others just a plot summary, some couldn't be bothered at all even if you were George Eliot come back to life and had just penned *Middlemarch, Part II*.

For those wary publishing souls who accepted queries but no excerpts by e-mail, I composed the following:

> My name is Frank W. Dixon and I've had two books published, *Plague Boy* and *Love: A Horror Story*. The former has been described as coruscating and blistering.
>
> After much internal struggling it pains me to inform you I've parted ways with my long-time agent Clint Reno and have decided to go it alone.
>
> My new book is called *Dead on Arrival*. It is about a suburban dad whose life is changed irrevocably one day when his wife and children perish unexpectedly. Within two days he is having the time of his life.

If you would like to read an excerpt of this work of sublime suburban mimesis, please let me know.

I sent that to eighteen editors. I then tweaked it for the more trusting types who would accept a twenty-page excerpt, tweaked it again for the not so trusting who only accepted ten-page excerpts. Taking snail mail, faxing, and e-mailing into account, I had to come up with eight different templates, eight variations on the same desperate theme, which was: *PLEASE READ IT, PLEASE LIKE IT, PLEASE FOR THE LOVE OF GOD PUBLISH IT!* By the second day I had sent out fifty-eight queries, including seventeen twenty-page excerpts and fifteen ten-page excerpts.

Though it didn't take up nearly as much time, all of this was more difficult than writing the book had been.

Now I could go back to playing poker and checking my e-mail for the avalanche of replies from editors. But what do I do, I fretted, if ten publishers want to publish *Dead on Arrival? How do I handle that?* I decided that I would simply call Ross F. Carpenter and say, "Ross, you're hired. Pick the highest bidder and do the deal. And, oh yeah, you no longer have to read the book."

I got replies on the first day, some within minutes: six editors politely passed, three impolitely passed ("I have no interest in such dreadful material"), four requested excerpts and three of those who had received excerpts subsequently requested the whole thing. Over the next few days, it got even more difficult to keep track of: some editors who had read the ten pages wanted twenty more, some who had read the twenty pages wanted only ten more, and, of course, there were some who had read ten or twenty who were telling me to fuck off.

But I wouldn't let them have the last word. I was the Big Man now. *Watch out!*

One editor who didn't want to read an excerpt—I don't think she even finished reading my e-mail query—told me, "I haven't read either of your two books (certainly not after I read Cody Marshall's review of *Plague Boy* in the *Times*) and, based on your summary and sales history, am certainly not going to read this one."

Well, the new tougher me couldn't let it just die like that. I e-mailed her back.

> I would really love to know what in the name of Almighty
> God does that (you not having read my first two books) have
> anything whatsoever to do with this (you not giving my third
> book a freaking chance)? This means you would've passed up
> on *Gatsby* 'cause you never read *This Side of Paradise* and *The
> Beautiful and Damned*. Now, I've Googled you, and your client list
> is unimpressive at best. I mean, I've never heard of any of them!
> So as of this writing, you are just as much a failure as I am. The
> difference between us, you ask? I may be a failure but as for you,
> you have to leech off of people like *me!*

To the editors who refused to read an excerpt, I e-mailed: "You're not going to even give it a chance?!" Sometimes that would get a reply, sometimes not. I knew they had stacks of manuscripts to tend to . . . but I wanted these *refuseniks* to spend more time reading my e-mail than they did that other stuff. "I am a published author of two slightly well-received books and you won't even read TEN pages of my new work? And you wonder why people watch *America's Next Top Model* while there are only three people who read fiction anymore?"

I was, I knew, burning bridges for any books I might write in the future, but I was cognizant of the fact that I might not write anything in the future now that I was making more from poker than from literature and that these bridges had never been built in the first place.

One editor e-mailed me:

> This is the most depressing and disturbing thing I've seen in quite
> some time. I could not read more than five pages of what you
> sent me.

I was aghast and wrote back:

Aren't literature, music, and art *supposed* to disturb? You think
Elizabethan audiences were in stitches when King Lear died, you
think Caravaggio's *Deposition* is a laff-a-minute riot, don't you
know that when people first saw Stravinsky's *The Rite of Spring*
they threw ratatouille at the orchestra and when they first saw
Un Chien Andalou there was a riot and for a while slitting eyeballs
became de rigueur?! Oh, why am I even wasting my time with
you?! Just keep publishing your drivel, why don't you.

The very worst angel of my nature now wanted *Dead on Arrival* to never get published, just so I could keep firing off my rage-infused hate mail. It was the best damn catharsis a fella could have that didn't involve expelling some sort of fluid or waste product. God forbid some editor would actually like my book and want to publish it!

To the editor who told me: "Women do the majority of fiction reading these days and this is a novel that would be and should be despised by women," I wrote back: "So you're just going to pander to the shopaholics and Devil Wears Pradas and Bergdorf blondes of this world? Excuse me but doesn't that make you a whore?" I didn't expect a reply to that but five minutes later came: "I'm not going to even dignify that with a response, Frank," to which I responded: "Um, you just did. Besides, my mother, who is a woman, would love to read this book and not just because she's my mother." One minute later I received: "Based on your writing abilities, Frank, I'm surprised your mother can read at all." To which I replied: "My mother, I'll have you know, has been a literacy volunteer since before the library in ancient Alexandria burned down so I request that you refrain from mentioning her. And how low have you sunk anyway that you would bring up my mother in this discussion? But I'm not surprised you took it into the gutter for that is where you truly belong."

A few editors, based on my summary or the excerpts they'd read, did want to read the whole shebang but eventually they turned me down. (Only now was the cruel irony of a book titled *Dead on Arrival* dawning on me.) Even though they had given me a chance, I let them have it, too. "Well," I wrote them, "I want to sincerely thank you for taking out the time from what I'm certain must be a busy day to make an incredibly moronic mistake."

Some editors, I sensed, wanted to keep the chain of hate going. For all I know, it was the high point of their workday. These editors I sort of respected—they were feisty—and there was one scrappy guy in his sixties who traded a total of thirty-one e-mails with me. (I'd like to believe that they admired my pugnacity, too.) However these exchanges eventually degenerated into schoolyard "are too" "am not" "are too" "nyah, nyah, nyah" affairs.

"Your book isn't nearly as good as you think it is," one editor wrote me. I replied: "You're right. It's not. It's better! So publish it." She wrote back: "Nope. It's just not good, Frank." To which I riposted: "You're right. It's just not good! It's great! So publish it."

"I'm sorry," another editor wrote me, "but we're going to have to pass on this. With the way this business is right now, it's just not what we're looking for."

I asked him: "Huh? 'The way this business is right now'? Can you please tell me about 'the way this business is right now'? Because frankly I am not familiar with 'the way this business is right now.'" When he didn't reply I asked him again. And again. Then I fired off an e-mail so offensive that I feared hearing from the police.

I was getting badly battered, I was losing the war, but at least now I was fighting back. And I was comforted knowing that I wasn't merely fighting for me, but I was fighting for every working stiff who ever got bawled out by a boss, I was fighting for every Little Guy who got stomped on by a Big Bully, I was standing up for the poor loser who knows he can't fight City Hall and for homeless puppies who get euthanized for having sad loveable eyes and floppy ears. I was Tom Joad fighting so that hungry people could eat, and for poor kids laughing when supper's ready. But mostly, yeah, I *was* fighting for me.

Feeling terrible had never felt so good.

An extra dose of insult and injury came my way one day from a likely source: Bev Martin. She told me she had just finished her third novel, which I didn't care about, and that her publisher was going to give it a massive push in the spring, which really annoyed me, and that movie companies were already clamoring for it, which infuriated me. But this wasn't, she pointed out, why she was e-mailing me now.

> soooo . . . what i really need is a favor. i met a criminally young and sort of sweetly naïve girl at a writer's conference last week. her name's Susan Jessup and she's only a few weeks out of the Babbo Writers Workshop in Ashland, NC, and lo and behold—she's written her first novel. it's dark but goodish and she said that YOU are her favorite author! when i told her i knew you she was ecstatic. anyway, could you/would you/can you please look at her ms. and get in touch with her? she's a doll, really, and merely seeks your sage wisdom.
>
> also, don't forget: Deke Rivers, Last Resort.
>
> Bev

I couldn't believe that her third book would be getting a massive push and that another one of her bathetic tales about a warped wealthy family would get sold to the movies; I couldn't believe that she had the nerve to ask me to get in contact with this young, criminally sweet Babbo writer after she'd initiated the whole *Saucier* debacle; I couldn't believe she had the audacity to again bring up Deke Rivers (didn't she know how insulting that was to me?). But what I really could not believe was that someone had read two books of mine and liked them both and thought that I had some wisdom to impart. That just didn't seem right.

I wrote Bev back and told her to give the girl my e-mail address and phone number. I'd love to help, I told her. I promised myself that if and when this Susan contacted me, I would be polite and helpful to her. What the hell? I had the time and money to be nice now.

Deke Rivers. Last Resort Press. Paying someone to publish *Dead on Arrival*. Then I could hire, I thought, an aggressive and insincere publicist to spread the word around, to bookstores and book clubs and the press. Maybe the worst idea of them all wasn't so bad.

❖ ❖ ❖ ❖

There must have been hundreds of manuscripts going unread in December and January—editors were too busy e-mailing me. Perhaps I had gotten them in such lousy moods that they wound up rejecting books which they, had they not been bubbling over with bile and nitric acid, would have gladly published otherwise. So be it.

One evening, two weeks before Christmas, I attended a reading at a Barnes & Noble on Lexington Avenue uptown. The author had penned a variation of *Jane Eyre* . . . the narrator was the character Bertha Mason, Rochester's insane wife, and it was written in some incomprehensible patois that was occasionally interrupted with outbursts of schizoid insanity. Having never been able to sit through the movie, having never been able to muster up the interest to read the book, and not paying any attention to the author reading, I had no idea what was going on. The author wasn't merely doing a reading; it was an attempt at performance art, and at one point she was yelling and hacking apart Jane Eyre's body with an invisible machete. Saliva flew from her mouth, her eyes surged out of their sockets, and I couldn't tell if the twenty people attending the reading were riveted to their seats or were too scared to leave.

Halfway through I stood up and interrupted.

"I represent," I told her, "the Brontë estate and we intend to sue!" I brandished my cell phone and said, "I've been recording this. How dare you appropriate this magnificent novel for your own personal gain. We just won four hundred thousand dollars from someone who put the umlaut in the Brontë name over the O and not the E. *That's* who you're dealing with here!"

She froze. Did she really believe I was serious and that the thirty or so grand she had received for penning her high-strung, forgettable work was going to be snatched from her savings account by Charlotte Brontë's great-great-great-great-grandchildren?

Someone tapped my shoulder.

"Mr. Dixon?" I heard a woman whisper behind me.

I turned around and saw a vaguely familiar face. She examined, for a second or two, at close range the new hair, new pounds, and new tinted shades.

"Yes?" I whispered back.

"I'm going to have to ask you to leave please," the store manager said.

"All right, but how do you know who I am?"

She told me that she used to work at the Union Square Barnes & Noble and that I'd once asked why that store had no copies of *Plague Boy.*

"I was the one," she reminded me, "who told you the book was out of print."

"Okay, I'm going now," I told her.

"And *please,*" the woman hissed, "stop what you're doing!"

They were on to me.

It was Glenn Tyler of Lakeland & Barker who had called me a Master of the Suburban Mimetic and said that I possessed some sort of secret sharer status. I had, he'd said, given him a kind of spiritual rash. I still have no idea what any of that means, but I do know that he was the Abraham and Sarah of all my rejection; on the genealogical chart of everything negative that had recently befallen me, it all stemmed from him. Therefore he had to pay, too.

I sent him an e-mail asking if he wanted to read a new book of

mine. (This was the first direct contact he and I had ever had.) I
didn't tell him what it was about or the title. A week went by and he
told me to send it to him; he was, he told me, familiar with *Plague*.
I sent him *DOA* and waited. It probably took only one paragraph
for him to realize he'd already read it. Graciously never letting on,
he e-mailed me: "I am afraid that I'm going to have to pass." Now,
he didn't know that I had read the rejection he'd sent Clint—I'd
been counting on that—so I wrote him back: "That's really all you
have to say about it? Three years, 750 pages, and all you can say is
you're passing? Nothing about me being a master of the suburban
mimetic? Nothing about a kind of spiritual rash? Aw, c'mon, throw
me some props here, G-Man!" When, as expected, I received no
reply, I e-mailed him: "Pussycat got your tongue, does it?"

That was the end of him and of me and him together, and to
my dying day I will picture Glenn Tyler covered head to toe with
the scaly, flaming purple rash that I gave him, scratching himself
so hard that every ounce of his sick spirit oozes out of the wounds.

Cynthia noticed that lately I was in an unusually cheerful mood.
"You must be having an affair, Chip!" she even once jokingly said.
"You're just so *sprightly!*" (Even Wifey was now calling me Chip to
my face every once in a while, as I was calling her Wifey to hers.)
She would come home from work and, after eight hours of bat-
tling editors and publishers, I was walking on air to open the door
for her.

"We should take another vacation soon," she said to me one
night in bed.

"Yeah, that's a good idea." And, man, did I have the money for it.

We discussed where we might go and, after considering Puerto
Rico, Hawaii, Barcelona, Napa and all the other usual places, we
settled on London. In February. "It will be freezing and wonderful
and we'll drink tea and keep warm," she said, sounding like three
Hemingway heroines all at once. "And if you want," she suggested,
"you can write during the daytime there while I walk around and
shop and keep our hotel room warm and pretty."

The next day the two-week vacation my wife and I had begun to plan took a new twist. Or to be more accurate, it got fatally mangled. I was at a private table with APG and told her about it and she said, "So, uh, why does she get to go with you and I don't?"

"Because," I reminded her, "she's my wife and you're not?"

"Not good enough. How about I just happen to be there at the same time as you?"

Right away I had a much better idea: I would go to London alone. The cover story would be I was refining and finishing the *Trilogy*. No, I'd tell Wifey, this isn't really a vacation for me. *This is work.* I'd tell her that after London—after three weeks in London—she and I would go someplace else, anywhere she wanted. Someplace exotic. The thought of Tahiti, for some reason, drives most women wild. But I didn't mention Tahiti just yet.

And in London I really *would* work on the *Trilogy*. It was already written; all it needed was a little nip here and a massive tuck there. So yes, I would stay in London for a week and work on it, Artsy would then join me for two; I'd work on the book during the daytime and she and I would dine like royalty at night. We'd shop till we dropped. We'd stay at Claridge's or the Connaught or some unknown boutique hotel where the room was tiny and the bed was uncomfortable and the cost was five hundred pounds a night.

I resolved that when I hit $400K I'd stop playing poker. Forever!

The plan was idiot-proof. I knew that Wifey would allow it: she wanted me to write and to get published again. The week I'd be in London alone, I resolved, I would starve myself into quasi-perfection, so that when Victoria showed up I wouldn't be such a chubby hulk. I'd eat a half a scone in the morning and walk twenty miles a day, then eat rice for dinner. And APG, I was sure, would fancy the New Much Fiercer Me.

The next day I woke up realizing that this was all an insane pipe dream and that APG didn't really mean it, but the first words out of her mouth—or her keyboard—to me that day were: "So have you been thinking of our fantastic London getaway?"

I confessed I had, then asked her how could she, a mother of two and a wife of one, manage to sneak away for two weeks?

She told me to hold on. She logged off and I stayed put and sat alone at our private table. Five minutes went by and she didn't return. Ten minutes. The Big Man sat back in his chair and stared into space. Were 2,000 people out there watching me wilt? Fifteen minutes. And then with a merry tinkle she sat right next to me as the Busty Blonde.

"Just called Mr. APG," she said. "I told him I wanted to get away & start painting again & really immerse myself in it for a few weeks. He bought it."

We played a hand and I quickly dumped $700 to her. "Hey!" I said. "That was my round trip airfare!"

"Just e-mail me," she said, "when you're going and I'll make it work out."

We played one more hand. I don't know if she lost on purpose but I won the airfare back with the next hand.

♠ ♠ ♠ ♠

That moment when I opened the door and saw the back of Diane Warren's head between my younger brother's legs . . . that was without question the *Hindenburg* "Oh, the humanity" low point of my life. Nothing will ever top that. Were I ever to walk in on Wifey naked in bed with the starting front seven of the Dallas Cowboys, that wouldn't do it. Because I've already had the shock of a lifetime. Dostoyevsky was once taken outside to be shot by a firing squad but lo and behold, he wasn't executed—it was just your typical cute Russian prank (*Gotcha, tovarich!*). As a result of this extreme close-up of the existential abyss, hundreds of thousands of people were later forced to read *The Brothers Karamazov* against their will.

Maybe we all get the personal lowlights we deserve.

So as a cheating victim I wanted to know just what I was getting into. I knew everything there was to know about Victoria G.

Landreth, but how much of the everything that she told me was true . . . and what else was there? But what I really wanted to know was: was I the only player on the site she was flirting with?

There was only one way to find out.

One day I told APG I had to bring both of my computers in to be fixed. She told me she would miss me and I told her I'd miss her too.

It was all a ruse.

I opened up a new account on the Galaxy and chose a name for my new persona. The handle I had in mind would certainly be available: the Suburban Mimetic.

For three days I spied on Artsy Painter Gal. Since the Suburban Mimetic wasn't on her Galaxy "buddy list," she would have no idea I was logged on. I watched her sashay from table to table, I watched her play dozens of hands, I felt it in the pit of my stomach when other male players attempted to flirt with her. She talked to them but never flirted and it warmed my heart. My e-honey was being true to me! Over those three days I even sat in and played a few hands with her—I purposely lost half the London airfare she'd lost to me—and struck up a potentially dangerous conversation. "So, Artsy Painter Gal, what do you look like?" the Suburban Mimetic brazenly asked her. "Eh, I'm all right," was all she said. She refused to play the coquette and I gulped—it was like the mushy point in the movie when the loser guy realizes that the pretty girl really likes him best after all.

(The Suburban Mimetic also played a few hands with History Babe, got her at a private table, and exchanged ten minutes of dirty talk with her. She told me, "Oh god oh god i am cumming now!" but I knew—in Vegas she had told me too much about her m.o.—that she wasn't in fact "cumming" but probably was slapping together a baloney and cheddar sandwich with her free hand.)

Three days later Chip Zero was back. Artsy told me she'd missed me and that she'd been miserable without me. My duplicity had paid off.

(If poker has given me anything, other than esteem, self-confidence and a lot of money, it is a knowledge of bluffing and about how anybody will believe almost anything.)

Everything I was doing emboldened me to do more. Winning money at poker was my safety net and gave me the courage to flirt and possibly abscond for three weeks to London with APG. That in turn gave me the courage to take on the publishing world, which gave me the courage to win more money at poker. My onions, reader, were now the size of cannonballs.

And it was with those dangling cannonballs that I phoned an old acquaintance.

> Martin Tilford: Frank Dixon? Good God! A blast from the
> past!
> Me: Martin, how *are* you?
> Martin Tilford: I'm good. You know, I have warm memo-
> ries of meeting you back—
> Me: Do they involve seared peppercorn tuna?
> Martin Tilford: Heh-heh. You remember that. By the
> way, I should tell you—I read *Plague Boy* and enjoyed it
> immensely.
> Me: What about the other book ?
> Martin Tilford: *The Horror of Love?* No, but it is on my list.
> Why are—
> Me: Hey, Martin, things were very bad. Remember?
> Martin Tilford: Things were bad? I'm sorry but I must be
> missing something here.
> Me: Things were very bad then but still we carried on.
> [Long silence.] You're not getting this, are you? Things
> *were* very bad. But still *we* carried on. We carried *on*.
> Martin Tilford: I don't know what you're implying. Uh, why
> are you calling, Frank?
> Me: Things were very bad then but still we carried on. That
> was the first line of my book. Remember now? You liked

the first line. You liked it a lot. And I was just wondering
if maybe you'd want to publish it since, you know, it got
off to such a great start. And if not, then maybe you'd
like to take me out and this time I'd be allowed to order
the burger that I wanted? Well? Martin?

He groaned, he sighed, he waited for me to continue; I didn't
and he hung up on me.

(To really rub it in, for the next four business days I called the
still-extant Café Quelquechose and had seared peppercorn tuna
delivered to him. I stopped when I realized that I might not be
torturing him with this and that he was probably eating it.)

A few days before Christmas I e-mailed Greg Nolan, my editor at Norwich Cairn Books, my U.K. publisher, whom I'd met
several times. When I told him I'd be in London in February and
had a new book I was shopping around, he suggested we do lunch
and asked me why Clint had not sent him the manuscript; when I
e-mailed him back telling him I was going it alone now, he told me
that he felt he couldn't read the book unless Clint sent it to him;
when I e-mailed him back saying that while this was fair to Clint
it wasn't fair to me, the book's author, he told me to contact Clint's
foreign sales representatives in London—maybe if they read the
book and liked it, he would read it—and I remembered then that
even though my books had gotten good reviews in England, they
had not sold terribly well there either; when I e-mailed him saying,
"Okay, does this mean we won't do lunch?" he told me, "Of course
we will!" He told me he would try to set up a reading at some local
venue. For some unknowable reason I told him to go ahead and
set it up.

Greg Nolan had taken a page out of Ross Carpenter's book.
No, it wasn't Ross's book—it was Franz Kafka's. I soon found out
that the people who handled foreign sales for the Reno Brothers
would not read *Dead on Arrival* either, not unless Clint submitted
it to them. The prospect that I would become the first American

author to win the Booker Prize (and that this in turn would get the book published in the U.S. and that all the publishers who rejected me would be humiliated) was starting to look quite bleak, and no longer was the irony of my book's title merely dawning upon me; now it was a rusty spike getting driven into my skull.

If Glenn Tyler was my Abraham and Sarah, then Clint Reno was my Adam and Eve.

It was his turn to pay now.

I created a purposely sloppy letterhead for a scruffy unbathed hipster named Joseph Kaye and made up a fictitious address for him in the once edgy Williamsburg, Brooklyn. I faxed a letter to the Reno Brothers and told Clint that I (Joey) was a twenty-five-year-old Yale grad who'd just undergone a rigorous five-week ordeal at the Babbo Writers Workshop and emerged one of the cream of the crop. I told him that my short stories had been printed in many alternative publications and on literary Web sites . . . and then I proceeded to make them all up: Swordshares, iLit, FUNKtional Illiterate Press, subfuscus.com, the Anti-Antioch Review, whipster .org, alternationation.com, literalorgasm.net, and so on. Would you, I queried, like to take a look at the 310-page work of fiction I'd just finished, which was "dickens meets pynchon meets 50 cent"? Fearing he might try to contact Joey K., I told him to ignore the letterhead information: I no longer lived in "Billyburg" but now lived in (the much more edgy) Greenpoint and would contact him.

I called the office a few days later and it was so easy to get through to him that it broke my heart. Courtney Bellkamp simply put hipster Joey on hold and then ten seconds later, Clint Reno picked up. Not so long ago, it had been that easy for me, too.

Putting on my best garbled Eddie Vedder voice, I (Joseph Kaye) told Clint what my new book was about ("sexually-racially-artistically confused hip-hop fuck-up torn between white boy ivy-league shit and hard-core rap underbelly, and it's sort of man's inhumanity to himself?") and how I'd won this and that minor literary prize ("and the total amount," I said, "of all the prizes came to about forty-five dollars?"), and Clint was very polite and interested. "Sure," he said, "e-mail it to me." He then asked me if I had been in touch with any other agents and I—truthfully—told him that I had not, that he was my first choice. "I was looking for an agent," I mumbled in all lower-case Vedderese, "And I read that you represent Frank W. Dixon, whose work I like really admire?"

"Yes, yes . . . I do."

Rat bastard sack of steaming, two-week-old, maggot-infested cowshit.

"And the weirdest thing . . ." Joey K. said, "is I think I saw you a few weeks ago on Spring Street talking to him?"

"Yes," he said, "I did run into Frank."

"He had doughnuts? And he dropped the box?"

"Yep, that was him."

"Okay, I'll e-mail the novel soon. . . . I just need to kinda like punctuate and uppercase it and whatnot."

Lying rat bastard. I *knew* it was him and not Vance!

But two weeks later I e-mailed him:

rmmbr me? yale babbo anti-antioch williamsburg greenpoint subfuscus? long story short i signed w/other agency. the carpenter group? their interest was genuine, solid, enthusiastic. the book was sold. $350,000, which is about $349,999 more than I thought i'd get. it drops in april. movie deal also done. $1,900,000. sorry, dude. maybe next book? peace.

joey k.

♥ ♥ ♥ ♥

On Christmas Day, right after we opened our presents, I told Wifey of my plan to go to London alone for three weeks and work nonstop on the *American Nightmare Trilogy*. I was going to throw myself into this, I told her; every second of every day was going to be about writing and I was going to tap every creative cell and tissue in my body even if I had to turn myself inside out. "You don't want to be there," I warned her. "It could possibly get very ugly." I said that after this nonvacation vacation, I would definitely need a rest and threw out Tahiti as a possibility. As I'd suspected it would, her face lit up when she heard that and she told me she would think about it.

"I hope this is okay," I said. The floor was covered with wrapping paper, opened boxes, mink-lined leather gloves, and a new pair of size six Jimmy Choos, and Celine Dion was wailing "Oh Holy Night" and the only thing glistening brighter than Cynthia's green eyes was the electric Baby Jesus teetering on His side on the treetop.

"No, it's okay," she said. "Tahiti sounds great!"

I knew she'd see it that way.

I was so touched by her excitement and her urge to be with me that I wanted to drop London and head to Tahiti with her that night.

"So where will you be staying?" she asked.

Now, thanks to poker, I could afford an expensive hotel in London. But I didn't want her to know where I would be, just in case she decided to pull the surprise of a lifetime and drop in on me (and Artsy). Also, as unbelievable as this may sound, I wanted a place where I couldn't get access the Internet so easily . . . or at all. For not only would I be there with Artsy but I really was going to London to write. To ensure this, I decided I wasn't going to bring my laptop, which had become such an integral part of me that it was like leaving my liver at home. I would just bring pens and pads and the *Trilogy*.

I'd be kicking it Old School.

"I was thinking of the Connaught," I answered. "It's a very writerly place."

The next day I called a respectable three-star hotel off Brompton Road in Knightsbridge. It certainly wasn't the Connaught but it wasn't a youth hostel either.

"Do the rooms have free broadband access?" I asked the reservations clerk on the phone.

"No, sir, I'm afraid we don't."

"Well, how much would it cost per day?"

"Sir, I'm afraid this hotel does not have it. We do have modem ports though. They're rather dreadfully slow."

"Perfect. I'll take it."

I booked a single room for one week, then a double room for me and APG for two weeks. Three weeks. No laptop. No poker. A huge part of me would be dead. For a while. In the pit of my stomach I felt Dostoyevsky's firing squad line up and take aim.

"I'm not going to bring my laptop either," Artsy e-mailed me the day after Christmas.

(Although holidays drastically reduce the number of people who play poker online, there still can be found plenty of sorry losers playing on Christmas Day, Thanksgiving, Yom Kippur, New Years Day. I had noticed this because I was one of them.)

❖ ❖ ❖ ❖

After I booked a flight that left for London on February 15th I unleashed the second wave of my attack; fifteen more editors and agents got e-mails from me. Of those fifteen, only five wanted to read *DOA*, and of those five, three told me it just wasn't right for them; the remaining two never returned my e-mails or calls. I didn't understand that: couldn't they even write me one single sentence telling me they hated it? Wasn't rejecting people—people who'd spent years writing their books—and reducing them to tears one of the grand perks of the job?!

Years ago, after writing the first three hundred pages of Book 2 of the *Trilogy*, my flight from London back to New York was an hour in the air when I realized—panicking out of my wits—that I'd accidentally left my carry-on bag, with the five legal pads it was written on, on the security conveyor belt back at Heathrow. But it didn't matter. Back in New York I sat down, tuned in, and hammered it out of me, every page and every word, right into my Commodore Amiga. Two months later British Airways returned my carry-on bag to me: there inside were my five legal-size pads, as well as some unused Durexes. Comparing what I'd written in London to what I'd tried to remember, I saw that they were virtually identical. Absolute magic.

So I wasn't worried when I could not find, despite turning my apartment upside down, the keys to the storage closet where all my past writings were kept. Yes, I could go to the storage facility and show them my driver's license and prove that I was really me, but I knew that once I wrote the words "Things were very bad then but still we carried on," the rest would pour out of me like blood spurting out of a severed artery. (If Aleksandr Solzhenitsyn in a labor camp could commit to memory entire novels that he hadn't ever typed, then I could do the same to novels I *had* typed *not* in a labor camp.) It would be just as it was the first time: I'd sit down at the library, take out my pad and pen, and let it flow. And I'd hone and polish it as it came back to me. Just as Michelangelo said that within a hunk of marble there was a statue waiting to be carved out, on the empty lines of those yellow pads lived my masterpiece, waiting, in Van Morrison's lovely words, to be born again.

"I'm with you in London now," Artsy IM'ed me a few days before my flight. "We're in our hotel room and it's cold outside but my head is on your chest and we're damp and naked. Far from the madding crowd, baby, we are with each other at last. At last."

Soon we would be eating food cooked by Marco Pierre White and Gordon Ramsay and walking arm in arm down Regent Street, loaded down with shopping bags, the smoke on our breath entwining in the air. I had seen her in a bathing suit at the Nirvana and soon I would see her all bundled up in a shearling, scarf, and fur hat, and I'd see her in nothing at all.

A few days before my flight I was playing poker and winning a lot, trouncing everyone—it was the day I went over $320,000 (only $80K more to go before I'd stop playing for good)—when my *Love: A Horror Story* Amazon ranking flashed in front of me.

I had gone, I saw, over the one-million mark. Not a million books sold, but somehow there where 1,000,251 books higher ranked than mine.

Who knew that so many books had ever been written? But they had been, and they were all kicking my book's ass.

Then I saw I had a new e-mail. I didn't recognize the sender's e-mail address at first—jtall@bhb.com—but a few seconds later it came back to me: Jim Tallman, Bedlington House Books. Bedlington was a boutique publishing house (that is, they paid their authors very little, nobody who worked there made much money, and hardly anybody read the books they published) and I'd sent him three queries about six weeks before. When he didn't reply I'd called him and gotten him on the phone and listened to him squirm while I asked why he hadn't replied. "Okay!" he caved. "I'll read your book!" I e-mailed him *DOA* a minute after that, and then he never got back to me. No longer the shy, retiring, pussy-footing type, I began sending him e-mail. "So?" went the first one. "Read it yet?" went the second. "Well, did you finish it and if so, what are your thoughts?" was the third. "Come on!" one of the last ones said. "Talk to me, Jimbo!"

I opened up his e-mail now and tried to make sense of it.

Toby:

Can't believe you ever actually worked with that pest. In a word: UGH.

Jim

P.S.: I'll let you know when I'm free. It's busy here.

I scrolled down to the e-mail from Toby Kwimper to Jim that Jim *thought* he was replying to.

Jim:

If I were you I'd just e-mail him back a nice brief note saying that the book wasn't for you. After that, you could relocate to a city far away and change your name and profession. BTW, you're

not the only one. At least three other editors have told me about
his irritating behavior in the last few weeks.

    Toby

    P.S. Yes, a lunch is in order. Just tell me where and when.

It made sense now. Jim Tallman was looking to Toby Kwimper,
my former editor, for counsel. Below Toby's e-mail was Jim's initial
e-mail to him about me, which had started it all.

Toby:

    Toby, hello. I'm writing you because I'm in a bit of a
predicament. Frank W. Dixon has badgered and harangued and
begged and beaten me into submission so that I'll read his new
novel. I don't know if you are good friends with him or not but,
frankly, he made a massive nuisance of himself.

    I cannot read the novel. I gave it to my assistant but she said
she was so turned off by the first ten pages that it viscerally upset
her.

    He keeps e-mailing. He seems like someone who longs to hear
the word NO, but I just do not want to be the one to do it.

    HELP! and let's have lunch sometime.

    Jim Tallman

    Bedlington House Books

Jim thought he was replying to Toby but he had the thought of
me—the pest, the irritant, the massive nuisance—so much on his
mind that he'd sent it to me instead.

That correspondence hurt but not as much as it should have.
I don't remember the exact date, but a long time ago I gave up on
being loved by everyone.

I didn't mind being a private nuisance, and I certainly didn't
mind viscerally upsetting anyone, but one day I discovered I was
also a public nuisance. I was scrolling down through gawker.com
one day when I came across:

Don't you just hate it when you haven't written the Great
American Novel but you think you have? Doesn't it disgust you

when your first book gets a lot of undeserved publicity but doesn't sell and then your next book gets even less publicity and sells—oh, at last count, what was it—zero copies? What to do? You write a third book and when even your own agent shreds it, you shop it around yourself. We kind of like it that you harass every tweedy, bespectacled, martini-swilling, self-loathing editor on Grub Street. God knows, they have it coming. But now they're getting so riled up . . .

continue reading »

I didn't continue reading. I was humiliated, I had brought it on myself, I had it coming, but that didn't make it any better, and besides, all those editors deserved what they got, too.

My jihad was over. The original idea, years ago, had been to establish a reputation with three minor books, then get the *American Nightmare Trilogy* published. Now I was going to turn that on its head. The *Trilogy* would get *Dead on Arrival* published and the rest would be history. I wouldn't harass any editors anymore. Not for a while at least.

Now I knew what it was like to be a door-to-door vacuum salesman, the guy that barges in, dumps a handful of dust on the floor, then sucks it all up and makes the sale to the housewife. But I was selling myself and it hadn't worked. No, I wasn't the vacuum salesman, I wasn't the vacuum. I was the dust.

♣ ♣ ♣ ♣

On the morning of February 15, I kissed Cynthia good-bye when she left for work. She wished me luck, told me to call often. I told her I would . . . though I didn't let on I'd be calling just to make sure she was in New York and not in London.

When we parted, once again I felt all the warmth sucked out of me at once.

I spent the rest of the day—never taking a break—playing poker. It was like an alcoholic going on a binge the day before checking himself into rehab. I lost, lost some more, lost more than that, climbed back up, struggled and fought and wound up $10 ahead. Ten hours for ten dollars—a mockery of the minimum wage. The walls of my apartment faded out, I wasn't really sitting on a chair at a desk in the Western Hemisphere on Planet Earth . . . I was light-years away, floating semi-comatose in an opalescent nebula of real-time gambling space.

I had to be at the airport in two hours and decided to eavesdrop.

I saw History Babe and Wolverine Mommy and Second Gunman at a table yukking it up. Cookie joined them and played a bit. Then Hist left and got a private table with Hands Brinker and he told her how much he wanted to lick her all over. I saw Bjorn 2 Win win four grand from a table full of irate Spaniards. Bjorn was, of course, a sore loser but an even worse winner and really rubbed it in. "I hate this game," one of the Spaniards said, "but I hate you even more, *puta!*" A few minutes later I saw Kiss My Ace and Boca Barbie talking in cutesy little poems to each other. It was like watching two kids feeding each other cotton candy.

In ten minutes the Town Car would be downstairs, ready to whisk me away to JFK Airport and to London, to the small library in Kensington where the Muses would sing to me and I could pour out all my soul's honey and fire, and into the arms of Artsy Painter Gal.

I was just about to leave when I came upon Pest Control and Bubbly Brit Bird.

> **Pest Control:** oh god no. i wasn't ignoring you! i wasn't.
> **Bubbly Brit Bird:** well? please. talk 2 me. what's wrong then?
> **Pest Control:** it's not good. i'm haven't been home for a few weeks, georgy. not good.
> **Bubbly Brit Bird:** where are you then?
> **Pest Control:** in hospital. and i'm not getting out.
> **Bubbly Brit Bird:** oh god, i'm sorry, phil. my sweet philly.
> **Pest Control:** emphysema. very very bad. i'm on oxygen. a tube most of the time into my throat but it's no use, georgy. it's very bad.

Bubbly Brit Bird: why didn't you tell me this? you know how much I care about you. all the times I couldn't find you here i thought you wuz avoiding me.

Pest Control: i just didn't want you to know. don't want u 2 feel sorry 4 me.

Bubbly Brit Bird: but i care! oh, i feel so bad for you, philly. are you in pain now?

Pest Control: pls don't feel bad for me. i've had good life. and i got to know u at the end. you made me so very happy, okay? :-))) not much pain. just v. tough breathing.

Bubbly Brit Bird: is there anything i can do? u have no idea how much u mean 2 me. i can fly over and see you. i know your wife is around but maybe you could sneak me in?? just for 1 sec? i want to see u!

Pest Control: my sweet georgy. not enough time for that. not much time left at all.

Bubbly Brit Bird: oh my phil. i miss you. i miss you. pls don't go.

Pest Control: i'm sorry. i wasn't avoiding you. never would do that. just v. sick, that's all.

Bubbly Brit Bird: pls, phil. tell me if there's anything I can do. anything at all.

Pest Control: just play a few hands with me now. that's all i want. we'll play. okay?

14

Ice Cold

A rriving in London on a cold and gusty Friday morning, I took a taxi to the unspectacular five-floor Royal Brompton Hotel where my drearily appointed room looked onto a narrow sidestreet on which stood an Indian restaurant, a fish and chips joint, a French bakery and launderette.

I permitted myself that day and the weekend to take in the city. The plan was: three days of tourist stuff; then five days of solid nonstop writing; then Artsy would arrive.

I stuck to my draconian diet, having only white rice for dinner the first night. During the day I walked about fifteen miles, all in a frigid wind. As I walked, small scraps and then whole sections of Book I of the *Trilogy* came back to me, word by word, paragraph by paragraph.

I didn't miss poker at all.

Saturday it got colder, but I went to three museums and ate a half a scone in the morning and more white rice at night. I was hungry but resisted the impulse to eat, even with the curry, croissant, and fish and chip aromas drifting in from across the street. The second day I walked nineteen miles and on Sunday I did it again. By evening my lips were chapped and my back and calves throbbed with an invigorating agony.

I would stop now and then at shops, cafés, etc. (Every once in a while an Internet café would pop up but I walked by; I didn't want to put myself in a situation where one click could bring me to a table.) All the bookstores, I'd noticed, had this one particular book in the windows; it was written by a writer I'd never heard of before,

Gerald Waverly, and was called *Nuts*. I must have seen a hundred copies before it dawned on me I was looking at the same book each time. It had a picture of a hand of poker on the cover . . . yet even then I didn't think of poker.

By Sunday night I must have walked fifty miles, and I took a bath so hot I thought it might set off the hotel's sprinkler system. Was it my imagination or were my corduroy pants hanging looser? The last thing I saw before going to bed was the snow starting to fall, slashing down on the empty street and the awnings below.

♠ ♠ ♠ ♠

I woke up Monday and trudged two miles through the falling snow and the two feet of already fallen snow to the library in Kensington. The whitened city was turning whiter, but I couldn't wait to sit down and get started, and it was if the decades had never passed and I'd been sitting in the library only the day before, forging my groundbreaking masterpiece.

CLOSED TODAY DUE TO BLIZZARD, a sign on the library door said.

I began another long walk and bought a heavy-duty parka and tundra-strength winter boots on Oxford Street. At twilight the snow stopped falling, and the layer on the ground, with the light dying on it, turned toothpaste blue. Icicles formed on Westminster Abbey and the Victoria Albert Museum and by late evening the snow was dark gray. I stopped into an Internet café on King's Road, but not to play poker. There was only one e-mail of note; it was Beverly Martin telling me to contact Susan Jessup, the young authoress who idolized me.

That evening I called Greg Nolan of Norwich Cairn and left a message on his voicemail, asking him if he'd set up a reading for me and if so where and when.

On the way to the library the next morning I stopped into a bookshop that was just opening up. I picked up a copy of *Nuts: How I Bluffed, Deceived, Scammed, and Defrauded Strangers,*

*Enemies and Very Good Friends and Lied to Just About Everybody
and Won £2 Million Playing Poker.* Below the title was the phonetic
pronunciation of the word "nuts" and three definitions—it was
styled like a dictionary entry. The first definition read "in poker,
the very best hand possible." The second was "testicles, bollocks."
The third definition was one word only: "insane." I read the jacket
and discovered that this Gerald Waverly had written a "searing,
scathing, scalding and hilarious" memoir about online poker. To
protect his identity, his face was not revealed in the jacket photo:
the tall stacks of pounds, euros, yen, and dollars in his hands clev-
erly concealed his face.

A few miles later, I turned onto Kensington High Street, which
was bereft of its usual bustle. Sooty snow had already been plowed
from the street and was piled onto the sidewalk. As I walked, I felt
a sudden throe of extreme existential hollowness and stopped and
examined myself in the ice-glazed window of a shoe store. I had on
my backpack, gloves, sunglasses, and scarf. Something crucial was
missing though. I resumed walking, feeling even more hollow than
before, and realized what it was: my laptop. I was suffering from
Phantom Limb Syndrome.

The library was open.

I sat down at a table on the second floor, took out my pens and
pads, and wrote the words "Things were very bad then but still we
carried on." I looked at it, crossed it out. Now, just because I'd begun the Troika that way so many years ago, why did it still have to
begin the same way? I could write it another way—Martin Tilford
be damned—so I wrote: "We still carried on then but . . ."

As I toyed around with rearranging the words, I noticed another
table, the long side of which was flush against a wall. There were
computers on this table and library users were accessing the Internet. I swallowed and could almost hear cards shuffling and chips
clattering and I felt like a coiled-up cobra hearing the first chirps
of a snake charmer's flute.

I was writing "Then things were very bad but . . ." (and thinking of "Ishmael, call me.") when my cell phone buzzed: it was, I saw, someone from Norwich Cairn. I couldn't take the call in the library, so I put my coat on, went outside—it was snowing again—and played the message.

"Hello, Frank, this is Penelope Something calling from Norwich Cairn. Yes, you're on for a reading. Be at the Leaky Crank Pub at eight o'clock Thursday night. It's a very nice venue. Ask for Nigel Somebody and he'll tell you what to do. We put a rather large advert in *The Pavement* newspaper last week. Also, Greg had to leave town at the last moment to attend the Odense Book Fair for a fortnight and I'm afraid he can't have lunch with you. Cheers."

A reading. Thursday night. My first reading ever. Gulp.

Back in the library I began to wonder which book I should read from at the Leaky Crank. There was the funny, poignant London chapter from *Plague*, but the locals might be offended when ill Londoners began dropping like flies. There was any section of *Love*, but that book died a quiet death in the stores and might die a second, much louder death aloud. When I started shuffling, in my mind, through the pages of *Dead on Arrival*, I nearly shot out of my chair when I realized: *Holy shit, I don't have a book to read from!!!*

I stuffed my pads and pens back into my backpack and flew down the stairs and ran out the door. Into the snow to head east, where all the bookstores were.

As I walked through the biting wind, I worked out the time frame: if I called Cynthia and she sent a book to me via FedEx it probably wouldn't get to London in time. I went to every single bookshop on the way, and when I got to Charing Cross Road I hit every bookstore there, too.

At Foyle's Bookshop I told a man behind the counter, "Look, I'm desperate here. I need to get a copy of any book by the American author Frank Dixon as soon as possible."

He returned two minutes later triumphantly bearing *The Shore Road Mystery* and *The Mark on the Door*, and I told him that I was interested in the other Frank W. Dixon, whereupon he handed me

a little pink form and I filled in the name of the books I wanted and
the author's name. Then I had to fill in my own name and phone
number. It was embarrassing to me that Frank Dixon was this desperate to read the complete works of Frank Dixon so I jotted down
the name Lonnie Beale.

"Can you get this to me no later than tomorrow afternoon?" I
asked.

"We will do what we can," he promised me unpromisingly.

My pink form was spiked on top of forty others, and it occurred
to me that they might do what they can but they were also doing it
for dozens of other people and I didn't stand a chance.

I walked up to Bloomsbury, all the while afraid my eyelids
were going to freeze open, to the Regent's Park area, then east
to Clerkenwell, where a good portion of Book 2 of the *American
Nightmare Trilogy* takes place and where I could find no bookstore.

I stopped inside another Internet café somewhere and went online, hoping that some insane fan of mine had posted a chapter or
two of *Love*. There were no chapters and, I was quickly reminded,
there were no fans either.

I logged on to the Galaxy and found Boca Barbie at a table.
"Hey, Chip," she asked me, "have you seen Kiss around today?" I
told her I hadn't played poker for a while and she said: ☹. A few
minutes later APG and I were at a private table. I didn't play. "I
thought you weren't bringing a laptop!" she said and I explained
my whereabouts and why.

I told her that I had a reading and she told me how proud she
was of me. When I asked her if she was still coming she said and
I quote: "I'm with you already, Chip, and our bodies are spent and
raw and we cannot tear ourselves apart from each other. We're
animals!"

I called home that night and told Wifey, who was at work, my
predicament.

"So where were you," she asked, "when it occurred to you that
you didn't have a book?"

"In the library. Why?"

"*Where* were you again, Frankie?"

"In a library." A library!

Just to be safe I gave her the hotel's fax number and told her to fax Chapter 13 of *Plague* and any ten pages of *Love*. "I'm on it!" she said, eager to help.

The following day I would visit every library in London. If that didn't work, maybe Foyle's would come up with a copy. I looked out the window and saw snow pouring down again. I couldn't see anything but snow, and this time it didn't look like it was going to stop.

♥ ♥ ♥ ♥

The next day the libraries were closed again: London had gotten pelted by fifteen more inches of snow and it was eight degrees out. Cars were buried within bone-white monoliths of powder; buses and the tube weren't running. Stiff Upper Lip City's lips had frozen stiff.

True to her word, Cynthia faxed me what I'd requested. But it hadn't come through properly. The pages were smeared and black and the man at the front desk told me the hotel's fax machine had been having problems "for quite some time now."

When I left the hotel the next day I thought: *I could just recite the first chapter of the* Trilogy *by heart . . . if it comes to that.* I knew I could pull it off.

My first stop was the Kensington library. A librarian told me they did have *Plague* but it was out presently on loan. "Do you have *Love: A Horror Story?*" I asked her. She checked and said no. I asked her when *Plague* was due back and she said a week ago. I asked her for a list of every library in central London and quickly got one. When I walked out of the building each and every snowflake looked like typewriter letters falling around me . . . they converged in the air to form the words of Book 1 of the *Trilogy* and I was being deluged in slo-mo by sentences, paragraphs and chapters.

I lumbered over to Foyle's — in vain I tried every library en route—and a different but very similar man there told me they hadn't gotten around to my request yet. "I need that book," I said, "in any way, shape, or form that you can get it." The spike had tripled with pink slips, I saw. "Please," I said, offering him twenty quid, "can you put my request on the top?"

No, he could not. But at least he didn't keep the money.

I looked at the list of libraries and began walking. West, toward Notting Hill. In some places the snow was white, in others, black or gray, and the footing was either crunchy or icy. The quaint Georgian buildings around Regent's Park and Bayswater looked like toy houses, cars skidded or crawled along for fear of skidding, the bitter wind whistled in every direction. Tomorrow night I would—or wouldn't—read from a book, then it was back to writing again. I bent forward as I turned onto Moscow Road . . . somewhere up ahead was a library. The wind died down, but when I stood up straight, I lost my footing—it was as if an incompetent kiddie-birthday-party magician had pulled the ground from under my feet. I fell hard on my knee and thigh and very quickly seven or eight hooded, goose-downed people were looming over me, making sure I was conscious (I was) and hadn't broken anything (I wasn't so sure).

"I'm all right," I said, looking up at their blurred forms and at the sky above them.

"That's going to hurt a lot more tomorrow," one of them warned me.

They helped me up—I nearly fell over again—and then politely shoved me on my way, but the pain in my knee was shooting currents of abject misery down to my toes and up to my neck.

No library had my books. Either the books were out or they'd never had them.

I limped back toward Brompton Road and, on the way home, every step down into the snow sent a wicked jolt through the leg. But I bought a lamp-size bottle of Scotch on the way. In my room I looked at my knee and thought of going to the hospital, but by the

City of San Diego Public Library
Logan Heights Branch

Title: Pocket kings : a nov
Date Due: 7/13/2015,23:59

1 item

Renew at www.sandiegolibrary.org
OR Call 619 236-5800 or 858 484-4440
and press 1 then 2 to RENEW.
Your library card is needed
to renew borrowed items.

time I drank a quarter of the bottle I couldn't make it to the door
and my knee wasn't hurting that much anymore. I called Wifey at
work and told her that no library had my books and that the fax
hadn't come through.

"You're going to have to e-mail me the book," I slurred, "just as
like a contingency plan thing." I was so hungry while I was talking that I was chewing on the pillowcase. "Send me *Dead on Arrival*." She didn't utter a peep so I reminded her, "It's the last book
I wrote. It's on my desktop computer."

I gave her my password and then she said, "Hey, did you hear
about Harry Carver?"

"No, what about him?"

"He sold a screenplay! For almost a million dollars!"

He sold a screenplay . . . a million dollars. Just as I was digesting
that, just as I was realizing that this was the screenplay Harry had
wanted me to write with him, Cynthia added, "And he wrote it
with your other friend Lonnie! Did you know that?"

No, I told her just before saying good-bye, I had no idea.

(No wonder I hadn't been able to contact either one of them
when I was in Las Vegas: they were probably together writing the
screenplay . . . in Las Vegas.)

The bruise on my leg was the shape and color of a map of Green-
land, but I was able to somehow make it to the hallway vending
machine. I got some ice, limped back to my room, and applied it
to my leg and my Scotch. I giggled drunkenly: the injury had been
caused by ice and here I was applying ice. I drank some more whiskey and giggled again.

When I woke up the next morning, a note on Royal Brompton
Hotel stationery had been slipped under the door. It must have
been written by the night desk guy, whose spelling made Ross F.
Carpenter look like a four-time Scripps Howard champion: "Foils
cold and they sad they have copies of yor book."

❖ ❖ ❖ ❖

London was mostly ice now. Trees and traffic lights had fallen onto streets and parked cars from the weight of ice, and a water main in St. James had burst and you could skate on the streets there. All of Whitehall Street, empty and silent and tomblike, looked as if it had been hosed down with crystal.

Foyle's was open and mostly empty and I showed yet another different but entirely similar man there my pink form. He disappeared up some steps. If I read from *Love* the audience would be putty in my hands. I would kill. The London chapter of *Plague Boy* was a bit dicey but would still go over well. And I'd have all of *DOA* to read from. The man was coming back down the stairs, his hands full of paperbacks.

"Here they are," he said. "The complete works of Frank W. Dixon."

In his hands were books in French, German, Italian, Spanish, Japanese. These weren't my books! But wait . . . *they were my books!* These Brits had gotten me the foreign language editions of every book I'd ever had published, but there was no English to be seen. I stood there, my leg aching, my stomach yearning for just a teaspoon of sawdust, and thumbed through a Japanese paperback and shook my head.

"This is it?" I asked. "Nothing in English?"

"No, Mr. Beale."

I picked up the German edition of *Plague* and leafed through it. Could he see my heart sinking? Could he tell how much I despised him? Did he know any German translators?

I bought the books, walked out, and threw them into the first trashcan I found, and even the jaws of that trashcan dripped with jagged fangs of ice.

I walked west, along Oxford Street, then went down through Kensington Gardens, which was lonely, sibilant, and fjordlike. Under the leaden sky the iced-over Serpentine and Round Pond looked as if they'd been filled with concrete, and the mostly black snow crunched underfoot. Back at the Kensington library, I asked the same librarian as the day before if the deadbeat who'd taken out *Plague* had returned it. No, the deadbeat had not.

It was coming on one o'clock and I called Wifey in New York. Seven hours to the reading. Yes, she told me, she had e-mailed *DOA*. I thanked her and she wished me luck. I thanked her again and she came up with another brilliant idea: go to the Norwich Cairn offices . . . they'd probably have copies of my books. *In English*.

The Norwich Cairn offices were all the way in Shoreditch, many miles away, and so I limped back east. (All this walking was great for me . . . my pants *were* hanging looser.)

Norwich Cairn occupied three floors of a remorselessly nondescript flat-brick building. For an edifice so melancholy, though, everything inside was modern and bright. The carpets were orange, the furniture was magenta and sea foam. In the lobby Norwich Cairn's current titles were framed and hung on the wall; there were dozens of them and I remembered how proud I was when one of my books was up there, too.

"Hi," I said to the waify brunette receptionist, "my name is Frank Dixon and . . ."

I wanted her to shriek and hold her hands to her cheeks and say *Oh crikey it's you I read both of your books and I luvved them they were so fanTAStic I nearly pissed me knickers!* But she looked at me vacantly and waited for me to continue.

I told her that Norwich Cairn had published two of my books. No change of expression. I told her I had a reading tonight that Greg Nolan had arranged . . . she lifted an eyebrow a tenth of an inch. I told her that Penelope Somebody had contacted me and I needed to see her right away.

She picked up her phone and I looked through the glass wall behind her, at editors, designers, salespeople, and assistants walking in the hallway, smiling at or ignoring each other. A minute later Penelope was standing right in front of me.

"Frank Dixon!" she said when she saw me.

My coat and hood were still on and I think my eyelashes were dripping melting ice.

I told her I had no book to read from, although I added that my wife had e-mailed me my latest one. "A book," I simply had to get in, "that Greg refuses to read." She told me to sit down and wait and that she'd go get the UK editions of *Plague* and *Love*.

I sat and waited and thought of hamburgers, barbecued ribs, General Tso, hot apple pie. When Artsy got here I was going to take her out to the best places . . . I had already made reservations at six different restaurants, all of them Michelin-starred.

Penelope came back and told me I was out of luck. Norwich Cairn had, she said, "pulped both books." What does that mean? I asked her, picturing a tall glass of orange juice with my books sinking toward the bottom. She explained that the books were out of print and Norwich had handed over the unsold copies for recycling.

"But you're okay for the reading tonight?" she asked me.

I stood and thought about it and, as I did so, saw behind the glass behind the receptionist a man who looked just like Greg Nolan, who was supposed to be at the Odense Book Fair, walk past, coming out of one office and going into another.

"We want you to read there," she said. "People would get interested in you again."

"Uh-huh."

The Odense Book Fair? Really? Was there actually such a thing?

It took three minutes to lay a guilt trip on me about the ad for the reading they'd placed in *The Pavement* before I promised her I'd go through with it.

"And afterwards," she said, "I really do think you ought to see a doctor."

I must have looked like hell because I hadn't even told her anything was wrong.

♣ ♣ ♣ ♣

I had to find a computer-and-printer setup to download *DOA* and knew just where to go: a library with internet access. It was four lousy goddam degrees outside, not including the wind chill, but I hit three libraries and four pubs. But it was like dominoes falling: the libraries were closing one by one, due to the cold weather, just as I hit them. The pubs, however, were not.

I walked back through the park. By 5 p.m. I was on Tottenham Court Road, where I got gouged for a laptop and small printer. I brought my new purchases into a pub in Soho and brooded over three more drinks—it was the happy hour and the place got respectably crowded considering it was now zero degrees out. *I'm going to get the three of us a taxi,* I slurred to my wounded and my good leg, *and take us home. Enough of this walking!* It must have been a sign I'd been drinking a lot that even my thoughts were slurred. But I couldn't find a taxi and had to drag the laptop and printer a few more miles through the flesh-splitting wind.

Back at the hotel I told the desk clerk to arrange a taxi for me promptly at 7:30.

It took me only five minutes to set up my account and get things going. The problem, though, was the Internet. Having courageously insisted on a hotel with no wifi, I was reduced to using the molasses-like modem connection and the phone's data port. *Oh God, what if Cynthia screwed up?* What if she hadn't sent me *DOA* but only thought she had?! I knew I could just recite any part of the *Trilogy* from memory and hopefully wow the trousers off the crowd. When I logged on to my e-mail there it was: *Dead on Arrival,* both as a Word document and a PDF.

When I realized I had no paper to print on, I hobbled back downstairs and told the desk guy I needed paper and saw hail the size of grapes pelting the windows in the lobby. I was given forty sheets of hotel stationery: the paper wasn't the right size and wasn't blank on both sides but it was all I had, and when I went back upstairs I took a long pull from my bottle of whiskey. I put the paper in the printer and pushed PRINT but the paper got

TED HELLER

jammed. I fished it out, tried again. Another jam. Another pull. I tried to print again and a page came out, but it was illegible. *Aha!* I believed I knew what the problem was and I adjusted a few things and pressed PRINT again. Two pages glided out as gracefully as a champion pairs dancing team taking to the ice, and then my phone rang.

"I'm afraid, sir," it was the guy at the desk telling me, "that we were not able to get you a taxi due to the weather."

"And you're telling me this *now?!*" I yelled. Forty-five minutes to the reading.

I slammed the phone down. I'd have to walk to the Creaky Lank or whatever it was called. And I'd have to start out in a few minutes. I selected twenty pages to print and began to change clothing. I was gazing at the now grape-jelly-colored bruise on my thigh when I heard a violent thwacking noise . . . it was my printer choking on twenty pages of paper all at once.

It wasn't going to work.

I'd have to, I now realized, recite Chapter One of Book I of the *Trilogy* and I changed, secreted what was left of the whiskey into mouth and into my new parka, and got going. *What I'm going to read now,* I would announce, *was something that I originally wrote here in London many years ago and have returned to London to write again. I hope you like it.*

I limped through the dark and deserted frigid streets and arrived only ten minutes late. By the time I got there my bottle was empty. And so, pretty much, was the Leaky Crank.

♠ ♠ ♠ ♠

Things now begin to take an unfortunate turn.

I approached the tall, thin blond bartender, who told me in an offhand manner that he was Nigel, and I ordered a Scotch and told him I was Frank Dixon. Neither relieved, overjoyed, nor interested to hear this, he said, "Yes, so?" I told him that I was here to read my book. He poured the Scotch, looked at me and said, "So where's your book then? . . . Start reading!" He assumed, I could tell, that I was going to just open up a book and start reading to myself.

It wasn't your classic London pub, it was more like a student lounge in a community college. Large, dumpy chairs and couches, wobbly wooden coffee tables and side tables, floppy chenille pillows, stained dhurries on the floor, posters for plays that had closed ten years ago. The jukebox was on, and there were only six people present, four men and two women, not including the staff (Nigel and his barmaid, a slatternly, raven-haired woman). One of the patrons resembled Frank Lloyd Wright at his most imperious looking—he had the *Telegraph* on his lap and was murmuring to himself. It wasn't a promising picture.

"No, I have a *public* reading to do here," I said to Nigel. "Didn't Penelope from Norwich Cairn call to arrange this?" He summoned over Moira, the raven-haired slattern, and they chatted, then he came back to me and said, "There was a call like that, but we're not really so keen on that sort of booky stuff here."

"I came to London strictly for this reading," I lied. "They told me they put a rather large advert in some paper called *The Pavement?*"

At his table Frank Lloyd Wright, probing his ear with a long, slender finger but still able to listen in, let out a guffaw that readjusted the ice in my tumbler.

"*The Pivement?*" Nigel echoed incredulously. "That's a newspaper for homeless people!"

Well, the homeless read too, I wanted to tell Nigel. Instead I pointed to the patrons and said, "For all we know, these people could be here to hear me read."

"Who, them?" he said, pouring me another drink. "No, they're always here."

Moira chimed in good-naturedly: "Oh, Nige, let 'im read 'is book!"

I said, "I'll read but do I have to pay for my drinks?" He shook his head and I said, "Then can I have another?" He poured and I said, "Can you at least turn off the music for this?"

Why did this have to happen to me? Why did I ever want to be a writer? Not only was I a battering ram, I was also the wall the thing was battering. The best thing that could have ever happened to me would have been if I'd just failed outright. Or better yet, I should never have committed one word to paper. This perverse desire of mine to matter was destroying me.

Moira got up in front of everyone, brushed her black hair back with her hand, clanked a pint glass with a knife and said, "Awright, everybody, we got a real special guest here tonight who flew all the way from Amerryca just to read. 'is name is . . . What's your name again?"

I stammered out my name, and the door opened and a couple, all bundled up, blew in. Moira said to them, "Jeff! Anna! Are you 'ere for the reading?" and Anna answered, "What reading?"

I staggered over to a patch of dimly lit space between two couches. Moira said to Nigel, "Nige, turn the music OFF!"

"What I'm going to read now," I announced in a Dewars-mellowed tone, "was something that I originally wrote here in London many years ago and have returned to London to write again. I hope you like it." Frank Lloyd blurrily folded his *Telegraph* and clasped his long hands on his table.

"I hope I like it too!" another man sitting by himself said to a chuckle or two.

"Ohhh, Trev!" Frank Lloyd moaned to him. "Will you please shut up for once in your godforsaken insufferable life! Everyone is so bloody tired of it!"

The Clanky Reek Pub was whirling. But I began . . .

"Things were very bad then but still we carried on. Time is a . . ."

It didn't sound right.

I said, "Let me try that again." I thought a beat and then said, "Then things were still very bad but we carried on. Time is a funny thing . . ." That didn't sound right either.

I took a deep breath, closed my eyes, opened them and began again.

"We then carried things on very bad but . . . No. The very things we carried then were still but bad. A funny thing is time . . ."

I had the undivided attention of everyone except for Moira, who was vigorously polishing a side table. It was time to move on to the next sentence, which was . . . which was . . .

There was a second sentence—it was out there somewhere, I'd written it, it did exist—but it wasn't coming to me. (Ironically, it had something to do with the quirky nature of time and memory.) It quickly occurred to me that I could just segue into the first sentence of Book 2 of the *Trilogy* and I did so, but lost the thread right in the middle of it, whereupon I remembered the second part of the first sentence of Book 3, so I cut and pasted them together to form one whole unlovely unit. My mind racing, I dashed to a fine sentence I'd remembered earlier in the day in the park and said it aloud: "And then I saw famous Round Pond for the first time, which was just that, a round fucking pond." After that, nothing came to me. Not a syllable. "You Don't Have to Say You Love Me" by Dusty Springfield came on—to *that* I could remember all the words—and had this been a Hugh Grant or Colin Firth romantic comedy I would have begun singing along and everybody would have joined in and adored me. Roll credits.

"And that," I announced sheepishly to all present, "is as far as I've gotten. But . . . but when I finish it I would love to come back to London and read it to you."

There was a smattering of applause from everyone, led by Moira, who'd tucked her rag and Lemon Pledge into her armpits just so she could clap.

I went back to the bar, ordered another drink and sunk my head into my hands.

Oh, Lonnie Beale, why hath I forsaken thee?

"This one," Nigel said, "I'm afraid I've got to charge you for."

I drank it and reeled to the door to leave. Had I not been

drinking, I think I still would have been reeling. Outside, the ground was frozen and the night was silver, ghostly, and daunting. As I gazed into this Shackletonian bleakness, Frank Lloyd Wright called out: "When you finish your book, I'll be sure to buy a copy."

I believe he really meant it.

♥ ♥ ♥ ♥

The next morning I limped down to a hospital on Royal Hospital Road, where I was X-rayed, given thirty ultra-powerful prescription painkillers, and told I had a "savagely deep" thigh bruise and a "horribly brutal" hairline fracture.

I didn't go to the library that day. I stayed inside my room and grooved on the awesome opiate high. I don't know if the pills were supposed to kill the pain or simply make me not care about it. In the end, I don't know which one happened.

Tomorrow my mistress was coming!

I nodded out with a bag of ice over my leg, and when I woke up I thought I'd urinated in the bed and was appalled. When I realized it was merely the melted ice, I took two more pills.

The snow and ice outside were melting. The temperature had risen to a balmy thirty-eight degrees.

Coated with sweat I crawled out of bed around dinnertime and went online and Googled "Odense Book Fair" and found there indeed was such a thing and that Greg Nolan had been in attendance . . . three months ago. Then I looked up *Nuts* on Amazon U.K. It had only been out two weeks but was, at that minute, ranked twelfth. "An engaging and thoroughly ferocious read," the *Observer* called it. Poker Book Lover, from Wigan, had given it three stars and said: "I would have given this book five stars but Gerald Waverly comes across as so despicable, scheming and heartless that, in the end, I felt let down. Is there really scum like this out there? He makes Bernie Madoff look like Mother Teresa."

Amazon itself weighed in:

AMAZON.CO.UK REVIEW

In his riveting memoir, Gerald Waverly, a self-professed "scheming sociopath, morally bankrupt confidence man, irredeemable oenophile and pathological liar" describes with bracing, nearly toxic wit how he used every devious trick in the book to win unfathomable amounts of money playing poker online. "I am the sort of nasty chap," he warns us, "who when a woman tells me she recently got engaged, thinks of slicing her finger off for the ring." Not for the squeamish, Waverly lets fall not one droplet of sweetness or sentiment. "These people weren't people," he writes of his marks, "they were suckers, fools, bank accounts waiting to be emptied." And empty them he does. Going to hysterically elaborate lengths to cultivate friendships in order to destroy them, using an hilarious assortment of guises and tactics, the pitiless Waverly (he informs us he has a first at Cambridge in physics) confesses that the only tricks "I would not stoop to defraud another player were the ones that I had not yet thought of, and those were few." By the end, Waverly ends up a millionaire, but it is he whose moral bank account has been emptied. Whether he realizes this or not is conveniently never mentioned.

It took me about three minutes of poking around to find out who Gerald Waverly's editor was: Greg Nolan at Norwich Cairn.

I went into the Galaxy. But not to play. I found Second Gunman, who'd just won, he told me, $3K from Bjorn 2 Win in one hand, and I told him where I was and why. I found Kiss My Ace and told him that the other day Boca Barbie had been looking for him. "She found me," he said.

I took three pills that evening, only two more than the recommended dose, and fell into a long fantasy/dream: I was at a fabulous PEN pool party at an exclusive resort in St. Barts; my date was Artsy Painter Gal, and all the writers, artists, and VIPs loved her. Richard Ford, Jonathan Safran Foer, Michael Chabon, Gary Shteyngart, and the rest of them were there, drinking and lingering around the starlit pool and talking books, art, politics, and book contracts. Near a trellised wall Adam Gopnik and Anäis Nin were making out, and cavorting near the diving board were a naked Sal Rushdie and a naked Marty Amis and also naked James Frey and his naked date . . . who was the one and only Lilly! He was wheeling her around in a red wheelbarrow in the rain, and even though she was dead she was the life of the party. Damien Hirst came over and shook her hand and she thanked him for doing such a marvelous job preserving her. *You finally made it, Chip,* APG said to me. *Great job.* The Mitch Alboms were there; not Mitch Albom and a wife, but Mitch Albom and his very own deceased self, a sportswriter angel who'd descended from Heaven just for this shindig. Jonathan Franzen traipsed over with a blonde under each arm, and they had an Oprah Book Club sticker on each nipple. *Great job, Frank,* he said to me. *Great job.* Safran Foer or Dave Eggers came over and started talking in tiny footnotes that appeared at his ankles. He told me[4]. . . . I asked him, *Huh? What do you mean?* and he said[5] . . . and walked away. Then James Frey wheeled Lilly over to me and she said to me, *Did you hear about Jill Conway's new book?* (For a mangy, pathetic crackwhore who'd committed suicide, she didn't look half-bad.) *No, Lilly,* I said to her, *I haven't. It's another book about food,* she told me. *The book actually eats itself page by page as you read it! It's going to turn postmodernism on its stomach.* Molly Bloom, naked on a chaise longue and sipping a melting margarita, said to me, *Yes, Frank, great job, yes, Frank, great job, great job, yes.* I asked Artsy, *What have I done? Why is everyone saying great job?* and she smiled and said, *This is your book party! You're the guest of honor! Your poker memoir got published!* "But I didn't write a poker

---

4. "Great job, Frank. Really, just a great job."
5. "Great job. Seriously, man, congratulations."

memoir!" I tried to say but couldn't. Suddenly the party was over, and workers were sweeping up bottles, glasses, other orgiastic detritus, and all the scattered footnotes into dustpans, and I snapped out of it in my sweatsoaked sheets and it was Saturday morning in London and in a few hours the real Artsy Painter Gal would be landing at Heathrow.

◆　◆　◆　◆

It was all a big misunderstanding. That's what it was.

I ate my half a scone, then gathered my possessions, including my notebooks and new laptop and printer, and moved into the double room, which had a nice view of lively Brompton Road. I took a shower—and I badly needed one after the previous clammy day.

By noon APG hadn't shown up and I began to panic, but only just a bit. Planes were landing at Heathrow but there were many long delays.

At four I went to the Galaxy to see if she'd sent me an e-mail saying she'd changed her mind. There was no such e-mail.

Afraid to leave the room in case she showed up and found me absent, I didn't even get my usual portion of rice that night. I just stayed in the room. Although I did start eating British candies from the hallway vending machine at regular half-hour intervals.

The phone rang at eight fifteen and I ran to pick it up. *Darling,* I expected to hear APG say breathlessly, *there was a terrible foul-up with the flight and I'm in Cardiff now but will be in your arms in two hours.* But it was a man's voice on the other end: his name was Jean-Luc and he was calling from Gordon Ramsay's and wondering why my party of two hadn't shown up for dinner. "Because my party died today!" I said before I hung up on him.

I stayed in the room the next day and paced and paced and finally at noon took three more pills. At three the phone rang and it was someone from the River Café calling to confirm my reservation for two that night. "We'll be there," I promised her.

Outside the street was bustling and sunny even though all of London was turning into black, crystally mire. The Great Thaw. It was Sunday afternoon and people were out and shopping and slogging through what looked like ankle-high caviar.

I went online. There was no e-mail. I kept going online. Nothing.

Had Mr. Artsy Painter Gal found out about our assignation and thwarted the whole thing? Most of me hoped it was true: I longed to be with my loving wife in our comfortable home and wished I'd never set this absurd tryst up.

Two more pills and a few hours later I went onto the Galaxy, and there she was at a table in High, nonchalantly playing with four other people. She had just raked in $5,500 — the cost of a first-class round trip airfare from L.A. to London — with a full boat, Queens full of 9s.

I stayed out in the ether and didn't play.

Chip Zero: NH.
Artsy Painter Gal: Thnx.
Chip Zero: Can you meet me at a PT asap?
Artsy Painter Gal: You know I'd follow you anywhere, baby!

A minute later it was just Artsy as the Icy Blonde and me as the Big Man at a table.

Chip Zero: So, uh, where are you?
Artsy Painter Gal: You know where I am.
Chip Zero: Where?
Artsy Painter Gal: I'm in London! With you!
Chip Zero [looking around and not seeing her anywhere in London]: You *are?*
Artsy Painter Gal: Yep. Where are YOU?
Chip Zero: I'm in London too. When did you get here?!
Artsy Painter Gal: At 9 a.m. yesterday just like I said I would, baby.
Chip Zero: What room are you in?
Artsy Painter Gal: I'm in your room of course!

WTF?!?! Was she in the single room that I'd abandoned a few hours before?

Chip Zero: I'm in Room 325 now.

Artsy Painter Gal: So am I. I'm with you, baby.

Chip Zero: I'm in London. I'm in Room 325. I'm here at the Royal Brompton Hotel. It's Sunday. I'm here.

Artsy Painter Gal: And I'm with you. And it's 80 degrees and sunny out, baby. And Mr. Artsy Painter Gal is with the kids in L.A. and Mrs. Chip Zero is doing whatever.

Chip Zero: Uh-huh. And?

Artsy Painter Gal: And we had a wonderful dinner at Gordon Ramsay's last night and you and I made love all night and we walked all around today and went shopping. We cuddled tight in the room and tonight we're going out to dinner again and we'll do it all day and all night, baby. And tomorrow I'm going to paint while you write.

I had to quickly decide: do I take the moral high road here and make her think I was in New York after all and hadn't really come to London and wasn't in room 325 at the Royal Brompton and had not ever seriously believed we were actually going to commit adultery, or do I take the ignoble subterranean route and let her know where I am and plunge her face into a toilet bowl of guilt and reproach and flush the bowl over and over again? Do I just let her have it? I could, I realized, simply play her game, the talking-dirty-in-the-present-tense fantasy game, and say something like, "Yes, last night was wonderful, darling. You're with me now and I'm kissing you and holding you tight, lover." I'd definitely be saving face if I did that.

Nah. I let her have it.

Chip Zero: JESUS FUCKING CHRIST, I AM REALLY HERE! I AM IN LONDON RIGHT NOW BITCH AND I THOUGHT YOU WERE REALLY COMING TO BE WITH ME GODDAMMIT!!!!!!!!!!!!!!!!!!!!

Artsy Painter Gal: No! Oh God.

Chip Zero: YES!

Artsy Painter Gal: I'm sorry. Oh I'm so sorry. I feel terrible. Are you really there?

Chip Zero: Yes!!!!!!!!!!!!!!!!!!!!!!!!!!!!

Artsy Painter Gal: ☹☹☹☹

Yes, a great big misunderstanding.

I took three pills, ate some more candy, and took the tube to the River Café and told the maître d' when I checked in that I'd be only one that night.

♣ ♣ ♣ ♣

I moved back into the cheaper single room and stayed two more weeks, just as I'd planned, and never went to the library or wrote another word. But I did return, two times, to the hospital to renew the prescription, and it occurs to me now that the happiest times in my life weren't when I was happy at all but was when I was just too fucked up to be sad.

I rarely left the room except to eat . . . and I ate huge portions and drank well. I stuck to the story: to every nosy maître d' who asked me why I was one and not two, I replied, "Because my party died."

Monday night, the day after I realized I'd been stood up, I fell asleep but woke up in the middle of the night. Someone or something—Wifey, a tarantula, a Moors Murderer, a large rat, Artsy—was in the room with me. Whatever it was, it occupied the chair against the wall. I was too afraid to turn the lights on to look. It was breathing, pulsing, emitting heat, it was alive, and in the darkness the thing kept getting bigger and was taking over the room . . . it was like the apple in the Magritte painting and was going to overwhelm me or eat me alive.

It was the new laptop.

I began playing poker again. Morning, afternoon, night. I didn't stop except to eat or shower and I wasn't, I confess, doing too much showering. I had obscenely good luck . . . it bordered on cruelty what I was doing to other players, but I kept at it. And I relished it.

If I was logged on, Artsy Painter Gal didn't come on. Of course not. She was as horrified as I was. Albeit for completely disparate reasons.

After a week of playing and winning tons and tons of money, I logged on one day as the Suburban Mimetic. I didn't want APG to know I was around. Sure enough, there she was, at a table in Medium. Calm, cool, collected. I played a few hands with her. The next day I won over five grand from her with three Aces, which I played with slow-cooked, sadistic perfection. "Nice hand, Suburban!" she said to me, "but not so nice." I waited a second and said, "thnx."

The next day I discovered her at a table with Cali Wondergal, History Babe, Toll House Cookie and a few others. Wolverine Mommy showed up and . . .

Wolverine Mommy: Hey, guys!

Toll House Cookie: Hey, Wolve.

Wolverine Mommy: Anyone seen Chip Zero around?

History Babe: No, not for a while. APG?

Arty Painter Gal: I think he may have gone away for a while.

I had only two days left in London and couldn't wait to go home. After an enormous meal in Mayfair I came back to the room with some take-away curry and fish and chips from across the street and logged on again as the Suburban Mimetic. I found APG in Medium and played with her and six other people. I didn't say a word. Kiss My Ace joined the table, said hello to Artsy and played a few hands. I won $700 with Kings and 5s. Kiss My Ace asked APG, "Hey, is Chip around?" "No," she answered, "haven't seen him." The cards were dealt, then she asked him, "Where's Boca?" He answered: "At work right now. No computer access." She shot him back a ☺.

After the next hand Artsy Painter Gal suddenly vanished, followed, a second later, by Kiss My Ace.

A minute later they were at a private table and were all over each other.

15
Just a Game

The human brain, the most splendid, obvious proof there is that Charles Darwin might have been on to something, isn't born wanting, needing, or knowing about gambling, cocaine, alcohol, or cigarettes, but let it lose a hundred bucks in a slot machine, or lay out a few lines on a mirror, etc., and soon it won't think of anything else. Work, children, health, food, sex, and responsibility all take a distant back seat. The unknowable, intricate, gray tripartite wonder that came up with the wheel, *King Lear*, pizza, the lightbulb, the Little Black Dress, the Infield Fly Rule, *North by Northwest,* and "A Day in the Life" is reduced to three pounds of useless mashed potatoes. Soon you will be robbing your mother, defrauding your father, selling your wife, and emptying your kid's piggy bank. The addicted Homo sapiens is the only animal who realizes it is an addict and would ever make an attempt to recover—would any self-respecting coke-snorting rhesus monkey ever check its hairy ass into rehab?—and thus these brilliant noble creatures are the only animals who fail at it. We think we're kings of the jungle but aren't really such bad-asses after all. It doesn't take much to bring us down to rhesus-monkey size: a hit of Vicodin, a glass of fermented barley, a chocolate bar, a skim latte, a pair of expensive shoes, or a round of Mortal Kombat or golf.

I can either gamble and not write or I can write and not gamble. Even though when I gamble I win and when I write I lose.

At least I know I have a problem. That's half the game, isn't it?

♠ ♠ ♠ ♠

I returned from London on a Monday afternoon, jet-lagged out of my wits. I called Cynthia at work, but her voicemail kept picking up. When she didn't come home that night, I called her cell and left her a message ("I'm *baaaaaack*"), but she didn't call. My e-mails went unanswered too. I kept checking but was too out of it to think straight.

The only message that showed up came from Susan Jessup. "Hey you, Frank Dixon!" her e-mail began. "Attached please find MY VERY OWN FIRST NOVEL! Woohoo!" She told me how important my first book was to her (she had even, she said, read my second); I wrote back telling her I'd look at hers. I skimmed the first chapter and read the second and—unbelievably—it was pretty good.

I'll do what I can to help, I wrote her. Just give me some time.

I fell asleep thinking that Cynthia would slink into the bed in the middle of the night and fill me with the comfy warmth that any exhausted traveler needs upon his return. When I woke up at about 3 a.m. and she wasn't there, I panicked and thought of calling the police. But I fell back asleep.

I woke up and played poker, and right after the sun rose, I did something I thought I'd never do: I e-mailed Deke Rivers at Last Resort Press. I thought he would wait a few days to get back to me and that we'd make an appointment to meet in a week, but he got back to me a few minutes later and said I could swing by his office at two that day. He told me to send him *Dead on Arrival* right away. "I'll hop all over that puppy, Frank," he wrote. This for me was scraping the brackish depths of a sewer with a butter knife, and I felt like a two-star general who became a bellhop just because he liked wearing epaulettes.

I took a long, hot shower and imagined myself as a low-level Mafia guy in a dead-end alley somewhere in New Jersey. We were just outside the DeLillo Sausage Factory at midnight and the stench of offal was rife, and ten other mafiosi were walking slowly toward me carrying baseball bats . . . they wore violet Adidas tracksuits and were going to beat my brains out: Herman Melville, F. Scott Fitzgerald, and the Jonathans and Davids and Brett Jay McEllisses were coming for me . . . they were going to feed me half-alive into the meat grinder and turn me into sausage. "Don't do it, guys, please," I begged. They came closer and I cried: "You can't do this to me! I'm a made guy!" Fitzgerald and Safranzeneggerthemgart weren't impressed so I reminded them, "I've had two books published!" The sausage grinder started up behind the brick wall and they raised their bats and I yelled out, "YOU CAN'T DO THIS TO ME! MY FIRST BOOK GOT A B-MINUS IN *ENTERTAINMENT WEEKLY*!!! IT WAS ONE OF THE *DES MOINES REGISTER*'S TEN BEST BOOKS OF THE YEAR. YOU CAN'T! GUYS, I'M CORUSCATIN'!!!" It didn't matter . . . they were taking their Louisville Sluggers to my head and kicking my ribs in, and inside the factory the grinder was spinning and humming for me.

There was no sign of Wifey. I phoned her father's office, but he was, his secretary told me, out of town; I tried her mother in West Virginia, but she wasn't home. Worried now, I headed out for the meeting at one thirty. As soon as the meeting was over I would make every phone call possible to find her and, if need be, go to the police. It was possible, I knew, she'd had to go out of town on business, or maybe her mother had needed her suddenly.

Getting off the elevator, I felt like I was doing the shabbiest thing I'd ever done . . . it was like a coed in the 1950s going to get a back-alley abortion or a forty-five-year-old perv meeting a twelve-year-old he'd been having online sex with. Last Resort Press was comprised of four small offices and a reception area. It could have been a dental suite at one point; all the other offices on the floor belonged to dentists, orthodontists, endodontists, or other mouth-based people. I checked in with the receptionist and sat down next to a slender woman with large black eyes and eyelashes, black leather everything and long, straight metallic black hair. It was obvious she was an eccentric, self-obsessed poetess, and I went through all sorts of yogic contortions in my seat to let her know I didn't want to talk.

Deke came out and we shook hands. (His grip was reassuring, All-American, and frightening.) Square head, an overgrown, graying crew cut, ruddy complexion, a tobacco-brown suit. He could have been the head of about six hundred different small-town chambers of commerce.

"I've already knocked off a hundred and sixty pages," he told me when I sat down in his cluttered office. Deke spoke with a gruff voice and had to clear his throat every ten words.

"Then you've come to the—" I began.

"The part when the wife and kids die? Oh yes. This is solid stuff."

Was he going to ask me why had I come to him, why I couldn't get it published elsewhere, and how much I was willing to pay to have it published? How did this vanity press business work?

"This is professional grade, Frank," he said. His feet were on top of three manuscripts on his desk and there was a speckled wad of gum on the sole of one of his Wallabies. By imagining myself in a large vise I was able to keep from squirming. "I'd really love to publish this. It's just A-one, top-drawer material."

"Thanks." The vise tightened and my shoulders were starting to crimp.

I wanted to know what Last Resort would *not* publish. There were book covers on the walls: *The Reasons for My Suicide* by Ginny Pierson, *A Middletown Childhood* by Victor Blumberg, *Destroying Planet Earth* by Zarbakon-VI, and a book I wouldn't have minded reading called *The 152 Chicks I Did and the 12 I Didn't and Why* by Vinnie G. If a Park Avenue society matron got her poodle a computer and the dog hammered out gobbledygook for three years, would Last Resort publish it? Did they ever actually edit anything, suggest changes, cut something? If a ranting psychotic came in off the street with all his ravings on 10,500 single-spaced, drool-drenched pages, would they print all twenty volumes as is?

On the other hand, though, maybe this was every single novelist's wet dream. No suggestions, no cuts, no interference. Total tamper-proof, uncontaminated, free-range fiction.

"I'd like," Deke said, "to recommend a few changes though, Frank."

"Okay. Shoot."

"For instance, how would you feel about maybe nine-elevening it up?"

Right away I knew what he meant. And I wasn't shocked. For months, from editors and publishers, I had expected this suggestion. Simple nonclever stories about human beings and their travails weren't enough anymore. If it was going to click, it had to be written by an exotic multicultural woman or a Harvard-educated, snarky male media darling or a silver-tongued, dagger-witted, snaggletoothed, Johnny Depp–cheeked, Oxbridge-educated Brit; or it had to be about 9/11, or about immigrants assimilating in the U.S. and struggling charmingly with American things like shopping malls, cable TV, ATMs, and Jell-O, or about ex-pats hitting it big in the Moscow underworld, or about rich blondes exfoliating at Bergdorf's, or about a girl's sexual relationship with her father or growing up in a zany New England family or meeting the lovable transgender lifesaving dogs of dead sportswriters in Heaven, or about being raised by crack-smoking truckstop wolf whores and Bloods and Crips in order to escape Nazis.

"You want, I take it," I said (and already he was nodding), "the wife to die, not in a car crash as I have it now, but to die on September Eleventh, is that it?"

"Think about it. It'd really grab the critics that way."

"So the wife is in the Twin Towers. She's at work, she gets killed, the husband gets the call or he sees it on TV. But everything after that . . . it stays the same?"

He took his feet off the desk, leaned forward and said: "Or there's this. And it just struck me this instant. Now, believe me we do this a lot and, considering your famous Hardy Boys name,

maybe it'd be a mistake. But we change your name. You write it . . .
as a woman. You're Felicity, you're LaKeesha or Candy. Make up
a last name. Berkowitz, Jackson, MacTavish. You wouldn't believe how popular the name Felicity is among female readers—we
focus-group these sorts of things and the numbers are through the
roof. Or we go with something exotic like, say, Boompha Jalalabad.
You know, you jump on that Jhumpa Lihiri–Azar Nafisi–Thrity
Umrigar *What I Talk About When Kite Running in Tehran* band-
wagon. And we could change all the genders around. It's about
a housewife whose *husband* gets killed on nine-eleven and *she*
lives it up afterwards. She starts doing all the same things . . . you
know, sleeping around, drinking, drugging, and gambling and
everything."

"So instead of my male widower sleeping with his dead wife's
sister, now it's a female widow sleeping with her dead husband's
brother and all *his* friends?"

"You got it! Written by Felicity MacTavish or Boompha
Jalalowitz."

Deke Rivers wanted it to be a chick book. Had he leaned forward close enough and had I leaned in, too, I would have seen Kate
Hudson dancing in his eyeballs.

"I'm telling you," he said while I sat there numb and slack, "this
is just what the doctor ordered. They'd eat it up, they really would."

I pictured the illustration on the cover: a thin but chesty, smartly
dressed woman wearing all sorts of expensive pink clothing and
overloaded with pink accessories—Kate Spade handbag, oversized
Gucci shades, Jimmy Choos— blithely applies pink lipstick while
the pink Twin Towers crumble harmlessly around her in a cloud
of bubblegum-pink dust.

Deke told me that he personally could go over the manuscript
and change the names and genders and get it back to me; he said
we could hire the best publicists and send copies everywhere once
the book was printed. I was too stunned by all this to reply and was
on the verge of an outer-body experience (just for relief, my soul

was about to rove across the hallway to an endodontist's office and get a root canal).

Deke walked me out to the elevators. We shook hands, the elevator came, and he asked me to think about his suggestion.

So I pay *you*, I wanted to say, and somehow *I* end up being the whore???

Instead I told him I would think about it.

❤ ❤ ❤ ❤

When I got home Cynthia—to my relief—was sitting on the couch with her legs crossed and the latest copy of *InStyle* on her lap.

"Where were you?" I asked her. "I've been really worried."

"Where do you think?"

"I don't know. At a work off-site? Your mom's?"

"So? Did you get a lot of work done on the *Trilogy*? When do I get a chance to read it?"

"When I put it all together. I have to clean a few things up."

She flipped *InStyle* onto the coffee table and it made a loud clang.

"So tell me . . ." she said. "How long have you and this Artsy Painter Gal been involved? And don't tell me you're not."

"We're not."

All the air around us abruptly vacated the premises.

"Oh, yes you are."

I took my coat off and sat down on the couch, whereupon she stood up and went to the dinner table and sat down there.

"You snuck off to London with your *poker* mistress?!"

"How did you know about this? And it's 'sneaked,' not snuck. And she is not my mistress."

(I could have said "Poker is my mistress" but opted not to.)

"What I know or the fact that I know doesn't interest you . . . it's *how* I found out that fascinates you, isn't it?" I nodded and she went on. "When you asked me to send you whatever the hell that depressing, unreadable book is called, you gave me your password."

I don't know what pissed me off more, my being foolish enough to trust her with my password or her calling my book unreadable. I think it was the former. (Quickly I wondered: *Would Cynthia like* Dead on Arrival *as penned by Boompha Felicity Jalalowitz with the pink cover, expensive accessories and new 9/11 theme?*)

"I read some e-mails," she said. "That's what I did."

I resisted telling her how unethical that was because I knew there was no way I was going to win with that. She explained quickly to me that she had spent the previous night at a Tribeca hotel and was too angry to see me or talk to me.

"I can't believe you sometimes," she said.

"Neither can I. Listen . . . I went to London. That's true. I really did plan to write, I swear. I don't know what you read but I promise you: nothing happened."

"You're lying! You betrayed me."

"I maybe was going to but she never showed up!"

"She didn't show up?"

"No! I swear to God . . . she stood me up! And probably nothing would have happened anyway."

She smiled. The fact that I'd traveled all that distance and spent all that money to cheat but wasn't able to . . . she was loving it.

"Well, I still want you out of here."

"No, you don't."

"I do!"

I wasn't expecting this. I had been planning on a hot romantic two-week tryst that nobody would ever have found out about; now I was being thrown out of my own apartment for an affair that hadn't even happened.

"Please don't do this to me," I said.

"I'm giving you ten minutes. Pack your stuff. Get out."

She didn't smile or scowl, and in a weird way her face looked like the high school yearbook picture of some girl that nobody else in the book remembered at all.

I began packing, slowly at first, but then sped things up when she said, "Eight minutes." Jamming underwear into a suitcase I told her, "Look, I'm a loser," hoping that she'd say to me, "No, you're not!" Instead she said: "Yes, I know." "No," I said, still hoping again that she'd contradict me, "I really am." She said, "Yes, you are. You have accomplished nothing in your entire life." I put a few socks into the suitcase and said, "Hey, I did get those two books published," and she said, "But they didn't sell. Six minutes." "So you really think," I asked, "that I'm a loser?" and she said, "You always tell me you are! And yes, I see now that you're right." A few shirts fell out of the suitcase and I said, "Look at me, I can't even pack. I can't do anything," and she said, "You're right. You're lousy at every single thing you do. And you have five minutes. And I can't stand your new hair, by the way." Incensed, I said, "Hold on . . . you really think that I'm not good at *anything?*" It was hurtful to me that my wife was finally agreeing with me. "Yes, I do!" she insisted. "You're not good at anything." "Oh yes I am!" I said. "Oh, and what's that?" she sniffed. "Poker!" I said.

Four minutes after the echoes of her little snort died down, I was gone.

❖ ❖ ❖ ❖

I moved into a ten-room, $850-a-night *très charmant* hotel on the Upper East Side and stayed there four or five days. Without my laptop. The plan was to purge myself cold turkey of all the pills, booze, gambling, lousy food, and wicked fun. I wanted to see if I could go a few days without playing poker. And I could. But after I checked in I began vomiting and trembling wildly; I had chills and sweated nonstop and wept on and off, and my body was wrenched and twisted and a lifetime supply of mucus kept flowing out of me. I lost track of time and the world, and time and the world lost track of me. I refused housekeeping: every time there was a knock at the door, I called out, "Please just leave me alone!" There were all sorts of fancy shampoos and conditioners that I repeatedly tried to shatter before realizing—it took two days—that the bottles were plastic. I barely made it to the bathroom when I had to go. Until then I didn't think it was physically possible to shit, pee, throw up, sweat, cough, be wide awake yet also be asleep and dreaming, to feel pain and relief all at the same time, but now I know it is.

I called Wifey but she wouldn't pick up. In my mind I wrote gorgeous *Faerie Queene*–length love poems for her but then tore them up and burned the scraps.

I wanted to murder someone but didn't know precisely whom to kill.

Stone cold sober, I urinated my initials on the wall. I also urinated a cross, a swastika, a star of David, and finally a smiley face on the floor near the window. I shouted curses and cruel insults at passersby outside the window and carved my misery into the faux–King Louis the Whicheverth armoire with my fingernails and teeth.

Curled up on the floor and shivering, I believe I may have called Deke Rivers to shoot the breeze. He had read the rest of *DOA*, he told me, and would publish it for a fee to be named later, but he still thought I should "nine-eleven it the hell up" and reverse the genders. I said something about all agents nowadays being interested only in money and not art and how the literary world has changed for the worse, and he said, "It's true, Chip, and it's just a goddamned shame, isn't it?" "Twenty out of twenty agents," I lamented to him, "would rather handle *The Da Vinci Code* than the *Blood Meridian*s of this world, wouldn't they, Deke?" "You're darn tootin' they would, buddy! Frank, they handle *The Da Vinci Code*, these agents'll tell you, so they can afford to handle the *Blood Meridian*s of the world, but uh-uh . . . they handle *The Da Vinci Code* so they can afford their summer homes." He cleared his throat and a quivering jellybean of phlegm oozed out of my phone. "The world, Deke," I said, "has become a bad place." "It's commerce taking over art, that's what it is," he told me. "Just a sad commentary on our times." I thanked Deke for hearing me out and he said, "Any time, Frankie, any time."

I hung up—but maybe that phone call never really happened.

Sometimes that hotel room was spinning slowly one way and I was spinning a lot quicker the other way. At night I thought the patterns on the Egyptian cotton sheets and on the comforter were hearts, diamonds, spades, clubs. Cards were whispering into my ear unspeakably horrific things. The 3 of Diamonds, for example, cackled to me: "Tonight your asshole is going to suck you up and swallow you alive."

My cell phone rang on day three or four and I was so sure it was Wifey calling that I picked up. But it turned out to be Susan Jessup and she sounded liked she was ten and was trying to sell me Girl Scout cookies. So, she said, didja really read my book? I told her I had and that I'd liked it a lot. While I clutched the night table, she asked me if I wanted to meet for a coffee and I said, Okay, sure. She told me she was in New York and it turned out she was only ten blocks away.

We met at a Starbucks and I hadn't done anything to fix my appearance. My stained, sweaty dress shirt was mostly dangling out of my pants, my breath reeked, my skin was a dull, undiscovered color, and if a tick or a louse or cockroach fell out of my hair nobody in Starbucks would have been shocked. Susan was twenty-three years old, the daughter of two teachers, had shoulder-length blonde hair; everything she wore was probably from Express or H&M, and I could tell that the very sight of me in this condition was causing her tremendous discomfort. She squinted and tried to get me in focus, but it didn't happen.

I sounded like I was drunk and hadn't slept in a week, but she never asked me if anything was wrong. Maybe she thought I always was in this shape. Was this for her like me thinking I was going to meet John Lennon but instead having Charles Manson show up?

"So," she said when we sat down, "you really, really liked it?"

"You want to write books? This is what you want to do?"

When she nodded I thought: Wow, if this sweet young girl were my daughter I would be the luckiest, most delighted father alive.

"You're sure about this, Susan? This is the course you're setting for yourself?"

"Yes. This is what I want to do. So? My book? How can I make it—"

"I read some of it, yeah," I mumbled. "But not the whole thing because I don't read books anymore. There's better ways to waste my time. So I guess I lied. And I'm sorry. I liked what I read, but the thing is I'm not going to read it. It's not—it has nothing to do with you, I promise. I'm probably not going to read anything ever again. Now here's my advice." I paused for a deep breath. "*Don't . . . listen . . . to me.* And this isn't against you personally because you seem very nice and very intelligent. For your own sake, just toss it out. Stop writing. Stop reading. Every word you read is a lie. Writers are liars. Pathetic, whiny, uninteresting, self-obsessed, lazy liars. Nobody means what they say anymore except for me right now. *Nobody!* They're worse than politicians. All just a bunch of whores! If you're an honest, sincere person, you won't do this. Please don't do this to yourself! Find something else . . . do charity work . . . build huts for lepers or plant trees or answer phones for PBS or Jerry Lewis! But really, you should just give it up. There's no hope! And that is my advice."

I tried to stand up but tumbled to the floor. I looked up and saw she was in tears. I was in tears, too. *Oh God,* I said looking up at her, *I'm so sorry!* I was trembling again, head to toe. I told her I'd been going through a rough time lately, that my wife had tossed me out of my home, and she grabbed my hand and helped me up and out onto the street.

If not for her I would have fainted, or something worse might have happened, and when we parted two minutes later we were both still sniffling. I promised her I'd be okay.

The next day I checked out of the hotel and left $1,000 for the poor chambermaid, whose supercharged Dyson vac and bottle of Windex would be no match for the fetid havoc that awaited her. I got a *Times* for the taxi ride downtown and read that the movie rights to a book written by a pseudonymous British author had been optioned for $900,000 by Pacer Burton's production company. The book would soon be published in the U.S.A. and was called *Nuts*.

Whether it was cold or mild that day or snowing or a hundred degrees out, I have no idea.

When I got home it was four in the afternoon. I showered and hoped to God Cynthia would take me back and for an hour and a half I rehearsed a summation that Émile Zola, Clarence Darrow, and Johnnie Cochran would be proud of. Yet some part of me wanted her to walk into the apartment with some hunky revenge-fuck lover so I could stand up, point an indignant finger at her and say, "Aha! *J'accuse!*"

When she walked in—alone—she wasn't happy to see me.

"This is difficult for me to say," she said, "considering how much you mean to me, but out means out."

I fell to the floor, grabbed onto her calves, and she said, "It's not going to work."

I stood up and asked her, "Okay, then what will?"

She told me I looked terrible and she cooked me some bland pasta, but she wouldn't sit at the table while I ate it. We stayed silent until the last noodle was down.

"So you have to leave now," she said.

I told her I had nowhere to go, then said: "Give me ten minutes."

I checked into another hotel, then flew to Detroit the following night. (I tried to tell Wolverine Mommy I was coming to Michigan but couldn't find her online.) It was obvious from the roiling sky lowering in on me that it was going to snow. After gorging on five Cinnabons at the airport, I rented a Hyundai Cilantro and drove north. The snow was falling but I made it to the Mackinac Bridge. I kept driving. WELCOME TO PURGATORY, the crooked sign said. I checked into the Purgatory Inn, and Wolve came to visit and that's when I began writing this. This cathartic, redemptive, lifesaving memoir.

♣ ♣ ♣ ♣

Rarely leaving my motel room—where was there to go?—I wrote
for several weeks in Purgatory. It was hard to tell when it was day
or night. I also played poker. And won as usual. But winning wasn't
fun anymore. Even the sadistic thrill of crushing inferiors was gone.

"So are you going to tell me," Wolve asked me one night, "what
happened with you and Artsy?"

"Nothing did," I told her. "It's time to move on."

Artsy Painter Gal no longer existed as such. But Victoria G.
Landreth was out there somewhere, playing under a new alias. I just
knew it. I would spend hours watching players play and chat and
see if I could discern who she was. Sometimes I was sure I'd found
her but then I could tell—from a joke, phrase, a word, a raise, or
a bluff—it wasn't her. I would play at tables and sometimes when
a new player like Ruthless in Seattle, Ickie Vickie, or Little Red
Whorevette joined me, I thought it might be her. Maybe it was. But
she didn't mean anything to me anymore. She was like a case of the
mumps I'd had when I was two. It was just something that happened.
Or didn't happen. The only thing I wanted was my old life back.

Cynthia wasn't taking my calls or answering my e-mails or text
messages. Had I sent smoke signals, she would have ignored those,
too.

But I was writing again. That was a start. And it felt great.
There was hope. And this time the hope didn't involve landing a 6
on the river to complete a gutshot straight.

"Cynthia," I said in one desperate phone message to her, "I'm
writing again! I swear I am. And guess what? It's a memoir. About
this whole mess! That's a good thing, isn't it?"

For all I know she fast-forwarded through that message and
never heard it.

But one afternoon, perhaps five weeks into my Purgatory so-
journ, my motel phone rang. It was Wifey. (Caller ID had tipped
her off as to my phone number.) I was so excited to hear her voice I
almost began to weep. But there was little joy in her voice.

"So where are you exactly?" she asked.

I told her where but left out the Wolverine Mommy part. I repeated that I was writing again but either she didn't believe me or didn't care. A few months ago when I told her that I was writing or had just won $500 playing poker, her face would have lit up. But now? Everything about her was not illuminated. And it was all my fault.

"Look, the reason I'm calling is," she said, "Second Gunman just called—"

"Huh? Johnny? From England?"

"Yes. Him. He called from Blackpool. He said you might be in trouble. Some Swedish man is in New York now, he said, and—"

"*What?!* A Swedish man?"

It was so pleasant hearing her voice that I was having trouble keeping track.

"And he wants to kill you. That's what Second said."

Sweden. Who in Sweden would want to kill me? Who in Sweden wanted to kill *anyone?* Other than Olof Palme, has anyone ever been killed in Sweden?!

"Apparently," she continued, "you won a lot of money from him?"

Bjorn 2 Win. It had to be him, I knew. I'd beaten him for about fifteen grand all in all. He lost so easily to me that sometimes I actually felt sorry for him. It was like taking candy from a baby. For all I knew, he *was* a baby.

"Is it Bjorn? Did Second say it was Bjorn 2 Win?"

"Yes. That was his name."

(No wonder Second was warning me, I thought—he was the one who advised me to play Bjorn whenever I hit a serious losing skid. *He feels responsible.*)

I didn't know what to say. Just the fact that my wife was talking about people named Second Gunman and Bjorn 2 Win was a sign of the walking-talking catastrophe I'd become.

"Well, at least I'm not home in case he finds me."

"But I am! What if he comes after *me?*"

"You didn't beat him at poker. I did."

(Yeah . . . but she *was* wearing the chinchilla coat that cost exactly sixteen grand, paid for with the money I had won off of Bjorn 2 Win and countless others.)

"Don't worry," I told her. "If he really wants to kill me, I'll just give him his money back."

I could give it to Bjorn, I figured, then probably win most of it back from him once he returned home. It was my money after all! Even though it was his.

The wind howled and shook my flimsy door and I asked Cynthia, "Hey, do you want to come out here? I'll pay for the airfare and everything. It's really nice."

There was only silence on the other end.

Just as I begged, "Please take me back!"—right between "take" and "me"—she hung up.

A few nights later Toll House Cookie found me online. He told me he had some news for me and my initial thought was, *Uh-oh, his wife suspects that his nonexistent Cousin Cleon really didn't die and I have to cover for him.* But that wasn't it. He asked me for my phone number and that's when I knew it was serious. He logged off and called me and told me he'd heard on the Galaxy that Bjorn was in New York buzzing around for me.

I didn't know whether to stay hidden in the Upper Peninsula or return to New York.

Marvis gave me a third option. There was a motel near his toll plaza. It was thus only a few yards away from the Holland Tunnel and I would be close to my home, my former home.

"Okay . . . sounds doable," I said to THC. I told him I'd be in New Jersey within two days.

When I hung up I pictured a lugubrious six-foot-eight Swede carrying a hatchet and lumbering around the streets of Manhattan at three in the morning. He was stopping strangers and asking them, "Do you know where is Frank Dixon?"

On my last night in Michigan, Wolve baked me a seven-layer chocolate cake, which she and I ate in less than ten minutes. We kissed on the cheek and said our good-byes and she returned to her three young boys and to nurture the next generation of doctors, civic leaders, fry cooks, and crystal-meth dealers.

The next morning I drove back down to Detroit and flew to Newark. By then—about a month ago—I had won over a half a million dollars. $650,000 in less than a year! A Queen-high straight on the river netted me $14K against the fearsome SaniFlush and put me over $600K. "You're a damn good card player, Chip, you know that?" he told me.

I took a taxi from the airport to the Tunnel Motel. It was a dreary place, right on the highway, the kind of place that millions of people, on their way from New Jersey into New York City, have driven past and gasped, "Oh god, who would ever stay in a place like that?" (The answer is: Me . . . I would.) The last time I had seen this nondescript joint was the previous September, when Second and I came to New Jersey to pick up Marvis to go to Las Vegas. I had no idea that night, of course, that in a few months I'd be holing up there. It had barely registered then, and it was like John F. Kennedy looking across the street and thinking, *Hmm . . . that must be some sort of book depository over there* and then forgetting about it a second later.

I called Cynthia and told her where I was. She told me she hadn't heard from Second, and I assumed the coast was clear and that the Swede was back in Gothenburg chopping up stallions and mares. When I called her again the following morning, she didn't pick up the phone.

On my first night in New Jersey, the traffic outside kept me awake. It sounded like a dying person's wheeze, except the person never does completely die. Temporarily carless, I knew I could walk to the Holland Tunnel and into the city but I wasn't sure if that's permitted and I feared the way the *Times* might report it:

UNSUCCESSFUL AUTHOR PERISHES IN NJ–NY TUNNEL
Poker-Playing "Writer" Felled by Fatal Fumes, Coroner Suggests
Failed Novelist Was on Way Into Manhattan to Make Up With "Wifey"
*Author Was So Hated and Ignored by This Paper That
There Really Is No Reason for This Article*

The worst thing was the smog. It sat all over the hotel roof, it seeped in through the walls, and in the middle of the night, half-awake and half-asleep, I thought I was becoming a part of it.

It was a dreadful atmosphere to work in but I kept writing. I kept playing, too, but the more I wrote, the less I played. The more I wrote, the less I needed to play. Once I got started I couldn't stop. This was my salvation. Writing was a better, healthier, and more enjoyable addiction than gambling, even though gambling was a hell of a lot more lucrative. Playing poker, the gratification isn't delayed. Writing, you sometimes have to wait years for the full punishment.

Then one cold afternoon there came a pounding on my motel door.

Hoping against hope it was Cynthia, I arose from my unheavenly bed and put on jeans and a sweatshirt over my thermal underwear. (I'd begun sporting the Unabomber look since moving there.) Wifey knew where I was but even if she still felt one microbe-sized vestige of love for me why would she want to come feel it there?

It was Marvis/Cookie, I saw between the orange and black curtain. He had on his gloves and regulation blue Port Authority winter coat, and smoke was blowing out of his mouth as he bounced up and down in place, trying to keep warm. For a week he'd been bringing me pizzas and muffins and Whoppers, but he wasn't holding anything now.

I opened the door for him and the freeze outside nearly sucked me out of the room and blew me down the highway.

Marvis walked in and sat down on the motel room's one chair.

"Here," he said, pulling a Snickers out of his coat. "You want this?"

When I said no, he told me it was frozen solid anyway and put it back in his pocket.

"You know, you could buy a car," he said. "You got enough money."

"Maybe I will. Why?"

"I'm just sayin', that's all."

He looked at my laptop and told me that I played poker way too much and I told him truthfully that I'd been playing a lot less lately because I had started writing again. He waited a few seconds and said: "Did you know that Second Gunman is coming back to New York again?"

"No. I didn't."

One day, I reflected, I wouldn't mind seeing Johnny-Boy again. But that wasn't the day. Nor would tomorrow be.

"And that the Swedish guy is still here? Bjorn whoever?"

"He's still around?!"

"Dude must really want his money back, Chip."

I told THC that I'd won B2W's money fair and square, that it wasn't my fault I usually beat the Baltic Butcher, that a bet is a bet and that this wasn't just a game but was a business and it simply wasn't cricket for him to come and ask for his money back.

"I don't know if he's gonna actually *ask* for it," he said.

"So why is Second coming? And when?"

"He just said he was getting a plane, that's all. Frankly, I'm not too anxious to see him." He paused and said: "He did say he's co-min' to save you and Wifey's asses though."

"From . . . Bjorn?" Cookie nodded and I said, "Look, I told Wifey not to worry about him. He was coming after me, not her."

"Have you spoken to her recently? Are you sure she's still alive?"

Of course I was sure she was still alive! But then I thought about it. We hadn't spoken in days. So I wasn't so sure.

"Maybe tomorrow," I said, "I'll go into the city and make sure she's okay."

"Tomorrow? Jeez . . ."

"You think I should go now?"

"What if she's layin' dead on your living room floor with all kinda knives and axes through her or she's hanging from some hooks?"

"She's not! But just in case, can you lend me your car? Now?"

While we walked to the toll plaza, where his blue Malibu was parked, I imagined opening the door to the apartment and seeing my wife's bloodied body hanging from a hook and then I'd call the cops and they'd come to the apartment and take photos and they obviously would think that I killed her, which is what I'd assume, too, if I were them; then I'd have to prove I didn't and that I'd been staying in the motel the entire time.

Marvis gave me the car keys, and I said, "It's not like Bjorn brought all his butcher knives and axes and whatever with him to America, you know."

"But he did," THC said. "That's what Second told me. Dude brought all of 'em."

♠ ♠ ♠ ♠

After finding a parking space right in front of my apartment building, I nodded to the doorman, ignored his prying question ("Hey, where ya been?") and took the elevator upstairs.

I opened the door, walked in, and saw no corpse on the living room floor. Nor was Cynthia hanging from a hook, her olive shanks stripped of their delicious bounty. It was four in the afternoon, and if she were still alive, she would have been at work. I walked into my study. Nothing. No body. Then into the bedroom and bathroom. Nothing.

I lay down on my wife's side of the bed, curled up with one of her pillows, and slept for ten minutes. This was home. *Our* home. By far the safest, coziest place on Earth.

I saw that she hadn't thrown anything of mine out. Which was a positive sign.

But she had thrown *me* out.

I found a duffel bag and stuffed clothing into it. Some sweaters, a scarf, some shoes and gloves. I went to the refrigerator and opened it. General Tso and rice leftovers in a white container, some half-eaten lasagna, three bags of cold cuts packed tightly in some cream-colored wax paper. Another cold-cut bag in light blue wrapping. I took out two slices of prosciutto, dipped them in mustard, and they melted in my mouth. I undid the strange blue-colored wrapping but could not recognize what sort of meat it was and put it back into the fridge.

I left her a note: "Came by to get some stuff. Call or e-mail to let me know you're okay. I miss you and want you back. I'm sorry for everything. PLEASE give me another chance!"

When I passed the doorman on the way out—did he and the other building employees think that Cynthia and I were now separated? (and maybe we were)—it occurred to me that I still had no proof she was alive. Maybe Bjorn 2 Win had murdered her the previous evening and, after eating some of the lasagna, deftly sliced her into several hundred choice cuts and was now on his way to dispose of them in woods, Dumpsters, and landfills in the contiguous forty-eight states as he nonchalantly tooled his way around the U.S. If she had been murdered, my little note to her would surely wind up being used as evidence against me and would show how truly heartless and cunning I'd been, to murder her and leave a note that supposedly attested to my innocence but ultimately only demonstrated my sociopathic cruelty. "These are the words," the grandstanding Assistant D.A. would bellow as he wildly waved Exhibit C in the courtroom air and utilized some of the cheap alliteration that has occasionally marred this memoir, "not of a loyal, loving husband who misses his wife, but of a cold, callous, cruel, and calculating killer!"

So I went to the Starbucks across the street and took my old stool by the window and looked out into the frosty air, and at 5:40 Cynthia wheeled around the corner, wearing the chinchilla coat that all my skill and good luck had gotten her, and unwittingly walked past the blue Malibu that had conveyed her husband momentarily back home. She was bundled up and still in one warm, furry piece and was alone and very much alive, and I began blubbering like an idiot into my third hot chocolate with whipped cream.

I called her that night and she picked up the phone.

"Will you take me back if I get help for my problem?" I asked. "I'll check into a rehab clinic. I promise. I've looked into this Shining Path place in New Mexico. It looks perfect for my problem. . . . I'm like the dream textbook case for them! I think they can help me there."

"Maybe . . . I don't know" was all I could get out of her.

But it was something.

A few days later—I was writing ten hours a day now—I went onto the Galaxy and there was an e-mail for me from someone who had never sent me one before.

> Frank W. Dixon:
>
> Yes I know your real name. I know what you do. A bookwriter. 2 books. *Plague Boy. Love: A Horror Story.* I am in New York City looking for you now. I want my moneys back. I know where you live. I will be at your apartment on 16 Street tomorrow exactly at 1:30. Your wife will be at her job at the Soles Magazine at this time. We will play cards. It must be No-Limit. Three hands. Then I will go. 1:30 sharp. Do not disappoint me or I will come to New Jersey to get you. I know where you are.
>
> B2W

When I read that, I instantly forgot all about the miracle cure of writing. Opium poppies began to sprout, tall, white and beautiful, from the dull plaid rug on my motel room floor, their bulbs bursting with blissful sap. The poppies were growing and their stems were reaching for me, wrapping around me and pulling me down, and wires were shooting high voltage straight into my cerebral cortex, and the raging inferno had been rekindled in my groin.

I wrote back:

Okay, Swede, IT'S ON. But leave my wife alone. She has nothing to
do with this.

A minute later he wrote back:

You claim this yet does she not wear the expensive chinchilla coat
and shoes purchased for her with no doubt some of the moneys
that you have won from me?

I logged off, pulled the window blinds down, turned the TV and
the lights off, and propped the chair up against the door (which,
given the neighborhood and class of clientele, I probably should
already have been doing). A minute later my cell phone rang.

"Holy shit!" is how I answered the call. "Do you know what's
going on?!"

"I think I do, gobshite!" Second Gunman/Johnny Tyronne said.
Man, was it good to hear his voice. My personal cavalry galloping
over the ocean to rescue me!

"Where are you?"

He told me he was at a dive motel on Broadway in the twenties
and had landed in New York only two hours before. "Even the
feckin' bedbugs," he told me, "in this place are afraid to sleep here."

"You didn't have to come to New York, Johnny," I said.

"I couldn't have that Viking bastard cuttin' me best mate's head
off with a horse butcher hatchet, could I?"

I told Second that Bjorn wasn't out to kill me—most likely—and
that he just wanted a crack, in person, at winning his money back.

"A throwdown, one on one, head to head, mano-a-mano then?"

"Yeah. And it's No-Limit too. Tomorrow at my place."

Second asked me when Bjorn was coming over and we agreed to
meet at my apartment an hour earlier, at 12:30.

"Seriously," I said before I hung up, "thanks a lot for coming. I
appreciate it."

The next day I was back in my apartment at eleven forty-five.
I'd brought the laptop. All the lasagna and Chinese leftovers were

gone from the fridge, but there still was that mysterious blue package of otherworldly cold cuts. The place, I noticed with dismay, was starting to smell more of Cynthia than it was of the delectable blend of Cynthia-and-Me.

At twelve thirty the buzzer sounded and a minute later Johnny Tyronne was back in my apartment.

We shook hands. His battered suede jacket was gone and so was his mustache and stubble; he was wearing a long, nice black cashmere coat and had lost a few pounds.

"Your wife's not coming home?" he asked me. "There's no chance?"

"She shouldn't be. She's at work. Why?"

"Just because. You don't need any distractions."

I asked him what he'd been doing in Blackpool but he didn't tell me much. He seemed more concerned about the Once-and-For-All showdown than I was.

"Do you think," I asked him, "he'll want to play real cards or play online?"

He said he had no idea and told me to log on to the Galaxy. I opened up my laptop and did so, then he took a pack of cards out of his pocket and began shuffling them.

"Do you want to practice with real cards, play a few hands?" he asked me.

"For real money?"

"What kind of practicing, Frank, would it be if it's for fake money?"

He said we'd play five hands with real cards for real money, just to get me primed and ready, then we'd play a few hands online, him on my desktop, me on my laptop. When I reminded him that the Swede had insisted on No-Limit, Second asked me if I was really up for that and I told him I was.

I won the first hand. Three 6s. (Aw shucks . . . that was the first hand I'd ever won with on the Galaxy, way back when.) Up $3,500.

"Do you want me," he asked me, "to write a check now or should we wait until all five hands have been played?"

"Let's wait. I trust you."

"I was only kidding, mate."

I won the next hand. I was now up more than $6,000 on him.

We folded the next two hands. Then he won the next three hands and suddenly I was out almost $40,000.

My visitor came over to me, grabbed my elbow, and said, "You okay?"

Unfazed, I wrote him a check (from an account not linked to the site). I was ready for more. A lot more. It was time to move to the computers, where I was more at home. That was my bailiwick. A pitch right down my wheelhouse.

"He's a terrible, terrible player, this Bjorn guy," Second said. "He shouldn't even be allowed on the site." He grabbed both my shoulders, looked me straight in the eye, and said: "Look, it kills me to say this but you're one of the best players out there. Everyone knows that."

"They do?" I gulped.

He went into my study and logged on to the Galaxy and I brought the laptop in. He sat in my chair, rubbing his hands together, and I sat on the floor right underneath my self-portrait.

"He wants to play how many hands with you? Three, was it?"

I nodded and Second looked at his watch. It was 1:10. Twenty minutes and counting to Swedish Horse Butcher.

"We better hurry then," he said.

We created a private table in Ultra-High No-Limit. The betting would be through the roof. We both folded two hands, then . . .

My hole cards were two Kings. Two cowboys. Unbelievable. I felt the juice, the fireworks. It was as if someone was plugging me right into a power plant.

"You're sure you want to do this?" I asked him.

He didn't say no and I bet huge. He saw it and then raised huge. I reraised and he saw it.

Another King came up on the flop, along with an Ace and a 10.

"Second, I can't do this to you," I said.

"Play, Chip. It's just a game. That's all it is."

I was going to trounce him, I was going to smear him all over the rug. The pot went up, way up, past $70K, past $90K. Perhaps all the other 40,000 players currently logged on were now watching us. The turn card was a six. I bet $20,000; he raised me, I reraised. The river card was an Ace. I had a full boat, Kings full of Aces. I wanted to raise Second another $20K but felt sorry for him, so I only raised him half that . . . but he raised and I saw it.

Second Gunman wins $162,000 with a Full House, Aces full of Kings.

A fifty-pound lead baseball bat smacked me in the forehead. That's how it felt.

"Okay," I said, my mouth drying fast. "I think I'm ready now."

"Another one. You need to win again."

I looked up at him from the floor. He wasn't looking at me. The hole cards had already been dealt.

I had an 8 of spades and a Jack of spades. He bet, I saw it.

I drew a spade flush on the flop. I wanted to win my money back so I bet big.

"I've got absolutely nothing here," Second said. But he reraised.

He was, he told me, going to purposely lose the hand so I would win all the money back that I'd just lost to him. I kept raising, he kept reraising, I was barely paying attention until the pot went over $150K.

I showed my Jack-high spade flush.

He showed me his Queen-high spade flush.

His Queen was his only spade. The three of spades on the river had killed me. I was now down to less than $200,000.

"Chroist," he gasped, his hand over his mouth. "Sorry."

I took a very deep breath. Bjorn 2 Win would be there in twelve minutes. Second told me he was now going to turn all the money back over to me with the final hand. That was good because I had garbage for hole cards. He told me he had garbage, too. To get my $350,000-plus back we kept raising and raising. I still had nothing, just a measly King high by the turn, which was a dumb five of diamonds. I looked at Second and he was shaking his head in dismay. "I got nuthin' too," he muttered. I bet, he raised, I saw it. The river was a two of hearts, another dumb card. Maybe he had three twos or fours or nothing at all . . . it didn't matter.

The pot was a staggering $198,000. If ever in my life I needed an adult diaper, this was the time. But I was safe.

"I have a Jack high, Chip," Second Gunman said. "If I beat you with this, we'll keep playing until I can get all your money back to you."

"I have a King high," I told him. "Other than that, just the big squadoosh."

When I win, I thought, *I'll have all my money back. If I lose, I'll have only $1,000.*

We showed our hands.

Second Gunman wins $198,000 with two 2s.

"Huh?" I said. "You said you had nothing!"

"I thought I did," he said. "I didn't see that second two."

"Okay, let's play again."

He looked at his watch. Bjorn 2 Win would be over in one minute.

He stood up and walked to the living room. I looked up at the walls, at the two paintings on the wall. They were bad, yes, but weren't completely terrible. They were only terrible if you thought that they were any good. I stood up and went to the living room. Second was putting his coat on and was at the door.

"Where are you going?" I asked him.

"I'm leaving." His eyes darted side to side.

"You can't do that."

It was just past 1:30.

He opened the front door and took a step out and I grabbed him by his arm and tried to pull him back in. But he was big and strong and I couldn't get him back in.

"Don't your dare touch me, fucker!" he snarled, his whole aspect changing in a flash.

He sounded different, he looked different. It wasn't his voice anymore, it wasn't his voice or his accent and usual cadence. It wasn't him . . . he transformed before my eyes and passed from the person I'd thought he was—from what he'd made me think he was and from what I'd wanted him to be—into the person he truly was. Whoever that person is.

"You're not really Second Gunman," I said. "There is no such person."

He said nothing and tried to leave again. I grabbed his arm and pulled him back. He was on one side of the threshold, I was on the other. Bjorn 2 Win should have been there already. Three minutes ago. The air in the room was fizzing rapidly and I felt weak.

"You're Bjorn 2 Win." My voice sounded like I was lost and needed directions.

He didn't say anything.

"No," I said. "You're not. There is no such . . ."

Then a few words passed over my lips that I didn't even intend to utter: "You're Gerald Waverly? You are . . ."

He looked at me. There was no pity, no feeling, no joy, or sorrow. Just ice and vapor. I realized my arm was still on his. I was grabbing onto him, my fingers were clutching the sleeve of his cashmere coat as hard as they could. But it didn't matter.

He slipped away.

Epilogue: I Could Write a Book . . .

And now this shrill whine, this sickening saga of self-pity, this overlong grating lamentation, this interminable jeremiad, has come full circle.

Everything a writer says is true. Why? Because a writer said it and no writer is ever wrong about anything. Right?

So when George S. Kaufman claimed that satire is what closes on Saturday night, he was correct—he was a writer so he must have been right. Yet how do you explain the success of *The Producers* or *Scary Movie 31* or *The Office* or the Marx Brothers? A hundred essayists a year will be shamelessly unoriginal enough to remind you that Thoreau once wrote that most men lead lives of quiet desperation. And because a writer said it, it must be true. Yet you have to look no further than the memoir in your hands to see that at least one man's desperation is deafeningly not quiet. (Next time you look at Munch's *The Scream*, imagine every word herein shrieked out of that gaping maw.) A recent Times/CBS poll found that of the 68.8 percent of men who did lead lives of desperation, an overwhelming 83.9 percent were very loud about it. If Thoreau is right, then men are also going to the grave with their songs still in them. Speaking for most men, I can tell you that by the time we're dead, we're all completely songed out—there isn't a lyric left in our lungs. So Thoreau (and all those who quote him) had no idea what he was talking about.

Do good fences really make good neighbors? What Robert Frost wrote may look good in your *Norton Anthology* and in a thousand op-ed pieces a year about geopolitics and defense spending, but just the other day a Reno woman climbed over her white picket fence and shot her neighbor six times in the head. "The bitch," the killer claimed, "had it coming"—she'd been having an affair with her assassin's husband for five years. (Perhaps Frost should have said that tall, electrified barbed-wire fences make good neighbors.) The past is never dead, Faulkner (and thousands after him) told us, it's not even past. *Never* dead? WRONG! The past is often deader than a doornail. That money I lost . . . it's gone, it's past, it's really incredibly dead. (The past is also supposed to be another country. And what's past, we're told, is also prologue. The upshot is none of these writer geniuses had any idea what the past is.)

There are no second acts in American lives, F. Scott Fitzgerald and many generations of hacks since have informed us. But it would only take one person to disprove that, and I submit: Richard Nixon. And if that doesn't do it for you, how about Muhammad Ali, John Travolta, Bill Clinton or . . . F. Scott Fitzgerald? If an H-bomb had been dropped on Oxford, Mississippi, would Faulkner still have guaranteed us that Man will not merely endure he will prevail, and does anybody really still believe T. S. Eliot's assertion that the world will end with a whimper and not a bang? Happy families are all alike, Tolstoy (and millions since) said, but every unhappy family is unhappy in its own way. But my own family became much unhappier when we found out we were unhappy in the exact same way as the family across the street from us, and there was this very happy family next door to them who was happy in an entirely different way than the happy family immediately across the street, and this made both families even happier.

Highly unimaginative essayists remind us fifty times a year that Philip Larkin wrote that sexual intercourse began in 1963 between the end of the ban on publishing *Lady Chatterley's Lover* and the Beatles first LP. (I've read that quote, which wasn't even that clever to begin with, so many times that the words now put me to sleep even while I'm cringing.) But if this is true, then how were the Beatles and Philip Larkin and D. H. Lawrence all conceived?

Every word in these pages is true. It all really happened. I found out about online poker at a dice table at the Luxor in Las Vegas. I started with a mere $1,000 and in less than a year worked it up to over half a million and then lost $549,000 of it in one afternoon. Undone by two 2s. I really did go to London and got stood up. My books went out of print, Pacer Burton never did make a film of *Plague Boy*, and my wife gave me the boot.

And I really did check into the Shining Path Clinic just to get her back.

What is past is prologue. But the past isn't dead. So is the past . . . epilogue?

I have to write in order to keep from playing. It's a simple formula. If I play I lose even if I win. If I write I win even if I lose.

Whom gods destroy they first make mad. Well, maybe some of them. The others the gods just make lucky.

❤ ❤ ❤ ❤

The money was gone. I'd been had. To say that I felt used and hollow would only skim the surface. I was destroyed. The man who stood in the doorway for five minutes staring into dead space was not the same man who, only an hour before, had eagerly opened the door to let his "best mate," his "personal cavalry," into his apartment. This was the new me. Shattered, null, void, ruined. Emptiness on legs.

After Second Gunman left, I recovered my breath (it took some doing) and logged on to the Galaxy. Bjorn wasn't on. I went to his profile on the site and there was hardly any information there. He lived in Sweden, it said, and was a butcher. No birth date, no photo. He had last played, it told me, two days ago at 7:15 GMT. I went to Second Gunman's page. He worked in a hotel in Blackpool, it said. No birth date, no photo. He had last played two days ago at 7:20 GMT.

Drying out in the boutique hotel, I had wanted to murder someone but didn't know precisely who it should be. Now I had a pretty good idea.

I took a taxi downtown. Spring Street was crowded with people shopping and coming back from lunch. I walked past my old Dunkin' Donuts perch, then crossed the street. RENO BROTHERS LITERARY AGENCY, the label on the downstairs buzzer said. The antechamber was dusty, but the afternoon light beamed in and made the grime dance. I rang and a second later a female voice said, "Yes?" I said, "Buzz me in." "Who's this?" I was asked. "It's Thomas Pynchon," I mumbled and sure enough the door buzzed and I was allowed in.

I walked up to the third floor and headed toward my elusive Prague Castle, the Fortress of Rejectitude, the Stronghold of My Ontological Insecurity. I didn't know what I was going to do if Clint was there, nor did I care. I was running on autopilot and the pilot in question that day wanted to maim, cut, and kill. I rang the office doorbell and was buzzed inside.

"May I help you?" the pretty young receptionist said to me.

"I'd like to see Clint," I said. She looked vaguely familiar.

"And you are again?"

"You're Courtney Bellkamp. You were reading *Plague Boy* on the subway a few years ago. You're the only person I ever saw reading one of my books in public."

Realizing her mistake, she put her hand over her mouth.

I looked over her head and saw that Clint's door was open just a crack. The light was on. A few years ago I'd signed the *Plague Boy* contracts in there and had to stop myself from shedding tears of joy when Clint said to me, *You're gonna finally get published, man!* That was one of the happiest days of my life.

I started walking toward his office and Courtney said, "You can't go in!"

I heard a voice from inside Clint's office and could tell he was on the phone.

I had just lost over a half a mill to two 2s—why wouldn't I cave his skull all the way in?

I pushed the door open and saw my nemesis. Not one hair stray-
ing out of his ponytail, not one wrinkle in his suit. Tie puckered
to perfection. He saw me and widened his eyes for a second, then
raised a finger as if to say, *I'll be right with you.* But bloodthirsty
Capt. Autopilot pulled the phone out of his hand and slammed
it down. (The Captain was doing a much better job than I would
have.)

"Where's Clint, Vance?" I asked him, making him believe he
actually had an out.

"Clint is in Los . . ." Clint started to say, but he saw through it
and I shut the door behind me with my foot.

"So, uh, what's up with *DOA?*"

"With *what?* Look, Frank, we could have set up a mee—"

"No, we couldn't have set up anything. I know exactly how many
e-mails I've sent you! I know exactly how many times you didn't
answer me. Do *you?* Do you know the number? And you really
don't know what *DOA* is?!"

He looked at me. *Does this nut have a gun?* he was wondering.

"Two hundred and twelve e-mails! That's how many. I counted
them!" I hadn't counted and the number could not possibly have
been that high, but it was a good bluff. "Two hundred and twelve
unanswered e-mails."

I could see one or two orange hairs wriggling free now from his
rubber band.

"*DOA* . . . that's my book . . . *Dead on Arrival.* Remember it now?
I gave it to you and I even paid for the breakfast that day! And you
know what else? I went to a book party and got hit by a Drakes
Cakes truck when I left! I was in the hospital and had a patch on
my eye and my leg was broken and you couldn't even e-mail or
call?!" Even though every word was untrue I was working myself
into the lather I wanted to be in.

"Frank . . . I'm sorry I let you down. I know I did. And I'm sorry
for that. But there was nothing to tell you."

I had come here to wring his neck, to yank him by that ponytail and shake the freckles off his nose. But suddenly a fleeting sob escaped my throat.

"Sit down," Clint said softly. "Please."

I sat down. My sweater and coat were still on and it felt like I had a fever.

"Do you want some water?" he asked me.

Pouting, eyes welling up, I shook my head no.

He sat down, too, on his desk, a foot away from me. He could tell that I wasn't carrying a gun and wasn't going to hurt him and that I was crumbling.

"All right . . ." he began with some very agent-ish hemming and hawing, "I, uh . . . I don't know how to say this but . . . maybe, well, I'd say our business relationship at this point is . . . it's done. It's over. Right, Frank? You agree with me?"

I nodded and wiped away a tear.

"So do what you want with your book. You can shop it around. It's yours."

I didn't tell him I'd already done that and that there were no takers.

"But the other thing," he continued, "I want to tell you is this . . ." I waited while he looked me over, gauged my mood, and saw that my fury had turned into self-pity. "I'm a literary agent. This is a business. I'm not a brother or a father or a friend. Okay? I'll say that again: *I am not your friend.*" With every word he got louder. "Is any of this sinking in?" Still pouting, I nodded. "You take this whole thing too seriously and that's not the way to go about it. So what if you don't ever get published again. Big deal! Every day a million bad books are written that the writers think are masterpieces and they don't get published. Join the club." He blinked his eyes a few times and continued: "Just . . . stop . . . writing! Stop it! Forget about it. You're not going to be successful. You don't have what it takes. Now come to terms with that, will you?!"

"Yes I *do*." I sounded like a five-year-old. "I *do* have what it takes."

"You don't! You're just . . . you're just not that good."

"You're telling me," I said between whimpers, "that I'm not as good as . . ." I mentioned the usual suspects: Franzfoerthemshteyneggchabon.

"No. You're not. They're a lot better than you. You're not even close."

"Okay." More tears were falling. "I see."

"You know what you should do? Get a hobby. Some kind of hobby. Play tennis or something. Or you want to be creative? Is that it? You think you're some kind of creative artist? Then, Frank, why not take up something like—I don't know—*painting!*"

Of all the possible hobbies, pastimes, or crafts, he had to mention painting. It couldn't have been quilting, scrapbooking, batik or macramé. Clint had no idea about my time in Paris a long ago . . . but still it was a very low blow.

I stood up and looked at him and grabbed his tie.

Reader, I decked him. One sock to the jaw. A vicious right cross.

I knocked him hard to the floor—his head rebounded frighteningly off the radiator—and thanked him for his advice and left.

Heading down the stairs, I thought: *So should I send Clint my poker memoir when I'm finished? Who knows—maybe he'll like it, all will be forgiven and he'll shop it around!*

◆ ◆ ◆ ◆

It's true. I slugged Clint Reno. (That bitch had it coming, too.) He could have called the cops and had me arrested for assault and for impersonating a reclusive, successful, vastly overrated author, but he was probably too embarrassed. (If a headline were ever to read FAILED AUTHOR PUNCHES OUT LITERARY AGENT, nobody but another literary agent would ever take the agent's side.) I imagine that a few minutes after I left, Courtney was either holding a bag of ice to his face or sitting on it.

It's all true. It all really happened.

One memoir that isn't all true rests on my institutional coffee table at this very moment: *Nuts*, by Gerald Waverly. Waverly, I admit, possesses a flair for a tale and, unlike this memoirist, keeps his story moving forward with every sentence, which is quite an impressive accomplishment considering he is an unfeeling, cutthroat sociopath. Willie Sutton robbed banks because that's where the money was; Gerald Waverly robs people for the same reason but also because afterward people feel used, barren, and violated and banks do not.

Particularly fascinating in Waverly's 289-page rip-roaring memvel is when he states Americans make the best marks because they are "so trusting, so earnest, so desperate to be loved, so heartbreakingly gullible." According to *Nuts*, two years ago, Waverly, in the guise of a three-star chef named Simon Barker, wormed his way into the life of a Minneapolis realtor: they became chums, took a long weekend in Puerto Rico together, picked up hot Latinas. Then he defrauded the poor guy out of 420 grand. A few months later, pretending to be a roguish Welsh poet named Ewan Llewellyn, he did the same to a bipolar art dealer in Palm Beach. Three Queens ruined him. (That score was for 800K . . . so maybe I shouldn't feel so bad.)

But as is the case with other pseudomemoirs, I just cannot tell where truth ends and fiction begins. Some of it seems all too real, some of it stinks like week-old haddock and chips. Because in the final chapter of the U.S. edition, Waverly, now passing himself off as Nigel Hatcher, comes to America, *purposely* loses ten grand in a makeshift New York City casino (located beneath a hospital, not a bodega) run by colorful Brooklyn mafiosi (they even say "fuhgeddaboutit" to him once, which is, for my taste, one time too many), then ends up driving to Las Vegas in a stolen red Mustang convertible (no mention of Abdul Salaam, thus robbing F. Murray Abraham of the plum movie role) with a self-loathing literary has-been named Chet Morton (who'd had his only book hit the bestseller list ten years before and who plays online under the name the Big Man), and picks up, along the way, a handsome streetwise New

Jersey homicide cop named Delroy Johnson (poker handle: King of Spades) and a Pamela Anderson look-alike (poker handle: Astro Physics Chick). Exaggerations abound, embellishments bounce all over the place like Super Balls, and bald-faced whoppers spit in your eye. "I shagged Astro on the bonnet of the Mustang on Route 66 in broad daylight while the Big Man and King of Spades watched and cheered me on," Waverly claims. Huh? Route 66? "The Homicide Cop bruthah and the Former Writer and I had a pissing contest to see who could piss the farthest across the Rio Grande," he tells us. "I won." "I'm going to write a book about you, I think," the literary has-been slurs to Nigel Hatcher one night in an Amarillo honky-tonk. "Please don't," Waverly, knowing that a few months later he'll cheat chubby Chet for almost every penny, requests. (Don't worry, Nige, I won't!) In Las Vegas, Waverly not only wins $80,000 from Astro Physics Chick at poker in their high-roller suite at the Bellagio but then dumps her for three strippers. He buys a Bentley and gets into a card game with the hunky homicide dick and takes him for sixty large. By the time he's driven back to New York, not only has the washed-up writer developed a serious man crush on the dashing Brit ("He was even starting to talk like me," Waverly writes. "That's when I knew he'd be mine") but so has his wife, Mrs. Big Man, who literally gets on her knees and begs him to whisk her away from her humdrum New York life and take her back to London, where Nigel supposedly manages a successful hedge fund.

Well, at least in his version, I did at one time crack the best-seller list.

So who is Gerald Waverly? And who is Bjorn 2 Win?

"What I like to do," Waverly tells us in Chapter 3 ("How To Be a Nefarious Scoundrel"), "is present myself not just as a friend but as a hero. It was easy to do if I also manufactured a villain. It was easy being Luke Skywalker if I was also Darth Vader; it was easy being Churchill when I was also Adolph Hitler. It never failed."

Gamblers are paranoid by profession and should be. The odds are stacked against you and everybody truly is out to get you.

When Second came to New York, when we drove to Vegas and flew back, I never once saw his ID. Nor did I ask to, for why in the world should I have? "Gerald Waverly," the author tells us, is a *nom de plume* anyway. Was Johnny Tyronne his real name? He told me he worked at a hotel in Blackpool called the Four Swans. The day I lost all the money and decked Clint Reno, I Googled the Four Swans and learned that there did exist such a hotel . . . until five years ago, when it burned to the ground. I called Blackpool directory assistance: there was no Johnny, John, or J. Tyronne or any other Tyronne. Further digging uncovered five other hotels in England called the Four Swans. No Johnny Tyronne had recently worked at any of them. My best mate was the shadow of a phantom.[6]

There was no Bjorn 2 Win either. The day after I lost all that money, B2W disappeared from the site. He was the Darth/Adolph to Second Gunman's Luke/Winston. I tried to recall all the times that I'd played against the Baltic Butcher: not once had Second Gunman, despite having told me how pathetic a player the Swede was, ever been at the same table. Many was the time, moreover, that Second had *sent* me to play Bjorn. "He's dead money," Second often told me. (And I recall now how conspicuously agitated Johnny/Second/Gerald got in Las Vegas when I recommended we play Bjorn 2 Win for a few easy thousand. "It's not a good idea," he'd snapped. He even told me how sorry he felt for him. That bastard. And he, with his First in Physics at Cambridge, had also quoted Einstein to me—momentarily slipping out of character—about how God does not throw dice. That cold-blooded rat bastard.) For eleven months Bjorn lost to me, then he began threatening me.

---

6. Most of the names of characters in this memoir—Harry Carver, Clint and Vance Reno, Susan Jessup, et alia—are the names of characters in Elvis Presley movies. This is for legal purposes and because when I Googled the name "Johnny Tyronne," I discovered that Gerald Waverly had most likely gotten this name from the Elvis movie *Harum Scarum* (1965).

Winston feckin Churchill to the rescue.

There was no Bjorn 2 Win, there was no Second Gunman.

All his feckins and bloodys and gobshites and mates. Summoned right up from Central Casting, he was. He wasn't even an *original* fake! And I fell for it.

I think I can pinpoint the exact moment when he decided to make me his next mark. It was when I told him my real name and he checked out my lousy Amazon rankings. That's when he knew I was a soft target and could be had. Yes, that was it.

At Shining Path, while I held sweaty hands with my fellow addicts and lip-synched the Serenity Prayer, I could not stop myself from wondering: were the cards real? Were the games I played with Gerald Waverly on the afternoon of my downfall "honest" games? When we played with real cards, I won the first two hands, then he killed me the next three. (I was so whacked in the head that day that I didn't even cancel the check I wrote him.) Maybe he had stacked the deck, maybe he was pulling cards from his sleeve, a pants' pocket, or his asshole. But what I really think is that when we played online, when I sat on the floor under my self-portrait and he was at my desk . . . *I am convinced he had rigged the games.* The way the hands played out, card by card, bet by bet . . . it all played out perfectly like a script he had written. I was unwittingly starring in his movie, the movie of my own tragic downfall.

Second Gunman hasn't been on the site since that day. He's gone.

Show me a writer who isn't paranoid and I'll show you a deceased writer. Every year 200,000 new books come out, which means at least 199,999 other writers are hoping you fail. Critics lie in wait poised to tear you down. The odds are stacked against you.

In *Nuts* Waverly claims he occasionally uses other people as foils and shills. So then, was Artsy Painter Gal in on the scheme, too? Think about it. She formed a long-distance romantic connection with me, we conversed daily, she stood me up and vanished. And then—when I was vulnerable and wallowing in this nadir—Second Gunman, her possible accomplice, moved in for the kill. Yes, I did see APG in the flesh on Empyrean Island, I saw her husband and kids . . . but maybe they weren't really her husband and kids and were itinerant farm workers or out-of-work L.A. actors. Perhaps Gerald/Johnny/Second/Whoever paid Artsy and her "family" to go to that resort. Not only did they get a lovely weekend on Empyrean Island out of it but also an additional ten grand. That would be a drop in the bucket for Gerald Waverly when he finally cleaned me out.

All APG really had to do was pretend to like me for a little while.

Was History Babe in on it? Something about their relationship didn't seem right. Maybe Gerald flew her into Colorado so that we could pick her up. Maybe they're really husband and wife and it was some sort of perverted role play. Or maybe they're brother and sister.

The only one I trust is Toll House Cookie. But maybe I shouldn't even trust him.

Is it possible that the *Times, Time* magazine, and *The Boston Globe* were also in on the caper? They purposely gave my books bad reviews so that publishers wouldn't publish me anymore so that I would then take up playing poker and I'd believe it was the only thing in the world I was good at. And then Gerald Waverly would strike.

Maybe Hollywood was aiding and abetting, too, when they didn't make a movie out of *Plague Boy*.

Maybe *you* were in on it when you didn't buy my first two books?

No, there was no Second Gunman. And Toll House Cookie, History Babe, Artsy Painter Gal, Wolverine Mommy, and Grouchy Old Man didn't really exist either. Because neither did Chip Zero. Cartoon characters all.

There's another possibility that chills me. In the dead of night I shoot up in my bed and think about it until it makes me sick. Was Cynthia in on it, too?

How convenient was it: I go to London to hook up with a mistress I barely know, the mistress doesn't show up, I return home, Wifey throws me out, I lose $550K?

Is it possible that she and Johnny fell in love with each other the first time he visited? And that, while I was penning this book in Michigan and New Jersey, they were conducting a torrid affair with each other? Supposedly Second returned to Blackpool and the Four Swans after Las Vegas . . . but I have no proof that he ever *was* in Blackpool. Maybe while I was busy not getting laid in London at the Royal Brompton Hotel, he was getting busy with my wife in New York on Sixteenth Street and Eighth Avenue.

"I enjoy tormenting my marks," Waverly tells us in Chapter 5 ("I, Scumbag"), "after I distance them from their money." He leaves "calling cards" for his victims, he says, objects he knows will strike a raw nerve. After he bilked the Minneapolis real estate man, he left a chef's hat in the man's underwear drawer; after he took the bipolar Palm Beach art dealer for a ride, he left a Welsh dictionary in his medicine cabinet.

Those mysterious cold cuts in my refrigerator . . . was that Swedish horsemeat?

I'll never know.

♣ ♣ ♣ ♣

It was about three o'clock when I got home from decking Clint Reno.

I knew I had to be out of the house by the time Wifey returned. If she saw me—she had already imparted this to me a few times—she might get a restraining order, and a restraining order, I knew, would be a serious hindrance to us ever getting back together.

I gathered clothing into a suitcase for a possible long haul. In the living room I started hurling books onto the floor. *Ulysses* was the first to go, and with sadistic relish, I tore *The Waste Land and Other Poems* to shreds. Next was *Anna Karenina*, which I'd never even finished, and *Gravity's Rainbow,* which I knew I was supposed to think was a masterpiece but had never liked. I tossed out Homer, Virgil, Horace, and Ovid and chucked Chuck Palahniuk and Chuck Klosterman and dispatched *Dispatches* and sent *Lolita, Augie March,* and both *Lord* and *Lucky Jims* to their Maker. I showed no mercy. The last book I threw out was Dr. James's Olde Insomnia Elixir: *The Golden Bowl.* It was like *Fahrenheit 451*—which I also tossed out—when all the books go up in flames, except that's supposed to be sad and this wasn't. I was glad to be rid of them. I dragged four large Hefty bags filled with books down into the building's basement. They'd never be read, skimmed, or seen again. *Goodbye, Mr. Chips, Farewell, My Lovely, Goodbye, Columbus, Bonjour Tristesse* and *Fuck You, Charlie.*

Back upstairs packing my laptop, I espied the dog-eared copy of *DOA* that Cynthia had never finished. I tore it up, ten pages at a time. Then I went onto my desktop computer and found *DOA,* trashed it and emptied the trash. As of that second, it no longer existed anywhere in the known world (Clint had probably purged his copy a long time ago; Deke Rivers was massacring his). I went into a file cabinet and found a few short stories and outlines and first chapters of books I'd started. I destroyed them. EVERYTHING MUST GO. I went back to the desktop computer and dragged more of my writing into the trash. I ripped *Still-Life With Pear* off the wall and broke it in two across my leg, then cut it to pieces. I ripped *Self-Portrait With Headache* off the wall and broke it over my leg, but as I did so something behind the painting fell to the ground with a clank.

It was a key.

I left a note telling Cynthia I'd dropped by to pick up a few things, that I was going to seek professional help and make her proud of me. I took a taxi over to the storage facility in the twenties; the facility is one square block of twelve stories of wall-to-wall dust overlooking the Hudson. I showed my key and ID and a few minutes later I stood in an eight-by-twelve unit, where a low dangling lightbulb barely lit up my dozen or so cartons. The boxes on the bottom were starting to give way. Poems, short stories, watercolors, gouaches, oil paintings, plays, screenplays, everything. My entire creative output, my oeuvre, the issue of my spirit. Tens of thousands of pages. How many weeks, months, and years of my life had I wasted trying to make something out of myself? If someone were to tell me the exact number in hours and minutes it would stop my heart for good. I dragged a box out into the corridor, then another. Wheezing from the effort and the dust, I created three stacks of cartons in the narrow gray hallway. I grabbed a fistful of paper from a carton on top. It was a play I had written or cowritten long ago. This box was filled with plays I once thought would make me rich, famous, and honored. They hadn't. I reached into the next box down and pulled a page out and saw it was a lousy love poem (John Donne meets William Carlos Williams) I'd written for Cynthia when she and I had just started dating . . . when I saw that I toppled over the whole stack with a kick. I reached into the top carton of another stack and pulled out a thick manila envelope. I tore it open and pulled out the yellow clutter of paper within and looked at the front page and read it.

"Things were very bad then but still we carried on."

I left it all in the hallway and when I went back downstairs I told the two men working behind the desk to throw it all out.

♠ ♠ ♠ ♠

This is exactly where a flashier, more competent writer would have begun this story. At the end.

I spent another week at the Tunnel Motel in New Jersey, trying to track down Second Gunman and my money. I had once worked my original thousand-buck stake up to 550 times that . . . and I knew I could do it again. But I couldn't. Hanging out at the Low tables I got my remaining $1,000 up to $1,400 and moved up to Medium, but before I knew it I was down to $250. With her stack up over $140,000 Wolverine Mommy visited me at a table in Low—it was humiliating for me to be seen there—and asked me, "What are *you* doing down here?!" I dropped fifteen bucks to her two 9s and left without answering.

Never telling Cynthia about what Gerald/Johnny/Second/ Bjorn had done to me—or what I'd allowed to be done to myself— I left her an urgent-sounding message saying she had to call me, that my life was at stake. She called me back and I told her I was checking into the Shining Path Clinic. Even though she made no promise to take me back, she told me she was rooting for me and instantly I knew I'd made a smart move not telling her about dumping all of my dough.

Finally I was doing the right thing.

I flew here to the Southwest—I charged the flight—and checked myself in. Shining Path, one of the best treatment centers of its kind, stands on fifty acres (five of which are parking lots) and abuts a magnificent golf course; looming over an Olympic-sized pool is the center itself, a prismatic glass and steel building that looks like a swiftly rejected design for a World Trade Center replacement, only set on its side. The grounds are completely flat, not even a pimple, and the lawns are perfectly kept; the white gravel roads cross each other neatly and there are trees here and there, all exactly the same height. The whole place resembles a small architectural model of itself and when you stand or sit on the grounds you feel like a tiny plastic figure frozen in your tracks.

The ten-page form I signed upon checking in asked me what I did for a living. Having not been published for years, I wrote: "Unemployed writer." The center's Assistant Director admitted me; he was friendly at first but flatly refused to call me Chip.

It is a twenty-eight-day program. Individual therapy, group therapy, making your own bed (and lying in it—how fitting), cleaning your room, group and individual prayer. They put me in the Non-Substance Wing, which makes it sound as if it either is going to melt under the sun or float off with the first breeze. The patients in there are kept away from the junkies and alcoholics in the other wing, for the same good reason that in prison shoplifters should be kept away from murderers. In my section were sex addicts, hard-core masochists (there was a guy who loved to have cigars put out on his arms and legs), shopaholics, gamblers, video-game fiends. If there was a thing in the world that you could get hooked on, this is where you went to get unhooked on it.

All the rooms are small and identical and supposedly there are no special privileges: even if you were Prince Charles or Bill Gates, they'd stick you in a room with a plumber or truck driver. Or with someone like me. My roommate was Jared; he was from Tyler, Texas, and was only seventeen years old. Jared had what I thought at first was a savage purple rash around his neck. But, he told me, he was a "space cowboy": he was addicted to "the Choking Game," aka Space Monkey, American Dream, Knock Out, Hawaiian High, and about thirty other wonderful monikers. He and his buddies choked themselves until they almost passed out or did pass out. The rush as you lapsed into unconsciousness, Jared told me, was super awesome. *Whatever*, I wondered, *happened to good ol' circle jerks and the Soggy Biscuit Pro-Am?!*

Shining Path doesn't allow card playing. Computers and laptops are *verboten*. (Too many gambling, video-game, porn, Zappos, and eBay addicts trying to get cured.) The good part for me was this meant no playing; the bad part was it meant no writing.

Every day it was sunny, warm, zero humidity, no wind. The sprinklers always came on at the same time, to the second, and did the exact same water dance for the same amount of time. Even the grass takes part in the clockwork.

I attended two lectures — or confessionals — on my first full day. (Attendance is mandatory.) The first speaker was a sex addict named Tom. He really should have chosen a different poison for himself: Tom wasn't attractive or rich and was lumpy around the middle . . . it could not have been too easy for him being a sex addict. "I tried to kill myself five times," he told us as he nervously jingled the change in his pockets. The second lecturer was addicted to betting on the horses. "I tried to kill myself seven times," he said. At the next confessional the following morning, a woman told us about her addiction to self-mutilation, but there was a slight downtick: she had only four suicide attempts under her belt. Their stories moved many in the audience, myself included, to tears, but I also wondered how a person can possibly fail to commit suicide, given all those whacks at it.

I mentioned that to my counselor, a lanky social worker with the lamentable name (considering she was treating a card player) of Jackie King, and she threw me out of her office and told me to see her the same time tomorrow. The next day she told me that despite what I may have read about how winning releases certain pleasure-inducing chemicals in the brain, gamblers gamble not to win but to lose. When I told her that I didn't lose, she didn't believe me. You've hit rock bottom, she said, that's why you're here. With what Second/Johnny/Gerald had done to me in mind, I corrected her: "No. Rock bottom hit *me*." When I told her how wonderfully refreshing an ice cold beer tastes in August and opined that the single worst part of being an alcoholic is that, after you've kicked the habit, you're not allowed to ever have another drink, she threw me out again.

There were a few hot female patients there and there were rumors among the men that one or two of them were nymphomaniacs, but I missed Cynthia and wanted her back. I wanted to move back into my apartment, forget about cards and the $550K I'd been robbed of, and write an unlikely happy ending to this story.

I hadn't noticed it the first two days—everything was so new— but there were copies of *A Million Little Pieces* everywhere. There were plenty of Bibles, too, but Frey's mendacious masterwork was definitely Good Book No. 1. People not only believed the book, they believed *in* it. They were like pilgrims flocking from thousands of miles away to gaze at the Virgin Mary's tear-streaked face in an Egg McMuffin.

The library was filled with other substance-abuse and addiction and self-help memoirs, books with such lurid titles as *Hammered* and *Wasted* and *Cracked and Hammered* and *Wasted and Cracked* and *Drunk and Disorderly* and *Rich Coke Slut* and *Smacked-Out and Dead* and *Madison Avenue Meth Mama*. They made me cringe. Someone should just cut them up, throw two-thirds of them out, and randomly paste what's left into one book and call it *How I Grew Up in a Fucked-Up Family and Endured a Screwed-Up Childhood and Started Getting Stoned as a Kid and Then Totally Got Wasted with Booze and/or Drugs For Years and Lost Everything I Had but Somehow Lived to Whine About It to You for Profit, Catharsis and Fame.*

(Sometimes I think a National Book Award should be awarded to every brutalized person who ever suffered at the unloving hands of their own family, and to all the destitute people who got addicted to drugs, booze, or gambling and forfeited the treasure of their souls, and to all the trampled, powerless victims of poverty, disease, violence, war, and mass murder . . . who never wrote one single word about it.)

There is no coffee or tea at Shining Path because there are caffeine junkies; the gym only allows you in for a half-hour at a time because there are exercise junkies and the Runner's High isn't permitted; no iPods or other personal stereos are allowed on the premises lest anyone get addicted to love, hooked on a feeling, or develop a hard habit to break. Watching soap operas and game shows is banned, too.

Writing was forbidden. That is what killed me. They took away my sole salvation.

I was dying to write again, to feel that wonderful sensation of words flowing like honey from my soul, and since I couldn't, I made it my avocation to sit next to fellow patients reading whiny recovery books and harass them.

"What are you," one surly guy snapped at me in the lounge, "some kind of writer or something?" "As a matter of fact," I told him, "at one time I was." He said, "You know, I could write a book about this place."

I got up and left.

I didn't make any friends there.

On my sixth day at Shining Path I phoned Cynthia at work and told her, "I feel a lot better. It's working. It kills me to admit it but it's really working."

"Really? Already? It is?"

"Yes . . . I'm finally kicking this thing. God, what an idiot I was! To have risked losing you and to screw up my life like I did. Baby, it's as if I'm a new person. I'm getting better."

I told her I missed her and we both got choked up. She sounded happy for me. I told her that it was against Shining Path's rules for us to talk again during the remainder of my treatment.

We said good-bye and first thing the next morning I packed up and left the place.

Nobody tried to stop me. It wasn't a prison, there were no fences or guards with guns in towers. I reclaimed my laptop and wheeled my suitcase to the parking lot and waited for a taxi. It was sunny and warm and I was wearing winter clothes. The driver took me to the airport. I went to the ticket counter and was just about to buy a one-way ticket to New York but saw that there was a flight to Las Vegas leaving in an hour and a half.

I'm staying in Las Vegas now in a motel a mile from downtown. The Golden Palomino Motor Lodge. Thirty-two rooms, cable TV, AC, mountain views. Sixty-nine dollars a night. Built in 1954, the motel's layout is U-shaped and the view of the mountains to the west is spellbinding. If Man had not invented Las Vegas, you think as you stare out at the sunset, then God or firebreathing demons living in the Earth's molten core would have. Coronas of magenta, cedillas of lilac and violet waving over the mountains, and finally a fluttering of foreboding crimson and . . . blah blah blah. Nowhere else have I seen such fire take over a sky. The view of the swimming pool, which is the size of a train-station bathroom and is just as disgusting, is not spellbinding: the pool is kidney-shaped, if you had a severely damaged kidney, and the water is teal but it's a chemical teal, not a real deal teal.

I've been here almost a week and a half. Writing. Occasionally playing. But mostly writing.

During the week the place is fairly deserted. I occasionally hear couples fighting in foreign languages, I hear liquor bottles being thrown into trashcans, I hear men laughing, coughing, and cursing to themselves. The guy in a room down the hall lives here year-round; he's in his seventies and was a blackjack dealer at the old Desert Inn and now only has one arm. He won't tell me why but I have a feeling the story isn't pretty. The narrow Maypo-colored hallways reek of cigarettes, and the sheets have a brownish tinge to them but they seem to be clean.

A tall neon sign stands at the motel's entranceway. A muscular palomino, full-length, flicks on and off. The horse is considerably more orange than gold, and the sign, I've been told, has been on the fritz for decades. For a few seconds the neon horse is on all fours but then is supposed to rear up, then settle back down again. Sometimes it works, most times it doesn't, and yesterday I bet someone a hundred dollars that on the twentieth flicker it would work. We waited and counted and he handed me the money. But it wasn't an honest bet . . . I'd been studying the sign for days and knew its patterns.

Cynthia is convinced I'm still at Shining Path working out my problems, talking to fellow addicts and recovering. That's exactly what I want her to think.

My plan is to stay here for another two weeks. Then I'm going to fly back to New York, tell her I completed the program and that I'm a changed man and completely cured.

If I can pull that off, if she takes me back, it would be my greatest bluff ever.

I write, rewrite and, as you can plainly see, don't do nearly as much deleting as I should. It's what keeps me going and I'm terrified of stopping. At night I take a taxi downtown and play roulette for a bit. It is the stupidest game ever concocted but, hey, if it was good enough for Dostoyevsky it's good enough for the Big Man, too. I win, I lose, I break even, I come home.

Three days ago I took a break from writing and began playing poker again. I worked the stack back to $1,000 and then up to $3,000 with a King-high straight. I was talking to people, to new players on the site, and making jokes and making new friends. I never let on that at one time I had been one of the kings of this very strange hill. Yesterday I got my stack up to over $4,500. It took a while, it was tough, grueling going at times, but I hung in there and battled. Cocky, bold and foolish, I then moved up to the High tables. There, glowering behind his Aviator shades, sat the hooded, unknowable menace SaniFlush, all alone and waiting for me.

It was just me and him, and my heart began to pound.

High Noon with the Prince of Poker Darkness.

"Chip," he asked me, "where's the rest of your money?"

"You're looking at it, Killer," I told him.

He nodded, smiled wryly, and shrugged. I could *see* it.

Our hands were dealt and we stopped talking. It didn't look too good for me. There were three hearts on the table, and the way he was betting, I was certain he had a flush. I needed either a 10 or a 7 on the river for a full boat . . . it was the only thing that could save me.

By the river, every penny of mine was at stake. I sat on the edge of the bed with my knees knocking, my heartbeat quickening, and my stomach turning to warm slop.

The river card came up a 7 and I won over $6,000. It was a minor yes-there-really-is-a-God miracle and I almost thanked the Almighty for it.

Ten grand in three days. That's not bad. That's not bad at all.

No second acts, you say? Okay, think what you will.

I can stop now. After all, I'm a winner again.

IRIS JOHNSON

Ted Heller is the author of two previous novels, *Slab Rat* and *Funnymen*. He lives in New York.

Join us at **AlgonquinBooksBlog.com** for the latest news on all of our stellar titles, including weekly giveaways, behind-the-scenes snapshots, book and author updates, original videos, media praise, detailed tour information, and other exclusive material.

You'll also find information about the **Algonquin Book Club**, a selection of the perfect books—from award winners to international bestsellers—to stimulate engaging and lively discussion. Helpful book group materials are available, including

Book excerpts
Downloadable discussion guides
Author interviews
Original author essays
Live author chats and live-streaming interviews
Book club tips and ideas
Wine and recipe pairings

twitter **Follow us on twitter.com/AlgonquinBooks**
facebook **Become a fan on facebook.com/AlgonquinBooks**